The props kicked over, barely hinting at their true power. Just to see them free spin . . . It thrilled her to the marrow. She let up on the starters and the blades wound down.

"Whoa . . ." Awesome. A throwaway word through no fault of its own, but in this case it was completely right. "That's about the best time you could have with your clothes—ah, I mean, in a tethered plane."

"I don't know," Logan said. He had a truly goofy smile on and he was watching her with those cat eyes again. "I've never flown without clothes."

The Fly Guy

Laura Bradford

ZEBRA BOOKS
KENSINGTON PUBLISHING CORP.
www.kensingtonbooks.com

ZEBRA BOOKS are published by

Kensington Publishing Corp.
850 Third Avenue
New York, NY 10022

All Kensington titles, imprints, and distributed lines are
available at special quantity discounts for bulk purchases for
sales promotion, premiums, fund-raising, educational, or in-
stitutional use.

Special book excerpts or customized printings can also be
created to fit specific needs. For details, write or phone the
office of the Kensington Special Sales Manager: Attn.
Special Sales Department. Kensington Publishing Corp.,
850 Third Avenue, New York, NY 10022. Phone: 1-800-221-
2647.

ISBN 0-8217-8032-8   3 4633 00153 0649

First Printing: June 2006
10 9 8 7 6 5 4 3 2 1

Printed in the United States of America

To Harold,
who left me the sky.

Acknowledgments

Many thanks to Wanda Zalewski and Frances Olson for their unflagging enthusiasm for this project and their thoughtful input to the manuscript. Special thanks to pilots Captain Kenneth Olson and Captain Bryan Shewokis for assistance with the technical aspects of the story.

Finally, to Laura herself, without whose support and ideas this book would not have happened: we did it!

Chapter 1

Sarah waited, crouched in the underbrush. Dusk settled. Mosquitoes buzzed softly, occasionally reconnoitering her ears or tickling her skin, but none lighted. Good. The new repellant was everything the manufacturer claimed it was.

She touched the trim ring of the brand-new, certified-waterproof-down-to-200-feet-plus watch strapped to her wrist by its patented camouflaged Neoprene band. The softly illuminated dial informed her that the barometric pressure was rising; it was 2 A.M. in London, her wrist was thirteen feet above sea level, and the rest of her had been scrunched up in the prickly bushes for almost an hour. The wait was always worth it, but in the last few years she'd been having arguments with her knees about that.

A soft breeze off the ocean brushed her face. The wind was a friend this evening, carrying away the scent of her and her new toys.

Her hiking boots were a few days shy of broken in. She flexed her complaining toes. Okay, what a little wussie. And nobody needs that kind of gear just to hang out in their local neighborhood nature preserve, right? Correct, technically speaking, but Sarah was a writer.

Fiction, maybe? Very cool. Good money, lots of recognition in fiction. Maybe deep thought-provoking tomes? Groovy— the gal's a real egghead. But . . . no.

Surprise. She writes . . . she writes . . . Cripes, why was this so hard for her to admit? She writes outdoor equipment reviews for a hiking magazine.

So there.

Nothing wrong with it. Couple pages and one deadline a month. Opportunities to use kick-ass cutting-edge equipment on day hikes and backpacking overnighters in various New England locales—all reachable by car. That was key.

To her never-ending amazement, people—women, mostly— apparently paid attention to what she said. Or, rather, wrote. Most men never seem to listen to anything, so good luck there.

Her tassel-toed, loafer-loving editor was always telling her, his inflections so Bostonian as to be almost a caricature, "Numbers don't lie, Sarah. The market share of products you endorse significantly increases in the months immediately following your column. You are a cash cow."

Hooray for the numbers, but being likened to a barnyard animal, however, wasn't exactly tonic to a gal creeping up on the median of her third decade. As if on cue, her right leg cramped beneath her. She shifted position on the sandy soil and one of her knees popped, sounding like a firecracker in the stillness. Her body's list of complaints had lengthened of late, she was noticing, but she supposed that was to be expected late in the warranty.

So this lurking about in the woods—much as she loved it in its own right—was all part of the job. Someday, though, Sarah wanted to be what she thought of as a "real writer." A storyteller. Documenting people's lives. Doing important stuff. Deep stuff. The idea scared the crap out of her, but it dogged her every byline.

An early cricket chirped. The bushes rustled softly, maybe fifty yards away. Sarah imagined the house lights dimming. Another rustle, from somewhere across the clearing just in front of her. She eased out a pair of folding binoculars, the barrels protesting from newness as she gently persuaded them apart. She peered through the lenses experimentally.

Nice optics. Great field of view. Even in the low light, it was easy to pick out details of the scrubby, dwarfed woods around her.

There, on the far side of the clearing. Flashes of white, waist high, in among the gauzy, green shimmering of a scruffy silver birch. She held her breath. *Showtime . . .*

A delicate, dappled face emerged from the leafy cover, topped by ridiculous, endearing ears. She stifled a giggle at the stuff of Bambi: a beautiful doe. *A doe, a deer, a female deer . . .*

The doe's slim body followed, sidling into the clearing barely twenty yards from Sarah's position. The animal stood stock-still, poised for flight, delicately sampling the air.

Evenin', Mom. You're looking lovely tonight. . . .

The doe must have given some secret mother deer signal to her offspring, because all three babies abruptly tumbled out of the brush. The cutest things they were, too, once they'd regained their footing. Each one nuzzled Mom in turn, then started moseying around the clearing like they hadn't a care in the world.

Which they wouldn't, as long as Sarah was alive. No one was encroaching on their territory. Poor things.

Developers on the island wanted to get rid of them completely. Have a wholesale shoot off. Damn nuisance, all these damn deer. Shorn plantings, threats of Lyme disease.

Bothered the new home owners, they did. Sarah could recite verbatim the litany of arguments.

But worst than the frigging developers was frigging Crossly Field.

The name alone made Sarah want to spit like an old Italian woman. The tiny local airfield had reopened six months ago after having been shut down since before her sister, Beth, and Sarah were twinkles in their mommy's eye. Little planes now buzzed in and out of the airfield all day long, taking tourists on sightseeing trips along the shoreline.

Sarah did not like airplanes.

Lucky for the deer and her that the flight path for the one operating runway ran parallel to, and a good distance away from, the preserve and not directly over it.

Miserly Noah Crossly owned the chunk of Pear Island, named for its shape, that Crossly Field and the preserve were set on. Just after World War I, Noah's father—the family was obscenely wealthy—had made a deal with the town of Tidal: let us have our pet airstrip and you people can use the rest of the land for a wildlife refuge. For more than eighty years the agreement had held.

The barnstorming exploits of the Crossly family during the twenties and thirties were legend in Tidal. After WW II, Noah Crossly, a decorated hero of the Pacific air war, returned home to Tidal with plans to continue operating the airport, but a series of tragic events soured him on flying.

Mother deer finally abandoned her reconnaissance and lowered her head to nibble. The kids rooted out tender tufts of grass.

This place, these creatures . . . really, the preserve was heaven on earth. Concerned townspeople—*and* Sarah, not that it was all about her—had busted their volunteered humps over the last several years to install wildlife observation blinds, trail signs, even some boardwalks to provide handicapped access. School groups, the Council on Aging, and families used the preserve through three seasons. Nature nuts like Sarah were in and out all year long.

Now the airport wanted to build a second runway. With all its access roads and landing lights, it would bisect the preserve into two almost completely separate pieces. Larger planes—there was even talk of small jets—would take off directly over the preserve. The deer would be screwed. All in the name of serving the new, big deal condo owners who seemed to think that lifetime residents of Tidal didn't deserve a say in the future of Pear Island. But economic investment alone did not for an opinion make.

Suddenly, the doe tensed. Her ears swiveled and locked onto some foreign noise way beyond Sarah's hearing. Sarah crossed her fingers and willed her to stay. Wrapped contentedly in the innocence of youth, the kids grazed on. Long moments passed. Finally mother relaxed.

The family wandered to within twenty feet of Sarah's hideout. Close enough for her to pick up on the delicate eyelashes ringing Mom's striking dark eyes.

Beautiful. Absolutely beautiful . . .

Sarah was hanging her hopes on the fact that soon, any day now maybe, Bambi and friends might have a secure neighborhood, no strings attached. Tidal was due to inherit the preserve from Noah Crossly. A letter of agreement drafted in the twenties conveyed title of the land to the town upon the demise of the last heir of the Crossly line. Noah, now eighty-four, was in his final days. The entire parcel could be held in public trust forever. No second runway—ever.

Swamp peepers peeped.

Bullfrogs belched.

Sarah barely breathed.

Amazing . . .

Suddenly, Mother's ears twitched violently, and her head shot up. The kids, startled, bolted for the bushes. Mother let loose a stream of urine and bounded after them.

A fitting parting comment. Sarah rose inelegantly to her feet, because she too had heard the noise. An incessant buzz, growing louder by the moment.

Her body reacted instinctively.

Nausea swept over her. A curse stuck in her throat as it tightened. She shook her fist impotently at the purple sky.

The buzz swelled to a roar. Skimming the tops of the trees around the clearing, a small plane swept overhead, its wings and underbelly ablaze in orange and red, reflecting the last lingering rays of sunset. Unwanted memories swarmed.

Sarah tried to scream, but no sound came. Petroleum fumes filled the air. The raging heat of an African sun beat down upon her, driving her to her knees. Memories exploded in her mind. Scenes—horrible, jumbled—flashed through her consciousness like old-movie stills, curled at the edges, and burst into flame.

Her new, expensive, state-of-the-art binoculars slipped from her hand and hit the sand with a soft thud. That was the last sound she heard before she nose-dived onto a blanket of pine needles. *Fucking airplanes* . . .

In her last coherent moment, it struck her that the runway the plane appeared to be headed for hadn't yet been built.

Crickets chirped. The earth revolved. Twilight settled while Sarah dreamed.

But not a nice dream at all.

A deadly stillness settles over the scattered wreckage of the small plane. . . .

That was Spot's voice. A bit like Lon Chaney's, with overtones of Boris Karloff during the really scary segments.

Spot was an imaginary dog who lived in Sarah's head. No, he wasn't a real dog and, no, he didn't tell her to do evil things. Instead, he *kept* her from doing things. Normal things. Everyday things. Like taking a full breath or remaining conscious and upright around anything to do with airplanes.

And there . . . in the front seat, the pilot . . . Spot whispered into the stillness of Sarah's mind.

The native pilot, his eyes wide open and starkly white against his dark skin, stares unblinkingly into the far distance of the African Savannah. . . .

Spot was really in fine voice today.

A seeping wetness spreads across his torn shirt. . . .

The dog simply had no respect.

Could dogs have hunchbacks? Sarah always pictured Spot with one.

Was the stain just . . . sweat? Or something . . . else?

In her mind, his steely, horrid, doglike-but-sharper, more like a devil's talons/toenails clicked on the ground somewhere close by. He snarled, jaws dripping, razor-sharp teeth clacking. He was sniffing her out, probing her vulnerabilities, exploiting her unconsciousness.

Over the years, in an attempt to contain her imaginary canine companion, she'd built the psychological equivalent of The Great Wall of China in her mind. She'd chinked zillions of bricks into place between the pooch and her. It was tough work, slinging all those tons of mental mortar. And try as she might to seal up every tiny gap and cavity, there was always a weak spot somewhere and the damn dog eventually sniffed it out.

He gnawed on her entrails for fun, the bastard. Fortunately for her, they always regenerated in time for lunch. But still, it was damn inconvenient. How do you bring a date home for dinner when the damn dog wanted her for his?

Suddenly, the insane, bloodthirsty, idiot animal burst through the brickwork of his playpen. Spot consumed her.

* * *

The matter of how long Sarah remained unconscious was open to debate.

Her best guess? Somewhere between two minutes and half an hour. She could still make out details in the clearing and she hadn't wet herself. A voice injected itself into her tenuous hold on reality.

You're okay now. . . .

How nice. Someone was calling to her from *outside* her own mind. Thank heavens: a visitor.

The voice offered up more details: *You lost consciousness.*

Yeah, no shit. But, still, the voice seemed to mean well.

Too bad it lied.

Sarah cracked open one eye. A disembodied hand was poking a huge paper pill in her face. She thrashed her head violently to the side, abrading her cheek on—what? She forced her eyes to focus. Ah, shoelaces.

It was then she felt the familiar embarrassment that inevitably greeted her upon her return to Planet Earth. *Welcome home*—cough—*loser*.

She blinked grit from her eyes and focused on a hairy forearm, then slid her bleary gaze up to a nicely rounded bicep, over a shirtsleeve, made of a polished microweave nylon, along a well-contoured shoulder, around a button-down collar, and finally—voila! A face as reward for the effort.

A craggy face. Male. Not pretty by any stretch, not even handsome, but not unattractive, either. Experienced, people might say. She could barely say anything she was so wiped out.

"Hello," was the best she had.

"Hello, yourself."

Okay, so he wasn't a big talker either. Sarah elaborated, thinking someone had to. "I passed out."

"I know. I saw you go down. I roused you with smelling salts. You were not happy about it."

Gracious, he had good eyes to pick her swooning self out of all the brush that surrounded the clearing. Good eyes. Acute and cute. Ha! Must eat a lot of carrots. Green, were they? She widened hers in the low light. Yep. And one on either side of his nose. This was all good. Still mightily whacked, she chuckled inanely.

"It surprised me to see anyone down—I mean, *out* here," the craggy-faced man said. "I mean, there's nothing around." He looked around.

"Just me and the deer," Sarah said.

"Yes, the deer. I've heard about them." He said it like they were talking about the canals on Mars. He made another scan of the clearing, looking like an encounter-survivor who'd been beamed down in the middle of a mall parking lot and couldn't remember where he'd left his car.

Some kind of broad-leafed, generic crawling vine was minding its nonthreatening business on the trunk of a dwarfed birch near his sleeve. A cluster of leaves from it brushed his arm and he twitched away nervously. Obviously, Mr. Nice Voice wasn't some nature nut out on an evening of deer watching. Still, there were those eyes. . . .

"Think you can get up?" he asked her.

"I am woman," she groaned, levering herself to a sitting position.

"Excuse me?"

"Nothing. Thanks. I'll be okay."

He steadied her. Spot had scrambled the ballast in her hold and she was listing badly.

"What happened, anyway?" he asked.

"I had this little animal control issue." Her eyes focused

on some pine needles caught in resin stuck to one of her knees. She picked at the gunk.

"You were attacked?" He scanned the underbrush nervously.

"In a manner of speaking. But it's a . . . long story."

"Oh." Then he said the doom-laden magic words that everyone loves/hates to hear: "I've got time."

Tempting offer, really, to unburden herself to those green eyes. Stare deep into them. But, no. She had to be on *really* good terms with someone before she brought him home to Spot. "That's okay, really. Very nice of you, but trust me on this. Wait for the book; it'll be way better than the movie."

He angled himself so he could look directly at her. She sat up straighter and Orion tangoed in the darkening velvet above. He gave her a look that made her fervently hope that he didn't work for the Department of Mental Health, then made a conspicuous show of swiping at the tip of his nose with the back of a finger.

Sarah stared at him openmouthed.

He did it again.

She thought, *What's his—* Abruptly, she raised her hand to her own nose. Pine needles were projecting from her nostrils like boars' tusks. She turned her shoulder and performed the inelegant extraction.

That explained the look, anyway. She gave him points for hanging in there. "Yikes," she said.

"Is right," he said. "This happen often?"

"What, the pine needles?" She gestured at her nose.

"No, the other thing. The passing out."

"Oh." What the hell. "Well, I had a little . . . incident a while ago. Actually, quite a while ago. Almost"—like a gambler working against twenty-one, she hedged—"fifteen years ago. When I was a kid." Why was she suddenly getting cute about her age?

"And?"

Nosey, wasn't he? But because he was twisting her arm so badly she decided to keep going. "A plane crash. It still bothers me." Understatement of the year.

His eyes skipped a couple of frames. He was there, then he wasn't, and then he was back again. "Really. Let's get you to your car."

Screech! The conversation had slammed to a halt. They'd obviously stepped in something yucky. If he were with a friend she would have been concerned about the condition of his shoes, but as it was, the man was nothing more to her than a nice set of eyes, so she said, "Uh-huh, let's go," and slowly rose to her feet.

He kept a hand on her elbow. A nice hand it was, too. She was definitely still gaga. She leaned into him.

"Nice ones," he said.

Now she didn't know if the evening air suddenly chilled or what, but right out of nowhere she found herself with two tiny tents in her T-shirt.

"Your binoculars?" He was holding out the first subject of next month's "Gear Review."

Idiot. She nodded dumbly and slung them around her neck by the strap, where she should have put them in the first place.

"Ready?"

"Born that way." They took a few steps together; then he released her to the wild.

Stunted, scraggly stands of birch and pine dotted Pear Island. Fighting for purchase and freshwater, the trees shoot a tangle of shallow roots every which way just below the surface of the sandy soil. As the ever-industrious ocean winds strip away and redistribute the sand, these root bundles are laid bare, creating willy-nilly snares for the feet of the unwary. Sarah had spent most of her childhood dashing in and out of this twisted warren and considered herself beyond the klutz stage of life, but losing consciousness for—she still wasn't sure how long—put her in a whole other league.

"Oof—" She gracelessly hooked a toe on a particularly gnarled specimen and down she went, landing on top of the very expensive, very not-hers binoculars. They would undoubtedly leave an artistic bruise high on her rib cage.

"Shit. *Ow* . . ." Her conversation was deteriorating with every tumble. She gathered her legs under her and unconsciously hiked up her shirt to inspect the damage. "Damn," she cursed to the heavens. When she looked up she caught *him* looking. Usually a sports bra girl, that evening she was packing one of her few lilts of lace. She hated going to the laundromat and beggars couldn't be choosers.

"Sorry, I wasn't fast enough," the man with the nice eyes said.

To see everything? Sarah wondered. She hoped he didn't mean *to have avoided you altogether.* "S'okay. Ricochet Rabbit couldn't have caught me."

He laughed like he really remembered the cartoon.

She made to get up, again. Bing, bing, *bing!*

"Sit," he said, but not like you'd say it to a dog. Kindly. She fervently hoped he wasn't a stalker. What a waste of face. "Get your bearings."

"Good idea. Standing doesn't seem to be getting me much."

He laughed again. Not the vacant, just-doing-this-to-be-sociable kind, either. He really seemed to think she was funny.

Yeah, to watch.

Crickets chirped again, now that the crashing and bashing had subsided. The bullfrogs had never stopped. Life calling to itself. Someone had to say something, so she did. "It's beautiful out here, isn't it?"

He looked around him like she would have in the house-wares section: like he didn't have a clue what most of the stuff around him was. "Yes. Yes, it is," he said, vaguely.

"You come here often?" Didn't *that* sound incredibly stupid outside of a bar.

"I . . . uh, get pretty busy. Hard to get away."

"Yeah. Me too."

The colors in the western sky were fading. If you looked directly at the sunset, you'd never see the pastel hues thicken and darken, picking up color like a linen napkin dipped in red wine. You had to use your peripheral vision. There, rose became salmon. Indigo muscled in at the boundary of day and night. She finally said, "I think I could give it another go now."

He extended his hand. It had the expected number of appendages. She didn't have to count them individually to verify. Like the swallows to Capistrano, her wits had returned. He hauled her to her feet.

She took a few steps, holding onto his arm. Her legs lost their rented feel. "I'm good, I think."

"Glad to hear it."

She was glad that he was glad. She got chatty. Hey, nice night, nice arm, nice guy—apparently. She must have earlier told someone that she was coming out to the preserve, and, anyway, they were almost to the safety of her car. "Too bad what's going on about this place, huh?"

"How so?"

"I mean, the second runway?"

"No, tell me."

Instead of stopping to ask herself, *How could he not know?* she proceeded to tell him.

"The second runway? That jerk of a manager out at the field wants to build it? It's going to be totally fuc—I mean, frustrating, if it goes through."

"And what are you going to do about it? Careful of that root."

"Got it." She watched her feet move for a moment. "I don't have to do anything about it. The situation is going to resolve itself before long."

"How so?"

Again, did the guy live in an appliance carton? "You probably already know this"—she tried to read the expression on his face, but he was inscrutable—"but pretty soon the town is going to own all the preserve land. Once the owner, um . . . passes. He's eighty-four and not doing well." She explained the long-standing agreement between Noah Crossly and Tidal. "I know, I know. It sounds like everyone's just waiting around for him to die. But that crappy little airstrip has been squatting out there since the thirties, when Pear Island was just a fishing village. Kitty Hawk north. It's about time it got reined in."

"And you're the one to do it."

He didn't sound convinced she could.

"Yeah, well, me and the Friends." The Friends of the Preserve: a group of semifanatical, nature-loving Tidal residents.

He scoffed. "I've heard about them. They don't sound like any friends I'd want."

Maybe his eyes weren't so great after all. "Go ahead, laugh, but I've done the research. Once the town has clear ownership of the preserve land, we can block the construction of the second runway. Access roads, signal lights, stuff like that, have to go up and the manager needs rights-of-way granted to do that. Which we won't give him. With luck, that stinking airport's going to perpetually remain a one-horse show." She loved that last phrase. She made a mental note of it for inclusion in future Letters to the Editor.

Abruptly, he cocked his head like he was listening. Sarah

prayed it wasn't to voices that only he could hear. She picked out the roof racks of her Rav jutting above the line of brush ahead. Almost there. It was then that she too heard the droning in the distance.

"Frigging field," she said.

"Crossly Field," he said.

Quick comeback. Maybe his conversational skills weren't a total loss. "Same thing, isn't it?" She laughed.

He didn't. "No, it isn't."

Damn, just when she thought she'd be invited back for the cruise season.

"The thing should be shut down," she said.

"We all got to live," he said.

The simple statement rang with the metallic rasp of a rapier being drawn. Sarah stopped dead in her tracks at the trail marker set in the ground at the edge of the gravel parking area. The man with the nice eyes almost rear-ended her. She suddenly had a thought.

She rounded on Green Eyes. "Hey, you said you saw me pass out in the preserve, right?"

"So?"

"So, before I went bye-bye, how did you sneak up on me without me hearing you?" Daniel Boone he was not.

"I . . . saw you from . . . a little ways away."

Close enough to see her but not close enough for her to hear him. Right.

"How far away?"

"Ah . . . I don't know. Fifty feet? Something like that?"

In other words, directly overhead. He'd been in the fucking plane.

"You were in the fucking plane," she said.

Her hands started to shake. She jammed them onto her hips to steady them. "Why were you flying *that* low over the preserve in *that* particular spot?"

He'd been way off the flight path for the operating runway.

"I was on an . . . unscheduled flight," he said.

Unscheduled, her ass. She caught the ripe stench of hedging, a time-honored strategy she'd raised to the level of a personal art. Her gut sent her some very weird, very unpleasant messages.

"And your name is . . . ?"

"Logan Donnelly. I'm the new field manager out at Crossly." He stuck out his hand.

She suddenly wanted to wash hers. Should have known. Should have frigging known. It was always her that got stuck with the ace of spades in Hearts. Who always landed on No Parking.

"Well, well, well, Mr. Field Manager. At long last. Despoiler of green places, snake in the Garden of Eden, worm in the apple," she said, pleasantly. "How do you do?"

He took his hand back.

"Mr. Donnelly, I have only two things to say to you. One, Rachel Fucking Carson herself couldn't get that second runway open"—she grazed the front of his shirt with the tip of her index finger—"and two, I hope your stinking, inconsequential little operation gets blown into the sea."

She snapped a salute, spun on her heels, and stalked to the Rav. *Jerk.*

Bigger one, her. Absolutely shit judge of character. She patted herself down, searching for keys. Like an idiot she hadn't hooked them to the little ring inside the hip pocket of her hiking shorts. They must have fallen out when she conked out. Damn it, they were probably back there in the frigging sand somewhere.

She flinched at the touch on her arm. "Keep your hands off me," she said, spinning toward Donnelly. She aimed her finger at him again, this time like a derringer. "I know your type."

He put his hands up in mock surrender and took a step back. She resumed her full-body search. After a few moments he said, "Think quick." She heard a jingle and looked up.

She snatched her keys out of the air.

Asshole.

She spun her tires as she left the lot. Mr. Logan Donnelly, the brand-spanking-new "field manager out at Crossly," danced in the hail of flying gravel.

Chapter 2

Like an off-road racer on amphetamines, Sarah slammed the all-wheel-drive Rav through the twists, turns, and potholes peppering the dusty dirt track leading out of the preserve. Not until she hit the asphalt of the main road leading to the bridge over what was known locally as The Rip, a fierce little stretch of deepwater current that ran between Pear Island and Tidal proper on the mainland, did she calm down. She reminded herself that, on her salary, she could ill afford to replace the entire undercarriage of her vehicle.

The light on the front porch of her hovel came on automatically when she was about halfway up the front walk. In defense of her landlord, her rented house really didn't become a hovel until after she moved in. She retrieved the front door key from under a flower pot bursting with begonias. Thievery has become so sophisticated that "Look under flower pot" has been deleted from the procedure manual.

She let herself in, snapped the deadbolt home behind her, turned, and about jumped out of her skin. The silhouette of a man was framed in the kitchen doorway at the end of the hall.

"Jesus—" She stumbled backward, groping for the handle of the umbrella she kept in a corner next to the front door. Her motto? Impale first; ask questions later.

"Sarah . . ." the silhouette said.

Then she recognized the voice—which was a good/bad thing. It was one she thought she loved before she heard it more on voice mail than in person. It belonged to Rick, her ex–main squeeze. The man she'd been ready to spend the rest of her life with. Or so she thought until a noxious chemical accidentally spilled on him, morphing him into Captain Industry. *Wham!* Suddenly, he possessed the ability to open multiple warehouses in a single bound and spontaneously turn everything he touched—including her—into a business proposition.

She clicked on the hall light, illuminating what seemed to be the perpetually exasperated expression he'd been wearing since their little spat. They had been engaged. There were pictures around somewhere of her with a promontory-sized rock on her finger to prove it. But six weeks ago she had handed Rick—overhanded him, actually: fastball, high and inside—his ring back in a particularly graceless and ugly scene that took place over pasta. The symbol of their commitment she had pitched at him had bounced off his admittedly broad chest and landed neatly in his vermicelli with white sauce.

Now they were . . . taking some time.

"You left the key out," he said. "How many times have I told you about that? All some creep has to do is—"

"What are you doing here, Rick?" Her tone was neutral. The same gear their relationship was stuck in.

He came down the hall, arms extended in a full Welcome

Back, but she stood her ground. When he got within groping range, she made a quick little sidestep and dumped her stuff on the floor at the foot of the stairs. He immediately bent down, grabbed her backpack, and hung it neatly on a wall peg.

Sheesh. Enough to drive a person crazy. Wait—now she remembered. It had. "Rick, wait—"

He interrupted. "A man can't just drop in on his fiancée?" he asked. "He needs an invitation?" He took the umbrella from her.

"Ex-fiancée, Rick. We had an agreement, remember? To take some time? To think things over?"

"Well, yeah. But then to get married."

"Well . . ." Damn. Why was it so hard to give him up?

She stalled. "Look, Rick. I've got a lot of things on my mind right now. I haven't had time to think about . . . us."

His shoulders drooped and he put his hands on his hips.

"Sarah, I don't get you. I gave you over a month to . . . what did you call it? Reassess? Review? Reevaluate?"

He made it sound so cold. Part of her situational paralysis about Rick was that in a less than healthy way she felt sorry for him because he was involved with an emotional cripple: her. But if she wasn't careful, that feeling could prove her undoing. She'd end up allowing herself to be smothered by his immense Rickness.

"And now, what? You still don't know," he said. "You're never going to make up your mind, are you?"

He didn't hear that from her. But the man could read a situation, she'd give him that. Probably one of the reasons his business had grown so fast. Except she wanted their relationship to be more than just a "situation."

"Are you dumping me?" she asked.

"Dumping you?" He took her hands in his. "What are you, nuts?"

Don't ask a question if you don't want an honest answer. "I don't know. Maybe."

He laughed. "I love you."

And wasn't that just the trouble? He did.

He truly thought she was the cat's meow. He would be happy with her forever. She'd never have to lift a finger to support herself; he'd be the ultimate provider. And he'd never screw around on her. Yeah, yeah, everyone says that, but she really didn't think he would. He wanted her in his life and in his house and in his bed and on his balance statement for the rest of his life.

But where she really wanted to be was in his heart. And she wasn't.

So let him go, a normal person would say. As did the Greek chorus of everyone else in her life.

But Rick represented the ultimate rain check. An unredeemed winning lottery ticket. To her, though, its worth didn't lie in the actual cash value. It was the *idea* that she could cash in big any time she wanted to that was priceless. Rick was a hedge against . . . No. She wasn't going there.

"Yeah . . ." she said, apropos of nothing.

As with all chickenshits, her default strategy had been simple: Do nothing, cloud the waters, get people pissed. Delay, avoid, confuse—cha-cha-*cha!*

"You know I'd always take care of you, Sarah. Sickness, health, all that."

Because she was not an ice queen—her occasional bouts of cruel behavior notwithstanding—her eyes filled. He was genuinely offering her everything a lot of women would die for: a loyal, good-looking guy who'd love her forever in the best way he knew how. Tons of money. You couldn't laugh off the very tangible assets of Venture Adventura. But it was like the Zen thing: Grasshopper, what is the sound of one hand clapping?

Even coming from a writer that sounded pretty whacked to her.

Take Two.

What she meant is that she wanted a partner that could, well, supply the other hand. Someone who'd argue with her, bump up against her, scrape the velvet off her antlers with his. That was something deer did. Someone who didn't reflexively worship the ground she walked on. Someone who loved her—and this was the tough part—even though he really knew her. But Rick really didn't know her. And that was the rub.

She pressed her fists to the sides of her head. "Rick, I'm sorry. I'm not trying to string you along. I just don't . . ."

"Know yet?" he said. "I know." He kissed her forehead resignedly. "When you do, I'll be here."

Yikes. She *had* to find him a good woman. Shoot this thing he had going with her. Put him—and her—out of their collective misery, because she was a selfish jerk. She could never make a decision. What the hell was wrong with her? And why was her mother's voice suddenly in her head?

She sniffled and for one second she dropped her guard and allowed him to pull her close. He had just *the* best chest. *Mmmm . . .*

Rick's cell phone rang.

With the lightning speed of a gunslinger in the Old West, Rick had it out of its holster faster than you could say *amortization table*. Cripes.

"Hello? Yes, Mitch." His brows knitted: trouble in cyberspace. "Tell them I'll meet with them in"—she felt him check his watch over her shoulder—"twenty."

Hitch up the wagon, round up the posse.

"Right, Mitch. You, too." He snapped the phone shut without so much as a "bye." Big business is so touchy-feely.

He patted her butt. "Honey, I gotta go."

That she recognized from voice mail. "I know."

Halfway out the door he said, "Call you," for perhaps the millionth time since she'd known him.

"Bye," she said, as the screen clicked shut.

Her own phone rang. Numbly, she lifted the mobile from its cradle on the hall table. "Hello?"

"Ms. Dundee?"

"Speaking." Effing telemarketers.

"Robert Iverson here. From *Natural Spaces?*"

"Oh, yes, hello."

Robert Iverson. Ivy league, nice suits, hair going silver at the sides but still had most of it. He was the editor-in-chief of *Natural Spaces*, a magazine out of New York. Its feature stories were the height of *la-ti-da* in the world of conservation and focused on citizen groups—usually made up of people with hyphenated last names—battling to save green spaces. Her cash cow status had evidently attracted his attention. Nice, the job he'd interviewed her for. The reporter/writer position for the New England region was a lofty pulpit from which to preach about the Pear Island issue. And it was a step toward her dream of becoming a bigger, better writer.

"We'd like to offer you the New England region if you're still interested," he said.

Well, hang a bell around her neck and call her Bessie.

She gushed. "What an opportunity," "You won't be disappointed," the usual. They arranged a time for her to meet his staff.

She rang off and discovered a sudden passion for the Macarena.

Chapter 3

Even after she undulated at length up and down the hall, Sarah was still all jeeped up. Working for Iverson. Imagine that. Pay dirt.

She had to get out and burn off excess energy or implode. Sometimes she thought she was part Labrador retriever.

A brisk walk to the market calmed her down. She was in produce, squeezing a melon and minding her own business, when her best friend from high school hailed her. Joan was a real best friend because even if it was Sarah who'd put on a few pounds since the good old days, Joan would never, ever bring it up in conversation.

"Yo, Dundee. Heard the big news?"

"You're pregnant? Too late, got the full scoop at the pharmacy already."

"Funny woman. You gonna buy that thing or give it an orgasm?" Joan nodded at the melon in Sarah's hand.

Sarah looked around to see who might be within earshot.

"Noah Crossly?" Joan leaned in conspiratorially, like a spy passing on state secrets. "Passed away yesterday."

"No!"

"Oh, but yes." She, too, started to caress a melon speculatively.

Yikes, what do you say? *Sorry you're gone. When do we get the preserve?*

"I know how you feel," Joan said.

Somehow she always did.

"But it was expected and there's no grieving family in the picture, so let's hope things go as planned, eh?"

Joan was right, of course, but Sarah still found it sad that Noah Crossly had essentially died alone. But that was the way he had lived. We all make choices.

Joan gave a conspirator's wink and fished a crumpled sheet of paper out of her voluminous purse. "Hey, got a flyer with your name on it."

It was from the Friends of the Preserve. They were holding a public information meeting about the future of the preserve later in the week. "Count me in."

There was an unexpectedly large crowd on hand in the Tidal town hall Thursday night. Joan had saved Sarah a seat second row back from the stage. She looked like a fortune teller with all the jewelry she was sporting.

"Sheesh, SRO . . ." Sarah said.

"No shit, huh? People are out in droves."

"I thought this was just an informational meeting."

"No kidding."

"Love the earrings, dudette."

"What? A compliment?" Joan flattened her hand against her ample chest. "No comments about the hoops interfering with cell communications? You must be in a good mood." Sarah filled her in on the deal with *Natural Spaces.*

"I'm happy for you," she said, squeezing Sarah's hand. A *real* best friend.

Joan filled Sarah in on the group seated at the dais. "You know Susan Crawford, right?"

"Town counsel."

"Got it. Next to her, Hillary, obviously." Mrs. Harker, to Sarah—always. Her bright silver helmet of a hairdo shone in the overhead spotlights. She was basically a good egg, but she had been Tidal's elementary school nurse for something like thirty-five years. When someone discovers nits in your hair in third grade, your relationship with that person is fundamentally altered forever. Sarah was also pathologically mistrustful of alliterative names. After she retired from the school system, Mrs. Harker had been elected commander-in-chief of the militant Friends of the Preserve. She had constantly harried Noah Crossly for the last ten years of his life about fulfilling his promise to the town.

"Who's that bright, useless-looking guy?" Sarah asked.

"Crossly's lawyer. And ease up. I'm working on him. He might not turn out to be that useless after all." She leered.

Sarah didn't want to know more. "And the last guy . . . ?" Sarah couldn't see him; the podium completely blocked her view.

". . . is Logan Donnelly, the field manager."

"Him I know. We've met."

"Hubba-hubba. No fooling?"

"No, fool. I bumped into him in the preserve, unfortunately. It had been a nice night up till then."

Joan leaned in. "Hmmm. Woman with much gold in ear sense big story."

"Don't be an idiot. I passed out. You know—the usual. Plane low-buzzed me and down I went. He got me back to the Rav."

Joan frowned. "What was a plane doing that low over the

preserve, anyway?" Then she made one of her abrupt, eight-track topic changes. "And far be it for me to be the Voice of Reason, but did you ever think about getting a Med Alert beeper? It's not every day that"—she took another gander at the stage—"Harrison Ford's going to come along just when you need him."

"That's wasted on me," Sarah said, referring to her thumbnail characterization. "I'm obliged to hate his guts because he runs the frigging airport."

"When we own the preserve you might find him easier to take."

"There's only one place I'd like to take him and that's to court. Endangering me and the animals like that."

Mrs. Harker took the podium and the microphone squealed. Her silver helmet flashed under the stage lights. She looked like Diana on the hunt.

"Ladies and gentlemen, welcome. Thank you for coming out for this informational meeting. Without further ado, I'd like to introduce tonight's panel." Each of the participants stood and acknowledged the crowd as his or her name was called. Everyone on stage seemed subdued, as if there were some underlying discord among the group. Sarah's radar screen lit up.

"Hey," she whispered to Joan, "I'm getting weird vibes, here. I didn't expect a keg party or anything, but why is everybody up there so glum? It's a done deal. Just announce it already."

"I hear you." She looked concerned, too, and her radar was Defense Department issue.

Tidal's lawyer, Ms. Susan Crawford, spoke first. "Welcome everybody, and again, thank you all for coming out in such large numbers. Tonight we hope to provide you with sufficient information to keep you apprised of a very fluid situation."

"'A fluid situation'? What the hell does that mean?" Sarah whispered.

"Dunno yet." Joan's eyes scanned the panel members like she was reading their minds. She probably was, for all Sarah knew.

"I'd like to introduce Michael Brophy, counsel for Crossly Airfield," Susan Crawford said. "Mr. Brophy, would you shed some light on this matter for us?" She took a step back and motioned him to the microphone.

"Pontius Pilate," Joan murmured.

"What?"

"Crawford. She's washing her hands of something. I don't like this."

Brophy cranked the microphone gooseneck downward and it groaned. "Thank you, Susan, and greetings people of Tidal."

"He sounds like a space alien," Sarah said. Joan shushed her. She was not by nature a shusher. Translation: she was *very* worried.

Brophy cleared his throat. "I understand from my fellow counsel that the town of Tidal had a long-term . . . understanding . . . with Noah Crossly regarding the disposition of the Pear Island preserve land adjoining the parcel of land popularly known as Crossly Airfield."

Popular wasn't a word she would have gone with in the same breath as *Crossly*. Sarah sat up straighter in her seat. Brophy was spreading oil on the waters. Not good.

"It was understood that the transference of said parcel of land to Tidal would occur upon the death of the last surviving heir in the Crossly family line. It was the intention of Noah Crossly that this individual be Todd Crossly, his own son. Thomas Crossly, Noah's elder brother, was killed at Pearl Harbor in 1942, and Phillip, the younger, perished tragically in . . ."

In a freak accident right after the war. Yeah, yeah, this was the part everyone in Tidal knew. Sarah had been hearing about it ever since she was a kid. "The Crossly Curse" they called it in town. Noah was a nasty man in life, but his tragic loss of a sibling resounded within her. She also vaguely recollected hearing about another death at Crossly Field: a guy in the late sixties, early seventies had crashed out at the deserted field trying to make an emergency landing.

Brophy was still talking: ". . . unfortunate demise in"— he referred to his notes—"1970. This individual, later identified as Todd Crossly, had he not met his untimely death, would have inherited Crossly Field as well as the preserve land."

The pilot was Todd Crossly? That Sarah hadn't heard. Noah's *son?* From the reaction of people in the hall, everyone was as surprised by the information as she was. Mrs. Harker rapped her gavel and the side conversations silenced. She probably could have used her knuckles and had the same effect.

Brophy waited for silence before he continued. "It was commonly accepted that at the death of the last heir of the Crossly line the preserve land would automatically revert to Tidal under a written agreement."

So what was the problem?

"The problem is that the document outlining this agreement has apparently disappeared."

That got everyone's attention. People initiated cross conversations and a few Friends loudly offered some very unhelpful comments. Mrs. Harker vigorously exercised the moderator's gavel.

"The original, stored in town hall records, cannot be located nor can a copy be found among the late Mr. Crossly's papers or effects." Brophy massaged the edges of the podium.

Okay, but still no problem. Todd was an interesting, if not

somewhat macabre, side issue, but the last Crossly heir was as dead as yesterday's news.

The crowd settled as people gradually came to the same conclusion as Sarah had.

"Regarding the preserve land," Brophy continued, "the legal precedent we are operating under is that the final word regarding its present use, or any changes to that use, continues to rest with the surviving heir of the Crossly line."

Now she was confused. The surviving heir issue was clearly a moot point because there *was* no—

"Brace yourself," Joan whispered in Sarah's ear.

Brophy spoke directly into the microphone. "I must inform you that Noah Crossly was *not* the last heir to the Crossly line."

"Saw that one coming," Joan said into the shocked silence that lasted perhaps two seconds before the hall exploded. The crowd rose to its collective feet and Sarah had to stand on a chair or miss the show. People shouted and shook their fists. When verbal threats were made, the officer in back shouldered his way to the stage area.

"Crikey," said Joan.

Like you'd say "Survey says . . . ," Brophy lobbed his final grenade into the din. "The last heir of the Crossly line is"—he had to shout through the microphone to be heard—"Logan Donnelly."

The pandemonium in the hall ratcheted up about six notches. Brophy stepped back from the microphone as if he were expecting incoming missiles. The cop made a big display out of slipping his night stick out. Sarah saw him place a call on his shoulder microphone.

Logan Donnelly? The final heir? She struggled to comprehend the idea in the midst of the chaos erupting around her.

It was a pretty ugly, pretty scary scene for a while and it

was several minutes before the police officer got everyone settled down. Sitting down, at least.

Brophy came back to the podium. "In summary, as the surviving heir, Mr. Donnelly has continued proprietary rights to the preserve lands and may use them as he chooses. They will, of course, be transferred to Tidal, as per the long-standing agreement, upon the death of Mr. Donnelly."

Which half the people in the room obviously wanted to speedily render. More shouts rang out, but with the appearance of a second officer, everyone put a quick lid on it.

Brophy gestured for quiet. "Mr. Donnelly has made his intentions regarding the preserve very clear. He, perhaps, is the one to best outline them." He stepped down and Donnelly took the podium. Sarah hadn't noticed he had a slight limp. He had to crank the microphone upward. She'd forgotten how tall he was.

"Ladies and gentlemen, good evening." Predictably, he was met with a chorus of invectives from the crowd. Mrs. Harker's helmet caught Sarah's eye. Her frosty air of disapproval was better than most people's finger gesture.

"I can assure you that this evening's news, as shocking as it must be to you, was even more so to me, " Donnelly said. More booing. "When Noah Crossly engaged me as the manager of the field, I had no idea that I would one day be in control of it."

"Yeah, right . . ." echoed around the hall.

"I want to assure you that the preserve will continue to be used as it has always been. As a protected sanctuary for wildlife and the viewing of it by the people of Tidal."

What a stuffed shirt. What a blowhard. Sarah stuck her hand up in the air. Donnelly pretended he didn't notice her, so she waved it around energetically. "Excuse me!"

Sarah didn't remember until a long time later that Logan Donnelly had looked wearily behind him to his lawyer then, an action that somewhat surprised her at the time. Brophy had shrugged: *Better get used to it.* Donnelly resignedly turned to face his audience. Pro forma, he acknowledged Sarah's agitated arm antics. "Yes?"

Then, shading his eyes against the lights, he recognized her and became downright animated. "Why . . . we've met, haven't we? Yes, of course! It's my friend from the Preserve, Ms. Dundee."

Yes, they had met, but, no, she wasn't an old chum. She too well remembered the peeing and fleeing of beautiful Momma Deer. "Mr. . . . Donleavy, is it? Could you explain to us how flight paths directly above—and we're talking just a few *feet* above—treetop level will support and foster the protection of wildlife in the preserve?"

"Donnelly," he said.

"Pardon?"

"My name is Donnelly," he said evenly. "Not Donleavy."

Sarah conceded the point with a negligent wave. *Get on with it.*

"In every situation there must be compromise, Ms. Dungee."

Dungee. What a smart-ass.

He went on. "It's all about compromise. The town continues to get use of the land and I honor my grandfather's wish by reopening the second runway. Compromise, Ms. Dungee, compromise."

If he called her that one more time she was going to grab a baton from one of the cops and smack him with it. She held on to her temper by her fingernails.

"Compromise, Mr. Donnelly?" she said. The name game was getting old. "Compromise? Yes, I see you are very familiar with the concept." Sarah stood up and the cop gave her the hairy eyeball. What a baby; she was just a wee thing. "You've *compromised* the future of the animals in the preserve. You've *compromised* the viewing pleasure—isn't that what you called it?—of the people of Tidal. You've *compromised—"*

"Hear, hear!" rolled around the hall.

"We get your point, Ms. Dundee." It was Brophy again, moving in quickly and swinging the microphone away from Donnelly. "But the bottom line here is that Logan Donnelly is the rightful heir of Crossly Field and adjacent preserve lands. As such, he has final, ultimate, indisputable control of the disposition of the land."

"But—" Sarah sputtered, like a comic cartoon character.

"But nothing, Ms. Dundee," Brophy finished.

He caught the eye of the police officer. "I think it's an opportune time to adjourn this meeting. Let's let everyone sleep on it, shall we? Allow time for tempers to cool."

Nice thought, but hers wouldn't.

He motioned Donnelly away from the podium. "Please direct any further inquiries to my office. Thank you and good evening, ladies and gentlemen."

On the way out Joan said, "Well, that sucked."

So did Logan Donnelly. "We're screwed," Sarah said.

Chapter 4

The phone rang early the next morning. Actually, it was only early for Sarah. It was a little after nine, by the bedside clock.

"Hirro?" Her mouth was still sleeping.

"Oh—Sarah. Hillary Harker here. Did I wake you?"

The name snapped her awake better than any alarm ever could. "No problem. I was just . . . ah . . . getting up." A lie.

"Most unexpected result last evening."

"Yes, yes it was." She choked back a "ma'am."

"Of course we won't accept this lying down. Response plans are already developed."

She missed her calling at Normandy. "Really, Mrs. Harker, I don't think—"

"The Friends are picketing the airport."

And she was calling why? "That sounds um . . . great, Mrs. Harker. But, again, I really don't want—"

"I'd like you on the front lines, Sarah. You're a very visible member of our group."

Sarah wondered what group that was. "Ooookay."

Sarah also wondered if she could even *get* herself to the airport. And if she actually succeeded in making it there, for how would long would she stay conscious? Pitching face first into pine needles was one thing, tarmac another. But her fear of disobeying Mrs. Harker outweighed her fear of cosmetic dentistry. "Where and what time?"

"Ten o'clock this morning. We're carpooling. The rally point is the public lot downtown. We've gotten signs overnight."

Signs of what? Like omens? "Mrs. Harker, I care about the preserve, too, but I don't think we ought to base our response to Logan Donnelly solely on some sort of premonition. There's got to be a better way—"

"Sarah?"

"Yes?"

"Focus, dear. I'm talking about *protest* signs. To carry when we march? Alicia's husband had them printed overnight." Alicia Warren was Mrs. Harker's second in command. She also had silver helmet-hair.

"Right."

Although Sarah was determined to protect her deer pals and their habitat, she also valued her anonymous lifestyle. She'd gone so far as to refuse to have her picture printed in her "Good Gear" column. They could put someone else's face there if they really needed one, but not hers. Sure, she'd shot her mouth off at the town meeting, but that was because she was irritated. And afraid for the deer. Advocating for others, especially defenseless others, always got her dander up.

True, she'd written tons of Letters to the Editor, and, yes, she'd researched the legal aspects of the second runway. But that part was all done very hush-hush. Now Mrs. Harker was asking her to be cannon fodder, all because of her "visibility." Sarah suddenly wished she could make herself *in*visible.

"Mentally prepare yourself, Sarah," Mrs. Harker said. "We're not sure what we'll be up against once we get there."

Sarah checked her watch. How much mental preparation could a person do in . . . forty-five minutes, anyway? Probably just enough time to give the ol' bayonet a quick swipe with the stone, she guessed. Check the ammo clips, cinch up gear straps. Maybe instead she'd just brush her teeth and scrub the pillow lines off her face.

"Okay, Mrs. Harker. Ten o'clock."

"See you then, Sarah."

Yes, *ma'am!*

Sarah rolled into the town parking lot at ten o'clock sharp. She glanced at her watch. In military time that was about . . . ten o'clock. She got confused about that when the time went past noon.

More than half the spaces were already taken. Pretty packed for a midweek morning in Tidal. Serious-looking women with clipboards were working the crowd, taking people's names, presumably so they could notify the next of kin if anyone didn't return from the mission.

In keeping with the military theme, she'd worn a fetching blue and white camouflage top, sleeveless, with spaghetti straps. They'd never find her in the Arctic tundra.

She chose hiking boots over flip-flops. Assuming she even made it to the airport, they'd be on their feet for a while, and the boots would be an all-around better choice if they linked up into human chains and the police ended up dragging them away. Of course, she hoped it wouldn't come

to that, but in her limited knowledge of protest actions—
she'd seen the black-and-white footage of Montgomery,
Alabama—things done in groups, however benign they may
begin, seemed to have a way of turning ugly.

Deep down, Sarah knew she was as committed to saving
the preserve and the animals as the semiscary-looking people around her were, but she just didn't feel that a large-
scale, organized group protest best suited the cause. The
Friends were playing into Logan Donnelly's hands by coming across as a tree-hugging fringe group, as an eminently
dismissable wacko element. She herself preferred the inti-
macy of a close-proximity, one-on-one verbal knife fight,
where things got personal and you could slash at your oppo-
nent's honor and integrity. So much more satisfying.

One of the semiscary people around her turned out to be
Joan.

"You trying to blend into the landscape?" Joan asked, giving Sarah's top the once-over. "Wrong colors for this zone.
We're temperate."

"Ha, ha. But you're right. I'm kind of a fish out of water
here. Mass protest is not really my thing."

"Good thing you didn't grow up in the sixties," Joan said,
leaning on Sarah while she adjusted a strap on her sandal.
Joan evidently had more optimistic expectation of the morning's outcome than Sarah did.

"You'd have fit in perfectly back then," Sarah said. "I
know! When we get to the gate at the field, maybe we can
have a sit-in and sing 'Kumbaya.'" She batted her eyes excitedly.

Joan considered Sarah, head cocked to one side. "Say,"
she said, conversationally, "is it just me, or do other people
think your attitude blows?"

Sarah tuned her out because she knew Joan was right.

She *could* be a wet blanket sometimes. Okay, a lot of the time. But the thought of going to the airport really had her in a state.

One of the women with clipboards came up to them. They signed in. Sarah hoped her name wouldn't show up on some FBI watch list. A few minutes later, Alicia Warren cued them through a bullhorn to return to their vehicles; then she proceeded to line all the cars up with the precision of a funeral director.

Joan rode shotgun in the Rav. "10:20 A.M., mark," she said, poking at the buttons on her watch.

"What's with that?" Sarah asked.

"Hillary's got the departure time figured down to the minute. Why? I'm not privy. Something big's going on at the airport and she wants us to arrive smack in the middle of it."

Sarah's stomach flipped. Kill her with the planes, why don't you, then bury her with the publicity.

"Joan?"

"Mmm?" She'd switched to fiddling with the buttons on the radio.

"I don't know if I can do this."

"What, protest?"

"No. You know . . ."

"Oh, shit—the airport."

"Exactly." Sarah's throat felt like she'd swilled sand for breakfast.

"Nice time to think of that."

"Never do now what you can put off till later."

"Yeah, yeah. Story of *my* life. Let me think." Joan put her thumbs to her temples like she was trying to plug holes she'd suddenly discovered there, then said, "I got it. We'll use mental imagery."

"Joan, no voodoo please. I'm serious—"

"So am I. It'll get your mind off the planes. Let me drive."

"Okay." Sarah put on her blinker and checked the rear-view mirror.

"What are you doing?" Joan asked.

"Pulling over."

"No—don't! Hillary'll have our ass for dinner if we disrupt her precious convoy. Keep the wheel straight and get your foot off the gas."

"Joan, no. Please—"

Joan hiked her leg around the gearshift and slid her foot onto the gas pedal. The Rav shot forward.

"Shit, Joan! Stop—"

Sarah braked the Rav just in time to keep it from ramming into the rear of a huge white sedan driven by one of Mrs. Harker's contemporaries.

"Got it," Joan said. "Now, move your scrawny butt out of that seat. I got the wheel."

Somehow they did it. Joan ended up driving and Sarah wound up on the passenger's side.

"Shut your eyes," Joan said.

"What now?" Sarah said. What else could she do? Kidnap victims are advised to acquiesce to their captors.

"Picture yourself as . . . um . . . a tiger."

"A tiger? Why?"

"Because deer aren't dangerous. Christ. Will you please cooperate?"

"Got it. Claws? No claws?"

"Claws out, snarling."

Sarah didn't tell Joan, but she decided to become Spot. That didn't take much imagination.

"Okay. Now snarling." Sarah's fangs were dripping. She was cruising for fresh meat, pacing the length of that brick wall. Sniffing out weak spots. Spot for a Day. Not bad, actually, to be the aggressor for a change.

"How's it going?"

"It feels . . . ah . . . good, actually. Powerful."

"All that time with Dr. Loo? You should have come to Dr. Joan's free clinic instead."

"You'd look frumpy in a kimono." Dr. Cynthia Loo was Sarah's therapist. Lovely woman with a voice to match. Soothing, tranquil. She and Sarah had been playing Pin the Tail on the Doggie every Tuesday afternoon in Dr. Loo's office for years. Spot's wiliness made him an expensive pet to maintain.

"Incoming, smart-ass," Joan said.

Sarah heard the buzz. An airplane. She kept her eyes shut tight and kept snarling.

"Pretend that plane is threatening your cubs. Snarl louder."

In her mind Sarah snarled louder.

"I can't *hear* you," Joan said in singsong.

Sarah snarled audibly.

"You sound like Bambi with a wedgie."

Sarah cranked up her vocal cords and let loose her inner dog. The buzz from the sky was drowned out. Pretty slick. She kept it up. The closer they got to the field, though, the more planes she heard. Panic swam up at one point and she felt Spot's hot breath. Not coming out *of* her, coming *at* her. "Losing it here . . ." she told Joan.

"Hit this," Joan said.

Sarah opened her eyes. The flat of Joan's palm, fingers pointing up, was facing her. Sarah tentatively poked at it with a knuckle.

"For God's sake, you pussy," Joan said, "smack it!"

A plane sailed directly over the car, sounding loud enough to be *in* the car. Spot—the real one—sank his teeth into Sarah's ankle. She freaked, balled her fist, and punched Joan's hand as hard as she could. The Rav swerved; somebody honked. Sarah shut her eyes to await the inevitable crash, but the car rocked back into the lane. Joan didn't miss a beat.

"That's it!" she said. "Every time you get wigged out, smack—er—something. Here. Put my pocketbook on your lap." Sarah peeked and caught her massaging her hand.

When she heard the next plane, Sarah pictured herself on the top of the Empire State Building, holding onto the lightning rod with one paw and swinging at airplanes with the other. She slammed her fist down onto Joan's heavy leather bag until the infernal buzzing was driven out of her head.

"This is . . . stupid . . ." Sarah said, out of breath, "but it's . . . working. . . ."

Joan clucked. "And me without a doctorate. Open your eyes; we're at the gate. You owe me a tube of SPF fifteen, by the way."

She was right. Something was definitely . . . juicy around the flap of her bag. Sarah guiltily wiped cream off the leather with a fingertip and rubbed it onto her forearm.

The Rav coasted to a stop. There was a cop at the head of the convoy, motioning Mrs. Harker to pull off the road. Sarah put on sunglasses.

"I think he's telling Hillary it's private property," Joan said, squinting. "He's not letting us in. Donnelly must have gotten the tip-off we were coming." She followed the car in front of them onto the grass verge of the access road. Through the chain-link fence, not a hundred yards from them, Sarah saw a plane jump into the sky. The sun caught its wings, making them sparkle. She pummeled the pocketbook to within an inch of its life.

"Ye-ess?" Joan asked.

"I'm okay," Sarah said. "I'm okay. For now at least."

"Good. Feel powerful. Be powerful. Avoid sunburn at all costs. Give me some of that would you?" She pointed to the white trail of ooze now gushing freely from under the flap of her purse. Sarah scooped up a glob and handed it over. Again, Joan was a *really* good friend.

"You ought to put some of this on," she said, slathering her face. "You're already looking a little red."

"I'm pumped up. Like I want to enlist in the Marines or something," Sarah growled. Slamming things around really shook something loose in her head. Her mind was off the planes and onto what they were there for: the deer, the preserve. To fight for them. She was sure Dr. Loo would have been proud of her. She had "made her anger available." Sarah could hear Dr. Loo saying that in her lovely Asian lilt.

A woman was making her way down the line of cars and handing out signs on sticks: *Crossly Hides the Plane Truth, Runaway Runways Ruin Rights*—and Sarah's personal favorite—*Stop the Runway from Hell.* Alicia Warren's hubby had had a busy night.

Joan jumped out and grabbed the *Plane Truth* sign and Sarah ended up with *Hell,* so to speak. After an embarrassing little squabble, she got the one she really wanted. Why Joan didn't just deck her sometimes . . .

Mrs. Harker was packing steel—in this case a whistle—which she used to round everyone up at the gate.

"People, people," she said, standing on the running board of a huge SUV while an underling helped her balance. "Gather round. Time's wasting."

The rented cop grumpily watched from his post beside the front gate. Traffic entering the field was forced to make its way around the bulging entourage.

"This officer"—Mrs. Harker gestured toward him without turning her head—"has refused to allow us entry. Not that we expected anything less."

"With a good five-finger boost I'd have you over the wire in a heartbeat," Joan muttered in Sarah's ear. "Just think of the trouble you could cause inside."

A plane engine revved somewhere inside the fence and Sarah mentally kicked Spot away from her leg. "No, thanks," she whispered back. "This is close enough." She was pumped, not suicidal.

"We'll form a circle near the entrance," Mrs. Harker said. "As long as we keep moving and don't impede traffic we can stay as long as we like. We are guaranteed these rights under our Constitution."

Mrs. Harker made it sound like their Constitution was somehow superior to the one that served the other 220 million people in the country.

She was handed down off the car and people followed her to the gate, where everyone began milling around in a rough circle. People looked self-conscious and preoccupied, like they were wondering whether they'd left the iron on or thinking maybe they'd forgotten about a dentist appointment, but Joan got right into the swing of the thing.

"Crossly, Crossly, you guys frost me!"

Mrs. Harker shot her a look registered with Frigidaire, so Joan worked it around a bit.

"Buzz, buzz, buzz, buzz! That's all Crossly ever does!"

Some of the people in the crowd looked at Joan like they wished they *were* at a dentist appointment.

"Pretty good, huh?" she said, looking to Sarah for encouragement. Sarah pretended to have a sliver from the sign stuck in her hand.

"You watch too many football half-time shows," Sarah said.

"Really. So what're you bringing to the party?"

Sarah thought for a minute. She was a writer. Words were her life. She could do this.

She extemporized. "How about this? *'Logan Donnelly, you really suck. About the deer? You don't give a f—'* "

"Sarah!" She jumped and Joan laughed. It was Mrs.

Harker, calling across the circle to them. "Come over near me, dear. Let's marshal our forces, so to speak."

"She's separating us," Joan said.

"I feel like I'm back in junior high," Sarah muttered. She sheepishly cut across the ring of milling people to join up with Mrs. Harker.

"Sarah, I need you."

Sarah looked at her blankly.

"To help with the plan, dear?" she said, as if she thought Sarah was an imbecile.

"The plan?"

"To get in."

"In . . . ? As in . . . *in* the gate?"

"Yes." Her eyes were sparkling and the knuckles gripping her sign were white.

"But . . . there's a cop there."

"He is there"—she glanced disparagingly toward the officer—"because inside the gate, at this very minute, Logan Donnelly is rededicating the airfield as Crossly Memorial Airport. Can you imagine that?"

Yes, she could. Her blood boiled on cue.

"There is a television crew in there filming the ceremony for the news," she said.

A plane went by low overhead, probably coming in for a landing. Sarah barely noticed it.

"That bastard."

"Precisely."

Sarah played out a scenario in my head. "He'll get TV time on this second runway opening and everyone will assume it's a done deal, that the whole community approves of it."

"As they say after church suppers, dear, *bingo!*"

"We can't let this happen."

"My thoughts exactly."

That she and Mrs. Harker were in complete agreement should have thrown up a red flag in Sarah's mind. Maybe it did and the red on it just blended in with the only color in the visible spectrum she could perceive right then.

"Tell me about the plan."

Mrs. Harker nodded over her shoulder. "See Mr. Edmonds?" Sarah looked behind them. Ah, yes, the elderly driver of the Cadillac Joan had almost grafted Sarah's precious Rav onto when they were doing their frantic, front-seat fire drill.

"He's going to distract the officer at the gate," Mrs. Harker said.

"By?" Sarah desperately hoped it wouldn't involve the removal of any items of his clothing.

"Feinting a fainting spell."

Say *that* five times fast.

"Cool." There it was again. Another warning. She was using colloquialism with the lady in starched white whose office was right next to the principal's.

"When he hits the deck we make a run for it," Mrs. Harker said.

"Right past the guard—"

"Right through the gate—"

"And right into the middle of the ceremony!"

"Cool!" This time Mrs. Harker said it. The cock had crowed for the third time, but Sarah's ears were full of the rush of boiling blood.

With the casual cunning of an inmate on break in the prison yard, Mrs. Harker gave a knowing nod to Mr. Thaddeus Edmonds and down he went like a bundle of wet laundry. Panic broke out in the ranks. The officer came running over, yelling into his radio mike. Mrs. Harker's pals screened us from view.

Sarah grabbed her sign in a free hand and, with one mind, they made their dash for the gate.

"There!" Mrs. Harker screamed, once they passed the guard shack. "Over there!"

All Sarah saw were rows upon rows of planes, some of them tied down just like her family's African pilot used to have their plane. He'd rope their little plane to boulders in the afternoon when the hot, dry winds kicked up, threatening to flip the flimsy little thing onto its back.

"I can see the TV truck!" Mrs. Harker cried, in the nick of time. Sarah shook herself into the present. Mrs. H. had damn good eyes. And a pretty good set of lungs. Sarah was working to keep up with her.

Then Sarah spotted Logan Donnelly. Again behind a podium. Did the knucklehead own a portable one he just wheeled around with him?

"Twelve o'clock!" Sarah pointed. Mrs. Harker knew just what she meant.

They made for *him*.

Something, probably another plane, coughed into life in a row close to them, but Sarah was locked on target like a kamikaze, Logan Donnelly in her crosshairs.

They came at him from the side, so some of the people seated in front of him saw them charging before he did. The onlookers stared in disbelief. Sarah could just imagine how she and Mrs. Harker looked: a couple of mismatched warrior princesses in full-on battle mode, one scrawny and dirty blonde, the other elegant and matronly. Sarah figured that the protest signs probably tipped off that she and Mrs. H. weren't just hurrying to catch a flight.

Donnelly realized he'd suddenly lost his audience and followed their drifting gaze. The camera guy swung away from him and toward the charging duo. A guy with a lot of forehead and meticulously styled hair did a fancy lasso thing with a microphone cord to place himself between them and the rolling camera. They blew past a reporter from *The Coastal Press*.

Mrs. Harker beat Sarah to the edge of the seating area by full seconds.

"You!" Logan Donnelly shouted at Mrs. Harker. Rather unimaginative, Sarah thought. "And you!" He'd seen her.

"Queue up, dear, and keep moving!" Mrs. Harker called to her. Good soldier to the last, Sarah got "in line" behind her, which in retrospect seems an extraordinarily funny way to think about what she did, because it was only the two of them. The remainder of the day, from that moment on, became increasingly less hilarious.

They paraded around in—again, try to imagine this—a "circle" and Mrs. Harker, to not only Sarah's amazement, but that of every single person present, began chanting, "Logan Donnelly, you really suck. About the deer? You don't give a . . ."

Oh, yes, she finished it. Six and a half times before the wail of a police siren was heard.

Nine times—by then they'd turned it into a round—before Sarah felt her sign being pried from her grip. Nine and a *half* times at the point at which she desperately swung said sign at the closest thing to a pocketbook near to hand: Logan Donnelly.

The wood strapping and cardboard squarely impacted the crown of his dark head and the sign shattered with an incredibly satisfying rip, splinter, and tear.

In retrospect, Sarah was glad about the hiking boot decision. She lost a lot of rubber off the heels when the police dragged her sorry ass off to the cruiser.

Chapter 5

Joan, ever the pal, sprung Mrs. Harker and Sarah from the town pen.

That's a little dramatic, actually. She picked them up outside the police station after they were released later that evening on personal recognizance. Mrs. Harker and Sarah had called her on Mrs. H.'s cell phone, found at the bottom of a paper bag in which the police had placed their personal effects. *Personal effects?* You know, personal things: shoelaces, belts, drawstrings, anything else a body could use to hang or maim itself while in captivity. Gimping around the sticky floors of the Tidal lockup in heavy hiking boots with no laces wasn't easy.

All in all, though, incarceration hadn't been that bad. A few of the cops were kind of cute in a baby-faced, smooth-shaven, I'll-take-two sort of way. Mrs. Harker was the one who brought up that last point. Sarah hoped she would still be as enthusiastic at what? Seventy-something?

One of the guys gave them a couple of stale doughnuts for lunch, then a couple of microwaved Lean Cuisine's for dinner. Mrs. Harker and Sarah had no choice but to use the communal toilet in the cell, but Mrs. H. displayed an unexpectedly wicked sense of humor and an innate ability to make the most graceless of bodily functions an event. Aside from a potentially life-threatening case of waffle butt from the ventilated metal seats in the holding cell, they made it through their slammer time in pretty good style.

When Sarah got home around six-thirty, the damn message machine was blinking "Full." She was about to tap the rewind button when she halted her right hand in midair. *Yuck.*

She ran to the bathroom. She scrubbed her hands until they glowed cherry red. Got out the rubbing alcohol and wiped down the front door latch. And the house key. Then, recalling where her lily-white butt had recently rested, she took a shower. With antiseptic hand soap. Finally, she forced herself to stop thinking. It was a while before she made it back to the machine. Her mother's voice leapt out at her.

She and her mother had survived the plane crash.

"Sarah, I'm very worried. Where are you? As soon as you get home I want you to—"

Render a full report. Got it.

Next.

"Sarah, your mother here. Call me immed—"

Click. Violet's relentlessness was exhausting. It exacerbated the gulf that had steadily widened between Sarah and her since that awful day on the hot African savannah.

The other messages were from Robert Iverson; Violet; Logan Donnelly's lawyer, a Michael something; Violet again; and lest Sarah forget about her, Violet.

Michael something turned out to be Michael Brophy from the town meeting. Sarah had forgotten Joan had pointed him out to her.

He evidently knew her pretty well, though. Well enough to use her full name: Sarah Claire Dundee. In school, this had always meant she was in trouble. The trend continued. Brophy informed her that a restraining order had been issued preventing her from coming any closer than one hundred yards to either Crossly Field or Mr.—*bastard*—Logan Donnelly.

Like she'd want to.

A courier would deliver the notice to her in the morning. Goody, she loved getting mail.

Sarah placed a quick call to Susan Crawford, Tidal's town counsel, at home. She and Ms. Crawford didn't exactly travel in the same circles anymore, but they'd gone through the grades together, all the way up through high school. Besides, Sarah addictively watched *Law and Order.* She was David fighting Goliath and deserved publicly appointed, free legal counsel.

Susan assured Sarah that Donnelly's restraining order was in fact legitimate and, in terms of her continuing right to freely walk the streets, was worth very much more than the paper it was written on.

"Translation, Sarah? Resist the temptation to dick around with Logan Donnelly. The law is on his side."

"Thank you, Susan."

Sarah rang off politely enough but knew they probably wouldn't be doing lunch anytime soon.

She took a deep breath and dialed the number Iverson had left her.

A series of ultrapleasant secretaries volleyed her back and forth, then she heard, "Hello, Robert Iverson."

"Mr. Iverson? Sarah Dundee returning your call."

"Oh—Ms. Dundee, yes. Glad you called. How are you? Um . . . A few things have changed around here since we last talked."

"Oh . . . ?"

"Yes, Ms. Dundee—er, may I call you Sarah?"

"Sure, why not?"

Crap. This was gonna be the big Let-Her-Down-Easy scene. This'd be the first *and* last time her name would fall from his lips. He didn't want her anymore.

"Well, Sarah, I'm afraid the position we offered you—the one covering the New England region?—no longer exists."

"I see," she said, when she really didn't, but she had to respond with something other than "You *suck!*"

"It's been reconfigured, so to speak."

So to speak?

Disappointment, bitter as acid, rose in her throat. What was up with offering a person a job that didn't ever exist? Or maybe *it* did, but now they didn't want *her* to do it. Screw Iverson.

"Well, Mr. Iverson . . . say, could I call you Robert? Well, it sounds like we don't have much to talk about. Since I've really got to be going—"

"My, my, Sarah, you're awfully hard to talk to now that you're a celebrity." He chuckled.

She didn't get the joke. Time in the tank numbs a girl. "Pardon?"

"You haven't seen the TV?"

Dumbly, she looked at her ancient set in the corner of the sun porch cum living room grafted sometime in the sixties onto the rear wall of the tiny rented house built sometime before the Wright Brothers made it big.

"Still not . . ."

"The six o'clock news? You and"—there was a rustle of paper—"Mrs. Harker?"

"Were what?"

"Taking on Goliath," he said, chortling.

Phrase stealer.

"Turn. On. Your. Television." He enunciated each word slowly and carefully. Admittedly, her hair did have a little blond in it. Streaks, really, but they were completely natural.

Sarah did what Iverson said. And saw herself. And Mrs. Harker.

And the tracks the heels of her hiking boots had left on the asphalt of Crossly Field. Like bread crumbs, the rubber "contrails" led right to the rear door of a police cruiser. A smooth-shaven, baby-faced man in blue—she and Mrs. H. had found out at the jail later that the name of this particular one was Russell, prompting Mrs. Harker to dub him Satin Sheets—could be seen guiding Sarah's natural blond-streaked crown safely past the roof line of the sedan.

Violet must be so proud.

"I don't know what to say," Sarah said.

Oh, there was Logan Donnelly—*bastard*—picking splinters of wood off his polo shirt. The color looked weird against his trousers. Maybe it was just her TV set. She fiddled with the color knob. His skin turned a sickening green. She decided to leave it that way.

"So what do you think?"

Iverson had asked her something. The on-screen Martian had her mesmerized. *Bilious* bastard. "Uh-huh, yeah. Good."

"Great! We're all very excited here. The new position will really take advantage of your visibility. As I say, it will cover the entire U.S. instead of just the New England region, as originally discussed."

Excuse me?

"We want you on-site all over the fifty states, interviewing people on the front lines of preservation work. Your experience hiking, backpacking, canoeing, rock climbing will be enormously useful. We want you on the ground, so to speak, actually traversing, paddling, *climbing* these places people are struggling to save. Your unique combination of skills will bring a three-dimensional quality to our reporting never seen before."

Sarah put a hand to her chest to keep her heart from punching through. *Holy hand grenades, Batman.* All fifty states.

Surfing in Maui. She couldn't surf, but she'd learn.

The Grand Canyon: cathedral of everything holy and unspoiled. Pack out ya poop, but she'd deal.

Alaskan sled dogs. *Mush!*

"Did you say yes?" Iverson asked.

Close enough. She fought off hysteria and incontinence and framed her answer carefully.

"Yikes, of course! Yes! And thank you. Thank you very much."

"Great, great. The only thing the staff and I ask is that before we all get together—in, say, two weeks?—is that you capitalize on your newfound media exposure and put together an outline of your battle to save the Pear Island nature preserve. Just so we get a sense of your style and approach. How's that sound?"

Now it was *her* battle? But sure, whatever. She'd agree to run through brambles naked just as long as she got the job.

She said so more or less, omitting the naked part.

"Fabulous. Let me have my secretary call back. She'll set up a time for you to come in and meet all the staff."

Her new boss rang off.

She hung up and this time did the Washing Machine. *Oh, yeah . . .*

Ho-ly crap. Did that just happen? Tell the fricking stories of people all over the fricking *country?* Damn. It was just too good.

Ice cream with a cherry on top. The whole frigging *coun-*

try. See all kinds of exotic places. Go around and around the Earth, just like that little plane in the opening credits of Casablanca.

Zooom! She flew her hand around the hallway. Then doubled over.

Shit.

No.

She dropped to her knees, her brain liquefying. How could she be so stupid?

The plane, boss, the plane. She couldn't *drive* to Alaska, or Hawaii. Sure, the television networks allowed John Madden—another invisible pet owner for sure—to drive weekly his tour bus cross-country from football game to football game, but Sarah Dundee wasn't exactly packing the same level of market draw as Mr. Six-Legged Turkey. Iverson would laugh her out of his office. If he got so much as a whiff of Spot, his offer would retract like a bungee cord.

She was screwed.

By an ubiquitous, inconsequential piece of flying tin that stood foursquare between her and her future. And learning to surf. The statistically safest form of mass transportation available would, psychologically speaking, kill her if she boarded it. She'd be a full-time job for some unlucky air marshal. Years of dear Dr. Loo hadn't changed the simple fact that she was absolutely, completely, and totally chickenshit to get on an airplane.

Fuck.

Spot sensed Sarah was talking about him. In the back of her mind, he lumbered to his feet. Sarah lifted her right arm and held it out straight, palm facing the floor. She watched him hunt her down, offering no resistance. . . .

Tiny tremors rippled through her shoulder and, in a few seconds, her whole hand visibly shook and an icy numbness crept into her fingers. Objective and removed, she felt steel bands encircle her chest. Her throat constricted, cold sweat broke out on her face and neck, and nausea overwhelmed her. She dropped to her knees, then crawled to the wall and sat with her back against it. She fought the fighting urge to run—anywhere—and just . . . watched.

Her hands gripped her knees like they were sawdust baseballs and she could burst them if only she applied enough pressure. Her teeth ground together, masticating bitter memories. The smell of airplane fuel filled the hallway and the floor tilted sickeningly. With a will of their own, her eyes drooped shut and she watched while a crimson trickle slid down her mother's slack face.

Her father—*Oh, God*. His limp form in the copilot's seat, draped sideways across the body of their pilot. The orange heat of flames lapped the oak floor near Sarah's feet, and her legs drew back as if the blaze were real.

The fugue, like all the others, eventually ran its course. Feeling returned to her limbs, her breathing steadied, and her heart rate gradually slowed. But the attack had torn through her like a tornado in a trailer park. There was no resisting Spot in one of his moods; his power was awesome and absolute. Her psyche was in ruins.

She dragged the front of her top across her forehead to wipe the sweat from her eyes. She smelled like an amusement park ride on a hot day. Gripping the stair balusters for support, she pulled herself to her feet.

Standing there, in the middle of her hallway on a soft, balmy evening in July, she had to fight to convince herself that what she walked upon was solid hardwood, not melting aluminum.

Yes. There were the cracks in the floor where the boards didn't quite meet. Check. There: the dusty, white baseboards; the familiar wallpaper; the painted chair rail. Spot was temporarily sated. She was okay.

Walk the hall, now. Easy. Tiny baby steps.

Into the kitchen. She lunged for the edge of the oak pedestal table. Too fast. The world reeled and she lowered herself like an octogenarian into a captain's chair. She slugged coffee left over from the morning and quickly swallowed. Gross, but reviving.

The conversation with Iverson. It happened when? Minutes ago? Days? The mockingbird in her Birds of the Audubon kitchen clock obligingly warbled the seven o'-clock hour.

Shit. She was a mess.

She opened the back door for some air and peered through the screen. The backyard was beautiful. Yesterday, she had given the grass its semiannual cut with the crotchety landlord's crotchety old gas mower. She'd bagged the grass clippings and thrown them around the base of the evergreens for mulch. It still smelled fresh and green out there. A beautiful, pregnant, poignant, coastal Massachusetts evening. An early cricket chirped.

Life wasn't crazy; she was. Crazy, crazy, crazy. Patsy Cline, move over.

Was she always going to be nuts? Living a limited life tethered to a maniacal mutt?

There had to be a way out.

Dr. Loo, God bless her, couldn't seem to fix her. A succession of other shrinks had been working on Sarah since childhood. No joy there, either. She was beginning to think that she had to do it herself. Not alone, maybe, but mostly. By herself, she meant, mostly by herself. She sighed. She really didn't know what she meant.

It was frustrating. What end of a mad dog do you grab at? And even if she managed to get a good hold on him and fling him as far away into a dusty, unused corner of her mind as she could, wouldn't he just find his way home again? Home.

She'd given him one for twenty years. With three squares and cable. The question of the hour was: Why?

Never ask, she reminded herself, because you will receive. The insight sandbagged her: part of her would *miss* him if he left for good.

She struggled to round out the idea. Maybe he was her drug, her alcohol, her cigarettes, her reason—her *excuse?*—for not going all the way in her life. For not living on the edge. My God, she thought, she was like a battered spouse. Spot kept her safe, cocooned within a predictable pattern of abuse.

Now *that* was sick. She couldn't keep throwing opportunities—her *life*, for God's sake—away. She had to learn to live without Spot.

She paced the cracked kitchen linoleum and listened for the cricket. He answered. She paced some more, thoughtfully, only stepping on the faded flower arrangement at the exact center of each stick-on floor tile. Splashed water on her face at the sink.

There was some good news. Dr. Joan's *ad hoc* therapy on the way to the airfield that morning showed encouraging results, sort of. It enabled her to get her ass hauled off to the pokey, bond with the truly hysterical Hillary Harker, and entertain a B-grade fantasy about baby-faced officers of the law. Maybe there was hope out there yet.

Another buzz, not from the cricket. Sarah cracked open the screen door and searched out the sound. There, low on the horizon: a small plane. Laboring along, though, as if held back by an invisible hand. It slowly approached the house. Her insides churned. She was in no shape for a Round Two.

If she stood right there in her doorway long enough— maybe for a million or so years—intently observing planes go by, would she eventually give Spot the slip? Be able to just get on a plane and fly off and do a job?

Progressive desensitization was what the shrinks called it when you cuddled up next to whatever scared the crap out of you for as long as it took for your self-preservation instincts to realize that you weren't going to die. Eventually your nervous system got bored and forgot about the whole thing. Then you'd either be cured or in the loony bin eating moths by moonlight.

She let the screen door click shut. The July page of the calendar from Eastern Mountain Sports caught her eye. On the color spread above the weeks, a woman cliff climber, dangling from the fingertips of one hand, one toe jammed in a crevice, reached casually into her chalk bag, her muscles and tendons tense as piano wires.

Done that, had the T-shirt. Rock climbing had scared the shit out of her at first, but she started small, scaling big boulders. Then onto indoor climbing walls, then, at last, graduating to the real thing. Now she could probably climb just about anything in the Northeast as long as she trusted the person on belay.

The little plane was towing something. A banner. She grabbed binoculars from the ledge above the sink and stepped cautiously onto the sagging back porch.

Sightseeing Tours, the banner read. *Crossly Field* . . . then something too small to read.

Sightseeing tours. Could you imagine? Do nothing but sit there while some pilot ferries you around? God forbid you accidentally bumped any of the controls. With her luck she'd probably . . .

Probably what? She'd lost her train of thought. The plane had traversed the field of view of the binoculars—they were her own and couldn't hold a candle to the fancy ones she'd been testing—and she found herself focusing the binoculars *beyond* the plane, momentarily unmindful of its provocative power. She stared off into the ocean of wide-open blue sky beyond the white banner, now disappearing over the tree line.

Sarah knew from past experience that deep down inside her, locked in a little room one level down from the floor Spot patrolled, lived the most extraordinarily perverse part of her psyche. It was powerful and elemental. It made her buckle on her helmet for another stretch of white-water kayaking when the river had her as sore as ten rounds with a heavyweight boxer. It gave her the grit to strap on snowshoes and a forty-pound pack for a seven-day, winter wilderness, sleeping-in-ice-caves, gear-testing expedition when anyone with an ounce of functioning brain tissue would be curled up at home in front of a fire. It delighted in the fun part of her and encouraged the really stupid part and seemed to make no distinction between the two.

She had a visit then from her unknown, little understood benefactor when she thought about all that open blue up there just above the tree line. A thrill the size of Mount Washington ran from the tips of her toes all the way up to the roots of her hair.

Sightseeing tours. There wasn't enough Prozac in North America to get her cold turkey through that.

But . . . what about finding a good instructor who would help her sneak up on her fear of planes? Hell, her fear of being in the same geographic *quad*rangle with an airplane. Someone who would take it slow with her. Touch the plane on Day One, sit in it on Day Two, start the engine on Day Three, kick Spot in the balls on Day Four. Yadda, yadda. She might not even have to go up in one of those flying tuna cans. Just being around one of them long enough might help her get on a real airplane.

Big old jet airliner . . . Statistically safer than sitting in your own living room.

Car-ry me so far a-way . . . Like to Honolulu, where well-oiled guys in grass skirts and damn little else raced the waves in their native outriggers. Steve Miller rocked, still.

Maybe, with little steps and the right instructor, she could gradually conquer her fear. Not at Crossly, of course, because of The Bastard and his—*yawn*—restraining order, but somewhere else close.

She rewound the strap thoughtfully around the body of the binoculars and returned them to the sink ledge. She looked at the woman climber on the calendar again. She had done that. Maybe she could do this.

Her little buddy chirped.

Chapter 6

Sarah numbered the Internet among the most consistently supportive of her nonhuman friends, but this time it betrayed her. On the subject of local airports, it had only bad news to offer: Crossly Field was the only show in town.

Sure, if she'd been willing to drive up the coast seventy-five miles she'd have been in business, but one column a month didn't exactly get a girl a gas account. So, the next morning, ignoring the screams from every self-preservation instinct she possessed, she drove out to Crossly Field—oops: Noah Crossly *Airport*, don't you know—in disguise. With the kerchief and the bug-eyed sunglasses she looked like a cross between a fifties movie harlot and a battered spouse, but she couldn't chance Logan Donnelly recognizing her.

It proved extraordinarily difficult for her to navigate the Rav, *sans* Dr. Joan, through the front gate of the airfield. Yes, she could act like a card-carrying drama queen over silly little things, but this—this was something else again. The sign at the guard shack could have read "Abandon Hope All Who Enter" for all the cold sweat she pumped.

Difficult. It was very, very difficult.

Surprisingly, Spot kept to the shadows. Sarah assumed her hard feelings toward Logan Donnelly acted like an electric fence: Simmering Rage Repels Skulking Dog.

She bounced into the recently graded but still only gravel parking lot. At the far end of it, stuck on the front of a completely innocuous-looking building, was a cheery green and white placard that proclaimed one could "Learn to Fly Here." She didn't know what she expected. A neat graveyard with endless rows of white crosses each labeled with the epitaph "Previous Customer"?

Even though she'd grown up in Tidal, she'd never spent any serious time on the grounds of Crossly Field. Sure, on dares from town boys, she and Beth had hopped the fence as kids and she and Mrs. Harker had had themselves a whirlwind tour, but a person can only take in so much and effectively swing a sign. Everything about the place now had an in-progress look about it, with fresh paint and new shrubs juxtaposed with piles of construction debris.

The field was dead quiet at the moment; nothing moved on the runway, thank God. There were the little planes all tied down. A parched, sand-saturated African wind abraded the back of her neck. Spot growled and Sarah went a tad woozy. She pressed on, parking the Rav in front of the flight school building. She shouldered open the door and made to step out, but her legs went on strike. Her sports bra had become a federally declared flood zone. *Who* was nervous? Overriding the veto from her feet, she ordered her body to stand up. She tented her loose cotton top, surreptitiously flapping her arms to get air circulating.

"Trying to get off the ground all by yourself?" The voice came from behind her.

Feeling like a complete nitwit, she spun around. It was

Logan Donnelly. What a waste of an emotion. And a disguise.

"Really, I would think you had better things to do than loiter around the parking lot antagonizing the patrons," Sarah said. "Aren't there any green places left around here that need paving?" This to the man who could have her instantly thrown in the pokey.

He smirked. "So now you're a 'patron,' huh? The other day you were just a common criminal."

She reached into the backseat for her bag, tripped the door locks, and started walking toward the school entrance. She was wasting valuable oxygen talking to Logan Donnelly.

"So much for the restraining order," he called.

From her conversation with Susan Crawford, Sarah understood completely that he essentially controlled her destiny while she was on his property, so, naturally, she had to say something to piss him off.

She turned to face him. "Why are you so afraid of me, big man like yourself?" Maybe Russell served Healthy Choice dinners sometimes. They were pretty good. "Think I'm going to hit you again?"

"My lawyer felt obliged to serve you the order. I told him it would never work." He grinned—the bastard—jogged over to her and stuck out his hand. "The name's Logan Donnelly."

She knew that. "What?"

"The name's Donnelly, Logan Donnelly. I might be hard to recognize when my head's not sticking out of a sign. I'm reintroducing myself. You know, starting over? Now that you're a regular 'patron' and all."

He was *such* a bullshitter. "How nice of you to think of someone else for a change," Sarah said, removing the Audrey Hepburn sunglasses. The light was brutal. She put them back on. "I'm sure it's a first for you, Mr . . . er, Donleavy was it? As for seeing you around, I'm sure I'll be too busy for that."

"Lessons, huh?"

Was it written on her back? How did he know? "How did you know?" she asked.

"You've got that look."

"What 'look'?"

"Kind of desperate and damned. I thought you hated flying."

"That hasn't changed. Other things have."

"You pass out up there"—he pointed to the sky—"and 'things' will change even faster."

"I don't plan to go 'up there'"—Sarah belabored the making of air quotes—"right away. But it's nice of you to be so concerned, anyway." He wasn't scaring her off.

To her surprise, he said, "Watch yourself."

No, he could watch her. Leave, that is. "I plan to," she said, waving *ciao* cheerily over her shoulder as she marched off toward the flight school entrance. She felt his eyes following her. A shivery thrill bisected her navel. She chalked it up to nerves.

She must have been distracted because going in the door of the flight school she barreled headlong into a preppy-looking, middle-aged guy coming the other way.

"Oof! Sorry," she said.

"Ung . . . no . . . problem, young . . . lady," he said, in what sounded like an unnaturally high, strained voice. "Preston Lewis . . . flight . . . instructor." He winced, hitched his trousers, and gamely stuck out his hand.

Sarah took it. "Sarah Dundee, scared to death."

"Completely understandable. Here for lessons? Ah, no doubt. Let me get the door for you." He stood a little over average height. She slid under his arm.

"Lloyd should be out in a minute," he said.

"Thanks."

"He's the flight school manager."

"Thanks, again."

He gathered himself much like the visiting family of the mentally ill who are disinclined to abandon their loved one at the end of calling hours. "See you around, then ... Sarah."

He did a natty little touch to the brim of an imaginary cap and disappeared, whistling.

Did she *look* that crazy? More important, was she? After several minutes of humming to herself and trying to look everywhere but at the flying magazines strewn around the coffee table, a florid-faced, heavyset man came out of an office marked Director and spotted her staring off into space.

"Oh—here to pick somebody up ... ah ... after their lesson?" Clearly, in his mind, she didn't look sufficiently sane to receive instruction herself.

"Actually, no. I'm here—"

"Ah, for the Airview Restaurant. Great luncheon specials. Open in"—he consulted his watch—"ten minutes."

"Missed again. I'm here to sign up for lessons."

He looked at her like she'd just opened a trench coat and showed him all the sticks of dynamite strapped to her body.

"Oh."

"Indeed. So, can we get started?" Sarah nodded toward his office.

"Right." He wiped his hands on his stomach, took in her bare legs, and arrived at a decision. "Lloyd Higgins, flight school director. Come on in."

She nodded. "Sarah Dundee." She didn't offer her hand.

He motioned Sarah to go ahead of him into his tiny office.

He pushed an application form across the desk towards her, leaving it just short of her grasp. In reaching for it, she had to lean forward. He was all eyes.

She kept the door jammed open with her leg while she filled out the paperwork.

Sarah briefed him on the special nature of her particular "situation." The more she explained, the sweatier Higgins became.

No, she didn't want to learn to fly.

Yes, she knew this was a flight school.

She had a phobia. P-H-O-B-I-A. Lots of people had them. His eyes glazed over when she got to "progressive de-sensitization." After ten minutes, Sarah was ready to buy an ultralight plane and take herself up.

She had given it her best shot, but she felt like she was destined to lose the battle. In the short time she'd had to size Lloyd up, two things were clear: one, he fancied himself a ladies man; two, ladies belonged on the ground.

Especially a nervous, close-to-neurotic, afraid-of-flying lady.

"Look, Mr. Higgins, I didn't really want to get into my life story here," Sarah said. "But I'm being square with you. I could've been coy about the whole phobia thing and suddenly had an anxiety attack that would make things very uncomfortable for one of your instructors. But I didn't. I was honest with you. Now I expect the same consideration in return."

But she wasn't going to get it because he was too busy estimating her cup size.

"*Mr.* Higgins, *am* I getting through to you?" she barked.

His eyes shot up to meet hers. "Ms. Dundee, I'm just not comfortable with the risk this school would be assuming in accepting your . . . proposal."

You'd think she was applying to Harvard.

Fortunately, she could be truly evil when needed. She scraped her chair closer to his desk, which strained her shirt across her chest. Higgins's eyes zeroed in on her upper torso like heat-seeking missiles.

"I certainly respect your high standards, Mr. Higgins, I really do. And I'll be sure to reference them in the article I'm writing about"—*Holy shit, what?* The truth wouldn't work—"small regional airports and the quality instructional services they provide to the community."

There. A magnificent whopper. Top-ten lifetime. But it got Lloyd to break lock and tone long enough to make eye contact. They'd reached a milestone in their short, but tempestuous, relationship.

"An article? You're a writer?" He was all ears. Which was a nice change from all eyes.

"Oh? I didn't mention that? Sorry, Mr. Higgins. How silly. I'm in the middle of a piece for a national magazine."

"Really? How . . . interesting."

It *was* interesting wasn't it? For somebody who had trouble finding the floor with her feet most mornings, the subtlety of her so-called mind was often an unexpected surprise. All on its own, it had come up with a two-for-one deal: time at the airport to get her over the hump with Spot *and* provide a perfect cover story to collect inside info for the article outline Iverson wanted.

Hah!

If she were alone, she would have giggled. She refrained, afraid to lend support to Lloyd's hypothesis that she was a walking fruitcake. She waited patiently, keeping the tension high with shirtfront action while he wrestled with the quandary. He rubbed his chins thoughtfully, dividing his attention equally between her chest and her application. Sarah shimmied a few more times to stir the pot.

Finally, Higgins frowned and the skin on his forehead sausaged into a rasher of cocktail weenies.

"Well, all that's very interesting, Ms. Dundee, but I still don't think this will work."

Damn, thought she had him. But his resistance was stiff indeed, pun intended.

Note to self: Did Donnelly somehow give old Lloyd the old heads-up that she was coming this way? Donnelly's veiled warning said to her the answer was "No."

Sarah played her last card.

"Oh! I'm so silly. . . ." She touched her forefinger to her temple. "Didn't I mention, Mr. Higgins, that my magazine is paying for as many instructional hours as it takes me to get comfortable in an airplane?" Another gigantic lie. She mentally blessed herself.

His reaction was priceless. His jaw fell open, only to snap shut like a trout hitting on a mayfly. Then, cha-*ching!* Dollar signs lit up the cash register behind his eyeballs.

He made a final pretense of scanning her application. "Well . . . on reconsideration, Ms. Dundee, maybe there is some wiggle room."

Sarah wiggled. Kind of like a reward.

Higgins chuckled lasciviously and leaned close. His cologne broke over Sarah in waves. "After all, we at Noah Crossly Airport are always here for *you*, our valued customer."

It looked for a minute like he was going to touch her on the shoulder—*yuk*—to emphasize his point, but his hand thankfully never connected. Sarah feigned that his attentions didn't make her want to be sick all over his imitation wood desk. "Oh, Mr. Higgins. That's so wonderful!"

She made her eyes go wide, making herself dizzy in the process. "I'm sure if *you're* so sure about it, it'll all work out terrifically."

Sarah smiled artfully and fought to draw breath without gagging. It was a cheap, tawdry little scene, but damn she was good. In her imagination she blew smoke off her index finger.

Then, just to be sure they had their agendas straight Sarah narrowed her gaze and drilled Higgins. "But let's just remember I'm the student here, Mr. Higgins—the *customer*, you know? And I'm telling you, if this is going to work out I need an instructor who's gonna work with me." She scooted closer. "Otherwise, Lloyd . . ." She leaned in really close. He had very large pores. "The unlimited billable hours?"—she snapped her fingers and he flinched—"ain't happenin.'"

She sat back in her uncomfortable plastic chair and leisurely crossed her legs.

She watched him digest the notion of "unlimited billable hours" going up in smoke. *Snap!*

Sarah dangled a sandal from her toes. Lloyd's eyes ricocheted like pinballs.

"Okay, Ms. Dundee—okay," he said finally. "We'll make this work out somehow." He slipped on reading glasses and decisively flipped open a grubby schedule book. "I've got just the fellow in mind."

"Really? And you'll give him a full briefing on my . . . particular needs?"

"Absolutely." His pencil tapped on open blocks of time.

"When can I meet him?"

Lloyd chuckled. "One step at a time, Ms. Dundee. He's a fellow by the name of Preston Lewis." He penciled "Dundee" into a couple of spaces. "Yep, I think you and he are just made for each other."

Oh, great, Lloyd was a dating service, too. One-stop shopping. Learn to fly and join the Mile-High Club at the same time. Wait—*Lewis*. The guy she almost gelded in the doorway.

He seemed decent enough, the little she'd seen of him, although most of that was armpit. She recalled a snappy sport shirt, clean-cut good looks, and neat hair going silver at the sides. He inspired confidence. Good choice, Lloyd.

"He sounds fine. When can I start?"

"Nine o'clock sharp tomorrow morning." Lloyd tried to rise smoothly from his swivel chair but only managed to make himself look like a breaching white whale.

"Of course, with your particular . . . er . . . situation, I wouldn't rush it."

"Oh, right," Sarah said, smiling agreeably. "Unlimited billable hours." She made her eyes dreamy.

Lloyd rubbed his palms together like they itched. "Good day, Ms. Dundee."

Sarah added extra wiggle as she left his office. She could hardly believe herself sometimes. God.

"How'd it go?"

Sarah about jumped out of her skin.

"Do you make a living of sneaking up on people? Jesus . . ." She shook out the willies.

Logan Donnelly was in the shade, leaning negligently against the side of the flight school building. Sarah reminded herself to keep better track of him once she began the clandestine research for the magazine article. He was eating . . . *something* in a long roll. "What is that?"

"Hot dog." Not like one she'd ever seen. It wasn't of a color that one would associate with the animal kingdom. Covered in some kind of . . . calling it sauce would be generous. He had a bit of whatever it was sticking to his smug face.

Sarah motioned to her own chin. Donnelly swiped at his with the back of a hand.

Something compelled Sarah to ask, "What do you have against real food?"

"No time. This is quick," he said, wolfing a messy mouthful.

"Ah. No time. Yet you've got plenty enough to talk to me."

"I only asked one simple question. Which you haven't answered, by the way."

"Fine. It went fine." Happy now?

"Keep your guard up." He chewed around the words.

What was he, a certified paranoid? "Do you know what's in that?" Sarah gestured toward the hot dog.

"Why do I think I'm about to find out?"

An involuntary growl issued from deep in her throat. Why was she wasting *her* time? She shook her head and headed for the Rav.

Chapter 7

"Nine o'clock sharp tomorrow morning" came like eight seconds later. Sarah showed up at the airport with a rock in her stomach and spying on her mind. She prayed that her fifth-column work inside the enemy's stronghold would help her survive the next hour.

She looked over her spy gear before she left the car.

Camera? Check. Would it were a miniature one like the CIA used.

Notebook? Got it. She'd pretend to hang on Preston Lewis's every word.

Ziploc plastic bag? That *was* about the flying. It was stuffed in an outside pocket of a small daypack, where she could get to it quickly. Ever the planner, she'd eyed the volume of the bag at home and eaten a correspondingly sized breakfast. She slung the pack over her shoulder and locked up. She looked up to find Logan Donnelly again leaning against the side of the flight school building. Had he spent the night in that spot? He'd changed his shirt, so she guessed not.

The brim of his cap created a black band across his eyes. "So you're back," he said.

"Oh, yes. Yes, I am. Your charm and hospitality are irresistible. I can't keep away." Sarah flashed him a brilliant but completely insincere smile.

You keep your distance, I'll keep mine.

Of course *she* couldn't strictly adhere to that due to her fact-finding mission, but he could.

He stretched with the casual grace of a cat and said, "No need to be so cranky."

Sarah wasn't a cat lover, probably why they seemed drawn to her. "Don't you have some . . . responsibilities around here? Must you lurk in corners waiting for me?"

"Don't flatter yourself. Ultimately, I'm responsible for everyone and everything that comes through the gate."

"But I'm not okay with you having responsibility for me."

"But you're okay with him, right?" He twitched his thumb at Preston Lewis, looking natty in khakis, emerging from the Higgins Aeroservices office.

"Well . . . yes," she said. "He comes highly recommended."

Logan snorted. "By Lloyd, no doubt."

"Exactly. By Mr. Higgins." Great, now she was defending Lloyd.

He laughed. "Well, it sounds like you've got it all figured out."

"Yes, I think I do."

He seemed to find that the funniest thing of all. "Well, nice talking to you. I guess all that's left for me is just to sit back and watch the show. But don't say I didn't warn you." He tipped his hat and walked off in the direction of the maintenance hangar.

Watch the show, her ass. She'd give him a show. She barely checked the impulse to plant a kick in his retreating backside. He was *such* an irritant. One minute in his company and she could bite the heads off nails.

She hailed Preston Lewis.

"Ah, Ms. Dundee. Good morning. Lovely day!" He crunched energetically across the gravel toward Sarah. "Looking forward to our first lesson, are we?"

"Oh, indeed." She had unconsciously picked up on his plumy, BBC overtones. But, lesson? She wouldn't have exactly called what she wanted a "lesson."

"Well, let's get started then," he said, rubbing his palms together. "We're over there." He pointed towards the Tarmac where a group of people was climbing out of a twin-engine airplane.

It was an unexpectedly solid-looking craft. Standing on its fat tires in a three-point stance it looked . . . substantial. Nothing like the single-engine cracker box her family had flown in Africa. Nevertheless, she had to steel herself to follow Preston Lewis over to it. Her knees felt like someone else's and she could feel her mouth weld into a thin line. She had to watch her feet to make sure they continued moving.

Left, right. Left, right. *Hut!*

How badly did she want the job?

Left, right. Left, right. *Really bad!*

She held to the thought that if the going got tough, the tough could always call for Mr. Wizard. How did it go in the cartoons?

Twuzzle, twuzzle, twuzzle, twow. Time for 'dis one to come home . . . She'd repeat it over and over and be whisked to safety in the nick of time.

They were almost to the plane.

But where was the hail-fellow-well-met Preston headed? He'd gone right by the open door of the twin engine.

"Watch yourself coming around the tail, here," he said

over his shoulder, as he disappeared around the rear end of it.

Must be some kind of airplane etiquette thing: departing passengers come out one side of the plane and the next group goes in the other way. Cool. She was already picking up useful stuff.

She switched her pack to the other shoulder and rounded the tail, ducking as Preston had advised, only to find he'd apparently disappeared into thin air.

"Over here." Sarah turned in the direction of his voice and stared.

He was unlocking the doors of a large dragonfly. A plane just like the single-engine cracker box of her sweaty nightmares. The wheels on the thing looked like they came off a pop-up camper, and the Plexiglas windshield reminded her of the one she and Beth had on their Barbie coupe.

No.

What was it about the sins of the parents being visited on the children? Was she insane? Twenty years of therapy and she brought herself right back to where it all started?

Sarah eyed the unlikely conglomeration of cables, rivets, and sheet tin that made up the plane and felt the beginnings of panic. Metal bands squeezed her skull and her vision blurred. Her tiny breakfast slid greasily around in her stomach. In Africa, she'd seen the natives give their elephants sticks to grip within the curl of their trunks. When she had asked Tukaba about it—he had been their pilot—he had explained that elephants could be bloody minded and willful. Giving them a stick to hold kept their minds occupied, calming them. Sarah swung her gaze wildly, searching desperately for a stick.

She traced the line of a flimsy wing and it led her gaze to the flight school building in the distance. There was one, firmly stuck in the mud: Logan Donnelly. Still lounging in the shade, still holding up a section of wall. He tipped his hat at her.

He'd do.

She mentally unloaded. *Bastard*. What *was* it with him? Didn't he have something more constructive to do than hang around and gawk at her? And that frigging hat. She'd love to yank it off and stomp on it. Grind it into the—

"Ms. Dundee?" It was Preston Lewis.

"Come over here, please, Ms. Dundee. I'm going to walk you through the preflight check."

She checked the urge to lunge to one knee and flip Donnelly a double royal bird. She went around to Lewis's side of the plane but kept her eye on the figure in the shadows.

Preston launched into a diatribe that explained in minute detail all the external features of the Cessna. He stopped several times to have her walk through portions of the preflight inspection. *Why* were they checking the plane over Sarah couldn't fathom. Wouldn't any required checking have been done at the factory? After what seemed like hours, she sneaked a peek at her watch. Less than fifteen minutes had gone by.

Finally, Preston pronounced the exterior preflight inspection complete. Then they started on the interior of the plane. Preston hopped into the left seat. Sarah stuck her head into the tiny cabin. What struck her first was the smell. Sunbaked plastic, the tang of . . . oil? Yes. Something like a garage smell, but lighter. Spot bared his teeth. He remembered, too.

Behind the two front seats was an open area about the size of the rear deck of the Volkswagen Beetle she'd once owned. Her family's plane in Africa had had seats back there. Maybe the whole plane had been a little bigger? She couldn't remember, exactly. She threw her pack back there, as if to ward off whatever might be lurking. In other words: Spot. Indeed, the mangy mutt had sneaked on board ahead of her. He skittered to one side when the bag touched him. Did he add any weight to the plane?

"Stupid dog," Sarah muttered.

"Pardon, Ms. Dundee?" Preston had a questioning look on his face.

"Forget it."

Sarah grabbed hold of the door frame of the plane and hiked a foot into the cockpit. She thought she had her balance, but no. She toppled sideways into the cabin.

"Ouch!" Her head smacked into something.

"Damn!" Her elbow cracked against something else. Everything inside the plane seemed to be located in the most inconvenient place possible. It was like crawling up a porcupine's ass.

Preston Lewis said, "I told you to be careful, Ms. Dundee."

Yeah, twenty minutes ago. Preston flung himself into another monologue. Sarah took stock of her worst nightmare.

God, it was close quarters in there. She'd forgotten. Of course, she was smaller back . . . then. Just a girl. *Enough.* She shook off the memories. Spot blew woofies.

The freaking dashboard was right in her face and her legs—short little things though they were—were jammed up under it. The doors were open, but tendrils of claustrophobia sprouted from the floor and snaked their way up Sarah's legs. She never freaked out in caves. Spelunking wasn't exactly her favorite thing, but she'd been able to follow some pretty skinny guides through some pretty tight places. Yet on a relatively cool July morning there she sat, swimming in her own sweat.

It wasn't the size of the space, she realized, so much as the fact that it was designed to rise hundreds of feet above the earth. The thought of only a thin aluminum skin separating her from eternity made her crazy. She sensed creeping vines encircling her chest. To counteract the crushing sensation, she hung a foot out the open door.

Cleansing breath in, quick look at Donnelly. Still there? Yup.

Bastard. She emptied her lungs: Whoosh! Adios anxiety.

"Ms. Dundee . . . ?"

"Yes?"

Preston Lewis sighed. "Ms. Dundee? Please, for your own safety? Do pay attention."

She was. Just not to the stuff he wanted. No wonder she'd never done that great in school.

A few minutes later, after she'd given old Preston the third wrong answer to some arcane question about fuel pump something-or-others, he started on her again. "Ms. Dundee, I cannot overemphasize the importance of understanding the proper sequence of a thorough preflight inspection."

Blah, blah, blah . . .

"But you seem very distracted right now. Is anything wrong? Please tell me if there's anything I could do to help you better understand the process."

Lend her the video? Really, what the fuck did anyone care about fuel pumps? "Okay, okay. I'm with you. Go ahead." Cripes, ten years of the nuns and now Lewis.

"Very well. Now, about the carburetor heat . . ."

Jerk. Sarah went into screen-saver mode again.

Speaking of jerks, Logan Donnelly was walking away. Toward the restaurant. The Airview, Lloyd had called it. Donnelly had better get back in time for me to administer her next prophylactic dose of righteous indignation or dear Preston was in for a double dose of dipshit.

"Do you understand that, Ms. Dundee?" Lewis asked me.

"Er, yes. They should be in the 'up' position."

He looked at her askance, as the Brits would say, but resumed his monologue. Sarah scanned the parking lot expectantly.

Ah, Logan was back. Sipping at a coffee and chitchatting with someone who came out of the control tower to join him. A female "someone."

Short, dark hair. An attractive face. Compact athletic body; powerful, not graceful. A hiker type. You didn't get those kind of calves in a health club. Sarah looked down at her own legs, scrunched up under the dashboard.

Yep, solid. The curse of the outdoorsy chick.

Donnelly and his little friend leaned on the fence that separated the plane tie-down area from the parking lot. Sarah watched Donnelly sidle up closer to the woman. They were touching—the damn rearview mirror was blocking her view—arm to arm. Why did a plane need a rearview mirror anyway?

Preston Lewis said something that sounded like "pee-too tube." Seemed like a personal problem to Sarah, but she parroted something back at him. He seemed satisfied with the response, because he pronounced the preflight done.

The woman shoved Logan away playfully and sauntered off toward the control tower. Unaccountably, Sarah felt relieved. Logan threw his coffee cup into a trash barrel and headed off toward the hangars.

"Have you got all that?" Preston was staring at Sarah.

"Yes, of course. A-okay."

His look held the kind of pity reserved for those thought to be mentally compromised. Which, given her performance so far, was probably a completely justified impression.

But sor-*ry,* all the "preflight" crap was a waste of time as far as she was concerned. Yes, it gave the appearance that something worthwhile was actually happening. Otherwise, all an observer would see was a petite, dirty-blond, crazed-looking woman sitting in a plane talking to herself while a potential extra on Monty Python's Flying Circus stood nearby with steam coming out his ears. But, in the overall scheme of things, checking over the airplane mattered not one shit to Sarah because the plane was never leaving the ground with her in it.

Or so she thought at the time.

When she later reviewed the events of the day, Sarah realized that they had been writ clearly and large all *over* the proverbial wall, but she'd been too preoccupied with the vignette transpiring at the fence to stop and read.

She took a last look toward the parking lot. Donnelly had disappeared. Fuck him, she didn't need him. She screwed up her courage and asked Preston, "Do you think we could start the engine?"

He laughed. Not a very nice one. Sarah pitied Mrs. Lewis if there was one.

"A wonderful idea, Ms. Dundee. Buckle your seat belt."

Just to start the engine?

"That's good," he said. "Cinch up the shoulder harnesses, too. Good, good. Now, put these on." He passed Sarah a set of headphones with a boom microphone attached. "So we can communicate." That would be a first. After a few false starts, she got them on her head.

"There's a good girl." He fiddled with a few knobs and asked Sarah if she was ready. She gave him a thumbs-up. Hopefully the headphones would drown out the blast of engine noise she remembered from Africa. She pressed her hands over the outside of the plastic ear cups just for good measure. Where was Joan's pocketbook when she needed it?

Preston stabbed what Sarah guessed was the starter button. The engine coughed, the propeller spun arthritically, then the engine caught and roared. Not like a lion, but like fifty fricking lawn mowers with busted mufflers. It was a horrendous, terrifying sound. But Spot's growl from behind her was even louder. He was going ape shit and who could blame him.

"Holy crap!" she yelled involuntarily. She mustn't have had the microphone properly positioned in front of her face because Preston replied, "Good show!"

He pulled on a slide thing on the dash. It looked like something pirated from a snowblower. The roar decreased. His voice was in her ears.

"Try it, Ms. Dundee." He motioned at the slider. Sarah touched it like it was electrified, but when she pulled back on it the engine simmered down. She shut her eyes and pushed it forward and she imagined Spot's agitated pacing shook the plane.

"Good!" Preston said, like she'd discovered fire.

Sarah pulled and pushed on the slide a few more times and the engine obeyed her commands: Control. Control was good.

Dr. Loo would be so proud, she thought. Joan, too. She'd done good by Lloyd; Preston was okay after all. Sarah did wonder what her mother would think if Violet somehow learned what she was involved in. Sarah realized she didn't care anymore if Logan Donnelly had disappeared. "Could we go"—she didn't know how to word it—"for a ride?" Up and down the aisles between the tied-down planes.

Preston laughed, his eyes kindly on her this time. "Righty-o, Ms. Dundee." He must have thought he'd converted a heathen. He revved the engine and parts of the wing flapped up and down. Sarah didn't remember what Lewis called them. She shivered, a condemned prisoner hearing the dreaded drum roll in the courtyard.

Stand by, Mr. Wizard. The moment of truth . . .

A few moments went by. Nothing much happened. The headphones crackled. "Ms. Dundee?"

"Yes?"

"You've got to get both feet in the cabin. We can't go anywhere with you hanging out of the airplane."

"Oh." She pulled her foot inside and yanked the flimsy door closed.

"Is that latched?" Preston asked. "We wouldn't want to lose you."

Ha-ha. Very funny, and, yes, you probably would. She reclosed the door. "It's okay now."

Preston gunned the engine and the plane moved. Sarah hadn't anticipated the motion. When the tail swung around, she almost parted with some bodily fluids. The parking lot slid by the bow; then she saw a line of parked planes, then the open runway to their left. The plane bounced around, its wanna-be wheels telegraphing every flaw in the asphalt to her rear end. The sensation was akin to being trundled in a wheelbarrow down a rough garden path.

Sarah remembered the feeling from all the times Tukaba had taxied the four of them—Sarah, Beth, Violet, and her dad—across the hard pack of the improvised runway on the Serengeti. The harsh, baking African sun would take your breath away out there. She and Beth used to pretend they were sending telegraph messages with their teeth as the plane bumped along. Violet would warn them they'd have dentures at twenty-five if they kept it up. Sarah found herself wondering what, if anything, Violet remembered of those times.

Preston went for the slide thing again and the engine roared even louder. The plane seemed to leap forward, sending Sarah's elbows and knees into a collision course with protruding levers and gizmos. Something bumped her sneakers. She pulled her feet back and out of the way. The wheel in front of her twisted and turned with a life of its own, mirroring Preston's inputs on the set of controls on his side of the cockpit.

Another kid memory: she and Beth used to imagine a ghost operated the second set of controls on the passenger side of their airplane. Tukaba had sometimes let one of them sit in the right seat and hold on to the wheel—it was called a yoke, Sarah remembered him telling her—during taxiing. They'd loved it.

Beth . . . God, her dad. Sarah tucked the memories away deep. She would continue to miss them later. This right now was business; this was about her getting back what had been stolen from all of them.

Preston finally got up a good head of steam and the plane coasted along fairly smoothly, passing planes of various makes and conditions, all neatly roped down to rings set into the asphalt. After about a hundred yards, Preston slowed the plane to a stop.

"Whew," Sarah managed. "This baby really moves."

Preston chuckled. She wasn't joking. That little trip was her equivalent of Lucky Lindy soloing the Atlantic. She had survived. She'd kept breathing. And dreaming of Arizona and Alaska and Hawaii. A few more times up and down the little bit of Tarmac and her pulse would probably drop below 200. Then outta the stinking plane and into her nice, safe, earthbound vehicle. Live to taxi another day.

Somebody called on the radio. Whatever he said was pure, unadulterated gibberish to her, but Preston goosed the motor again and bounced the plane toward the runway. Sarah imagined that they—the people in the control tower—had given Preston permission to extend their gentle airing onto the runway proper. Cool. Close to the flame, but not in it. Perfect.

They reached the head of the runway and Preston swung the tail around to line up with the dotted white line running down the middle of it. Then he said, "Tower, this is LD one-oh-eight requesting permission to take off."

The radio came back. "Roger, LD. Please hold."

Sarah finally woke up. Things were suddenly not so perfect. "Ex*cuse* me? Did you say 'take off'?"

Preston winced. The boom mikes were sensitive, but so was she. About going up in the sky in a Pepsi can.

"As in off the ground?" she said. "Into the air, into the wild blue yonder, etcetera, etcetera?" She fought the impulse to finish the song in a mock baritone.

"Well . . . yes."

"Are you crazy?"

"I beg your pardon?"

"Crazy. Nuts. Are you?" She visually underscored the concept with slow, circular rotations around her ear with a fingertip. "Didn't Lloyd tell you about my little 'problem'?"

"Well, of course. But there's nothing to be afraid of, Ms. Dundee. Flying is perfectly safe."

"Hah."

Tell that to Spot. *He* probably needed the baggie.

"This wasn't part of the plan, Mr. Lewis."

"We'll take it slow, Ms. Dundee."

Her palms slicked with sweat. "Oh, no, we won't, Mr. Lewis. When I said 'a ride,' Mr. Lewis, I meant just that. A ride. *On the ground.*"

He looked at her like she had antennas instead of ears.

"You can't be serious, Ms. Dundee."

"On the contrary, Mr. Lewis. Completely."

A look came into his eye that again made Sarah pity Mrs. Lewis. "Whatever you say, Ms. Dundee. Now please relax. I've handled numerous jittery students before."

"Jittery" was she? She clenched her sweaty fists. She

wanted to dimple J-I-T-T-E-R-Y into the side of his head. Stupid, pigheaded, know-it-all—

On the other hand . . . he was right.

She *had* to do this eventually.

Shit.

Static filled the headphones; then the tower came on the radio. "LD one-oh-eight, you are next for takeoff. Waiting for traffic to clear."

Terror filled Sarah. Fear of going, fear of not going. Fear just because it was all she'd ever known since the Africa crash.

She was sick of it. Couldn't live with it anymore. "It" being Spot. She wouldn't. No more canine companion. Time to kick him squarely in the doggy digit and run for it. "Okay, okay. I'm sorry. I'm in. One quick trip up, then right down again, yes? With everybody still alive?"

"Ah, I'm delighted, Ms. Dundee. Good show, what?"

Sarah glanced at him to reassure herself he hadn't surreptitiously donned a white silk scarf while she'd been busy freaking out. Was it her or did he sound more and more English the closer they got to the air?

Preston pulled on what she had figured out was the throttle and the engine speed increased. The plane gave a lurch and inched forward on the Tarmac.

Ho-ly shit. She threw a death grip onto the edge of her seat.

Arizona, Alaska, Hawaii. It became her mantra.

Preston babbled something unintelligible to the tower, then waggled the control wheel and the floor pedals. All manner of external plane parts wiggled and waved. Something contacted Sarah's toes again, so she drew back her feet. With her luck she'd twitch and send them hurtling into a parked plane.

She watched the bits and bobbles of the plane gyrate until

her overactive curiosity got the better of her. Honestly, she'd stop and query the hangman as to where he learned his knots.

"What are you doing?" she asked Preston.

"Checking to make sure everything works."

Sarah laughed. This time he didn't.

"You mean sometimes it doesn't?"

"Oh, that's very rare, Ms. Dundee."

Now, she would have been happy with that answer. "Very rare" worked for her. Yet for some unimaginable reason—she was thinking maybe Preston did not fully comprehend the quantity of nuts in the fruitcake beside him—he elaborated.

"I remember once in, oh . . . the midnineties, I think it was. This fellow I knew had gotten up about a hundred feet, never having checked the rudder, mind you, prior to take-off—preflight, Ms. Dundee, preflight—anyway—"

The radio came to life. "LD one-oh-eight, you are cleared for takeoff. Begin your roll now."

"Roger, tower. LD out."

"Where was I? Oh, yes." He cranked the engine as loud as it would go. Still it wasn't noisy enough to drown out the rest of his story. "All of a sudden he came out of the sky like a brick and pancaked into a hangar. The plane caught fire and—wait! What are you doing, Ms. Dundee?"

Changing her mind.

Looking for an Exit sign. Really, was Preston deliberately malicious or just criminally stupid? Even Spot was scared shitless.

Sarah's hands fumbled on the harness releases. "No way," she said, quite calmly, she thought, given the change in circumstances. She twisted sideways and the seat belt bit into her abdomen. "No fricking way—"

"Ms. Dundee, remain facing forward, please."

"Shut this frigging thing off, Preston. I'm not going."

The plane picked up speed and the dotted lines on the runway blurred into a continuous white stripe.

"Ms. Dundee—"

"Fucking now!" This she screamed.

"Once we're airborne you'll see—"

She'd see shit. She burst free of the shoulder harness and knifed forward into the instrument panel.

Preston Lewis reached out a restraining hand and pleaded, "Ms. Dundee, calm down!" It sounded as though he finally realized he may have bitten off more than he could chew. "Once we start the takeoff we can't simply—great Scott!"

The plane had veered to the left alarmingly. One wheel lifted clear of the pavement, and Lewis corrected for it. Sarah had inadvertently kicked the rudder pedals on her side of the cockpit. The plane returned to the centerline but then swerved abruptly to the right. Astonished, Preston wrestled with the controls.

Ever the innovator, she had found a tried-and-true method for aborting a takeoff: randomly kick the pedals that she had remembered steered the plane while on the ground. Thank you, Tukaba. The airplane listed sickeningly to the left and slued toward the grass verge.

Preston Lewis again tried to correct, but Sarah kept her weight behind the pedals and he was forced to cut the power to the engine and brake hard. Tires squealed as they bit into the Tarmac, then telegraphed every anthill on the grass verge as the plane left the runway. After a wild fifteen-second ride during which she and Preston Lewis vied for control of the airplane, they came to rest on the grassy strip, perpendicular to the runway centerline.

For a few moments, all that could be heard in the cabin over the idling of the engine was the ragged rasp of their breathing in the headphones. Then the radio crackled.

"LD one-oh-eight, this is tower. Status please. Are you declaring an emergency?"

Preston Lewis reached out a shaking hand to click the radio mike. "Negative, tower. Request permission to reenter runway and return to taxiway. Over."

He'd lost his English overtones somewhere on the last quarter mile of runway.

"LD one-oh-eight. Glad to hear it. Permission to reenter runway now. Report to tower when you're in."

"Roger. LD out."

Sarah expected a tornado. What she got was a killing frost.

"Look, Mr. Lewis, I'm sorry about—" she started, but Preston would have none of it.

"Silence, damn you." Lewis swiped both hands down his face, as if he were trying to rid himself of a cobweb he'd stumbled blindly into, and blew out a breath. "*Never* in all my years have I ever had a student try to *crash* the airplane."

He savagely jerked on the throttle. Sarah thought the engine was going to fling itself out onto the grass. "Get your feet up on that seat and keep them there," he hissed. The tail swung around.

His rebuke made her feel like a six-year-old. With the single-mindedness of that tender age she unclipped her seat belt. "I am *not* doing this," she announced. "I am *not* riding in this plane anymore." She popped the door latch and kicked it open. It swung completely around on its hinges and slammed against the fuselage.

"Bloody *hell*, woman! We're on an active runway!" Lewis took one hand off the control wheel and grabbed for her, but Sarah already had one foot on solid ground and was in love with the sensation. Lewis killed the engine, and as the prop wound down she heaved the rest of her stubborn self out the door.

She heard Lewis's voice behind her. "Tower, this is LD one-oh-eight. We *now* have an emergency. Be advised passenger has left plane. Is crossing operating runway—"

Not caring to hear the rest of the indictment, she looked around wildly, her eyes lighting on the flight school building: a safe haven. She sprinted across the runway toward it, truly understanding the terror Cary Grant's character must have felt in *North by Northwest.* Dodged between parked planes in the tie-down area, tripped over tie-downs, finally reaching the parking lot fence. Winded and mortified, she hung over it, sucking in air.

Shit, shit, shit.

How to kill your dreams and yourself in one easy lesson. She'd completely screwed the pooch.

Her and her big ideas. Tackle something herself that twenty years of professionals hadn't fixed. Now everything was gone to crap. The job: Arizona, Alaska, Hawaii. They would forever remain just places on a map. Any shred of self-respect she ever had? *Pffft!* Gone like Preston Lewis's phony accent.

Vaguely, she wondered if she was open to criminal prosecution for screwing with the plane and almost killing Lewis. Not that she particularly gave a damn about *him* at that moment. Namby-pamby little jerk.

She kicked at stiff tufts of grass at the base of a fence post. Ants burrowed around unconcernedly down there. Tending their eggs, making new tunnels, trundling along under the weight of microscopic bundles of ant goodies.

It must be nice to have no consciousness, to not be cursed with wanderlust and desires. Why couldn't she be content with plying the safe, familiar back roads of New England, philosophically resigned to lugging her stuff around in the back of a ground-hugging four-by-four, earthbound like the happy little ants below? Instead, she was maniacally driven to explore, push the envelope, test the limits. Why?

Because she wanted a fucking life, that's why.

The toes of oil-stained, worn work boots inserted themselves into the homey, domestic scene transpiring in the grass.

"Look out!" Sarah cried. Little black bodies scrambled for cover.

"Developing a personal relationship with the insect world are we?"

She wearily lifted her head. It was Logan Donnelly, of course. Sarah squinted at him across the chain link. Her sunglasses were long gone in her flight for life across the runway.

Which he'd undoubtedly witnessed.

"You know, I'd really like to tell you where to go," she said. "But right now I just can't seem to find the energy. So why don't you just crawl back to your dirty little maintenance shed and leave me alone?"

Sarah realized she had never been quite so close to him before. Red-gold whiskers glowed in the morning sun. He rested his forearms on the top bar of the fence, just inches from her elbow. She'd seen that ploy before. She caught a whiff of machine oil and, to her surprise, something else not unpleasant.

Mint. Peppermint. His chewing gum.

"What the hell went on in that plane?" he asked neutrally, in spite of the expletive.

"A last-minute change of plans."

He snorted. "Preston's gonna have a lot of explaining to do."

Chapter 8

Later that day, Sarah's jangled nerves finally settled enough for her to think about her stomach as something other than a liability. She was scraping together random food items that, with a stretch, could be called dinner when the doorbell rang. She wiped her hands on a dish towel.

All she could see through the security peephole in the front door was a blurry shape. Whoever was out there was trying to look in at her while she was peering out at him. Creepy.

"Who is it?" She wished she still owned the cassette tape of dogs growling menacingly, but she'd dumped it a while ago. It riled up Spot.

A mumble reverberated through the thick oak door panels.

The best defense was a good offense, so Sarah decided to quietly slip off the chain and whip open the door. No pervert, but no religious activist either. It was Logan Donnelly.

She kept the screen door latched. "What do you want?" Kind of blunt, but, Hey, she didn't ask him to come.

He held up a familiar, green nylon daypack. Hers, of course. "I bring you this."

She hadn't even missed it. The ground loop had rattled every dish in her cupboard.

"You left it in the plane," he said. "I was going to tell Preston to bring it over himself, but he didn't look like he was in the mood."

She laughed, in spite of herself. This Logan Donnelly was such an odd man. He hadn't shaved, Sarah noticed, but he was wearing a fresh shirt. And Columbia nylon hiking pants. Professional interest: she'd done reviews of its stuff. He didn't look bad in taupe.

"How did you know where I live?" she asked suspiciously.

"Phone book?"

Duh. She took the latch off the screen door.

"You're holding that bag like it was a bomb," she said, taking it from him.

"Things seem to explode when you're around."

"Aw . . . you've seen my yearbook! That's just what it said under my picture . . ."

He looked confused.

"It was a joke. I'm kidding."

He smirked and relaxed a little. "Sometimes I just don't get you."

"Ah, something in common. Me neither." Why she admitted that to him of all people was a mystery to her, but it really had been one hell of a day. "You want to come in?"

"I'm not so sure that's a good idea."

"The cops confiscated my sign—or whatever's left of it. Let's chance it." She needed to sort out what had happened that day and, ironically, Logan might be the only person on the planet who could help her. He'd witnessed the whole mess, after all.

Logan paused, hand on the jamb. "Only if we reset the clock one more time. Go back to our neutral corners?"

"Absolutely. I'm really sorry about the sign . . . ah, incident, by the way. I'm not apologizing for the intent, just the execution of it."

He nodded. "Okay. I guess I get that."

He followed Sarah out back to the kitchen. She was suddenly aware of stray crumbs on the linoleum and every spot of gunk on the counters. Amazing the stuff you never see when you live alone.

"Want a beer?" She rummaged in the fridge, even way up back behind the ancient, half-full jars of salsa, and only found a single to fish out.

"It's your last one," he said.

"Hey, go for it. There's the quick and the thirsty in this house."

"I'm flying early tomorrow. I usually don't drink within twelve hours of going up. We'll split it."

O-kay. From the cupboard, she fished out what she fervently hoped was a completely clean glass. Hope is a fragile thing. Surreptitiously, she flicked a bit of crud off it with her thumbnail.

Sarah watched him pour half the bottle into the glass, putting on just the right amount of head, and he handed the glass back to her. He settled himself onto one of the bar stools. His feet rested flat on the floor. *Long legs.* Sarah's feet always dangled inches from the ground, just like a little kid's. "Bottoms up," he said.

"*Salud.*" Yum. Beer always tasted better with company.

He started the ball rolling. "So, about today."

She snickered. "Which part? The part where I almost wrecked a plane and killed my instructor? Or the part where I threatened to rat you out to the food police?" She supposed she might someday see the humor in the situation.

He picked at the label on the bottle in his hand. "The food thing"—he waved his hand dismissively—"is neither here nor there. You and I have a minefield between us. The preserve, the runway?"

Their eyes met and Sarah nodded. *Go on.*

"So I'm not surprised we're always at each other's throats about things that are tangible, tangent . . . what's the word?"

"'Tangential'?"

"Exactly. Tangential to the real issues. And speaking of real issues, why do you want to go up in a plane, anyway? I saw you in the preserve that day. You said 'No big deal,' but you looked like shit—pardon my French—after I buzzed you."

"How nice of you to say."

"What I mean is, anything to do with airplanes is pure torture for you. Why do it?" He took a swig of Sam, never taking his eyes off her.

"You're a pilot, but you could probably do other things. Why do you do what you do?"

"Because not flying is not an option."

"More common ground," she said.

"I'm not . . . following."

She told him about the new job, omitting the name of the magazine and any specifics. He remembered that she'd told him she was a writer, but a lot of people seemed to file that tidbit away. She felt obligated to qualify "writer."

"I do outdoor equipment reviews. For a magazine. I test the stuff, then do a monthly column."

"Ah, the reason you had all that expensive, new stuff in the preserve."

"There you go. I've got plans to do more, though. Something on a bigger scale." She didn't elaborate.

He asked her more questions about her aspirations. Sarah

suddenly found herself tongue-tied, blushing like a teenager. It was humiliating. She covered with a coughing fit.

"The stuff you, ah, want to write sounds interesting," he said, looking concerned at her hacking. He was working at it, Sarah realized, working to keep the conversation going. Interesting.

"Myself," he said, "I don't get to do much fun reading. I mostly keep up with technical stuff on flying. Maybe a Stephen King now and then. Oh, and anything I can find about antique airplane restoration. It's a hobby of mine."

She laughed. "You need to broaden your literary horizons, my friend, although Stephen King gets you some points." Ah, King. Like a lot of beers, best enjoyed in his native land: Maine, at midnight, in the deep woods. By flashlight. Scare the shit out of you.

Which brought Sarah around to thoughts of Spot. Maybe it was the alcohol, but she felt she owed Logan an explanation for her crazy behavior at his place of business. She gave it and he listened, not saying much. When she finished, he didn't have the put-down-the-gun-we-can-work-this-out expression on his face that most people did after she'd introduced them to Spot. His look was blank. Completely.

"That's it?" she said. "No reaction?"

"I . . . don't really know what to say. That's . . . some story," he said vaguely. To Sarah it looked like he was trying to remember if he'd left a propeller spinning somewhere.

"You okay?" she asked.

His eyes snapped back into the present. "Yes. Fine. This thing—a dog—lives in your head. And he sort of . . . haunts you."

"Right. But he's not real, though. You got that part, right? I'm not channeling or anything. He's imaginary."

"Right. Imaginary. Got it."

To her surprise, Sarah found herself hoping he did.

"Now, let's talk about you," Logan said.

"We have been."

"I mean about what happened at the field today."

"Like I already explained, I had a little accident."

"No, you had a potentially big accident that just didn't happen."

Go soak yourself, her mind thought, but her mouth said, "It looks like we have a difference of opinion on that."

"On a lot of other things, too. None of which will not go away no matter how much alcohol we consume together."

Just when she was thinking they could grow to be buddies. He meant the second runway. *Big* issue. Massive. As much as she—and undoubtedly he—would like to break away from its dark, seductive pull, they were inexorably dragged into its orbit.

"I *don't* want that runway," Sarah said, pleased that she was able to utter the noun *runway* without the adjective *frigging* in front of it.

"Why can't you just—" Logan cut himself off in midsentence and took a good pull at his beer. His cheeks were flaming.

Neither of them spoke for a half minute, each trying to behave, although Sarah doubted either one of them could explain why.

"Look, let's try focusing on one thing at a time," Logan finally said. "Let's try . . . what happened with Preston Lewis?"

Sarah clinked the glass against her front teeth. "Okay. He set me up."

"Did he."

He could make one eyebrow go really high. "The deal was that we were supposed to just sit in the plane for a while; then, if I felt okay, we'd maybe taxi around a bit. No way was

I taking off in the plane. I had to do something to stop the plane."

"He's a good pilot."

"A good pilot doesn't necessarily a good teacher make. That Lloyd's a piece of work, too, by the way. You're in charge over there, aren't you? You ought to get rid of him. Man can't keep his eyes to himself."

Logan put his beer down and laced his fingers together on the worn Formica bar top. "First, Lloyd is a fixture. He's not going anywhere. I *can't* get rid of him. My grandfather left the field to me with conditions, Lloyd being one of them. The more time I spend in Tidal, the more I'm finding out that old Noah never let anyone have anything without some strings attached. Second, from the way I saw how you sauntered out of Lloyd's office I'm thinking you used his wandering eye against him. You 'talked'"—he made air quotes and shimmied on his stool— "him into letting you take lessons."

Sarah opened her mouth for a comeback but shut it again. "So your point is . . . ?"

"My point is that you got caught in a squeeze play between Lloyd and Preston. They were duking it out to see who had the bigger pri—sorry—the most power over you. Preston wanted to prove how great an instructor he was and Lloyd probably wanted to milk what he saw as a cash cow."

Sarah winced. Did she have a dollar sign emblazoned on her forehead like Harry Potter's scar? She sighed. Logan was right, damn him. "Yeah, that's what I'm thinking now, too," she said.

She sloshed the last mouthful of beer around in the bottom of the glass. "But what do I do next? The closest field's over an hour's drive away. That's going to be an incredible pain."

"If it was even an option." He looked at her evenly.

She connected the dots. "Blackballed? I'm blackballed

from flight training?" Incredible. Was there a regionwide broadcast as soon as the wheels of Preston's plane had rolled to a stop? *"Calling all flight schools, calling all flight schools. Be on the lookout for a dirty-blond Caucasian female, midthirties, desperate look in her eyes. Do not teach. Repeat: do not teach. She is considered posttraumatic and dangerous. . . ."*

"I picked up some talk about it on the local bands just after noon. Sorry."

"Mentioned my name?"

"Of course not. But that won't make any difference."

"Mmmm." Sarah swilled the last of her Sam Adams. It was warm and bitter.

"But all is not lost."

"Un-huh." It was to her. Crap.

"I could help you out."

Say *what?* She put the glass down on the bar. "How?"

"I could be your instructor."

She steepled her hands in front of her mouth. This guy was a hoot and a half. Giggles rose from her toes and burst like champagne bubbles. She doubled over, belly laughing. When the fit passed, she rested her elbows on the bar and blotted her eyes with a paper napkin.

Logan was still calmly looking at her. "Now, why— whew!"—she had to fan herself—"would you ever consider doing that? Help *me*. The woman with the sign, remember?"

She reached across the bar and gently rapped her knuckles against his dark curls. "The woman who tried to decapitate you? Who'd gladly carpet bomb your airfield? Are you nuts?" Really, too funny.

"Maybe. But I don't want any accidents at my facility. My insurance ratings can't take the hit right now. Not while I'm still putting together financing for the second strip. I'm afraid that somehow, someway, you'll eventually con someone into taking you up. If I do it myself, I don't have to worry about the result."

"Wow." Touching motivations. Really heartfelt. Especially the part about the insurance risk. She bit her tongue and ordered herself not to look this particular gift horse in the mouth. "That would be . . ." She gnawed at the flesh on the inside of her cheek. It was hard. Catholic guilt made it tough for her to accept something from someone she'd trespassed against. "Great."

Although accepting his offer was a little tough, it *was* a no-brainer. A win situation for Sarah. Not for him, although he didn't know the half of that yet. Did he have any inkling that he was serving up the means for her to rain destruction—in the form of Iverson's investigative article—upon his head? People should be required to wear a hard hat around her.

"Good," he said, sealing his fate.

That was easy. But then Sarah wondered if there was a catch. Was she, the screw*er*, in fact the screw*ee?* Logan's offer seemed to be too good to be true.

"And before you go thinking I'm too good to be true," he said, right on cue, "I want something in return."

Ha-*ha* . . . the dirty bastard. Knew it. He and Lloyd—maybe even frigging Preston—had a bet on who could get her into the Mile-High Club first. Even a backstage pass to Crossly's inner workings wasn't worth that. Sarah stood and crashed her glass down onto the pile of dirty crockery accumulated in the sink. "Mr. Donnelly, I thank you for your generous offer, but I think it's about time you got back to—" But he wasn't done.

"If I get you up there, flying around? Comfortable in the air, more or less?" His eyes were boring holes into her.

Remember the sign, her look said.

He held her gaze, chugged the last of his Sam, and set the

bottle carefully down on its watermark. "You get the Friends of the Preserve to back off me."

Oops, deal breaker. "I can't and I won't," she said. "One runway's bad enough, but I can adjust. But no way, the second one. Everybody's hard work right down the tubes? The deer screwed? No way. Forget it."

Round and round we go. Arm in arm with the Friends, taking on Goliath to protect Pear Island. The article—and the job resulting from it—could potentially become a major weapon in the battle and she was committed to writing it, with or without Logan Donnelly's unwitting help. If he withdrew his offer to take her on as a, what, student? she'd just have to tackle the afraid-to-fly issue in a different way. Cook up another scheme to ferret out the info for Iverson. "I'm not calling Hillary Harker off, even if she'd listen to me."

"People do listen to you. You've got more influence in this town than you realize."

If he mentioned cash cow one more time, Sarah decided she'd kill him and bury his body under the front rosebushes.

"Probably because of all those Letters to the Editor you write."

Too bad, she had to let him live. But the letters? They had probably tipped him off as to who she was the first day they'd met in the preserve.

Maybe she didn't want to hit him with a sign anymore, but the intricate dance was making her get crabby and irritable. They were diametrically opposed on the preserve issue and she couldn't imagine them ever finding a middle ground. "This is going nowhere," Sarah said, flopping onto a bar stool. "You want to destroy the preserve and I want to protect it."

Logan stood and walked his empty bottle over to the counter. "Destroying the preserve is not my aim. Seeing

Crossly Field do well is. That was my grandfather's final wish, the real reason he pulled me into the project."

Sarah found herself suddenly intrigued about the *other* reasons.

"I've grown to love Crossly Field," he said, simply.

That seemed to me a little bit like falling in love with a lifelike blow-up doll, but because he looked so down, she said, "It *is* doing well, though. You've got the flight school, the Airview Restaurant—good fries by the way—a new control tower, hangars. . . ." She ticked off the positives on her fingers.

He shook his head as if he pitied her. He planted his hands on the edge of the bar top, fingers showing, thumbs underneath, arms locked at the elbows. "You know how much it costs to install and maintain that kind of capital equipment? You can't do it on French fries and one runway. I need commercial flights—as many as possible—going in and out of there every hour of every day, generating revenue. My long-term financial plan hinges on the second runway."

The Friends suspected as much.

"It fails, Crossly Field fails. Noah Crossly left me his baby. I've got to make sure it survives."

"But what about the deer?" Sarah asked. "*They* won't. You'll scare the crap out of them—and I mean that literally—when you add the new flight paths right over the preserve. What about *people's* rights to simply have a beautiful place in nature to escape to? One that doesn't have to 'generate revenue' or justify its existence in any particular way? Somewhere really special that can just *be* there, forever, for the people of Tidal. For me. Maybe my . . . kids, someday." Where did that come from?

"Sarah, Pear Island is under assault from all sides. Just look around. How many of those beachfront condos were there even five years ago? If it's not me wanting a piece of the place, it's the developers. At least I won't be bulldozing all of it. The animals can have their little eco . . . spot." He waggled his fingers to suggest deer happily comingling.

"Eco*system*," Sarah said. "Until *vr-r-r-room!*" She nose-dived her hand at the backs of his, feeling the briefest flash of body heat when she crossed them. "Party's over. Deer want off the island. They risk the traffic on the bridge or the currents of The Rip to reach the mainland, where they will be run over. Or shot. Or starve to death. How long do you think that community is going to last with jets zipping over their heads? A year? Two? My guess is not more than five."

It was disgusting. "Logan, your problem is that you really have no understanding. No, maybe intellectually you do. Wrong word. You have no . . . appreciation for nature, for wildlife. For their struggles to survive in places where people are squeezing them out. Have you ever actually spent any time in the woods? Watched any animals out there?"

"Sure. One time in Basic." He started rummaging through the pencil jar on the bar. Sarah wanted to slap his hand away before he reached the strata of sticky pennies at the bottom.

"Come again?"

"Basic training. In the Air Force." He looked up wistfully. "All I ever wanted to do was fly."

"I'll bet. And?"

"We had to do this survival training thing. A mission simulation. Forced landing in a remote area. You know, a live-off-the-land thing? They parachuted about six of us onto this little two-bit island off the coast of Georgia. Kind of like Pear Island actually. Sandy, scrubby. A nothing little spit of land."

She bristled at his portrait of the preserve. He must have sensed it because he looked up from the neat picket row of pencils he was creating. "Keep going," Sarah said.

"You had nothing with you but your K-bar knife, some matches, not even paper to wipe your—"

She held up a hand. "I've got the picture."

"Sorry. Well, I found out ahead of time where they were gonna be dropping us off and I had a buddy of mine fly us in supplies. Bedrolls, netting. We had fresh bread, butter, eggs even. It was great. We passed with flying colors. No pun intended." He chuckled at the memory.

"No offense, but you are such a scumbag. That's cheating." In one way, though, she identified with his objection to forced participation in what she could well perceive were mind-numbing group activities. Her mother was humiliated when Sarah was asked to leave her Girl Scout troop over a midnight prank involving the den mother and a purloined tube of Bengay. But Sarah, unlike Logan, had not signed up voluntarily. Besides, the training was for Logan's own good. "I can't believe you. What if you crash-landed somewhere"—a little too close to home; she grabbed at the edge of the bar to steady herself—"and you had to live off the land for days?"

"To stay alive I'd eat bugs, no problem. But eat them just for practice? No sir-*ree*."

You couldn't not laugh.

He chuckled, too, a rusty sound. "Great visual, huh?"

Sarah laughed again, reliving the Bengay incident. "Yeah." Logan Donnelly was a dangerous man, she realized. He made it difficult for her to hang on to her rancor. She said, "Here's another good picture: you saying good night."

Sarah walked him to the front door. "See you . . . ?"

"Nine sharp tomorrow."

"Done."

"Good night," he said, smirking.

Watching him walk away was so not worth her time that she wondered why she did it.

Chapter 9

Crossly Field had a surrealistic quality when Sarah arrived there the next morning. Menace permeated; danger lurked. Nothing was quite as she remembered it seeming B.G.—Before Ground Loop.

She leaned her trail bike against the fence at the edge of the runway.

She felt relatively calm, given where she was and what she was about to do. She had thought a lot about what Logan had said about the almost accident she'd almost caused. Getting ambushed by an imaginary dog paled in comparison.

No sign of the lumbering Lloyd around the flight school office, but she planned to give him a wide berth. The "Get Out of Dodge" flavor of their last encounter still lingered. Preston she could give a rat's ass about. He'd do well to stay out of *her* way.

She checked her watch. Where was the incorrigible Logan Donnelly this fine morning? Waited a few more minutes, saw a couple of planes take off. Very weird she didn't feel weird about that, but maybe Einstein had it right when he said everything was relative. The debacle with Preston, in spite of scaring the crap out of her, had yielded a new perspective: you were relatively safe around airplanes as long as you never left the ground in one. No need to call out the Dog yet.

9:05.

Be there at 9:00 sharp, he'd said the night before. Sarah remembered the scene in Charlie Brown when Lucy yanked the football away. Right when he was about to kick it. Logan had better not set her up if he knew what—

A plane engine fired up near the flight school. A Cessna emerged from the tangle of wings in the tie-down area. It taxied parallel to the fence and stopped on the Tarmac twenty feet in front of Sarah. The engine cut out and the propeller wound down. The side door popped open and beneath the door a man's leg slid into view: Logan's. She'd made a thorough yet unobtrusive study of them the other night after the minibuzz from the beer had hit her. It embarrassed her to admit that. About the legs, not the buzz. An expensive drunk she was not.

Today the long, lean, matched set was encased in another product recently reviewed—L.L.Bean Backcountry Hikers— in a fetching slate tone. Street clothes she might be shaky on, but trail fashion? She was a maven. Kelly green tennis shirt on top, tucked in. Not what she'd have gone with—maybe the short-sleeved, vented nylon number from the same line?

"Hey," Sarah called.

"Come around." The fence, she guessed he meant. He gestured.

She thought about hopping it, just to show off, but she'd

probably snag her shorts on the top, fall on her ass, and break something. Primly, she opted for the long way around. Calm, deliberate: that's the way pilots acted.

She joined Logan next to the plane.

"We'll start with the preflight check," he said. "You do it every time you even think about going up in an aircraft."

Good morning to you, too. What was his problem? And what was it with the preflight checks? He was the pilot; let *him* do them before she got there.

"Why do I care about a preflight check? You're the pilot," she said.

"I thought about what Preston Lewis was doing with you. He was on the right track."

Oh, boy. Was there the equivalent of the "Blue Wall" in aviation?

"I'm no shrink," he said, "but I think the only way you're going to feel okay about going up there is if you feel you have some kind of control over what's happening to you. What do you think?"

She remembered the feeling of revving the engine. "Okay. Maybe. But what does that mean?"

"It means you get lessons. Flying lessons."

Lessons? It might have been Spot she heard then, but again . . . maybe not.

"Hello? Did you hear me?" he said.

"Yes. Lessons. Flying lessons. I would . . . eventually . . . fly the plane." Big deal. Ha-ha. Fly the plane.

He nodded. "That plane."

This was serious shit here. "Yes." *Gack!*

That was Spot making a noise like a cat coughing up a hairball. His sense of humor was limited but incredibly well timed. "I . . . don't know."

Logan shifted his clipboard from one hand to the other. "Look—I want you out of my hair, you want that job. This is the way to do it."

"You saw what happened to Preston Lewis."

"We're not going up on the first day. We're not going up until you're ready. Take as long as you need."

Did either one of them have *that* much time? Sarah pictured the Sphinx completely reburied by shifting sand, the Leaning Tower of Pisa in shattered pieces on the ground—

"Within reason," he said. "I can't spend the rest of my life on this project."

Unlike her, who'd spent most of hers on it. Maybe he had a point, though. Maybe it was about learning to control—literally—her own destiny. "Okay. But we don't go up until I say."

"Again, within reason."

He did have an airport to run. Although how he did it from the shadows of the flight school building she couldn't imagine. But flying lessons. *Control.* Of *everything*. A little bird inside her fluttered hopefully from one rib to another. She was certain it left via the large hole in her head.

"Okay," she said. "Okay. Call me crazy, but okay. Th-thank you." Barely a stutter. Not bad.

"Moving along to the preflight, then," he said.

You're welcome. He could be *such* an ass.

"We start on the outside of the plane and work around it in a sequence."

No wonder Lewis was a popular instructor when you considered the competition.

"We always inspect the same things in the same order. Routine is what saves you."

Goody, routine. Her favorite. "Wait." She put her hand on his arm. His turn to bristle.

Sheesh. *Calm yourself.* "Whatever you say, but first I want to talk money. This is a business arrangement, not a favor."

"Fine. But after the lesson. When we're done here we can do up a contract."

"I did one with Lloyd. Can't we use that?"

"Well . . ." He adjusted his baseball cap.

"Well, what? I want this on the up-and-up."

"Then, frankly? You're shit out of luck. Lloyd would flip if he knew you were back in one of his planes."

"His planes? I thought you owned this place."

"Lock, stock, but not barrel. I own the field—the grounds and the facility—but Lloyd owns the school and the airplanes. Except for the ones that are privately owned and stored here."

"Then how did you get to use this?" Sarah touched the wing of the little Cessna. Spot grumbled halfheartedly. "Lloyd must be pissed about what I did to the other one." She checked out the tail numbers. Cripes, it *was* the other one: LD 108.

"I told him I would make all necessary repairs if he would allow me unrestricted use of it," Logan said. "Plus, I pulled it over here so he wouldn't see you."

"Wow, that's really nice of—"

"Just don't mess it up again."

Please tell her *why* he was like that. "You think I *wanted* to do that? You think I enjoy smashing up your expensive toy? Why I ought to—"

"You 'ought to' what? You got no recourse. You shouldn't even be on these grounds, legally speaking. Can we please get going?" He pointed to a lengthy list on a clipboard. "I'll get you a copy of this, but for now just follow along."

Sarah mumbled uncivilly and followed Logan to the front of the plane.

"Like I said, the preflight check. Every time you go up you do one. *Every* time."

Yeah, yeah. Same old spiel as Preston's. Get on with it.

Sarah realized he was staring at her. "What did I just say?" he asked.

"Um . . . every time?"

He shook his head. "I hope you're listening, Ms. Dundee. You're paying good money for this and you're not going anywhere until you prove you've got everything under control. *Capice?*"

Why did he suddenly sound like an Occidental Dr. Loo? Sarah gritted her teeth. "Yes."

He was right. She wasn't focused. But his being a prick about it was so necessary? She forced herself to concentrate.

"Duck under," he said, stooping beneath a wing. He pointed to a small bent piece of pipe protruding from the bottom surface of the wing. "This here is the Pitot tube. Air rushing in the front of it goes to a gauge on the instrument panel that tells you how fast you're going, more or less. We'll talk about the more or less later."

Ah, an old friend: the very same "pee-too tube" Preston Lewis had rattled on about.

"Wait. That 'more or less thing' you're talking about," Sarah said, surprised to be suddenly engaged. "It wouldn't have something to do with the speed of the wind, would it? I mean, if you're going with the wind the tube gadget would read lower than if you were going against the wind, right? You know, with all that extra air rushing into it?"

Logan had paused to listen to her. "You've already started reading about this, right? You're a writer, so naturally you think that you can figure everything out from books?"

"Well, no. I thought about doing that, but I haven't actually started yet."

"You just figured the speed thing out all by yourself." The tip of his pen was poised motionless at the tube opening.

"Pretty much. I mean, it's common sense, right? Air pressure, combined speeds, blah, blah, blah."

He laughed and shook his head. "You having any flashbacks right now?" he asked.

"No."

He seemed to find her answer amusing. He led the way out from under the wing, straightened up like it pained him, and brought them around to the rear edge of the wing. "These are the ailerons," he said, pointing to inset panels in the wing that looked too loosely attached to it. "In the preflight, always move them up and down, through the full range of their motion. Feel for anything restricting their travel. Don't put your hands near here, though," he said, pointing to a particularly nasty-looking hinge. "If the wind gusts, the aileron can slam down on your fingers and crush them."

Ouch. "Playing piano one-handed for a while, eh?"

"Maybe permanently."

"Yikes."

"Something like that."

After the preflight of the outside of the plane was completed, Logan sat Sarah in the cockpit and went through everything in there gauge by gauge, and lever by lever. Before she knew it, he said, "That's it for today."

"What do you mean 'that's it'? It's only"—she looked at her wrist—"oh."

Tempis really *fugits* when you're having fun. And she had had fun. Some of the stuff Logan talked about sounded a little familiar from Preston, but a lot of it felt like she was hearing it—really hearing it—for the first time.

"Same time tomorrow, if you're game," Logan said, writing on his clipboard.

"Nine A.M. sharp. And we talk contract, right?"

"Roger."

Two could play the smirking game. "You too."

She hopped the fence this time.

Chapter 10

Sarah arrived at the field a few minutes early for her Thursday morning lesson, so she poked around, looking for Logan. She heard him before she spotted him. His voice sounded odd and muffled and seemed to be coming from inside a big metal shed, a hangar, she supposed would be the correct term.

She peeked through the door of the building.

Logan's voice was radiating out of the bowels of an old, old single-seater airplane that was resting in something like a boat cradle on wheels. The plane was a dusty, rusty blue-gray with the faded remains of a grinning shark's mouth painted on its nose. The engine, the metal shrouding that should have covered it, and what had probably been a glass bubble canopy over the narrow cockpit opening were missing. Only stubs of wings protruded from the fuselage. Hinge-looking contraptions dangled loosely from the ends of the amputations and she could look right into the hollow interior of the stumps. The rest of both wings was clamped into a rack off to the side, looking like major work had been done to them. Shiny new metal patches stood out.

Logan was bellowing. "Maura!"

He was cranky.

"Maura! You still out there or what?"

Really cranky. Sarah felt like a spy, not that it stopped her.

"Right here, bub," said a second voice, higher and lighter than Logan's.

A pair of legs in coveralls moved on the far side of the plane and made their way around to Sarah's side. They belonged to the attractive, dark-haired woman she'd seen Logan chatting up–slash–hitting on when she should have been paying better attention to Preston as he cheerily drove their little airboat deeper into the alligator-infested swamp.

"Quit screwing around out there and hand me in that seven-sixteenths crescent."

Always a gentleman, Logan.

Sarah watched the woman unhesitatingly select something from a compulsively neat array of mechanic's tools arranged on a rolling metal table. She spun a gleaming metal tool between her fingers like a miniature baton.

"This one?" the woman asked innocently, knowing full well, Sarah was sure, Logan couldn't see what she was holding, because all anyone could see of Logan was one boot sticking up out of the cockpit. The rest of him was inelegantly stuffed up the ass end of the plane.

"Very funny," grumbled The Voice in the Tail. "Now how the hell would I know what 'this one' is when my head is stuck so far up the ass of this Hellcat I can hardly see two inches in front of my face let alone what you got in your hand?"

Jinx ya, Sarah thought. Getting to be a habit with this guy.

Anyway, this Maura must have been busting Logan's

chops big time for a long time before Sarah had gotten there. Good for her. *Would that it were me,* Sarah thought. Yet who was this Tool Time vixen? Sarah wondered, not that it was any of her business. A love interest? Too bad. Tough to have a thing going with someone you worked closely with. Been there, done that.

Sarah watched the woman climb the cradle and wiggle her upper body into the tight cockpit opening. The plane must have been some kind of military aircraft. It was lean and mean. There were neat, square shiny patches around the rim of the cockpit. Sarah wondered if they covered up neat, round bullet holes.

"That the crescent?" The Voice asked.

"Yeah, yeah, right here." Maura's voice was muffled, too. "Thanks."

"No problem."

"You can get your hand off my ass now."

"Spoilsport."

Maura wiggled backward out of the cockpit.

Grunts and groans came from inside the fuselage. Maura paced. She rearranged the tools on the cart. She found a broom and swept the already immaculately clean concrete floor. Finally, she said, "Look, boss, we've been at this for three hours. You done soon?"

"Err—!" Logan's foot spasmed, then relaxed. "There. Now I am. Take this stuff from me."

Maura climbed up and reached into the plane, grabbed hold of the end of a yellow electrical cord, and hauled something out. The Voice said, "Be careful, it's—"

"Ow! Jeez! Hot? No shit, Sherlock." She tossed a droplight back and forth between her hands. Sarah cringed, thinking about airplanes and burning flesh. Spot, lying on his side and breathing deeply—probably dreaming of chasing her—sloppily woofed. He'd been sleeping more of late.

Logan extricated the assorted parts of himself from the plane. He dumped a handful of tools on the rolling cart and took Maura's injured hand in both of his. She looked up into his face as he made his evaluation of her palm.

Sarah wondered what Maura was thinking.

"You'll live," Logan pronounced, returning Maura's hand.

"Good thing, too, you being without workman's comp and all," she said. "Oh—hi. Can I help you?"

The rest of Sarah's sneaky self followed her sneaky face into the shed. "I'm ah . . . looking for him." She pointed at Logan.

"You're early," he said.

"Well, yes, I suppose I am. If you'd rather I waited in the office . . . ?" She made like to go.

"No. Lloyd'll be all over you in there."

Maura sniggered. Logan shot her a look. "Maura Winslow, Sarah Dundee. Maura, Sarah."

"Hi."

"Hey."

Maura wiped her hand on a rag and offered it. The two women shook.

"Well, we're done here," Logan said. That didn't ring true from the vibes Sarah had picked up.

"What about my money?" Maura said. "Don't think I'm doing this for nothing, giving up my morning off."

"Ah, you forget. Slave labor's above the law. I'll buy you and Eric lunch, though."

"Huh."

"And speaking of the lad . . ." Logan said.

A boy of about sixteen came in carrying a case of motor oil like a stevedore would, boosted on his shoulder. "Where you want it, Logan?"

"Last locker on the left, thanks. And tell the guy on the

truck that he has to pump out the waste oil tank. We're chock full."

"You got it," the boy replied, walking away.

"My son," Maura informed Sarah.

"Oh, and Eric," Logan said, "be nice to the guy. Otherwise he'll spill crap all over the place on his way out."

"Right."

"Give him a reason, right?" Maura asked.

"Huh?"

"You gave Eric a reason for being polite. So the guy wouldn't spill oil, right? Otherwise he probably wouldn't have thought to be pleasant."

"Ah, Watson, my methods become clear."

Maura slapped him playfully on the arm. "You are such an idiot."

"Thank you. Where to for lunch, by the way?"

Maura arched one brow. "The Airview. Where else?"

"Do I detect you got a problem with that?"

Maura chuckled. "It's not me that's got a problem, pal," she said, backing up and holding up both palms. "Personally, I think seeing you and June in action is better than a Jerry Springer episode." She turned and walked out into the bright sunshine.

"Interesting gal," Sarah said, fiddling with one of the shiny doohickies on the rolling cart.

"Leave it alone," Logan said.

She assumed he meant the shiny thing, so she did.

"Let's get out of here." He headed toward the open hangar door.

Ten minutes later Logan had the 150 signed out. He walked Sarah through the preflight.

"Even if you just shut the engine down for five minutes to run in and get a cup of coffee, inspect the exterior of the plane all over again before you start up," Logan told her, running his hand along a wing. "Some nitwit could have clipped your wingtip or the prop when they taxied by. Do it every time," he said. "No exceptions."

Then he walked her through the preflight again, interior and exterior, and gave her a mnemonic device to remember all the things to check. "You find anything that doesn't look or feel right, go get a mechanic."

"Unless you're already in the air, huh?"

"Are you getting this here, or what?"

Jeepers, she was just trying to lighten the mood. "Sir." She stood straighter.

That got her one of those dark, disparaging, Mr. Darcy looks with which she was becoming all too familiar. "Get in."

Sarah did and buckled up. Logan hit the starter, and the engine gasped, coughed, then held. "You did a lot of taxiing with Preston. Think you're ready for something else?"

"What have you got in mind? Is this like a Twelve-Step Program?"

"No. It's more like the ol' One-Two. You're either in the air or you're not."

"Very funny. I guess I have to do it sometime, though, huh?"

"I don't know. How bad do you want that job?"

"Really bad."

"Then yes. Sometime. But I have to know right now if you're going to freak out up there. Think hard about it. You lose it up there, you could kill us both."

He raced the engine and fiddled with what she now knew were the fuel mixture settings.

Freak out, her ass. She didn't freak out. She had anxiety

attacks and became temporarily insane. And it *wouldn't* happen. *How* she knew she couldn't say, but she knew. She could do this. Now was her big moment, the hour of truth, the day of reckoning, the . . . the . . . God, was she gonna throw up when they got back down. "I'm ready," she said, looking him in the eye. "Really."

Logan was apparently satisfied with what he saw in her eyes because he radioed the tower. While he was waiting for a reply, he filled her in on the plan.

"Just a few times around the field. Nothing major—just get you up there. I'll do everything. You just watch. Don't. Touch. Anything."

"Okay." It came out like a squeak.

The radio crackled and the controller in the tower said something unintelligible. It was really much easier when the messages from the control tower were written in scrolling text at the bottom of the computer screen, like it was on a flight simulation video game at the pizza place downtown. But then she *was* a text person, after all. Anyway, she'd tried the stupid game on a dare, almost revisiting her barely digested pepperoni and mushroom slice.

The plane jerked forward. *Jeezum!*

"A very forgiving aircraft," Logan said. He pushed on the throttle and the engine roared.

No click and drag here. This was the real McCoy. Sarah had visions of winding herself around Logan's head like a scared cartoon cat.

"A lot of aircraft you have to tell what to do. This one practically knows what to do before you even input the controls," he said over the intercom. She guessed he meant that to sound reassuring, but it sounded a little bit like saying that one particular brand of dynamite was safer than another. Logan fed her more information, but she missed it because she was fixating on Spot, who had her temporarily convinced he was running alongside the plane and leaping at it. The little bastard had woken up abruptly and realized he'd missed his connecting flight. She imagined his horrid toenails scrabbling for purchase on the fuselage. To distract herself Sarah thought about Logan.

Some hard miles somewhere along the line had etched themselves into his face, making him appear older than he probably was, Sarah realized. He was likely just a few years older than her, say thirty-seven, thirty-eight. He'd talked about being in a rush to learn to fly, so he enlisted at what? Eighteen? That meant he'd been going up in the air and coming down again safely for something like two decades. He hadn't flown anything other than a round trip yet and didn't seem to have recently developed suicidal tendencies, in spite of having made her acquaintance.

But he did have a slight limp and sometimes walked stiffly. That bothered her. His impairment seemed to be on the opposite side from *her* souvenir from Africa: a patch of scar tissue that looked roughly like the state of Florida. It started at Tallahassee, just below her belt line and ended with Key West just above midthigh. Shorts did a good job of camouflage, but bikinis had never been a go. She fervently hoped that Logan hadn't acquired his boo-boo in an aviation-related "oops."

The engine noise in the cockpit was overpowering, despite the headphones. She found it hard to concentrate with the racket.

"It'll quiet down a bit once we're up," he said, reading her mind. "Whatever you do, no matter how scared you are"— he glanced at her scrunched down in the seat, gripping the grab handles for dear life—"don't shut your eyes. You'll get nauseous."

Too late. Where was that Ziploc bag anyway?

"We're going to get clearance from the tower now to taxi out to the runway," he told her. The engine roar got, if possible, even louder, and Sarah felt the tail of the Cessna swing around behind her. It was disorienting, feeling one's backside move sharply around one way while facing straight ahead. It brought back feelings of riding carnival rides. She'd never gotten sick on them. Loved them in fact.

"Control, this is LD one-oh-eight requesting permission to approach Runway Four-Niner for takeoff," Logan said into the radio microphone.

The radio crackled and a calm, light voice replied, "Roger, LD one-oh-eight, you are clear to approach runway for takeoff."

"Roger, tower. Thank you."

The voice sounded familiar, but Sarah couldn't quite place it. They rolled along through a series of turns, her with white-knuckled hands clutching the seat and eyes squeezed shut. No one could tell her anything. Logan was preoccupied with taxiing and offered no comments. After a few minutes, the plane rolled to a stop at the end of the taxiway, and he wound the engine down a bit. In the relative quiet, Sarah felt an enormous foreboding.

It was like reclining in the chair at that moment when the dentist leans over with the drill in his hand and says, "Now open wide." Will the experience be as painless as advertised? Was it too late to reschedule the appointment? Were false teeth really that bad? But, no, there was no escape. You were committed

Logan's voice cut through the smell of burning tooth enamel. "Tower, this is LD one-oh-eight requesting permission to enter active runway." There was a pause, then the usual verbal garbage. He replied, "Roger that, tower."

He goosed the throttle and the plane swung onto the runway. He wiggled the control wheel, shoved the rudder pedals side to side, and looked out the back and side windows. "Checking the control surfaces," he explained.

"For what?" Sarah asked, in spite of her anxiety.

"To see if they work."

She remembered Preston and her in exactly the same spot. Had it been only a few days ago? "You have a misplaced sense of humor, you know that?"

"I was serious."

"Oh." Maybe it was her that had a misplaced sense of déjà vu.

The radio, again. Logan's acknowledgment was terse. "Roger that, tower. Initiating takeoff roll."

He revved the engine and looked to be standing on the brakes. He turned his head to her. "You ready?"

Her mouth was as dry as an old sponge. She nodded weakly.

"You sure? You can't pull a Preston again. You kick the rudder pedals or go nuts? We could die. That simple. Your call."

The little plane vibrated like a poodle that desperately needed to pee. He waited.

"Go." Her voice was a croaking whisper.

He let up on the brakes.

The Cessna began to roll. Five seconds—Sarah glanced at the speedometer—thirty miles an hour. Ten seconds? It felt like a hundred. The wheels telegraphed every bump and divot in the runway asphalt. They were running out of control down along a gigantic washboard. Her eyeballs rattled in their sockets and her teeth were clacked. Jumbled scenes flashed through her mind. Her father, Beth. The floor seemed to be melting. She felt like Jodie Foster in the capsule in *Contact*.

The ride suddenly and magically smoothed.

Thank God. The plane had come to a stop. Logan had reconsidered. Sarah cracked open one eye. There were houses and streets and swimming pools flowing smoothly by beneath the belly of the airplane. Kids played on artificially green lawns the size of place mats. Trees everywhere, poking up like the crowns of diminutive broccoli. Logan hadn't changed his mind.

Involuntarily, Sarah rocked back in forth in her seat. A low, keening moan escaped her clenched lips.

"How you doing?" Logan's voice, through the headphones.

No words would come out. A blessing, maybe, under different circumstances.

"You're not sick yet?"

She shook her head. Yeah, well, at least she was good at something. Only engine noise filled the cabin for the next few minutes.

The headphones crackled. "We're on the approach leg. One more turn and we're headed home."

Go back? She hadn't even realized he had made any turns yet. He *was* smooth. Yeah, but how good would he be on a real flight simulator?

You nitwit. You're in a real flight simulator.

"Wait."

"Yes?"

"I want to open my eyes."

"Okay. But look at your lap first. Then up to the instrument panel, then the horizon."

She complied, her eyes but slits.

Ah, yes, there were her thighs. Very nice ones, despite the trembling. Despite the unfortunate purple cast of Key West peeking out below one hem. Sarah loosened her viselike grip on the seat. The instrument panel was right in front of her. Its businesslike collection of dials and gauges was reassuring. They had a lot of miles on them—well-worn veterans of many successful flights. They weren't designed to be disposable items. Planes didn't just go up once, then crash and burn. Just her family's bad luck to have been around when one did. Hysteria, ever an attractive option, fluttered beneath her breastbone, but she fought it off.

Okay. Now the horizon.

The low morning sun reflecting off a light haze seared her retinas. "Yikes—"

"You bring sunglasses?" Logan asked.

"In my bag. In back."

"Turn around and get them."

Like that was easy. "In back" might as well have been the Upper Cataracts on the Nile. Ya couldn't *git* there from here.

"You're not going to tip the plane over or anything," said Logan. "Go ahead."

Twisting, Sarah groped in the space behind her, snagged the pack, and hauled it up front. She slipped on dark shades and peered through the Plexiglas windshield.

The view through the Plexiglas windows looked fake, like a virtual sky, screen saver dotted with blossoming cumulus clouds. But it wasn't computer chip wizardry out there—it was real. So real it took her breath away. In a completely unexpected way.

"Holy shit . . . You do this every day?" she murmured.

Logan's spontaneous laughter rattled around her headphone cups. "Just about."

"Logan, this is, well, I don't know what it is. . . ." The cumulus cotton balls floating in the ocean of deep azure were morphing into different shapes right before her eyes, and she felt close enough to reach out her hand and touch them. "It's like the ceiling of the Sistene Chapel. It's like Mount Katahdin. In Maine? No wonder God spends most of his time up here, Logan. My word . . ."

She bubbled over with awe. Like a little kid in a candy store wanting to gulp everything at once, she brazenly looked down at the ground through the side window. Mistake. Trees slid beneath tiny, boat-trailer wheels. "Oh, God."

She whipped her head forward. Pinwheels exploded behind her eyes. Her toes tattooed the cabin floor and she clutched her old friends the seat handles. "Oh, crap."

"Keep looking forward," Logan said. "Keep your eyes open. Keep looking at the sky in front. Ride it out."

An apt phrase. The plane had become a bucking bronco. It wasn't bouncing—Sarah knew that intellectually—but her body thought it was. Too much, too fast. Circuit overload. She rocked and fought to keep her eyelids from slamming shut. "Mr. Wizard . . ."

"Time for 'dis one to come home," she heard Logan finish for her. Then he clicked the radio microphone. His voice boomed in her ears. "Tower, this is LD one-oh-eight on final approach. Request permission to land."

She willed one eye to open. Logan was fiddling with a small wheel recessed into the instrument panel. Something in the wings whined and the plane seemed to sink.

"We're not dropping out of the sky," he said to her. "It just feels that way. We're slowing because of the extra wing. The flaps are going down."

She came around enough to be embarrassed at her behavior. "Mm."

Poor Logan, stuck with her. But, hey, if you wanted to enjoy your time in the air, you didn't invite a crazy person along for the ride.

"You're probably not gonna like this next part," he said, working knobs and switches on the panel.

Really? She'd adored the rest.

"The landing, that is. There's a bit of a crosswind on the runway."

He said it so casually: "A bit of a crosswind." Was that anything like "reports of icebergs"? She screwed her courage up and peeked out over the nose of the plane. The runway was right in front of them. The lights, the white stripes, everything. She'd done a bit of informational on-line reading since their last lesson, so she found herself looking for the wind sock. Logan would have to do something special with the rudder pedals and the control wheel to get one wheel down first, but she hadn't quite followed the article on that point and the idea of a streaming video demo had scared the crap out of her.

"This is going to feel a little weird," he said, "because I've got to touch the upwind wing down first."

"Just tell me you've done this before, okay? Humor me?"

"About twenty-five thousand times," he said, as if he had actually been keeping track.

"Cool," she rasped. She turned her head a fraction to the left, just enough to watch Logan. His face was a study in concentration. He held the wheel lightly in one hand and played the throttle slide with the other. The plane didn't seem to follow his inputs like an obedient robot: instead, he and the Cessna seemed to be engaged in a process of negotiation. It would go one way; he'd persuade it in another. It'd go there for a few seconds, then change its mind again.

"Just as long as we all end up at the same place at the same time," he said. Sarah assumed he must have felt her eyes on him.

"Cool . . ." She desperately needed new material. And the john.

Lower and slower the plane went, until the perpendicular stripes on the apron of the runway merged into a broad white band. Seamlessly, the Cessna morphed from a graceful craft of the air into a clumsy, earthbound vehicle, bouncing and jiggling along the asphalt runway at sixty miles per hour.

Logan braked cautiously and the plane reluctantly slowed, its nose nodding and tires squealing resentfully.

In seconds, they'd left the runway proper and were on the taxiway.

Sarah let out a huge breath and nearly blew out her eardrums, forgetting about the mike on her headset. Logan grimaced but didn't comment. He bounced the Cessna off the asphalt taxiway and into the tie-down area opposite the fence where she'd left her bike. He shut down the engine, got out and jammed wedges under the wheels, then hopped back in and started making notes on a clipboard.

"I am so fricking glad to be back on the ground," Sarah said.

"I'll bet," Logan said.

What she really wanted to do was fall out of the cockpit onto her knees and kiss the grass under the plane, and—this is really corny—she wanted to kiss Logan like he was her hero. Stupid sounding, even by her standards, but he really did seem larger than life to her at that moment. To think that he did this stuff all the time, taking people's lives into his hands, bringing them up and down safely. At least on a stretch of rough water you could offload your canoe onto the river bank at any time. Just stop the presses and think about life for a while. Up there—she looked skyward, still in awe—there was no pulling your boats up onto terra firma.

"Amazing," she said, contemplating the blue.

"You want to go up tomorrow?" Logan asked, writing.

"Well, like they say, in for a penny, in for a pound. . . ."

He looked up, puzzled, his pen frozen to paper.

"It means yes, absolutely."

"Good."

She grabbed her bag and swung her legs out of the cabin. He continued writing. "See you."

"Uh-huh."

"Thanks."

"You bet."

How nice he shared in her joy and success. She thought about hopping the fence again—he was all eyes the last time—but Maura was standing right where she'd stick the dismount.

Chapter 11

Sarah took the long way around the fence to buy time to gather her thoughts for what she expected to be the standard "Stay away from My Guy" speech. She couldn't have been more wrong.

"Hey," Sarah said.

"Hey, yourself," Maura said.

Maura out of her jumpsuit was a little less muscular. In it, she had reminded Sarah of a girl in eighth-grade gym class who'd said she'd beat Sarah up if she got a better time in the final heat of the hundred-yard dash.

"Good lesson?" Maura asked.

"Yeah. But am I about to get another one?"

Maura laughed.

Sarah laughed, too, because for a long time she hadn't had to think about the possibility of getting beat up.

"Me and Logan?" Maura said. "No. He's cleared for take-off."

Hah! Meaning he wasn't always. Knew it. "And you need to . . . talk about that?"

"I don't know any other way to say this than to just say it, so here goes: don't screw around with him."

Jeepers, did she mean, like, "Don't have sex with him"? Sarah hadn't actually gotten that far in her thinking. Her fantasizing, maybe, but—"Good God, does he have . . . a disease?" Poor Maura, was she a *victim?*

Maura let loose another laugh, this one with a dash of pity in it. "He was right about you."

"Really. Anything else?"

She shook her head. "I can't say."

The hell she couldn't. Sarah pictured Maura and Logan sharing their nasty little thoughts about her. Screw them. She was a woman of the world. She'd shot Class 5 rapids, fallen off cliffs, braved smelly guys in small tents—

Wait. "He *talked* to you about me? Why?"

"We talk about everything. That's part of the problem. Sure, we've unzipped a few jumpsuits together. More than a few, actually. We lived together for almost three years. He's like a surrogate father to Eric. He brought that boy back from the brink, let me tell you. I'd walk on hot coals for him because of what he did for my son. And me."

Sarah decided she liked this woman. And she suddenly placed Maura's voice. She'd heard it over the radio in the plane. Maura worked in the control tower. Multitalented. "So what happened?"

"It got creepy, you know? He's more like . . . I don't know . . . a brother or something. Although I gotta say, he's got technique."

"That can be hard to find, nowadays."

"Tell me. It's been a long dry spell."

"Ditto." Sarah thought about Rick. About the stuff they'd done together, his . . . technique. She was starting to forget some of the details.

Sarah found herself explaining to Maura the deal between Rick and her. Nothing heavy: her neurotic indecisiveness coupled with semidependent personality tendencies exacerbated by a traumatic life event. Maura had the good grace to look interested.

Isn't it funny when you suddenly think of a person who hasn't crossed your mind in ages, Sarah thought, and bam! there they are? Either on the phone or at your door or right behind you?

Rick was *so* close behind her—lookin' so perfect in his faded old jeans, as the song goes—that she almost smacked him in the head as she visually underscored for Maura how screwed up their situation was.

To Sarah he said, "I've had more trouble finding you."

Sarah noted, Not "I've missed you" or even "How the hell are you?"

"Rick, how did you know I was here?" she asked, noting, not "I've missed you" or "How are you?"

Could, like, just anybody see a pattern here? Even *she* could. She and Rick had a really, really, *really* bizarre relationship.

"Your mother."

Sarah assumed it wasn't a curse, just information. Her own fault, really, he was at the field in the first place. If she'd responded to any of his 4,000 phone messages he probably wouldn't have sniffed her out like a truffle. He leaned in to kiss her. She twisted away and he got the corner of her mouth.

Sarah introduced her new, sort-of-friend Maura—with whom she'd just had a discussion about the sexual prowess of a man Maura had slept with and Sarah had kind of halfway fantasized about doing the same with—to her ex-fiancé, whose sexual prowess she'd recently categorized for Maura as an eight plus.

Okay, maybe her relationship with Rick wasn't the only weird thing going on at the moment.

"Pleased to meet you," Maura said to Rick.

"Likewise," Rick said, and Maura smiled, undoubtedly taken in by the Ray-Bans. Sarah wanted to tell Maura that she too had settled for a "likewise," in the old days.

Let go of her hand now, Sarah wanted to tell Rick.

"Rick and I are old . . . friends," Sarah explained, like nobody really knew the score.

"And Sarah and I are sort of . . . new friends," Maura explained.

Now that everyone was clear, Sarah thought she would take her leave gracefully. Short-lived idea.

Logan drifted over, carrying his ever-present clipboard. At that moment, for two cents Sarah would have stuck it in an orifice the sun didn't generally illuminate. "Ms. Dundee, I need your signature on this," he said.

He held the board out to Sarah. Did he want me to get over her fear of signing official-looking documents about airplanes? No. Across the front of a blank flight plan he'd scrawled *This guy bugging you?* Awww, call her sentimental. . . .

She dashed off a terse *Sweet of you, no.* She batted her eyes at him when she handed the note back. Logan looked like she'd just handed him a ticking package. Messing with him was a ball.

"Rick? Logan Donnelly," Sarah said. "He owns this place. Logan? Rick Ventura. He owns everything else." Sarah caught Maura gaving her a funny look, but the guys got busy shaking hands, adjusting pant waists, flexing knees—the usual stuff—and didn't catch the sarcasm.

"Nice spread you've got here," Rick said, taking in the

planes, the runway, and the hangars. He acted like he was native to Big Sky country, but he'd been out of New England about six times in his life. His empire, Adventure Ventura, was strictly on-line. Somebody could find whatever bit of outdoor gear he or she wanted on his Web site, from kayak to daypack, and he'd ship it anywhere in the continental United States within two days.

"Works for me," Logan said. The way *he* talked anyone would think he owned a hot dog stand on wheels. It surprised Sarah. He'd acted like such a big deal at the public meeting.

Rick said, "Sarah, whatever possessed you to try flying? Just the thought of it sends you into a fit."

She'd give *him* a fit. . . . He was just pissed that she never tried to get over her phobia so she could fly to, like, Albany, with him. "Well, Rick, you know. Right time, right reason." *Slam!*

"I guess." He removed his sunglasses and artfully propped them on a sophisticated coif he had adopted since Sarah had last seen him. He did have nice eyes but, unfortunately, knew it. To Maura he said, "And what do you do around here?"

He took his time reading the Crossly Airfield logo scripted onto her shirt just above her left breast. It wasn't that hard to read. She took it in stride.

Logan didn't. "Look," he said to us, *us* being principally Rick, "we're busy now. Why don't you come back later?" Subtext: *or not.* "Then we can give you a real tour of the facilities." *And lose you in the runway landfill* was my take.

Maura said, "Oh. I've got some time now for a tour. If you've got places to go, Sarah . . . ?"

Brave woman, Maura, letting her slip out the back, thought Sarah.

"Sarah, I—" Rick started.

"Great, Rick, you'll love it," Sarah said. She shot Maura a

meaningful look: *owe you one.* "Mr. Donnelly, let's finish that paperwork."

She grabbed Logan's arm and steered him away before the flames coming out his ears incinerated his hat.

"Call you," Rick said.

Sarah waved. *One million and one . . .*

Chapter 12

It was a beautiful July evening.

Sarah was comfortably ensconced in a deck chair on her back porch with the heels of her bare feet resting on the rail. The bugs weren't due out for another half hour, and the sky in the west was tinged with rose. The tips of the tiger lilies ringing the back deck had exploded into orange starbursts. A couple of hanging pots of impatiens filled out the color spectrum.

Gorgeous.

Her notebook computer was open on her lap, the stalled cursor blinking accusingly. She was a couple of weeks into lessons and the rough draft of the article Iverson wanted was almost finished. Spending time at Crossly had filled in a lot of blanks, and she thought she'd be able to convincingly render the day-to-day life of a small, seaside airfield, but she found herself struggling to convey the information she'd assembled on Logan. She was pussyfooting around, feeling caught: How does a person tuck it to the guy helping her to get the job that said person planned to use to eventually bury the guy and his beloved business expansion plan?

Water gurgled. The dirt dam Sarah had built around her latest gardening experiment, half a dozen tomato plants, burst. No matter, it was a crappy time of day to irrigate, anyway. Amazingly, though, her little crop was coming along remarkably well this year. Usually only cacti survived her unenthusiastic care, but the Big Boys she'd picked up as infants a month or so ago were already festooned with fuzzy little green spheres.

She set the laptop down on the deck boards and stepped out to the garden to readjust the flow. Who made up these names for plant varieties anyway? Jeepers. *Big Boys* . . .

Then she took another look at them. Actually, with a little imagination, the pairs of little fuzzy balls kind of looked like—

Get a grip.

The single life may have its advantages, but sleeping alone was not one of them. There were times at night when she could gnaw the bedpost in half.

Being in the close confines of the plane with Logan Donnelly for hours on end wasn't helping either. Joan called that one. Sarah knew Logan's left thigh better than her own. Every banked turn threw his leg tight against hers, sending shivers up and down her spine. When he held the control yoke—his hands over hers—to get her to feel the plane's responses, she was way too conscious of her own. It was a full-time job not acting out any of the really stupid impulses that had been flashing through her mind—and points farther south—lately.

Yeah, yeah, the next logical thing would be Logan inviting her up to his place to see his etchings. But it wasn't creepy like that. He seemed completely unaffected by any of the touching stuff. It was just her that was clogging the boom microphone with drool.

Life with Logan was actually okay now. Lessons had unexpectedly settled into a pleasant routine. Her mother always said, "Give something three weeks before you decide about it." Spot was still a backseat driver, er, pilot, but they were making headway in their troubled relationship and nothing—not even a maniacal dog—was keeping *her* feet on the ground. She was becoming an air addict.

So far, though, she hadn't paid Logan a dime for his time or the use of the plane. That made her almost as uncomfortable as having to write about him in the article. Oh, they'd drawn up a contract all right, and she'd tried to pay off at least some of the hours he'd meticulously recorded on his ubiquitous clipboard, but he kept putting her off. She didn't like being that much in his debt. One way or another, though, she was pretty sure she'd end up repaying. What worried her was how.

Apparently his budget plan didn't include installments tendered in sleaze, as she'd first suspected. For that she was grateful, because if it had she'd have no choice but to dump him. If that had happened, she would have desperately missed the lessons and him, too, she hated to admit. He was a tough instructor: meticulous, demanding, and thorough. She understood in spades why he wouldn't be every student's cup of tea. Yet she could measure herself against him. And when she did something correctly for the first time and he grunted an acknowledgment, it was unbelievably satisfying.

She couldn't imagine what a better pilot would be like, and she was positive—from some of the things he'd hinted at during times she'd surreptitiously switched hats from student to "interviewer"—that she hadn't seen one *tenth* of what he could do with an airplane. Yes, he was an irritating bastard with his compulsive need for perfection—definitely overcompensating for something—but she was nevertheless content.

Sarah bid good night to the Boys, shut off the hose, and shut down the laptop. She idly wondered where an earlier printout of the rough draft had gotten to. As she was half-heartedly pawing through the sucking maelstrom that lived on her kitchen table, she heard the doorbell ring—sharply, repeatedly, insistently. Somehow conveying life-or-death urgency through its impersonal electric circuit. She was halfway to the front door when it became a steady, incredibly annoying buzz. *Hold your horses, you horse's ass.*

With one hand on the front-door knob and one on the dead bolt catch, she was about to twist both when common sense kicked in. She was alone in the house. She pressed her eye to the security peephole.

Logan.

It was just Logan out there. She went for the locks and started to slip them off. Then she stopped and peeked out again. He was doing a Rumpelstiltskin impression on the front porch, stomping his feet and waving a sheaf of loose papers at the door. His ravings were soundless, the volume muted by the heavy oak, but his anger radiated clearly through the thick panels.

Sarah took off the dead bolt and inched the door partly open but kept the security chain on. Logan looked even angrier face-to-face.

"What the hell is this?" he sputtered, thrusting the papers he was holding halfway through the crack.

Ask and you shall receive. He was holding her missing rough draft.

He tried to shoulder his way in, but the chain stretched tight, jamming his arm in the opening.

"I've got a gun," Sarah said, randomly.

"No, you don't. For God's sake, let me in."

"Oh, right. I'm going to let some guy in who's frothing at the mouth and waving stuff in my face. Radio the tower for another approach, flyboy."

Sarah heard him sigh deeply. When he spoke, his tone was even, but the strain of trying to sound halfway sane was clearly costing him. "Sarah, for a woman who supposedly has some brains, you are an idiot sometimes. Do you think that dinky little chain would keep me out if I really wanted to get in?"

"No." She watched *Cops* sometimes. "But if you bust through it you're breaking and entering, and that changes everything." There was a silence, followed by another deep sigh.

"You really piss me off, you know."

She guessed that the clunk she heard was his forehead hitting the door.

"No, really? *I* piss *you* off?" she couldn't help taunting. It was a strong door. "Good. Now you know how I feel every time I'm stuck in the damn plane with you for hours at a whack."

Not completely true, but her brain cells were buzzing. She'd been sneaky and got caught. He had her cornered. Strategy? Muddy the waters. Squirt ink, and then scoot away in the opposite direction. She watched way too much *Animal Planet*. She opened her mouth to speak.

Before any sound came out, a dark thought wormed its way into her forebrain. "Hey, how did you get hold of these, anyway?"

She yanked the papers out of his hand. "Logan, you bastard." To hell with flight. This here was a *fight*.

She clenched the sheaf tightly in her fist, struggling to comprehend the gall of the man. "You shit, you've been going through my bag, haven't you? I swear I'll—" She raised her other fist to the part of Logan's face she could see.

Very quietly he said, "Based on the crap I read in those papers, you think I'm a lot of things, Sarah. But a sneak I'm not."

She stared past her hand hanging in space and into Logan's unblinking gaze. She began to feel like a real jerk. Most people would have already been there.

"June, down at the Airview, gave it to me," he said, bringing his face closer to the crack in the door. "She found it under one of the tables in the restaurant when she was cleaning up after lunch today."

The part of his face that was visible smirked. Smart-ass. So she liked their fries. Fuck him. That didn't make her a bad person. Jerk. As pissed as he was, he still had time to enjoy his little coup. Still, she must be losing her mind to have let the article leave the house. If she were investigating corporate corruption she'd probably be fish food by now.

"Look, let me in will you?" he said, as close to a whimper as she'd ever heard him.

"Don't whine. It doesn't become you," she snapped, when actually it sort of did in a puppy dog way.

She thought about things for a moment: He'd read the article so the damage was done. His introduction to it was not going the way she would have liked, but she'd sweet-talked her way through stickier situations. The fact that he could be such an egotistical bastard also worked in her favor. When she did the draft, she'd struck a compromise between her need to expose his threat to the preserve land and the feeling that she owed him something for helping her, so she'd slanted things a bit to make him look like a hero. It wasn't the easiest piece she'd ever written.

So, given all that, what was he cranky about? And could she take advantage of the situation? Maybe dredge up more info on the tantalizing inner workings of his mind even at this late date? Time to go fishing.

"I'm a writer, Logan," she said. "You knew that. Everything that happens to me—everyone I meet—is grist for the mill. What can I say? You inspired me."

Silence from the other side.

"You've been hurt before, Logan, haven't you? That's why you're so suspicious of my motives, right?"

"I'm not talking through the damn door, Sarah," he said. "Let me in."

My, didn't he want everything. But for the sake of a better final copy she'd grant his request. *Zip* went the security chain. "I'm not in the habit of letting lunatics into the house," she said, stepping aside.

"And *I'm* not crazy about people publicizing my private business without my consent," he said. His eyes skimmed up and down her body. Sarah hadn't ever been conscious of him eyeing her quite that obviously before.

Maybe it had to do with the fact that all she was wearing was an undersized, partially damp T-shirt—the landlord's cheap hose had given her a run for her money—with nothing on underneath it but a pair of almost nonexistent running shorts. Time for the buddy-buddy approach.

"Ah, what are you worried about?" She waved her hand airily and casually covered as much of her breasts as she could behind crossed arms. "I'd never be able to publish it without your permission anyway. I just dashed something together to see if I had a story before I bothered you with it. Not to worry. You have final approval. Really."

"Sorry, Sarah," he said, "but this is where I get off. I'm not *ever* going to approve *any* part of this. I don't want you writing about me, period. And another thing"—he pushed his ball cap farther back on his head and jutted his chin out—"I'm not the big flying ace you make me out to be in the article. I'm just a regular guy working to make ends meet. Looking forward to the Friday night beer. Taking it one day at a time."

Yeah, right. Regular guys inherited entire fucking airfields all the time.

He pulled the papers from her hand and flipped to a page. "I mean, look at this crap." He read:

> *The sharp rasps of my nervous breathing were the only sound to break the steady drone of the single engine of the Cessna 152. My flight instructor, Logan Donnelly, remained silent and steadfast at the controls. His hands, steady and sure . . .*

"I mean, I'm no literary critic, but how stupid is that?" he asked.

She frowned. Hearing it come from his mouth? Really stupid. Hokey. Sophomoric. Iverson would have laughed her out of his office if she'd handed that in.

"And this?"

> *Logan Donnelly's hands rested inches from the control wheel on his side of the crowded Cessna cockpit. He was poised to rescue me should I, a fledgling student pilot, make an errant move.*

"I mean, really . . ."

"Okay," I said. "I get you don't like it." Neither did she. In truth it made her want to barf. "But what I *still* wonder is: Why are you so afraid of a little publicity? How could it *possibly* hurt you? Cripes, Lloyd will probably kiss the ground you walk on for all the free advertising the flight school will get out of this. The article, if it gets accepted, is a win-win thing for everyone. It's really no big deal."

"No big deal?" He looked like he could spit nails. "You paint me like some kind of parijia—what the hell is that word?"

"Pariah?" There were times being a writer was a good thing.

"Yes. Exactly. Like my whole aim is to use Crossly Field to completely annihilate anything four-legged or green. Then, in the next breath, you make me sound like a damn knight in shining armor. I'm nobody's hero. . . ." His voice trailed off and his eyes glazed over, as if focused on something only he could see.

Now *there* was a phenomenon she could write a book about. Sarah recalled seeing that same sudden disconnection ripple across Logan's face at other times, too. Like that day in the preserve, the first time they met.

And now it was happening again, right in front of her. She realized she was seeing the Lurking Thing, species and genus *Spotus Loganimus*. The beast she'd only caught glimpses of. The missing link that would unify the random puzzle known as Logan Donnelly. She was seeing his—*dum, dum dum*—Big Secret.

Abruptly, Logan returned from wherever he'd been with a souvenir: blue-white anger. "Don't try to minimize the issue, Sarah. This article is a bald-faced exposé. Nothing less."

Sarah watched the muscles in his jaw work. "No, it's not," she said.

"You come out smelling like a rose."

That was the thanks she got for trying to make him look like a good guy? She planted her fists on her hips, not giving a damn that his eyes again strayed down the T-shirt now stretched tightly across her chest. "You're overreacting. As usual, I might add."

A nontruth because it was usually her flying off half-cocked, but she was mad now, too. "Besides, the way the piece looks now is not the way it has to get submitted—like I said before. I can change the details to protect your precious anonymity."

"That makes me sound like I've got something to be ashamed of. Like I'm hiding from something," Logan said. He reached up and plucked at the shoulders of his shirt.

If the shoe fits . . .

"Aren't you?" Sarah said, cocking an eyebrow. "From exactly *what* I don't know, but you are hiding." She considered him. "Because I just can't figure you for small-town airport life. It's like you're in self-imposed exile. All nicely hunkered down at little Crossly Field. A big fish in a very small pond."

Right then would have been a great time to shut up, but being her, she of course didn't. "It's nice and cozy and safe at Crossly, isn't it Logan? Except you're more than a little scared of somebody accidentally flipping over the rock you're hiding under. Just why *are* you under there, anyway?"

The movie screen behind his eyeballs lit up again for just a millisecond, but long enough for her to confirm that she was pushing the right buttons. Or the wrong ones. She glanced out the screen door. People were laughing over a board game on the porch of the house across the street. She gauged the distance to the safety of the sidewalk.

What if Logan were an axe murderer who chopped his victims up into neat little bits when they got too close to His Big Secret? Not likely. He didn't possess the creative nature of the truly evil. He seemed like a basically normal guy who was desperately trying to convince people that he was dangerous: Stay away! Don't ask questions!

But she was determined to dissect the mind of the man behind the curtain.

And, damn it, she wasn't in his face solely because of his

reaction to the article. It was more than that. Here she was busting her ass to confront Spot head-on, while this guy—a talented and capable person, much as that stuck in her craw—gutlessly ran for cover from whatever was after *his* ass. He was acting like a chickenshit and she expected more from him.

"You, sir," she pronounced, "are a coward." She poked him in the chest.

"Look," he said, holding his hands up like he was trying to stop a train from running him over, "I really don't want to get into this with you. It's old; it's ancient history; it can't be changed; it doesn't really matter anymore—" He stopped abruptly, as if he realized he was getting too close to an edge. "That's it. I'm done." He squared his shoulders.

"Again, you are such a wimp," she said. "How can you bail out on me? Me, the woman afraid to even look at a plane who now daily shoehorns her fanny into a tiny little excuse for one—with the likes of *you,* I might add—to confront the very thing that scares the living shit out of her. I *did* what I had to do to slay my personal demons. What's wrong with *you?*"

He sighed. "It's not the same thing." He looked up at the ceiling as if the answer to her question was printed there.

"Hey, what's the difference? Fear is fear," she said. That was a reach and she knew it. People have all kinds of horrible things locked up inside them. Things that made Spot look like a lap dog. But she was unwilling to concede the point. "You look it in the eye, ruin a good pair of underwear, and move on. You're *allowing* whatever it is to beat you, Logan."

His eyes swung down to meet hers. The gray was the dirty-laundry color of the ocean after a squall has beaten it flat. He puffed out his cheeks and let his breath out. "Damn it, Sarah, let it go. It's not the same thing at all. What you had

to get over was between you and yourself. There is no getting over what I—aw, forget it."

The weariness in his voice closed the book in the middle
of a very interesting chapter.

She clapped her hands together once, briskly. "Well,
Logan, you're a big boy and it's your business, but if you ask
me, you look like a dirigible that's floating around on half its
gas. There is no way I would cart around something as big as
what you're carrying. *No* way. I'd do whatever I had to do to
give it the slip. Life is too short."

"I guess that's one of the things that makes me and you
different."

"Trite. You can do better."

"Maybe," he said, "but you can forget about this thing."
He handed Sarah back the draft. He turned toward the door
and rested his hand on the knob. "So, I'll see you tomorrow,
right? Nine o'clock?"

She folded her arms again and rocked on her toes. The
free show was over. "Yep, I'll be there. With bells on. Even if
I am scared shitless."

"I'll show you how to get out of a stall," he said, ignoring
my jibe.

"Something you need a little work on yourself," Sarah
mumbled.

Logan pulled his lips back in a stillborn grin and started
to ease himself out the door.

Then it struck Sarah—a bit out of character for her, she
realized—that the human being in front of her was in genuine pain. "Look—wait, Logan." She uncrossed her arms
and pressed her palms flat against her thighs. "I feel bad that
you feel bad. I really wasn't trying to make you look like a
jerk in print. Completely the opposite, in fact." She reached
out and touched him lightly on the wrist.

Shadows were falling in the front hall and she couldn't see his face clearly, but some of the heaviness seemed to leave him.

"Don't ruin the moment by apologizing," he said.

"You jerk, I wasn't." Sarah slapped him on the arm. "I didn't do anything to say I'm sorry for." She caught his look and added, "Yet."

He laughed. "You are such a distraction, you know that?"

Clumsy her: she flinched at the backhanded compliment, knocked into a shelf, and brought a whole packing crate of *The Stupids* smack down on her head. "Tell me about it," she said and placed her hands on his waist.

The discouraged eyes instantly transformed to a vivid and piercing green, their luster becoming like moonlight on a calm, flat lake. He trapped her hands in his and pinned her gently against the hallway wall. The length of his thighs felt terrific against hers. She lazily sank into the contact. He slid his hands along her forearms and lightly grasped the crooks of her elbows. "Good pilots stay completely focused," he said.

"Maybe I don't want to be a good pilot right now," Sarah said, surprised her words were a honeyed purr. "Besides, we're not in the cockpit." *That isn't exactly true,* she thought, as she felt him stiffen against her belly.

She traced the line of his shirt collar where it met his neck, and the stubble of his beard electrified her fingertips. Locked in a death spiral and going down fast, she traced the corner of his crooked grin with a tentative fingertip. She sensed Logan gamely wrestle with the controls, fighting the plunge, but it was a battle he fought alone. Mesmerized by the irresistible spin, she drifted down . . . down . . . down. Suddenly, Logan tossed her a parachute: he pushed himself away. Cool evening air skittered between them. Her lust spiraled into the sea. More bite marks on the bedpost.

"Whew . . ." she said, dazed, half grateful, half regretful that there had been someone in charge in the left seat. Because she believed that individuals should not go unrewarded when their efforts were valiant, she kissed Logan. She intended it to be a brief, gentle, thank-you-for-being-in-control-when-I-wasn't smacker, but it instantly escalated into a needy, greedy, Oh-my-*God*-it's-been-so-long kind of suction.

She hooked one leg around the back of his thigh—his right one, she realized. The one she knew so well from long hours in the plane. The long, *hot* hours. Long and hot. With the ball of her heel she explored the length of it, from knee to hip pocket. Hiking kept a girl so flexible.

Logan's hands took a while getting there—likely about two seconds in real time, Sarah vaguely thought—but they sure knew just how to cup her rear end when they arrived. Caressing, kneading, then, yes! *lifting*. She rose from the floor like helium balloons were attached, and her ankles had a lovely reunion just above Logan's . . . hell, *yes*, he had a firm little butt.

Then Logan's hands. Ohohoh *boy*, more of that. She heard herself pant around lips locked onto his. Like two drowning people sharing an oxygen cylinder. Damn being a writer. Sometimes it got in the . . . "Oh, my God!" she cried aloud.

His hands had slid up her bare back, then around to the front. All the parts fit together perfectly. Her breasts, his palms. *Sweet Jeez!* Her nipples felt like two ripe—*damn* the writing thing—*ahhh* . . .

She slid her hands down from Logan's shoulders to his belt and took the main line south. It was easy to stay on the trail. A well-marked ridge. A *long* ridge.

Ungh. That sound came from her, she realized. Logan was tracing the line of her panties, hooking his thumbs in the elastic. Something ripped.

She fumbled with the front of his shorts. Snap! Zipper teeth on her fingertips. Stuck. Room—she needed room.

"Logan . . ." As if reading her mind—like one mind they were, right then, she knew—he allowed her to slide down the length of his body. She lapped at his neck, bit his T-shirt front, slid the frustrating zipper all the way down.

He about jumped into her hand.

She circled him with two fingers and pumped tentatively through the fabric of his undershorts. He buried his face into her neck and Sarah felt his knees go weak. He was actually trembling. Pump. His turn to *ungh!*

Pump.

He knocked her hand away clumsily and sank to his knees in front of her. Another rip and then cool night air and lips on her breasts, her stomach, her—*ssss!* She clutched the hall table for support, her other hand on his shoulder, he tugging at her hair as his mouth tugged at her. *Gah!* She leaned back, consumed. The walls around her melted and she floated through colors, mists and then the torrent came. Swift, unstoppable, it took her out to sea.

Moments? minutes? hours? later she returned to consciousness. Fearing herself alone on the raft drifting on a flat sea, her eyes flew open.

Logan was motionless, watching her from his knees. Puzzled, Sarah glanced down, and then farther down. No, he was still in launch position. Certainly none of the urgency had gone out of the mission. Weird.

"Fine, thanks," Sarah said. "And you?" She stooped and reached for him.

"I'm good," he said, straightening.

She felt him. "I could make you even better." Pump.

Predictably, *ungh*.

"Sarah, look, I—"

Pump.

Again he moved her hand away. This time she felt his body turn to steel—all over.

"Me instructor, you student," he gasped. "Not gonna work."

Sheesh, some kinda willpower this guy had.

Sarah locked her arms around his waist and suckled his neck. "Did for me," she purred in his ear.

He gently pried her off of him.

Again with cool evening air. What gave with this guy?

He straightened his clothes and slid out the screen door. "Latch it," he ordered.

"Like it would keep you out if you really wanted to get— or stay—in," she said, doing it. She pressed her forehead to the mesh and braced her hands on the frame. She felt robbed. Christmas had come early to her humble hallway, but she never got to meet Santa. Robbed.

"Sarah." Logan's voice was ragged. She felt him tremulously touch her hair through the screen. The contact was so gentle she barely sensed it. It was as though he were imprisoned on the scary side of the jailhouse mesh and she was a surprise visitor he'd given up hope of ever seeing again.

"Why did I come here tonight?" he asked, sounding as unglued as she felt.

"To yell at me."

"Ah."

Crickets chorused in the still night air.

"But I can always do that tomorrow in the plane, right?"

"Uh-huh." Her legs were Jello. Heat lightning flashed in the distance.

"Nine o'clock, at the fence?"

"Wouldn't miss it."

"Bye."

"Uh-huh."

Not until the sound of his footsteps had faded away did she muster the strength to shoulder the oak door shut. The dead bolt snapped home with a soft, regretful *snick*.

Chapter 13

Sarah barreled through the front gate of Crossly Field at 8:57 the next morning.

In a cloud of dust and flying gravel, she skidded her trail bike to a halt. *Whoa, Silver!* Last night had left her edgy. She had expected to find scorch marks in the front hall in the morning. She chained the bike up to the fence at the edge of the runway and wondered how Logan would be.

He bounced the Cessna out of the school lot a minute or so later and jockeyed the plane through the tie-down area and onto the taxiway. It slowed it to a stop opposite where she was waiting and he clambered out. Like she had all the time in the world, she moseyed around the fence and over to the plane.

"Been waiting long?" he asked.

"Oh, a little while," she replied vaguely, brushing a stray hair back into place under the edges of her cap. Flirtation 101.

"Liar," he said. "I saw you pull in about two minutes before I got here."

Busted.

He leaned into the cabin to get something. He was wearing shorts this morning, and worn, but clean, construction boots. And his shirt coordinated nicely with the rest of the ensemble, for once. He looked like a well-dressed landscaper. With a wicked, white scar on one leg that started below sock line and tracked upward almost to the hemline of his shorts.

Ouch. That must have hurt. Hers had.

He pulled—what else?—his clipboard from the plane. "Let's see how well you remember the preflight. Go."

No "Good mornin'." No "Nice day, huh?" No nothing.

Okay, maybe he had short-term memory issues. Maybe he just didn't remember who he was sucking face with last evening. Really, it was one thing to be businesslike, but his social skills went to absolute hell around an airplane. She swung her pack into the left seat. But two could play that game. "Let me see," Sarah said, coolly. "The preflight. Because you've already started up the plane and taxied it over here, can I assume that you've checked the gas?"

"Do you mean did I check the gauge readings on the panel? Or do you mean did I visually confirm the tanks were full?"

"The second thing, the visual inspection, of course. You didn't bring a stepladder with you, so I couldn't get up there to visually inspect anything, now could I?" That drew a smirk. Ordinarily, the preflight check called for the pilot to clamber up a ladder, remove the fill caps from each wing, and dipstick both wing tanks to verify that their actual fuel load agreed with what the panel gauges said.

"You don't have to be sarcastic," he said. "But you do have to be more specific. Little miscues like that can lead to disaster."

Sarah could see his point. She herself always went over

every detail of a hike or a river trip three times if she was group leader. "Did you check to make sure the fill caps were back on tightly?" she asked.

"Yes, I did, and they were. And that's more like it."

She was absurdly pleased at his praise. "Okay, master switch on." She reached in the open door and depressed a large red button next to the pilot's control yoke. The fuel indicator needles obligingly swung to read "Full."

"Turn master off, and fuel shutoff valve on. . . . Oh, course it's already on. You taxied over here."

He nodded. "Good you looked."

"Cabin check done. Now the tail."

Sarah walked around to the rear of the plane, checked that the rudder gust lock was off and that the control surfaces felt secure and moved smoothly through their full range of motion. She felt Logan's eyes silently watching. It was a little unnerving, but not anywhere near as unnerving as having something she missed on the walk-around screw up in the air. She made her way along the leading and trailing edges of the right wing, checking for dents and dings and inspecting the control surfaces, just as Logan had showed her the day before. It was amazing how little she remembered of Preston Lewis's spiel and how much she recalled of Logan's. He might not act very sociable around airplanes, but he had a knack for explaining them.

He told her not to drain fuel from the wing tank sump drain, that he had already done it on both tanks, but he made her go through the motions of the procedure and describe the how and why of each step.

"And if the fuel was completely clear when you drained a sample, that would mean it was okay, right?" he asked—way too innocently—without raising his eyes from his clipboard.

Now wasn't he the trickster. "No," Sarah said. "It would

mean someone had mixed two different grades of fuel together and that is absolutely not right."

He nodded again. "That fools a lot of people."

She wasn't "a lot of people," now was she? Sarah opened the engine side panel on the nose of the plane and checked around for any animal or insect nests, not that there would be any because old LD 108 seemed to be a busy girl with little free time to gather dust, er, bugs. The oil level was fine, the carburetor air filter was clean, and she was about to tap some fuel from the fuel strainer when Logan stopped her.

"Good you remembered, but why wouldn't it be a good idea to drain fuel right now?"

"Ah. Hot engine. Possible *kaboom*."

"Something like that."

"But you've already checked it this morning, right?"

"Yes."

Sarah nodded sagely. The match returned to *love, all*.

She shut the engine panel, checking to make sure it was latched securely, then inspected the propeller. No nicks, no dings. Landing light just below the prop? Looked good.

Sarah made her way down the left side of the plane repeating the procedures she'd done on the right. Logan made notes on his clipboard the whole time. When she finished with the preflight, she stood, hands crossed in front of me, like a graduate waiting for her name to be called. It seemed to take forever for Logan to finish his notes. Sarah wondered if he'd explored the possibilities of having his damn clipboard surgically grafted onto his left hand, what with all the advances in cosmetic surgery.

Finally, he stopped with the chicken scratching and looked over at her.

"Not bad for a first try," he said.

What the hell? *Not bad?* She'd like to see anyone else go

through all the steps she did after just seeing them once. Twice actually, but the time with Preston was next to useless.

"You missed the landing gear check."

Shit, she had. She ducked under the wing and squatted down next to the left wheel. Good tire pressure. No fluid leaks. Brake cables tight. She repeated the inspection on the front and right-side gear, talking the procedure through so Logan would know she knew what she was looking for. Maybe there were consolation brownie points to be had. "Okay. That wraps it up," she said when she was done.

He made more notes, then swung a long leg up and into the cabin. "You all set to go up again today?"

Sarah clambered into the right seat, only bumping her knee once this time. Progress. "I think I'm okay. No nightmares last night."

He passed on the loaded remark.

"Buckle up, then." He depressed the master switch and hit the ignition. The prop ground around a few times, and then the engine gasped and held. He fiddled with what she'd learned was the mixture control knob. She clicked the door shut, slipped on the headphones, and adjusted the boom microphone.

"I saw you fooling with that knob almost the whole time we were flying around the other day," Sarah said over the headset. "It's the fuel mixture, right?"

His voice crackled in her ears. "Yes. As you gain or lose altitude, the engine needs a leaner or richer mix. Of gas I mean, more or less gas, accordingly." He looked at her questioningly.

She nodded. *Comprende.*

The radio sputtered its unrecognizable nonsense in an encore of yesterday, and this time she thought she caught the word *runway* and then maybe *rollup*. Logan replied and within minutes the Cessna was poised at the end of the runway. They finished their engine *run-up* that must have been what she'd heard—which Logan talked her through, then radioed for permission to take off. Sarah could hardly hear his call or the reply from the tower over the roar of the engine.

"Roger, LD one-oh-eight. Cleared for takeoff." Maura's voice.

Logan popped the brakes and the little Cessna sprang out of the blocks. She shimmied; she shook; she rattled; she rolled. The dotted lines on the asphalt blurred; then all vibration abruptly ceased as they stepped into the air. She was made for the sky, not the ground. Even Sarah could sense that.

Details of the terrain below immediately jumped out at her as they ascended. A crisp white line of breaking waves laced the lapping green edge of the surf on the weather side of Pear Island, the color of the ocean deepening to azure farther off the shore. Her favorite sandbar painted a soft tan strip against the blue maybe 400 yards offshore, running parallel to the dazzlingly white crust of beach. As they passed over The Rip, lobster boats sliced wide *V*s in the current. The wakes spread, intersected others, and spawned new, churning wave formations.

The rough and tumble placement of in-town homes and buildings contrasted sharply with the precise layout of newer housing developments, cars crawling along their crisp, unfortunate grid lines. Again with the swimming pools, their light colors and regular shapes an applied study in geometry. A few more minutes inland and farm fields with perfect cornrows undulated to follow the hillocks and drumlins left by the same forces that had scraped Pear Island into existence 10,000 years ago.

Sarah had kept her eyes open through the first five minutes of the flight, her hands lying flat and open on her thighs, and she was feeling rather proud of herself until six minutes into the flight, when something went bang. The wings of the plane threatened to vibrate themselves free from the frame and she was bounced around in her seat like a passenger in a toy car speeding down a washboard. She grabbed for where?—in the Rav there were overhead handles—but clutched empty air. "Wha-what the hell?"

"Turbulence," Logan replied, as casually as if she'd asked him who pitched for the Red Sox in last night's game.

"But it's clear all around us. No clouds. Nothing." Her body was playing Twister, The Millenium Edition, and her heart was threatening to jump out of her throat. There was *nothing* to hang on to in the cockpit. She fought the impulse to grab on to the control yoke moving eerily in front of her.

"Convection currents. It's like going through chop in a boat. We could lose it."

"By doing what?" She fervently hoped it didn't involve inverting the plane.

"Climbing."

Sounded easy enough. "How high?"

"Up to those cumuli." He pointed to a blossoming mountain of whipped egg whites off to their left. "A couple, three thousand feet up, probably."

"I don't think so."

He chuckled. "Thought you'd say that. Anyway, we'll probably break into some clearer air soon."

A few minutes went by with the engine roar and the ever-changing clouds their only company. Logan made minute movements with the control yoke and fiddled a bit with the mixture knob as they cruised, but he offered no conversation. The bumping and rocking went on and on, but he didn't try to explain it away or minimize it. By all accounts she should have escalated to full freak-out mode by then, but despite being fair to medium scared, she couldn't seem to muster the psychic energy to be nuts. Couldn't imagine why

Spot wasn't actively patrolling the wall. She wondered if the hypnotic drone of the engine had lulled him to sleep.

Sarah took in the ocean of sky surrounding them. The ever-changing mountains of cloud captured her attention, just as they had on the first flight, only then she'd been too scared to look at them for long. When she and Beth were little, they'd lie on their backs and stare up at the sky, watching the masses of white drift by. The panorama of shapes had been a canvas for their youthful imaginations. They'd argue about which burgeoning tower looked more like a tree, which fat pillow was most like a turtle.

But nowhere were the shapes more convincing or mercurial than on the African plains, especially at sunset. Purple cheetahs stalked orange gazelles, and rose-hued elephants lumbered placidly across the horizon.

Her stomach abruptly knotted. Spot exhaled humidly on the back of her neck. "Do all planes have a space behind the seats?" Sarah asked.

Logan actually laughed. The sound filled her headphones. "Why?"

"Just wondering."

"You don't look so good," he said, glancing at her.

"Oh . . . I was just reminded of an old friend."

He cocked an eyebrow. "And you want to bring him along?"

"More like leave him behind."

"The dog, right?" To her surprise, he said that with a straight face and an absence of sarcasm.

Sarah nodded, feeling stupid.

"You want to go down?" he asked.

What—right there in the plane? While he was flying? The sick bastard, now that he'd had time to reconsider her offer of last night. What was wrong with . . . oh.

"You mean 'to the ground,' right?"

"Well . . . yes."

Really, there were moments when she was simply unburdened by thought. And, yes, yes she did want to go down—to the ground. But she wouldn't. This was business. Hell, this was war. She grinned gamely. "How about a few more turns around?"

"No problem." He gently banked the plane.

She watched him execute the maneuver. Their shoulders made contact halfway through it, but it suddenly seemed silly to keep space between them.

Quite a mystery she'd fallen upon, this Logan Donnelly. A flying bundle of contradictions. Socially retarded around a plane, he nevertheless gave her more information in ten minutes than Preston Lewis had imparted in an hour and a half. And no one could tell her anything. Just ask Joan. Logan was compulsively safety conscious from what she'd seen so far, yet he volunteered to take up a fruitcake like her. And somewhere in the middle of that enchilada, wrapped up in an enigma, was the basically regular guy she'd split a beer and an orgasm with. But she couldn't get her head around all that right then, what with the beauty on display all around the airplane. And the heat in the cabin was making her drowsy.

Logan slid down his window. "Go ahead and open yours, if you want."

"I'm fine." They weren't in a fucking school bus, after all. Touch the window? Get sucked out of the cabin. Go ahead and laugh. It's easy when you're safe on the ground.

To distract herself, she watched Logan drive. *Fly,* rather. His hands rested lightly on the yoke, and when it twitched in the turbulence, he twitched it right back. His hat, a Sox one this morning, was pulled low over his eyes, and behind dark glasses, his expression was unreadable. Sarah took obscure pleasure in the fact that his shades didn't sport a fancy name brand. He had the gum going, but he wasn't working at it, just thoughtfully turning it over.

Rarely had she ever seen anyone so completely . . . *present*, she supposed would be the word. Dr. Loo was like that: serenely alert. Now *there* was a truly weird juxtaposition: Logan Donnelly and the lithe and lovely Cynthia Loo.

Suddenly Sarah got it. Why he wasn't yapping at her. He was giving her the space to do whatever she needed to do: scream, thrash, even jump from the plane? Probably not that. He wouldn't want to adversely affect his insurance rates. But he understood what she was dealing with. Why couldn't he just say so? Why does a guy on the brink of a big bang just slip off into the twilight, for that matter. That she *really* didn't get.

Oddly enough, having been given permission of a sort to do all manner of crazy things, Sarah didn't feel the need to do any of them. Not that she was completely enjoying herself, but it wasn't so bad this time being "up," as she was beginning to think of flying. The sense of unlimited space— being literally above the cares of the world below—imparted a new perspective: she was free . . . to remake herself. Sarah thought of the woman climbing her way up the Eastern Mountain Sports calendar hundreds of feet below in the kitchen.

What else? What else was she feeling?

Safe? A glance over the edge of the cockpit sent that idea spiraling down in flames. Spot snarled.

Secure? With her ass hundreds—she peeked at the altimeter—no, *thousands* of feet above the good, green earth? Nope.

What was it then? She heard Dr. Loo say: *What are you fee-ling, Sarah?*

In all her years of therapy, she couldn't remember ever having genuinely tried to answer this basic question. What she *did* recall were the gazillions of hours she'd spent jacking up her psyche in the hopes that her private horror movie would eventually spool through or oxidize from age and rip itself to pieces, anything, to grant her some peace.

That was it.

Peace.

She was at peace.

Resigned to whatever would happen while they were in the air.

Despite all Logan's skill, despite her careful preflight check, the plane could crash two seconds from now. There wasn't a frigging thing either one of them could do about it. On the other hand, they could fly around together for the next fifty years and never have so much as an engine burp.

All of a sudden the air around the plane smoothed, and the washboard effect faded. They rolled along freshly laid asphalt. The contrast was startling.

"We've left it behind," Logan said.

More than he knew. Sarah breathed deeply, letting air into places in her chest that hadn't sipped pure oxygen for two decades. Moisture filled the corners of her eyes; then a fat tear splashed onto her folded hands. The engine droned. A horse with a rider slowly materialized out of a massed formation of vapor off to the left. Her dad would have been snapping pictures like crazy. So much time she'd invested in being nuts. . . .

Logan's voice brought her back. "Found what you were looking for?"

Sarah nodded, blinking away tears. "Can I"—her throat was full of gunk—"learn to do . . . this?" She gestured at the control yoke, moving of its own accord in her lap.

"I could show you."

She thought about that. "When?"

Chapter 14

Sarah took over the controls of the plane for ten minutes. Goodness. Sex paled in comparison.

Before she left Crossly Field, she set up more flying times with Logan and tried to get him to draw up a contract, but he was too slippery to pin down.

She took the long bike route back to the house, stopping off for a quick dip at the public beach on the way. The tide was full in, and she did a brisk Australian crawl out to her favorite sandbar. She lolled around in the relatively warm, shallow water, basking like a nurse shark, gazing up into the wild blue she had traversed but minutes before. A faint buzz and a glint of silver over the ocean to the north of Pear Island told her someone else was up, but he was too far out to track. A leisurely breast stroke brought her back to shore.

She was sweaty again by the time her front tire banged open the gate into the backyard, and she had sand in her shorts, which always made her irritable.

"Say," said Joan, looking Sarah over from the vantage point of Sarah's one comfortable lounge chair, "aren't we just a mite flushed? With victory, or methinks . . . something else? *Dum, dum dum . . .*" Joan's feet were in the small wading pool and the hose was trickling into it.

"Oh, really, just come by any time. Don't bother to call first." Sarah leaned her bike against the tool shed. "I suppose I should be glad you've got your clothes on."

"Ha! Remember that one time—"

"Don't remind me." Sarah wiped sweat from her eyebrows. "Whew, it's hot out there pedaling . . ."

"Depends on what you're pedaling." Joan grinned sloppily.

Sarah dropped her pack on the back porch deck and flopped down on the bottom step.

"Gimme," she said, holding her hand out for a swig of the wine cooler Joan was Bogarting.

"No backwash, promise?" Joan said.

Sarah gargled noisily, then returned the bottle—*her* bottle, she realized, one of three left from the four-pack she'd purchased the night before—to Joan. Correction: two left. There was a dead soldier lying prone in the grass beside Joan's chair. Rather, *her* chair.

"So about this pilot," Joan said, straightening up.

"You want something to eat?" Sarah said.

"Of course, but don't change the subject. Rather than a high-fat, high-cholesterol snack, it'd be much healthier to munch on a nice, well-balanced slice of gossip, don't you think?" She bounced her eyebrows suggestively.

"God, you never give a girl any space."

"Absolutely correct. Where were we? Ah, yes! Lurid details."

"Details? About what?"

"*Lurid* details. About you and that *hot* flyboy."

"What are you, crazy? I'm flying with him, for Pete's sake. To get over my phobia thing. So what?"

"*So what?* I hear you almost crashed up a plane on one guy, and then you had this *other* one over for S'mores and Monopoly."

"We didn't play Monopoly."

"T'ja. No kidding. That's just what I'm afraid of."

"You've got a dirty mind."

"Mother of God, girl, just say he ain't married."

"No. He was living with this woman I met. But she said it was over. Then, I think, he had a thing—quite disgusting, actually . . . she's a baby—with this waitress at the airport restaurant, but that was just on the rebound or something like that. . . ." Sarah had pieced that much together from her conversation with Maura.

"'Something like that' covers a lot of ground, kiddo."

"I really don't want to know the details."

"Better not to sometimes," Joan agreed.

"But wait. How did you find out he was over here, anyway?" Sarah asked. *Survey said:* her mother.

"Your mother. She got it from Mrs. Calloway." Sarah's neighbor across the street. Nice lady. Liked to sit out on her front porch on nice evenings. Kept cats. And binoculars, evidently.

"I think it's great, Sarah. A nice change from Rick the Dick."

"You're whacked."

"No, really, Sarah. You've let just the right amount of time go by between telling Rick to buzz off and meeting this new guy. I was reading this article in *Cosmo* and—"

"Joan, drop it will you. I haven't done anything of the kind."

"About which part?"

Sarah picked at a splinter of wood popping up out of the decking.

"Sarah?"

Someone could get that thing right in the foot. Right up under the toenail. That would hurt.

"Sarah, why do I get the feeling there's more going on here than meets the eye?"

But not as much as Joan's cross-examination.

"Okay, Sarah, dear. I'll fill in the blanks myself. You just nod in agreement. Here we go: What's the big deal, right?"

Sarah nodded.

"You're not the kind of gal to have a relationship with two men at once, right?"

She nodded.

"So now that you've made it clear to Rick that it's over between you two, you're free and clear to pick up with some-one else, right?"

The splinter would not break loose. Maybe if she just twisted it?

"Sarah, this is where you nod."

Then sort of tugged on it.

Joan said, "Oh shit."

"Something like that," Sarah said.

Joan massaged her forehead with her fingertips, just like Dr. Loo often did in the long afternoon sessions. "Sarah . . . you did end it with Ranger Rick, right?"

"Don't call him that."

"Which means no, correct?"

What could she say?

Joan wailed. "How could you?"

"We've been taking some time. You knew that. What with him being Mr. Entrepreneur, it's been . . . convenient just to let things go."

"Jeez, Sarah. Even by my standards—and they are pretty low as you know—this is a royal fuckup."

Sarah took another swallow of wine cooler. "And this is getting warm."

"As am I. Just sweep everything under the rug, right? Case closed?"

"There're chips in the bread box." *Case closed.*

"Okay, so Rick is off limits. But what about Donnelly? How does he fit in?"

"Particularly crappy. He's eventually going to screw us over on the preserve." The animals, the school kids, the families on picnics. "Remember?"

"Re*mem*ber? Who sprung you and the septuagenarian sexpot from the pokey, you knucklehead?"

"I never should have told you about Mrs. Harker. But Logan's just helping me out. He's willing to take me—"

"I'll bet. . . ."

"*Up* and help me get over Spot."

Finally the annoying splinter broke free. Hers, all hers. She flicked it between her fingers out onto the lawn.

"Why, pray tell, is he willing to help you—the sign incident aside—when the help that he's giving you will ultimately lead you to a job that will give *you* the means to screw *him* over?" She shook her head like there were mayflies buzzing around it. "Whoa . . . I just used every brain cell I've got."

"Then I'll keep the answer simple: he doesn't know."

"That you'll slam the second runway for your very first assignment?"

"Yes."

Joan sucked her teeth thoughtfully. "Well, hey, there's nothing wrong with having him for a boy toy while you can."

"Joan, there's nothing going on. And I wish it were that simple. Cripes, I don't know. First I thought he—Logan—was a complete asshole; then he seemed to take my side when I bashed up the first plane. He's really not that bed—I mean *bad*," she said. Joan's expression said *Yeah, right*. "Which only makes the whole issue of how to protect the preserve doubly difficult. Plus, I think he's got something going on in his head."

"I should hope so."

"No, I mean like I do."

"Oh, boy."

"Please. I mean some kind of mystery/secret/bad hidden thing. Like with Spot? It flashes across his face every now and then. Now you see it, now you don't. What it is exactly, I don't get. Which bugs the shit out of me, by the way."

Joan smiled knowingly and began tearing the Bartles and Jayne's label from the wine cooler.

"Then we had a great time the other night. Sure it was awkward at first—"

"Were you drinking?"

"Just a little bit."

"Uh-huh."

"Really, just half a beer."

"*Half* a beer and he looked good? Girlfriend, he must be hot."

Sarah shot her a look. "Anyway, I sort of thought that after the lessons were over—"

"You could start another kind of lesson?" Joan cackled.

"Shut up. But now . . ." Sarah discovered another splinter, this one on the post next to her. "I don't know. I saw him today and he . . . he changes like a chameleon, you know? Today he was 'the pilot.' All business, like last night never happened."

"Did you kiss him?"

"Joan . . ."

"Hey, go easy. I'm on your side. I'm just trying to diagnose the situation. Think of me as your doctor." She persuaded a stubborn corner of the sticker with her thumbnail.

"Yes, then."

"Did he kiss you back?"

"*Oh, yeah.*" Sarah felt her face redden.

"Tongues?"

"Oh, yes, he has a very nice tongue. And more."

"Oh, boy . . ."

"All of that." Sarah decided to keep the odd little secret of his refusal of an offer of parallel play to herself.

Joan frowned and hummed tunelessly for a while, spreading the label from the bottle out onto her knee, trying to make it adhere. Sarah got bored with her deck renovation project and went hunting for a snack in the kitchen. Joan was still deep in thought when Sarah came back out with carbohydrates. She and Joan fought off a cloud of buzzing yellow jackets and made short work of half a low-fat pound cake. Finally, Dr. Joan gave her diagnosis.

"The real stuff's better."

"What?"

"The real stuff—you know, with all the calories, all the fat, all the sugar? Way better than this stuff." She pushed the empty cake box away disdainfully.

"About my 'situation,' Joan?"

"Assuming everything you've told me is true—" She glanced at Sarah.

Sarah spread her arms wide: *You've got it all*.

"There are three possibilities," then, Joan said. "One: he's a psychopath."

"And this is supposed to help me feel better how?"

"Honey, the truth will set you free. Two: he's a classic manipulator. Taking you for a ride for all he can get and is just pretending to be a really nice, trustworthy guy with a few interesting problems the mysterious nature of which—if you were completely honest with yourself—probably make him even more attractive than he already is."

"Ouch. How do you do it?"

"You think that's a trip? Try door number three: in fact he

is a really nice, trustworthy guy with a few interesting problems the mysterious nature of which *definitely* serve to make him even more attractive than he already is."

Crap. Sarah stamped her feet like there were fire ants in her shoes. "Argh! Jeez, you should start your own psychic hot line."

"Good, ain't I?" Joan said, a diabetic-who-ate-the-pound-cake look on her face.

"Damn. That's exactly what's been bugging the shit out of me about this whole thing."

Joan cocked her head.

"What I mean is, I'm usually pretty levelheaded about men, right?"

Joan coughed something that sounded like *"not."* Sarah chose to ignore her. "But with Logan, I just don't know. I get such mixed messages from him that what I think about him changes moment to moment. And I don't even know why I'm putting myself through all of this over him. What do I care? Or more to the point, why do I care? We all know how this story ends. Probably with another sign over his head once the second runway opens."

"But what *really* scares the crap out of you is possibility three, right?"

"Right."

"So what do I do?"

"About what? Rick? Logan? Both?" Joan drained the last of the cooler and pulled her feet out of the wading pool.

"About any of it," Sarah said.

Joan crumpled the label. "Sarah, these things take time. Take the lessons, get to know the guy, finish the lessons, then, hey, let whatever happens, happen. Simple." She flapped her hand at a determined yellow jacket, dragged the empty sponge cake box toward her, and began to reconnoiter the interior for crumbs.

"And in the meantime do something about Rick, right?"

"Well, I gently suggested that early on."

Sarah scrubbed her face with her hands. "I'm going frigging crazy, you know."

"No, really?"

You had to laugh, so they did.

"Sarah, honey, seriously. Do something about Rick," Joan said. "Then let nature take its course. I've *seen* those little planes they teach people in. You're gonna learn a lot about your flyboy jammed for hours and hours together in one of those things. Bet on it."

Sarah grabbed the empty bottle. Joan abruptly severed her relationship with the sponge cake box and crushed it up for the trash. "Hey, maybe you'll get lucky and crack one of his little mysteries while you're flying around up there," she said.

Sarah said, "I'd be happy just to crack one of my own."

Chapter 15

After Joan left, claiming a date with some healing stones, Sarah paced the house, restless and nudgy, finally sliding into one of those moods where even she couldn't stand herself. Joan was right about her relationship with Rick. It had flat-lined months ago. She resisted pulling the plug, and not because she was faint of heart. She'd been in a lot of tight situations in which she had had to use her head and keep her cool or get seriously screwed. But she dreaded the moment of standing alone when the haunting click-click-hiss of the ventilator keeping her and Rick's perverse union alive finally ceased.

Her eyes lit on the shopping bags malingering in the hall. Components to a flight simulator. She'd picked the system up at the Northshore Mall one night when she wandered over there for some fast food and free air-conditioning. It had looked pretty neat in the store. A control wheel and foot pedals came with the package.

She grabbed a Popsicle and lugged the bags upstairs to the spare room. She liberated the system pieces from enough plastic blister pack to mold three kayaks, found the installation manual, plugged everything in, and booted up the computer. The program loaded from a CD and in three minutes a length of virtual runway loomed in the depths of the monitor.

Sarah's palms slicked with sweat. She was facing the virtual controls of a little airplane. The engine was running and a propeller was slowly spinning in front of the virtual windscreen. Cripes. At least she had the luxury of sitting there and freaking out for as long as she wanted. Nobody behind her would be beeping a virtual horn.

The motor droned. Spot woke up, looking rather thrown together, and shook his head so vigorously that his stubby, hornlike ears made a clapping sound. Sarah couldn't believe she was doing something this crazy, either. After a few minutes, boredom won out over anxiety. She began exploring the instrument panel, mousing her way around the various gadgets on it. A box appeared over a lever and declared it the throttle. She clicked and dragged and the engine raced. Memories of her experiences with Preston Lewis made her stomach lurch. Probably a good time to stop and click on the box that said "Tutorial." Find out what all the little doodads and geegaws did.

Nah. Instead, she clicked on the "Fly Now" box in the corner of the screen. The hard drive ratcheted wildly and a new runway view materialized on the monitor. Directions from the virtual traffic controller scrolled across the bottom of the scene, informing her she was cleared for takeoff.

Her mouth dried up like the Serengeti. Every one of her bells rang long and loudly. *It's only a game. . . .*

She raced the engine, popped the brakes and the virtual plane started rolling forward. Dials on the control panel spun as the plane accelerated. She nudged the foot pedals she'd placed on the carpeting under the desk and the nose of the little plane obligingly swung left and right. A pixelly challenged blob in the distance reconfigured into a fence and a row of lights. Time to get up in the air. But how?

Another message from the tower scrolled across the bottom of the screen. *You are committed to takeoff. You must lift off the runway now.*

How comforting to know someone was watching out for her. She giggled hysterically. The fence got closer. The lights got bigger.

She wiggled the wheel. The plane rocked from side to side but did not rise into the air. There was a sudden crunch and, reflexively, she let go of the wheel and shut her eyes. Pinwheels went off behind her eyelids, and her throat constricted.

Bullshit. This was bullshit. It was only a game.

But her overstimulated neurons weren't buying that. Spot decided he needed exercise. Sarah rested her head on the edge of the desk and rode out his attack. As the damn dog trounced and bounced and snapped at her vitals, she searched for anchors in reality: kids' voices from the yard next door, the texture of the rug under her bare feet. Finally, it ended. Spot voiced a final, exclamatory *woof* and hopped back over the wall to rest up for the next sortie.

Sarah lifted her head, but that was a short-lived effort. It flopped back down onto the desk. For perhaps the thousandth time in her life she swore that there was nothing in the world she wouldn't do to get rid of Spot. But, as always after making such a proclamation, desperation set in. Helplessness and hopelessness, hated twins, wrapped wraithlike arms around her, lapping up whatever stray juices Spot had missed. Stealing her present, mortgaging her future, fucking up her chances for a job she really, really wanted.

A job that would mean national recognition. Hope for the

preserve. A chance to write about things that really mattered to people, that touched them, that touched *her*.

So she decided that if she had to force herself to sit in front of the stupid computer and bash up a virtual plane 100,000 times to give Spot the slip, that's what she'd do. Ah . . . grasshopper, the journey of 1,000 miles begins with one step. How long *would* it take to complete 100,000 simulator flights? Ten-minute rides, five on 2X speed. Ten an hour . . . The math eluded her.

Sarah straightened up and cracked her back. Spot growled halfheartedly. She'd outlast the little bastard if it was the last thing she did. She grimly clicked on "Try Again." The cockpit view and runway appeared. Messages from the tower scrolled. Groping around, she found a button on the wheel that made easier work of gunning the plane than clicking and dragging the on-screen throttle lever with the mouse. She let in the throttle and rolled. The damn fence loomed in the distance, taunting her. She pulled back on the control wheel about halfway along the runway length and the plane struggled to rise but couldn't break free of the ground. The speedometer read fifty miles per hour. Probably not fast enough.

She shoved the throttle to the stops and seconds later the plane lifted off, clearing the virtual fence by what seemed like inches. She forced herself to lighten up on the control wheel as the thin plastic creaked in protest.

The virtual ground fell away beneath her and her terrified toes tried to drive themselves through the weave of the carpet. She forced them onto the rudder pedals. Instinctively, she nudged them and the wheel toward the direction of the runway, her last known safe location. The view out the virtual cockpit windscreen was unnervingly real. Her body involuntarily leaned into the turn. About halfway through the bank, a loud horn blared.

Horrified, Sarah tightened the turn radius to bring the runway into view. The virtual cockpit began to shake horrendously, and the next thing she knew she was looking straight down at the ground. She yanked desperately on the control wheel as the good earth raced closer and closer. The screen went black for a moment; then the hard drive gerbiled and the monitor presented her with a replay of her aborted flight as seen from the perspective of an observer positioned outside and above her aircraft.

She watched herself slam straight into the ground.

Flight terminated! scrolled unnecessarily across the bottom of the screen. Shit.

Spot rolled over and yapped, then went back to sleep. Sated from his recent feast, he evidently felt obligated to fulfill only the most basic of contract obligations. He had enough sense to realize that she was not operating in reality at the moment. Good management decision to save his best stuff for the real thing. He snorfled and Sarah imagined spit running out his lower jaw.

She clicked on "Fly Now" again. This time she got the plane into the air, made a few turns, figured out how to retract the wheels, and then slammed the plane into the ground trying to land with the wheels up. The replay of the flight was unexpectedly hysterical.

Fricking video games. They were harder than they looked. Maybe it *was* time to click "Tutorial."

Chapter 16

Sarah checked her watch for the tenth time in half an hour. It was 9:45 in the morning. The intense summer sun was rapidly heating the Cessna, and the tension in the cabin was palpable, like a low-hanging, pressurized front nagging at her like a migraine. She adjusted the Cessna's radio headset for a more comfortable fit and squinted against the early morning light. Even through her sunglasses, it etched into her eyeballs like acid.

Logan was making her fly touch-and-gos. The deal was to fly a pattern around the airfield, perform a half landing by touching down lightly on the wheels, then immediately hop back into the air. To make life even more interesting, he insisted she use different flap settings for each touch—a seemingly small change to the uninitiated like Sarah—but the different flap configurations proved to have a huge effect on the handling of the Cessna. Each separate pass was a new experiment and the exercise taken as a whole was a royal pain in the ass. After a while she got the hang of things, but

Logan made her keep going. Which, because she was a gal who abhors hiking the same trail twice, seemed pointless.

Lifting off from her fifth touch in forty-five minutes, she was ready to stick a knitting needle up her nose just to break the tedium.

"Again," he said.

"Again?"

"Return to altitude, reenter the pattern, and bring her around. Again."

He never stopped. He was aviation's answer to the Energizer Bunny: *Dum-dum, dum-dum, dum-dum!* Sarah was beginning to wonder if asking Logan for lessons had been a good idea.

"Look," she said, taking a look around the immediate air space in anticipation of her first ninety-degree left turn into the new pattern, "the monotony of this is driving me crazy. Let's take a break. Go on to something else for a while, okay?"

"That's the whole point."

"*What* is?"

"The monotony." He was writing—need she say *on the fucking clipboard*?—and didn't look up.

"What are you talking about?" She wanted to bite off the boom mike like a baby carrot and spit it at him.

"It's all there in the accident reports," he said.

"And . . .?" She made a churning motion with her free hand.

"Keep both hands on the wheel at all times."

The last person to say that to her was her dad, when he'd let her drive his beat-up old Jeep Wagoneer in first gear in the cemetery early Sunday mornings way before she had her permit. *Ten and two, Sarah, ten and two . . .* he'd nag. She was a hellish pupil even then.

"And you should review a few."

Accident reports, she assumed he meant. Sounded like a fun beach read. Not.

"Pilots get bored," he said. "Makes them careless. You have to learn to stay sharp all the time. Keep focused."

When she was running tour groups with Rick, Sarah always kept current with incident reports regularly published by the National Forest Service. They documented type of injury, location, precipitation conditions, man-hours of rescue time, yadda, yadda—just to remind herself of the price of one bad call out on the river. She accepted Logan's premise. It was the delivery that grated.

The head-on collision she and her instructor had had in the front hall a few nights ago hadn't helped her attitude, either. Intrusive recollections of their little "close encounter"— she couldn't seem to dispel them completely no matter how hard she tried—sprayed gasoline on the simmering fire beneath her growing irritation. Every little thing *he* did was now immediately magnified to epic proportions. She was at a 9.5 on her personal ripshit scale and desperately needed to distance herself from him for a while, but the tiny cabin didn't afford her that luxury. They were squeezed in shoulder to shoulder and there was still fifteen minutes left in the lesson. When she was struggling with her temper, a fraction of time could seem like an eternity.

"Watch your altitude."

Her attitude? "Huh?"

"Your altitude? Watch it. You're descending."

"Oh, right." *Into thoughts of murder*. She eased back on the control yoke.

"Where's your mind this morning, anyway?"

"Right here, boss. Right where it should be."

He looked up from the instruments and gave her a dark look. "Keep it that way."

Screw you. Where was she? Ah, yes. Her irritation with . . .

him. She couldn't bear to even *think* his name because he was being such an insufferable prick.

"Check your altitude again."

Damn it. She'd drifted a hundred feet too high this time. The three-dimensional flying puzzle was enough to drive a half-crazy person crazy. She dropped the nose a few degrees. Logan's voice filled her headphones again.

"Why are you doing that?"

He had never been obnoxious before with his corrections, just insistent. But this morning—and it could be just her edginess talking—she was picking up sanctimonious overtones.

He persisted. "Will it have the desired effect on the aircraft?"

"No. And I know, I know: 'When landing, pitch controls speed, power controls altitude,'" Sarah said, parroting his own words.

A few seconds more went by.

"Well, then . . ." he said.

God, his voice. The headphones brought it right inside her skull. She fortified herself with a quick look at the wide-open blue filling the Plexiglas windscreen and pulled gently on the control yoke. Then she backed off the throttle.

Logan, as usual, damn him, was completely correct. In a few more seconds, the climb indicator headed back down the dial. She leveled the plane off at the altitude he wanted.

"Clear the area," he said.

She visually searched the skies around their little 150. They were alone. Just a girl, her imaginary dog, and an ego-maniac. "All clear."

"Turn left ninety degrees onto the downwind leg," Logan ordered.

As if she didn't know it was time to change heading. She

looked down, found the Route 128 interchange she used for a reference point, then banked the wings.

"Starting turn." Etiquette demanded—Logan had, as well—she use the phrase "initiating turn," but, sorry, her elevator didn't descend to that level of geekdom. *She*, thank God, did not have to change into a robot every frigging time she got into an airplane. A touch of rudder saw the bank angle indicator tilt neatly around the center axis of the gauge and stop on twenty degrees. Piece of cake.

"Hold this altitude and watch the compass," Logan said.

He should just tape the soundtrack to this portion of the show, then set it up to play an endless loop. Honestly. How much slow flying and banked turns could a person do? It wasn't like she wanted to fly for United or even get instrument rated. She backed into this torture because she wanted to get on a commercial airliner without the use of adult diapers. Then she'd unexpectedly gotten hooked on flying. Now she wanted to take advantage of her newfound skill and simply see a bit of the countryside from the air. That was all. No big deal. But, no. So far all they'd done was stay within a five-mile radius of Crossly Field—oh, pardon, Noah Crossly *Airport*—while just out of reach to the east, the tans and blue-greens of the North Shore coastline tantalized.

The headphones crackled: "You're almost through your turn. Level the wings, and back off on the rudder so you don't slide by. I want you out and level at exactly two-eighty west."

Before he'd even finished the command, the wings of the little airplane on the bank angle dial had smoothly slid to horizontal and the compass settled down on 280. Sarah allowed herself a smug smile.

"Not bad," Logan said.

Not bad, my ass. The turn was perfect. She'd even managed to avoid shoulder-to-shoulder contact with him during the bank.

"Fly approximately two minutes on this heading. Then, at your discretion, clear the area and commence—" he began, but Sarah couldn't take any more of the canned presentation.

"For God's sake, Logan, I know. 'Commence a ninety-degree turn left onto base leg.' I've heard it a thousand times. Let me just do it, already."

He became, if possible, even more remote.

Shit. She was an ass. Professionally, she owed him more respect than that. She opened her mouth to say something, but he beat her to it.

"All right, then. I'm turning this next landing completely over to you. You will perform a touchdown and then return the airplane to level flight in the pattern at traffic altitude. Apparently, you feel you're ready. Begin."

Sarah was speechless. Well . . . of course she *was* ready. She glanced down to the ground unrolling hundreds of feet beneath the boat trailer wheels of the Cessna. Toy cars streamed along Route 128. The tractor-trailer rigs looked like a person could reach down and pluck them off the highway. The Cessna's engine droned, suddenly seeming a very tenuous link to the familiar world a fifth of a mile below the little craft. Sarah became acutely aware of the frailty of the aluminum skin barely separating her posterior from a long drop through thin air.

She blew out a long breath. The roar in the headphones almost blasted out her eardrums. Too late to turn back now. She'd shot her mouth off but good. Hopefully, her own words wouldn't ricochet and hit her square in the ass.

Sarah cut back on the throttle and the Cessna settled into level, descending flight: 500 feet per minute on the vertical speed indicator. A quick visual scan of the area pronounced it clear. *Crap*. Carburetor heat. A bit far along the leg to turn it on—it took a few minutes to kick in—but she'd lost precious time recovering from Logan's surprise change of command.

Still time to back out, but fuck that. He'd never let her live it down.

She sensed her focus automatically sharpen as she began to concentrate solely on flying. She took a visual bearing on the ground. The end of the runway was at a forty-five-degree angle behind her, so she kicked in ten degrees of flap and adjusted the trim to hold airspeed.

She stole a sideways glance at Logan. He was staring straight ahead, sitting so still that if she didn't know his eyes were open he would have appeared asleep. Her dad used to have that same look when he was in the right seat of the old Jeep. Being a kid, she'd assumed her driving had thrown him into some kind of paralytic shock, but Logan's hands were palms down on his thighs, as far back from the yoke as possible, signaling instead that Sarah was totally responsible for the airplane.

She eased in another ten degrees of flaps, and as the airspeed dropped off, this time she held the nose level by adding power. Whoever said mistakes were the best teacher was one smart cookie. She wondered if Logan picked up on her improved technique, but a glance confirmed he was still imitating a cigar store Indian. Screw him. He wasn't value added. She could do this approach in her sleep. She thumbed the switch that connected her to the radio. "LD one-oh-eight requesting landing clearance, Crossly Field, Runway Four."

"Cleared for visual approach," the voice on control responded.

Maura.

"Roger. LD one-oh-eight now on visual approach," Sarah replied.

She exerted pressure on the yoke and rudder pedals. Three seconds later the engine hiccuped and the entire plane began shimmying. Not a tear-the-front-of-the-plane-off shaking, but a discernable vibration nonetheless. What the hell? Mixture, maybe? She spastically twiddled the fuel mixture knob. The engine smoothed.

Whew, her first almost emergency. And she'd done just fine on her own. Of course, Logan didn't so much as flinch during the whole episode. He was evidently content to watch her fry. She took another visual bearing on the runway off to her left.

It wasn't there anymore. Rather, it wasn't where it was supposed to be. While she'd been dicking around with the engine, they'd flown farther along the base leg of the pattern than she had realized. Crap. She searched the ground again. Gone also was her reference point for the approach turn.

Wait. There it was, the Pear Island bridge. Thirty seconds behind them. Damn the engine. She wished for that half minute back again. Now there was nothing for it but to make a late turn onto final approach. Otherwise, she'd have to navigate completely around the traffic pattern again to set up the landing approach while Logan sat still as death beside her, wreathed in reproachful silence. Shoot her now. The late turn would require a steeper turn, but the longer she put it off, the steeper it would have to be. Now or never.

A quick scan of the sky. Clear. Sarah shoved on the rudder pedals and banged the yoke in the direction of the runway.

Halfway through the turn, the vibration was back.

The fucking engine again. Who did the maintenance on these frigging planes? You took them up in good faith, assuming they'd run right, and suddenly the controls turned to oatmeal. One minute she had resistance, the next, mush. Her mind kicked into high gear. Problem? Not enough air over the control surfaces. Solution? More power, more push to the pedals and back stick to tighten the turn. She made it so.

In a heartbeat, all hell broke loose.

Chapter 17

The stall warning horn blared, and the nose of the Cessna slid across the horizon like ice cream off a warm plate.

Shit. Shit. Shit!

Before Sarah could make any control inputs, the plane accelerated and the wings wrenched abruptly left. Sarah's stomach hit the floor. She finally got a decent visual on the prodigal bridge. It filled the windscreen. They were diving directly for it.

"Logan!"

He'd already reacted, jamming the throttle full to the stop. The yoke spun beneath Sarah's hands, and as much as she instinctively wanted to cling to something solid, she understood that Logan had retaken control of the plane from his side of the cockpit. She forced her fingers to loosen their death grip.

Logan increased the pitch altitude to an obscene angle, and the Cessna shot toward the bridge. Even in her terrified state, a small part of Sarah's brain kept working: *He's swapping altitude for speed.* Speed was control. Control was life.

She'd given up control. Lost precious speed. Fucked up. She prayed they'd live long enough for Logan to have the luxury of killing her on solid ground.

Go, go, go! Faster!

The plane rocketed downward, eating up the distance between the concrete monstrosity spanning The Rip and their fragile tin bird. *Closer* . . . Sarah could see cars. People fishing. *Closer* . . . Children were shooing a dog off the roadway. The 1 percent of her cortex not immobilized by terror understood Logan was timing his pull-up. Too soon, they'd have insufficient airflow over the wings and unceremoniously pancake into The Rip like a sparrow into a plate-glass window. Too late? A lot of other people would join them in the batter.

The fishermen saw the Cessna first. They dropped their gear and scattered like ants under a magnifying glass, some of them grabbing for the kids.

Sarah realized she and Logan had but single seconds left. She thought about Joan, how much she'd miss her goofiness. And about Violet. Mom. So many memories of how they used to get along—before the African crash made emotional cripples of both of them—were still alive in Sarah. Ever mindful of her mother's admonition about accidents and good underwear, Sarah remembered she had unsuspectingly donned some of her finest that morning. Yet how little she had done to bridge the chasm that had inched wider between them with every passing year since losing Dad and Beth. Sarah took some comfort from the fact that at least *her* long separation from them might soon be over.

Killed by her own stupidity. What a sucky epitaph. Too bad she hadn't stayed afraid of flying. On the lighter side, if they didn't make it, at least she'd have the satisfaction of watching Spot bite the big doggie dish in the sky.

The moment of decision came and went and Logan obviously made the right one, because there's no such thing as a posthumous autobiography. The Cessna missed the bridge by little more than inches, though, Sarah thought, because the fishermen had felt compelled to duck behind the concrete railings as it flashed by overhead. From below, it must have been an awesome-slash-scary sight: engine roaring, wings wobbling, woman screaming.

When she looked back, Sarah saw one driver had rear-ended another and steam shot out from under the hood of the trailing vehicle. Kids with their arms outstretched madly circled each other in reenactment. Adult fists angrily waved in the general direction of the Cessna. Pretty much what you'd expect at these sorts of things.

They hurtled down the length of The Rip, past the lighthouse at the northern tip of Pear Island, sitting right where the stem of the real fruit would be, then slowly bled off speed as the plane clawed its way back up to 500 feet, then finally to 1,000.

The radio crackled to life. Even across five miles of empty air, Sarah picked up on the professionally masked terror in Maura's voice. *Please, God, not on my watch,* it said. "LD one-oh-eight, respond. Are you in distress?"

Not anymore they weren't. Sarah made the inelegant discovery that there was no spit left in her mouth.

"I repeat: are you in distress? Please respond."

Maura was dying up there in the tower. The plane was too far away for her to get a visual, although her radar blip and the Cessna's transponder code would inform her 108 was still a viable craft. Logan spoke: "You've got to tell them something."

Sarah's knees knocked together like castanets. Her palsied fingers fumbled. She clicked the radio button. "Tower, this is LD one-oh-eight. We experienced . . . technical difficulties. . . ."

How stupid did that sound? But she didn't want the whole East Coast knowing about her fuckup. "We're fine now."

Logan keyed the radio. "Crossly Tower, this is LD one-oh-eight. We experienced engine difficulty on approach and aborted. No assistance is needed at this time. We are reentering the traffic pattern and will request clearance to land in approximately ten minutes. Over."

Roger that. Way better than her pitiful speech.

Maura's relieved voice came back. "Copy that, LD one-oh-eight. You had us worried there. Will wait for your clearance request. Tower out."

"Clear the area; then reenter the traffic pattern," Logan said.

"*What?*" How nice to know that walking out on at *least* a hand job was not the craziest thing the man beside her had ever done.

"I said clear the area; then reenter the traffic pattern. Let's get this plane home."

"I can't."

"Yes, you can."

"No, I can't."

"You can and you will."

Was he out of his mind? Remove the question: he was. "What makes you think I could have a near-death experience, then pretend it never happened?"

"You've had twenty years of practice at it?"

"Fuck you. Countless fucking hours of therapy. You think I *like* falling on my face?"

"You're a chickenshit."

"Again, fuck you."

"With a limited vocabulary. I thought you called yourself a writer?"

Sarah wanted to tear the cabin apart. Hurl the headphones

across the cockpit. Hurl herself out the door and ruin her asshole instructor's precious fucking insurance rating. Instead, her rage melted around her like a thick ooze, deadening her senses, insulating her from the sharp edges of a too-present world. Trapped like a bug in amber, she became mesmerized by the wild blue staring in the windscreen at her. The endless, azure space that minutes before had seemed so inviting and secure. Now Sarah realized that all it promised was strict adherence to the cold laws of physics. And she was an earth-bound interloper, rising too far above her station, flying too close to the sun. She caught a whiff of heated wax and imagined the final cries of Icarus as gravity played its hand. The people on the bridge ducking . . .

God, her hubris could have killed them, too.

"No," she said, forcing the words out through thick lips, "I can't do this."

"Sarah, we didn't die. Nobody did this time."

This time?

That was supposed to reassure her? Why not something like "It wasn't that bad, really" or "We weren't in any real danger"? Her laugh was a hysterical bark. Why didn't they just fly back to the fishermen and yell down that they had strafed them on a lark, no harm meant. After all, nobody died this time. Hah!

Sarah watched her derision escalate to a full-blown howl. Maybe she should have screamed, "Sorry! Student driver!" out the side window as the locals kissed the pavement.

Tears rolled then, accompanied by wracking sobs and gasping breaths. The frenzy lasted a while, eventually degenerated into a soupy mess, given the headphones, the proximity of the boom mike to her nose, and the lack of readily available tissues. She gave points back to Logan for refraining from well-intentioned "there, theres" and back pats. He was flying along like nothing was happening.

Sarah pressed her sleeves and the front of her sweatshirt into mop-up service and settled into a state—as best she could describe it later—of detached calm. She was no stranger to a dizzying whirlwind of emotions, only this time when the tempest set her down, she was back in Kansas, standing on solid ground. The emotions she was feeling were genuine, the aftereffects of a real threat to life, not just a rehash of ancient crap. A nice change.

She took a deep breath and wrapped sweaty, sticky fingers around the control yoke.

She groped for the rudder pedals with her toes, checked the gauges and oriented herself to the horizon. She was scared shitless for sure, but it was time to put all that away in a drawer for now.

Bottom line: the plane had to get down safely.

"I got the plane."

Logan removed his hands from his control yoke and set them back in his lap again.

Sarah said, "I'm clearing the area visually and resuming traffic pattern." She shouldered goo off the tip of her nose.

"Roger, that," Logan said. "You are clear my side for ninety-degree left turn into traffic pattern."

"Initiating turn." This from *her* mouth. Suddenly, maintaining focus wasn't the issue it had been just a few, short, hair-raising minutes ago. Another lifetime ago.

A twenty-degree bank returned the plane to pattern. Two more lefts and she was flying base leg.

"You know what happened on your last try?" Logan asked.

"Yes."

"Tell me."

"I fucked up big time."

"Care to elaborate?"

Sarah sighed. "I didn't adjust the fuel mixture before

turning onto base leg, so I was distracted by a rough engine during the final approach turn. I elected to force a landing rather than go around and set up for a better approach."

The same mistake she'd made the very first time she'd flown the computer simulator. She braced herself for a reproach.

"And?"

"And I elected to turn at too steep a bank, lost airspeed over the wings, went into a stall, and almost fricking killed—"

"I was there for that part, remember? But was the airplane trying to tell you anything at any point during the turn?"

"Yes." He wasn't making this easy. Recriminations were beginning to look better and better.

"What?"

"The vibration and then the sluggish control response were warning signs that a stall was imminent." Just like on the simulator and just like he'd once demonstrated for her.

"Why did you ignore the signs?"

"Because I didn't want to do another go-around."

"Why?"

She hesitated. "I . . . I thought I would be judged somehow . . . lacking." She felt microscopic suddenly, too small to reach the controls. The Cessna twitched and she settled it with rudder input.

"Land when ready."

That was *it*? That was all? She'd almost sent them spiraling in for the big dirt nap and he just says land the plane?

Slam! That thought was tossed into yet another drawer. Later, when the plane was down.

"Reviewing prelanding checklist," she said. "Mixture, okay. Carb heat . . . on." Sarah touched each control as she recited the checklist. "Flaps ten degrees." The runway was now about forty-five degrees ahead, off the inside wing tip.

She thumbed the radio mike. "Crossly Tower, this is LD one-oh-eight. Requesting landing clearance. Over."

"Roger, LD one-oh-eight. Cleared for visual approach. Be advised there's a ten-mile-an-hour crosswind."

Lovely.

"Roger, tower. LD one-oh-eight turning on final now." Sarah cleared the area, then banked twenty degrees, using the rudder and ailerons, and added power to keep the Cessna in trim. "Adding another ten degrees flap," she announced. "Descending"—she checked the altimeter—"five hundred feet per minute."

The wind sock at the end of the runway was streaming left to right, so she backed off on the throttle and cheated the nose toward the left side of the Tarmac.

"Full flaps." She spun the wheel on the panel to the "Full" position and the flaps clunked down all the way. A touch of power brought the nose up again. Left rudder kept the Cessna on line with the apron of the runway, and left stick dipped the left wing into the crosswind.

With the airspeed pinned on the requisite sixty-five miles per hour, they crossed the diagonal yellow stripes marking the beginning of the runway. The weather wing twitched in the gusty crosswind, demanding to be let up, but Sarah held her ground on the controls and started the flare. The nose of the Cessna rose gently and seconds later, with a satisfying chirp, the left wheel touched and stuck. She cut power, and the right settled, followed by the nose wheel. She hauled back on the yoke and gently applied the brakes.

"LD one-oh-eight leaving runway," she radioed. "Thank you, control."

"Roger, LD one-oh-eight. Glad you're back."

Yeah. And not in a wooden box.

* * *

Sarah followed the taxi lanes back to the flight school lot. Logan hadn't spoken since he'd told her to land. She would have paid a lot more than a penny for his thoughts. They were down, and the inevitable was coming. Not before she killed the last obligatory switch, but it was coming.

As they exited the taxi lane and bounced onto the apron he said, "Park it out here."

In other words, don't bring it into the flight school lot. Logan had been letting her put the Cessna to bed after each lesson. Since she'd gained some legitimacy as a student pilot, he'd told her Lloyd had stopped flipping out about her using one of his precious planes. She couldn't imagine what her good-faith account balance would be after the morning's major withdrawal.

"I've got another student later today."

Ah, her replacement. Before her seat was even cold.

She jigged the Cessna around in a tight circle and left it facing the runway, ready for Logan's next flight, then chopped the power. The engine gave a last gasping sputter and the prop freewheeled to a stop. She snapped off the fuel pumps and the master switch.

After the continuous drone of the past hour, the silence was deafening. They slipped the headphones off and shoved open the doors. A light breeze wafted in, clearing out the sweet, close smell of hot motor oil. Metal ticked and cooled.

Logan seemed in no hurry to leave or speak. Not at all the bum's rush Sarah had anticipated. As usual, he and his clipboard were cutting a fine cameo of a fusty monk illuminating an ancient manuscript. The seconds dragged by. She didn't think it was appropriate to whistle.

So give, already, she wanted to scream.

She'd just missed killing them with a random act of aviation. Why wouldn't he just yell at her, call her a hazard, kick her out of flight school, quote from accident reports, quote from Scripture—anything. Just not this total silence.

Finally, he clicked his pen, settled the clipboard crossways on his thighs, and slid one long leg out the door. He rested his foot on a wing strut and blew out a long breath. "You're probably wondering why I'm not yelling and screaming about what happened up there."

"Well, actually—"

"I'm not, because you weren't the only one at fault."

Répétez, si'l vous plaît?

He did. "No, you weren't the only one at fault." Then he sighed.

Sarah shifted in her seat. This was a new angle. Not that she understood it, but it beat a slow death by denigration. A narrow shaft of sunlight illuminated her dreary prison cell.

"Well, sure. Anyone could see—" She'd allowed tremendous relief to take temporary control of her mouth. "Wait. What are you talking about? *I* almost turned us into a water feature. How was that *your* fault?"

"Because I set the trap you fell into," he said, staring, like she had often found herself doing, into the improbably blue sky, as if searching for strength that could not be found on terra firma.

"So you were *expecting* me to screw up?"

"I figured the odds were that you would, yes."

"So that's how you were able to react so fast when the stall hit."

"Well, yes and no. The stall gave plenty of warning. You didn't have to be a test pilot to see it coming. The vibration, the slushy controls. That part was your screwup. You should have caught it before it happened."

Sarah's face got hotter than the engine.

"Today was a life lesson, served up in a relatively harmless package," he said. "A chance to see what can happen up there."

Harmless life lesson, her ass. It was almost a harmful *death* lesson. "A lot of people would have been pissed if you'd killed me, you know."

She didn't think he heard her. He was still looking at the sky.

"Someday you might thank me for it," he said. "If it keeps you from becoming a part of the landscape when you're out there flying around on your own, it was worth it. That's going to be a major point in the report I'll have to file with the FAA."

Flying on her *what?*

"Excuse me? You can say FAA report and flying on my own in the same sentence? After what just happened you still see me as all-by-myself-pilot material?"

He sat up straighter in the seat and looked around the cabin, everywhere but at her. "The screwup you made up there was a big one. But you learned a lot from it. More than just about stalling, I'm thinking. About how a pilot has to be clear thinking at every minute, that you can't let emotions— anything—affect your judgment. But pilots are also human. Even the absolute best ones make stupid decisions."

Why did she think that they weren't just talking about flying anymore?

"Your attitude pissed me off," he said. "Finally, I'd had enough. I figured, screw you, go ahead and do it on your own."

Whoa, new concept here. She got to *him?* She'd been told she had that effect on people, but still . . .

"I suppose I can understand your reaction," she heard herself say. "Especially since you went out of your way to help me get over my phobia and all you got for your trouble was a ration of shit. Not all of that was deserved. Notice I didn't say you deserved *none* of it."

He laughed. "Guilty."

"Indeed, because you can be a royal pain in the ass. God, you're like an old woman sometimes with this safety and "practice until it's automatic" crap. I mean, I'm sure you have the best of intentions, but don't you turn people off of flying because they get bored and pissed off?"

"It happens. But I'd rather have them go to someone else to get the "anybody can fly" attitude. That way if anything ever goes wrong up there that they haven't been trained to handle, it won't be on my conscience."

Sarah waggled the yoke. "I guess I see what you mean." Damn, agreeing with him seemed to be habit-forming. "Flying isn't inherently dangerous. I know that now. Weird thing to say after almost crushing us into a paperweight, but it's true. Flying is safe. It's *people* who aren't. Every time you go up you bet that your skills are superior to whatever hits the fan."

She looked over at the end of the runway she'd just brought their aluminum cocoon in on. It painted a benign scene. Orderly rows of yellow landing lights. Wind sock billowing in the gentle breeze. Oh, sure, *now* it was gentle. The lost pride, the crosswind struggles, the ground loop landings, the flights that never arrived. They left no trace, no warnings for the unwary.

Logan's job was to train people to recognize those dangers and get themselves and their human cargo up and down safely in spite of them. Not an enviable responsibility.

"Logan, I think I just figured something out." She turned to find him watching her.

"It had to happen sooner or later."

"Shut up. What I mean is, *almost* messing up—up there,"

she said, pointing toward the soaring blue vault, "means you're still alive, right? You beat it." She thought about that for a moment. "Huh. It's really pretty basic stuff, flying."

"It's funny you say that," he said, sliding his leg higher on the strut and sinking lower into the seat. "I used to think that too. That up there things were black and white. They were absolute. You did everything by the book, everybody came out alive and kicking. You didn't, you ended up a smoking hole in the turf. Simple, like you said."

A gust of wind kicked up a dust devil out near the wind sock. The tunnel of fabric fled from it. "And something changed your mind?"

"Yeah. I found out that there are no guarantees. You know that in your head, but until you see it . . . feel it . . . you don't really know that . . . playing by the rules and being the best doesn't"—he searched for a word—"insulate you from screwing up, from . . . failure."

The *F* in failure was capitalized, she understood. An imaginary dog yelped.

It wasn't Spot. He was cringing in a remote corner of her mind, wearing doggie diapers. The openmouthed bridge kiss convinced him to consider a change of address. She suspected he'd learned there were safer places to haunt than Sarah Dundee's psyche.

She wondered again if Logan kept a pet, too.

Assorted insect life whirred and chirped in the grass beneath the belly of the Cessna. A grasshopper flicked into the cabin and landed on Sarah's leg, his long legs tensed, ready for evasive action. Who did that remind her of?

Logan jammed his clipboard in a slot between the seats, laced his fingers together, stretched his arms forward to touch the windscreen, then let his hands flop into his lap. He sighed.

"I have absolutely no idea why I'm talking to you like

this, especially since you'll probably use whatever I tell you in your damn article, but what the hell. After all, it'd make sensational copy. You know, the tragic hero angle?"

The none-too-subtle scorn was not lost on her. "Look, the only thing that's tragic here is your attitude, pal. I'll write the runway article as I see it. I told you that before. But I'm not about to take advantage of anyone—not even you—to fill out a story. So it's whenever you're ready."

By the evening of that same day, he was.

Chapter 18

The mosquitoes were just coming out. Logan slapped at one. "Bastards."

Sarah laughed. "We all got to live," she said, recalling the exact words he'd delivered to her several weeks ago in almost the same spot as they were right then. She let the little buggers gnaw on Logan for another few minutes as they negotiated the winding footpath, then stopped and handed over the bug juice she'd spritzed herself with before leaving the parking lot of the preserve.

"Just found this, did you?" he asked, taking the bottle from her.

"Yeah, just," she said, failing to hide her smirk. Not very Christian of her, but get backs were *so* therapeutic.

"I really don't understand the attraction," he said, squirting. Sarah's first response almost was to tell him that she, like the mosquitoes, had wanted to bite him hard a time or two herself, but then she realized he meant *her* attraction to The Great Outdoors.

And speaking of not understanding things, there was

something she was having a hard time with also: her sudden preoccupation with Logan. After she'd been treated to a tantalizing peek into his inner workings at Crossly Field that morning, she hadn't been able to get him out of her thoughts. She remembered the bridge scare a few times, too, but mostly she just thought about Logan. Around five o'clock he'd phoned and told her to meet him just before sunset at the bottom of the half-mile trail that led to the lighthouse at the far end of Pear Island.

"Spray the brim of your hat, too," Sarah told him, watching him anoint the rest of himself with the bug juice.

A few more minutes down the trail they arrived at the grassy area surrounding the base of the lighthouse. There was no keeper's cottage, Pear Island Light being a very modest beacon by East Coast standards. Sarah thought they'd be swatting mosquitoes as they ate their picnic supper on the grass, but, to her surprise, Logan had a key to the iron tower.

"We lease the attic space above the light chamber from Tidal. Loran—navigation equipment?—is being installed up there," he explained, "For when the second runway opens."

If it opens, Sarah mentally corrected. She stood back as Logan tugged open the creaky steel door. Cool, dank air streamed out. He slung the carry strap of a soft-sided cooler over his shoulder, and they wound their way up the metal stairs. It took them a while to make the climb, because as they ascended, Sarah had to stop at every slit window to exclaim at the changing view.

At the top of the tower, there was a round glass room where the beacon lived. The panorama from there was spectacular. The entire length of Pear Island, from its pronounced "stem end" to the north down to the trailing sand spit at its Rubenesquely rounded south end, was spread before them. The preserve, the parking lot—Logan handed her binoculars—wow. The space where she usually parked and, farther along, the Bridge of Death, a summer tango of cars crawling across it. Off to the left, Crossly Field. She could almost make out figures moving inside the control tower. She wondered if Maura was on duty. Over thirty years she'd lived in Tidal. *This* was a novel experience. Not as high as in the Cessna, but what the view lacked in scope, it made up for in detail.

She swung the glasses toward the open ocean. Next stop? England. On the horizon, streaks of what she imagined was rain connected a wall of angry-looking clouds to the sea.

"Something coming in?" she asked Logan.

"It's been building all day. Fast moving, possible lightning around midnight."

"This place grounded?" she asked. "If we get hit, I'd rather not be quick fried to a crackly crunch."

"No worries. This thing's been here for what . . . ?"

"Since the late eighteen hundreds, I think."

"There you go. Built like a battleship. Besides, we'll be long gone before the lightning gets here."

Or they could stay and watch. Boy, that'd be worth the price of admission. Up close and personal with Mother Nature. Right in the center of the flash and bang. *Man*. She said as much to Logan.

"Not happening." She'd never heard his voice so tight before. Not even during the bridge brush.

"Okay, whatever." Her stomach growled. "Hey, what'd you bring?"

"Fried chicken, fries. From downtown," he added unnecessarily. He didn't seem like a guy who cooked. He settled himself on a low shelf that circled the base of the huge Fresnel lens.

She knew the technical name of the thing because Logan had told her all about it on their hike to the tower. The whale-oil lamp inside the lens had been replaced with an electric light . . . ? She couldn't remember when. She hadn't been paying attention. The tide was full and two-foot breakers curled along the beach in perfect, tight coils. Sandpipers dodged in and out of the wash. Lovely. One of those times she wished she'd inherited her dad's knack with a camera, instead of her mother's temper. *You really should call her more often,* she'd chastised herself. Violet shouldn't have to get updates on her daughter's life by watching the local news.

Sarah kept a few treasured Before the Crash photographs of the family displayed around her disaster of a living room. One of her favorites was a self-timed shot—her dad was famous for his last-second slides into the frame—of the four of them: Beth, Sarah, Mom, and Dad. They were standing with arms around each other, the easy grins a matched service, dusty khaki clothing, posed in front of the little plane that later . . . Sarah stopped herself. Enough to admit that she missed all of them intensely. Even though she still had her mother, most of the time it didn't feel that way.

A *zip!* brought Sarah back to reality. Logan had the lid of the cooler undone and Sarah watched him fish two Styrofoam containers from the depths of it and free them from towels he'd thoughtfully wrapped around them. The outsides of the containers were slick with what Sarah could only imagine was some species of transfat.

"Aw, Jeez, Logan. Don't you know that stuff'll kill you? That there's a heart attack in a box." Steam rose up when he popped open the lid on the first container.

Damn. What a way to go. "I'll take that one, thanks," Sarah said, pointing and reaching.

"Beer?" Logan rummaged around and brought out a couple of bottles of low-carb something or other. Not a Sammie, regretfully. He twisted the tops off and handed one to Sarah. The glass was slightly warm from resting against the dinners, but what the hell. Life was good.

"It's probably illegal drinking up here, huh?" she said, feeling like an outlaw and enjoying it.

He shrugged. "You're with management, sort of." He lifted his bottle in a toast. "Here's to us. To life. To not dying today."

"Cheers." It was cold and good. The toast, and probably the sentiment, improved the flavor.

Sarah settled herself beside him on the shelf and balanced the Styrofoam tray on her knees. They ate in companionable silence. The clouds colored as the sun went down over Tidal. It turned obligingly to a big orange ball and took about a minute to vanish below the tree line. The strobe inside the lens stole some of the ambiance the darker the sky became, but Sarah's overactive writer's imagination softened the scene by conjuring up the soft glow of whale oil and linen wicks of days long past.

"Works for me," she said, muffling a belch behind a wad of paper napkins.

"Definitely comfort food," Logan said.

"A comfortable spot, too."

"For sure."

Dude . . .

She deposited her now-empty tray off to the side and shifted her butt to a better position on the shelf. The beer and the high fat content went to work on her and, by degrees, she became slit eyed and lazy.

Logan finished his dinner, then pulled a brown paper bag out of the seemingly bottomless cooler. An aperitif, perhaps?

"SweeTart?" He held the sack out to Sarah.

"No kidding?" It was full of penny candy. She rooted around. "Whoa, Runts? I love these things!"

He laughed. "Me, too."

Sarah soaked up the fabulous view and let her mind drift while she softened up one of the tasty, but rock-hard, banana pieces. "God, Pear Island is beautiful."

Logan sat up. "How about we take a break from that? Just for one night?"

"From what?" She was truly taken aback. "I was just admiring the view."

"From the 'Thing Between Us.'"

Sarah heard the capitals. "You started it," she said.

"No, I didn't."

"Yes, you did."

"Didn't."

She said, "This is fun until someone gets hurt. Let's really stop now."

He said, "But it's like a hangnail, you know? It keeps catching on everything. You get frustrated and finally bite the thing out of there."

"What an elegant simile."

"You're a writer. I'm working to impress you."

"I was joking."

"Me, too."

Sarah decided she was too lazy and relaxed to play "Top This," so she conceded the game for the sake of keeping the match friendly. "Look, Logan. I've been thinking it over. I understand where you're coming from about this second runway. I just *hated* it so much at first that I even thought that you and your fancy lawyer might have gone so far as to deliberately bury the 'lost'"—she made air quotes—"agreement. You didn't, did you?"

"No." The word fell out of his mouth like she'd asked him if he'd ever worn women's clothes.

"I don't think so now, but that's what I thought then."

She read his eyes, just to be sure. He was telling the truth. She shifted position on the ledge. "I couldn't see—oh, God, I can't believe I'm saying this—the 'economics' of the situation. I understand now that you're trying to run a business. You're trying to make it work. You've got employees—Maura, the maintenance guys and the Airview people—counting on you. They're all depending on you. I get that."

"Good." He sounded surprised. "So what's the problem now?"

"The problem is that you still don't get it."

"Get *what?*"

"*It.*" Sarah gestured to the world just outside the tower.

"Aside from being Stephen King's best book, I'd argue, what is *it?*" Logan made an awkward copy of her hand motion.

"The heart of the matter, Logan. Pear Island's been sitting here for something like ten thousand years—since the end of the last ice age—and it's going to be here long after we're gone. You don't screw around with stuff like that."

"Don't look at me like that," he said.

"Like *what?*"

"Like I'm the anti-Christ. If it wasn't me you were dealing with, it'd be the developers. You prefer them?" He snorted. "At least I'm not bulldozing the preserve. You can keep it, but this runway is going through. It's happening. You've got to get used to that fact. Don't get sucked in by Hillary Harker and her bunch. They think if they stop me they're stopping progress. Fat chance." He rooted around in the candy bag like he was looking for a lost winning sweepstakes ticket.

Sarah forced her fingers to unclench. "Logan, I just don't want to see one more place fucked over. Pear Island feels like a last stand, like the Alamo. My Alamo."

"Be prepared for a siege," he said, one hand shaking the sack and the other sifting through the contents.

"God, do you have to touch every piece?" she said.

"I like the little red ones . . ." he said, eyes on the prize.

And all along she'd been thinking they were having an intelligent conversation. She pondered the cannon she was inexorably inching into firing position: the reworked article. When she lit the fuse on that baby, you'd hear it all the way to Alaska. Hawaii, even.

With an exclamation of triumph, Logan popped whatever he found into his mouth and then, with the awareness that constantly surprised Sarah, said, "And then, of course, there's the fucking article. I was ready to strangle you over that. I don't mean that literally, by the way."

She nodded, appreciative. The world had become a dangerous place.

"I mean, I was pissed. Here I was, by helping you, unwittingly handing you the ammunition you needed to really screw me over. But the more I read, the more stupid I realized the article was. You were shooting rubber bullets. It was so inane and so stupid and so—"

"Logan?"

He paused.

"I get it?"

"Right. But then I realized what was behind it. You were trying to split hairs, trying to do what you needed to do to get your job and, at the same time, keep me from coming off like a total asshole. And then I didn't know if I really liked that either. Because you know the one thing left after everything's said and done?"

She couldn't imagine.

He shifted on the hard metal ledge. "The truth. You're left with what is, and you deal. Whatever it is, it's better than some fantasy about the way things are gonna be. Witness June at the Airview."

Witness Rick. She said, "Well, I'm glad you understand what I was trying to do, at least. It was . . . sophomoric. But I really felt stuck, you know? I wasn't going to do you dirty, no matter what. But you're right. Mincing words is insulting to both of us. Trying to paint you as something you're not is no good. So I'm going to rewrite the article. I'll be as surgical as I can with the redo, but I am talking about the runway's threat to the animals. Like I already said: this is my Alamo."

He started to break in, but she was on a roll. For all she knew, it might be her last opportunity to work on him.

"It's like with Teddy Roosevelt, Logan. Thank God he knew what natural spaces were because if he hadn't passed the preservation acts we'd have fucking hotels all along the rim of the Grand Canyon right now. The laws came about because of his viewpoint, his understanding his . . . *appreciation* of nature. Of wilderness. Of how important it is to people's heads, their hearts, their . . . souls, if you'll allow that."

"Yeah, but—"

With a raised hand, Sarah cut him off again. "I think if you had more opportunity to appreciate nature, you'd see it differently. Just like I did about flying. I felt like I was coming home up there, as stupid as that might sound. And you know what? I think that if you spent some time out in the wilderness you, too, might find a shelf for some of the things rattling around loose inside you."

Her scoff covered another of his attempts to interject. God, she hated it when her mother got on a rant like she was now. "Don't even speak to me about that whole Air Force survival training thing. That was just a joke to you. Something to beat, to get through. Again, I'll bet if you went out there in

Zebra Contemporary

To start your membership, simply complete and return the Free Book Certificate. You'll receive your Introductory Shipment of FREE Zebra Contemporary Romances, you only pay $1.99 for shipping and handling. Then, each month you will receive the 4 newest Zebra Contemporary Romances. Each shipment will be yours to examine FREE for 10 days. If you decide to keep the books, you'll pay the preferred subscriber price (a savings of up to 30% off the cover price), plus shipping and handling. If you want us to stop sending books, just say the word... it's that simple.

FREE BOOK CERTIFICATE

Yes! Please send me FREE Zebra Contemporary romance novels. I only pay $1.99 for shipping and handling. I understand that each month thereafter I will be able to preview 4 brand-new Contemporary Romances FREE for 10 days. Then, if I should decide to keep them, I will pay the money-saving preferred subscriber's price (that's a savings of up to 30% off the retail price), plus shipping and handling. I understand I am under no obligation to purchase any books, as explained on this card.

NAME _____

ADDRESS _____ APT. _____

CITY _____ STATE _____ ZIP _____

TELEPHONE (___) _____

E-MAIL _____

SIGNATURE _____

(If under 18, parent or guardian must sign)

Offer limited to one per household and not to current subscribers. Terms, offer and prices subject to change. Orders subject to acceptance by Zebra Contemporary Book Club. Offer Valid in the U.S. only.

CN066A

Thank You!

THE BENEFITS OF BOOK CLUB MEMBERSHIP

• You'll get your books hot off the press, usually before they appear in bookstores.

• You'll ALWAYS save up to 30% off the cover price.

• You'll get our FREE monthly newsletter filled with author interviews, book previews, special offers and MORE!

• There's no obligation — you can cancel at any time and you have no minimum number of books to buy.

• And — if you decide you don't like the books you receive, you can return them. (You always have ten days to decide.)

Be sure to visit our website at www.kensingtonbooks.com.

ll..l..lll....lll..l.l.l.l..l.l..ll.l..l.l..lll.l..ll..l

Zebra Contemporary Romance Book Club
Zebra Home Subscription Service, Inc.
P.O. Box 5214
Clifton NJ 07015-5214

the woods now, you'd get a whole new attitude about the value of the preserve. What do you think?"

She knew what he'd say before he even opened his mouth.

He opened his mouth and said it. "I don't know . . . I like nature—don't get me wrong. I like looking down on it. I'd rather fly over a nice, green forest than a city, probably. But other than that . . . I . . . I don't know. I could take it or leave it. It doesn't really . . . *matter* to me."

"You're hopeless," she said, not really meaning it. He wasn't hopeless. Neither was she. She was beginning to see that. But they—big T—were.

For a while, they were quiet.

"Hey, Logan."

"Mmmm?"

Sarah glanced at him. His head was back, resting against the base of the lens. His eyes were closed and he had a bulge in his cheek. He was working on some kind of jawbreaker.

"Be careful with those things," she said. "You'll break your teeth."

"Yes, mommy."

Sarah laughed.

Logan opened one eye and looked sideways at her. "There's more, right?"

"Actually, no. Not about . . . 'the thing.' I was thinking about something else. Something you started to talk about right after we landed? You were saying that one time you had some kind of big . . . problem in the air?"

Whatever he had in his mouth shattered.

"I've had lots of them. Take you, for instance." He tried on a grin, but it was the kind you hide behind.

"Ha-ha, very funny. You're the life of the party. Seriously, something really went wrong for you once, right? I mean, the limp and all?"

He worried the fabric of his trousers—Columbia, slate, nylon with mesh-bottomed, draining side pockets; she'd done a review on them last summer—where it stretched over his bad knee. Just when she began to think he was in danger of abrading a hole right through the material, he spoke.

"Oh, hell. What have I got to lose after all this time?"

Quite a lot, Sarah suspected.

He laughed bitterly. "Oh, yeah. I had a 'little problem.' You could say that." He kept his eyes on the evening sky.

"You want to . . . tell me about it?" Eggshells crunched beneath her feet.

He cut his eyes to her and licked his bottom lip. She was suddenly conscious of the fact that in spite of her having put her life in his hands, she really didn't know much about him: his background, his mental state. He looked . . . dangerous . . . right then.

But she wasn't about to run out on him, either. Wherever he was heading, it didn't look like a place anybody should go alone. She braced herself to hear a tale of aviation daring do.

"I killed a family."

Or not.

"A *family*? Of *what*?" An image of shorebirds popped into Sarah's mind. The kind that hung out in flocks on runways and got inconveniently sucked up into jet engines. He must have mowed down a bunch.

"Of four."

Not a very big bunch.

Wait a minute.

"*People?*" He must have thought she was an imbecile. Oh. My. God. Of course people.

"No, chickens. Of course people, you idiot." He glared at her. "Are you following along, here? I, Logan Gerald Donnelly, killed a family of four."

Mr. Perfection, Mr. Check Everything Three Times killed a family of four? And lived? It didn't make any sense. And his middle name was . . . what did he say?

Her mind had gone numb. "Oh, my God, Logan." What happened? she started to say, but then rethought. This was scary shit, here, this killing people stuff. Maybe he'd done it in cold blood. Deliberately. With his bare hands. No, that wouldn't work. He said it was in the air. Assume he meant when he was flying a plane. But maybe he put the plane on autopilot and flung his victims out the door.

Maybe she didn't want to learn about his past. Maybe Sarah Dundee was his next victim and he'd lured her here to this remote lighthouse to throw her off. Sarah checked the windows. Except for little vents at the top, the metal sashes appeared to be welded shut. She wrestled with the logistics of that for a moment. Then the sheer stupidity of her inner monologue stopped her in her tracks. She was definitely high on saturated fat.

This was Logan here. A basically okay person when he wasn't planning the wholesale loading of wildlife into box-cars. Sarah forced the tremor from her voice. "Tell me about it."

Logan took his baseball cap off, brushed his hair back, and then tugged the hat back on. He blew a breath up into the ceiling of the tower.

Ancient crap stirring. Who better to know?

"I did ROTC during college and joined the Air Force right after I graduated. Flying military jets was all I ever wanted to do. I got my wings and command of my own bird, made it through the Gulf War—which I will never talk about, so don't even ask me. The military was my whole world. For twelve years. Until it happened. The accident, that is."

He stretched his bad leg out, as if it, or the memories, pained him.

"I was flying a Pitt, a stunt plane, biwing. A beautiful job." The hint of a smile lifted the corners of his mouth. "Handled like a dream, full aerobatic capabilities. A real machine." He shook his head ruefully and glanced outside the windows, but there was nothing to see. The falling darkness had turned the glass walls into mirrors.

"I took her out on loan from a civilian buddy of mine. Just up for an afternoon of loops and rolls. Nothing out of the ordinary." He said this without a touch of cockiness. Evidently for him that stuff really was nothing. Me, I didn't even like it when roller coasters did weird stuff.

"I had my eye on the weather when I went up—the service said a front was moving in—and I could see a wall of clouds coming on as the afternoon went by. It looked like it was going to slide on past, but it veered off all of a sudden and the leading edge of it headed on a collision course with the field."

"I radioed traffic control and they cleared me for an immediate visual landing. I was in airspace dedicated to acrobatics and the tower radar showed nobody near me, so I set up for a quick approach. In the time it took to do that, the ceiling dropped like a hammer and the visibility went to about two hundred feet. We'd all underestimated the speed of the thing.

"But still no big deal, I remember thinking. I terminated my approach, then radioed for vectors away from the storm. I'd wait it out, away from the main body, then follow the tail end down flying IFR."

He glanced to see if Sarah picked up on the acronym, and she nodded: Instrument Flight Rules. Another thing about aviation she'd probably never figure out if she lived to be a hundred.

"So what went wrong?" Sarah asked, not really wanting to know, but finding herself hanging on every word with horrified fascination.

"They circled me around for a while, playing tag with the back end of the front. It was a nasty bugger, lots of lightning. Damn . . ." He pulled his feet under him, just like she did in Dr. Loo's office when things were heating up.

"Logan, go on. This is all good," Sarah said, trying to capture the soothing essence of Cynthia Loo's voice. "Let it come out."

"Finally, I radioed in a low-fuel situation and they vectored me down. I went into the pea soup and was banking for the setup when all of a sudden this giant fist slams down on the starboard wing. The Pitt practically inverted, and for a few seconds I partially blacked out. I heard crap whanging off the Plexiglas of the cockpit, hitting the fuselage. I woke up and got myself and the plane under some kind of control, but the upper airfoil on the left side had ripped half off and the lower one was missing about three feet off the tip."

"Holy shit . . . You hit something?"

"That's what I thought at first. There were some killer cell towers around the field. Maybe I clipped one of them in all that soup. But both altimeters told me the same thing: I was way too high for that. In the meantime, the rest of the top wing decided to shred its way back to the fuselage. That did it—the Pitt was going down. I took a quick bearing and headed the nose toward where I thought the woods were. Then I radioed the tower and bailed out."

"Out of the plane? You jumped?" Scenes of World War I flying aces found dead in cornfields, their bodies crumpled in heaps, feet from farmer's ponds, danced through Sarah's head.

"I had a 'chute on. Standard thing doing aerobatics. You wear a parachute just in case. Came down about a mile from the field. But I didn't quite get clear of the Pitt. Caught my leg on something on the way out."

"And the family? How do they figure in?"

"Their plane was what ran into me. They were lost, probably terrified, flying VFR—you know, Visual Flight Rules—in and out of the breaks in the cover, transponder *off,* if you can fucking believe it. The tower missed them on radar because of all the electrical interference. The list of things they screwed up goes on and on. Bottom line, though? I had a parachute and they didn't. I saw them impact just about the time I came floating through the bottom layer of clouds."

What did one say? *Gee, too bad? Gosh, it wasn't your fault?* All the usual platitudes fell short.

"Yikes." Sarah exhaled, dizzy. She hadn't realized she'd been holding her breath through his account. Suddenly, and unaccountably, she felt angry. Not at Logan but at the family. At the victims.

"What the hell were they doing up there when they didn't know what they were *doing*? You don't screw around in an airplane. You have to know your shit." Hours in the cockpit listening to Logan's harangues—and their little adventure at the bridge—had taught her that much.

"Look, Logan. You did everything you could," she said. "The guy flying didn't have a clue what he was doing up there. He should have protected his family better. If it wasn't you they ran into, it would have been someone else. You just drew the short straw."

There was a *really* long pause before he spoke again. Obviously, she wasn't as accomplished at separating her own feelings from her clinical responses as dear Dr. Loo. Apologies all around.

"I can't believe you just said that," Logan finally said. "Not that I've told all that many people about it. But no one's ever said what you just did." He snorted. "I just can't believe you, sometimes."

Well, me neither, Sarah thought. Cripes, she'd blown it again.

They were all right. Joan. Her mother, God forbid. No wonder she never had serious, long-term relationships. What a well of compassion she was, what a spring of solace, what a . . . jerk with a capital *J*. She was truly a heartless witch.

So you could have knocked her over with a piping plover feather when Logan said, "But I think you're right."

Sarah coughed like something had gone down the wrong pipe. What did he say?

"Huh?" She whacked herself on the chest.

"It's funny, but I've kind of been thinking that way myself lately," he said slowly, unaware of Sarah's self-flagellation. "I've kept myself swinging on the hook for a long time about this."

My God, here it comes, she thought. *Shut up, shut up, shut up,* she willed herself.

"I left the service as soon as my hitch was up," he continued, "even though I'd always planned to be a twenty-year guy. I drifted around for a while, trying different things, then trying nothing and drinking too much. Until my grandfather's private investigator—I didn't know Noah Crossly was my grandfather then—showed up at my door out of the blue one day. He pitched me a very interesting proposal: re-open Crossly Field."

Sarah nodded. Logan's fingers walked their way into the paper bag and explored meditatively. They extracted a miniature foil packet of SweeTarts.

"I realized that the thing I still did best, no matter what happened before, was flying. So I took the manager's gig. But what's always made it hard for me was having to keep this thing covered up."

"But it wasn't your fault. So what if people found out?"

"Because when they did they'd treat me different. Like a . . . charity case or something." He aped, "'Oh, poor Logan, what he must be going through.' God, I hate that crap."

Sarah took an offered SweeTart. "But how would they find out?"

"Most of them wouldn't, but an article about my life could spill the beans pretty good." He met her eyes.

"And picture yourself in bed—" He stopped and looked away, as if he'd crossed a line. "Never mind."

"Please don't treat me like a child, Logan. I get the picture. It's an emotional time bomb, yes? The closer you get to somebody, the louder it ticks?" Spot growled, mostly for show. He was one whipped pup since the bridge.

"Exactly. No matter how good it got, I always felt like there was this unspoken thing between me and whoever."

"And it was only a matter of time before the bomb went off and wrecked everything."

"Right." Then he shot me a wicked smile. "Hey, you're really good at figuring out what makes people tick, ha-ha. You should be a writer."

Sarah's heart skipped, much as she hated to admit it. Logan was being a smart-ass, but the writer thing sounded good coming from him.

"Hence, the whole June thing?" she said. "Shallow gratification? No deep stuff? Nice and safe?"

"Yeah, something like that." He had the good taste to look somewhat sheepish. "She was an out-and-out bombshell." Sarah clucked but kept quiet. Unfortunately, the memories seemed to warm him. "And, boy, did she elevate my ailerons—"

"Down, boy!" Sarah snapped her fingers in his face.

He laughed and Sarah watched him fight his sled back into the grooves. "But she and I had no mutual interest besides the most obvious one and I refused to let hormones run my life."

Then she knew. "She shut you down, huh?"

"Pretty much."

"Hubba-hubba," Sarah said, shaking her fingers like the tips were scorched.

"Enough."

She cocked her hands behind her head and made a round-house cut. "Swing and a . . . *miss!*"

"You made your point, already," he said, straightening the brim of his cap after its brush with her imaginary bat.

"I hope so." It was hard to resist coughing *Cradle robber!* into her fist, but she did. Maybe she really *was* a better person than she gave herself credit for.

"Noah Crossly gave me a second chance," he said, suddenly serious. "I owe him a lot. My life, maybe. At least the second runway. He wanted Crossly Field to be a success and I intend to make it one. He came to me—completely out of the blue—with no knowledge of me other than I was a good pilot, as far as I knew at the time. I didn't realize that he'd set the whole arrangement up until just before the meeting at town hall. He gave me the chance that he'd probably wanted to give to my dad."

"Give your dad?"

"My father wasn't attempting an emergency landing on the abandoned field."

"How do you know? You were just a kid."

"Because I'm a pilot now. My father was delivering a definitive answer to *his* father. Noah."

"Right. But to what question?"

"Do you have the guts to reopen Crossly Field?"

Sarah imagined Noah hounding his son relentlessly about it.

Logan continued: "'Fragile,' I'd hear my mother say to

people about my father after he came home from Vietnam. Posttraumatic stress they'd call it today. Noah just called it being a coward. My dad cracked under the strain."

"And Noah wanted to pass on the 'opportunity' at Crossly to you out of what? Guilt over how he treated your father?"

"Maybe he felt some, I don't know. I think he probably just wanted to finally get things the way he wanted them the last time around."

Any way you cut it, old Noah Crossly didn't have much of a human side. "Tough old bird," she said.

"Apparently."

Something had been bothering Sarah since Michael Brophy's bombshell revelation at the informational meeting. "That day—the meeting in town hall—when your lawyer announced that you would be inheriting the field?"

Logan looked over at her and nodded. "Uh-huh."

"I was so angry about the preserve that I totally missed the point that you had just been handed the real truth about your father's death. I went after you mercilessly. I'm . . . sorry about that. Not about defending the preserve, but about cutting into you right at that moment."

"Looking back, would you do anything different now? I mean, assuming you knew only what you knew about me then?"

"No."

"Well, it really wasn't personal, was it?"

They had both been in difficult positions. "I guess not."

"But thanks, anyway."

Sarah had to smile. "What did you think happened to your dad—before you found out the truth that night, I mean." God, the man had a lot dropped on him at that town meeting. All in front of John Q. Public, too.

"My mother had just said he had left us. No specifics.

Just that he gave his life for his country. Which, in essence, he did."

"Have you talked to her since you found out?"

"I can't." He peered into the wall of black mirrors surrounding them. "She's dead."

Open mouth wide and insert foot firmly. "Gosh, I . . ."

A low rumble reached them then, curled up as they were so cozily at the top of the tower. Sarah had briefly forgotten there was a world outside.

Thunder. The storm at sea was moving in. Logan's arm, pressed against hers, stiffened. "What about your folks?" he asked, absently.

"Planes giveth, planes taketh away."

It seemed he had to tear his attention from the gathering show outside. "Say?"

"My little phobia? Souvenir of the Dark Continent."

He shook his head. "I . . . ?"

She had spent all of her adult life circling the field, she realized at that moment. It was time to land. She let it all out in a rush. "My dad and my sister, Beth, were killed in a plane crash in Africa. My mother and I survived. I was fifteen." Her courage suddenly deserted her. "End of story."

"I doubt it," Logan said. He flexed his leg and Sarah again found herself mesmerized by the wicked white line running up it.

"We were in Africa: me; Beth; my mom, Violet; and my dad, Sherman."

Logan smiled.

"I know, Sherman, right? But he was a dear. I was fourteen; Beth was sixteen. Dad was on one of his sabbaticals—he was a professor of cultural anthropology—and he took us all to Africa with him this time. Every day this native pilot, Tukaba, would take us up in this little plane. Something like the Cessna, I think, now. We'd land at all kinds of different villages. Dad would collect oral histories from the people—"

"Sarah?"

"Right." She was allowing herself to drift away from the pain. "Anyway, this one takeoff didn't work out. We crashed. I—" Words jammed sideways in her throat. She rubbed the length of her windpipe.

She glanced at Logan. He was quietly watching her. He nodded: *Go.*

"I-I woke up first and I thought Dad and the pilot were covered in sweat, but then I realized that wasn't what it was. Mom was bleeding, too, in the backseat beside me. Unconscious. I looked where Beth should have been and there was nothing. No seat, no nothing." Her eyes glazed. She felt Logan's arm go around her. She allowed herself to move deeper—deeper than she had ever gone with Dr. Loo—into the labyrinth.

"I looked around the ground outside the plane and saw . . ." What? "Pieces of wing, Logan. Jesus Christ. Engine parts. Bits of tail fin. All thrown around and twisted up."

Logan's fingers dug into her arm.

More images came.

The cabin floor, hot under her feet. A great wracking sob doubled her over. "I lost my shoes, Logan," she cried. "My shoes are gone." Why that mattered so much she didn't know.

I'd lost my shoes . . .

The voice in her head that used to be Spot's had suddenly become her own. He had abandoned her to her memories.

Then: *God, Beth.* Where was Beth? Sarah remembered feeling around for her sister. Where there used to be plane and seat and sister, there was nothing but open space. A gaping hole.

Wait. That smell. What was it? Stinging her eyes, choking her . . .

Later, Logan told her she'd gasped for air like she was drowning.

Sarah heard Logan's voice then, but it was reaching her from a long distance away.

Fuel, gasoline. That's what the smell was. . . .

A bright yellow-orange blossom snapped her head around. She banged her head against solid metal. The next morning she'd find a goose egg over one ear.

"Sarah!" Logan's voice again. She had never heard him yell before.

Eager tongues of flame licked the shattered cabin windows. She grabbed for Violet, fought her free from the grasp of her seat belt. She and her mother tumbled through the torn opening, free-falling onto the baking sand of the plain.

"Logan!" *Somebody help me.*

Arms enveloped her. "Logan! I can't do this!" Her mother was dead weight, moaning softly. Had to get her away from the plane. Ten feet Sarah pulled her. Ten feet away from her father, her sister, their pilot. Then ten more agonizing feet. Twenty feet now. Twenty feet away from the life they all used to have. The seconds ticked off in her head. Thirty feet. Not far enough probably, but all she could do.

Sarah and her mother were hammered to the earth when what was left of their plane and their family exploded.

In the cool quiet of the tower, Sarah screamed. Screamed and screamed, Logan told her later. Then a TV screen in her head played the National Anthem and the world cut to black.

Sarah opened her eyes to find Logan staring down at her. "You ever consider a kennel?"

"Wha—?"

"For the damn dog."

"You met him." Sarah struggled to sit up.

"Yup." Logan got his hand under her and helped the process along. "Was he along for the ride when we almost . . . ?" He flew one hand into the palm of the other.

"Oh, yeah." Sarah rubbed a growing bump over one ear.

"You smacked your head against the ledge," Logan explained.

"Ow. Excitable object meets immovable one."

Logan smiled. To Sarah it was a lifeline. She wrapped her arms around him and they clung together, rocking, quiet.

"That dog really had you going," he said into her neck. "You tried to drag me down the stairs at one point," he said.

"Bad dreams."

"I guess."

"He gone?"

"I hope." Sara considered. "I thought he was before, you know, after the bridge. But now I think, yes, for good."

Logan broke the hug to look in her eyes. "Why a dog?"

Sarah shrugged and laughed. "I dunno. I guess if I did air-conditioning repair or was an architect or a pastry chef, I probably wouldn't have had a Spot running around loose in my head. But being a writer . . . ?" It was the first time ever she had said it that directly aloud. "It seems to attract an odd crowd."

Logan crossed his eyes and lolled his tongue.

Sarah slapped him on the arm. "Dope. What I mean is, I'm not callous about the tragedy I went through; it's just that you do what you have to do to survive. Me? I got a dog."

Logan nodded. Sarah could sense his assessment. "Huh. That's really something. Gonna miss him?"

"There's a hole there now, but I'm sure it'll get filled by something else. Hopefully, by something a lot more fun."

Still in a close embrace with Logan from the waist down, she felt him stir.

"Mmmm . . ." He leaned in and muttered onto the skin just below her ear, "Think of the possibilities."

He was preaching to the choir as far as she was concerned.

She went for the gold. Sarah traced the length of Logan's bent legs with her palms. He flinched when her fingers crossed the white line of his scar. "Sorry," she said, lightening her touch.

"So am I," he said. "I'm damaged goods."

She nuzzled his neck and moved her hand higher on his leg. "Good thing I still got my sales slip, huh?"

He groaned.

"Besides," she said, "you showed me yours, now I have to show you mine." It had been dark in the hall last time, and Logan had been extraordinarily focused on one particular point of contention. It was doubtful he'd taken in the entire map of the southern states. *Taken in* . . . Yes, he certainly had taken her in. She felt herself melt.

She brushed her lips against his mouth and ran the tip of her tongue lightly along his lower lip. Like he was starving, Logan made a feast of it and soon Sarah was gasping for air.

Somewhere along the line she must have graduated, she thought. Sure, she'd miss the student discounts, but *this*—she went after his mouth again—was *way* more fun.

Hands were everywhere. Whose hand, the exact location, all details lost in a blur of heat and anticipation. Suddenly a blinding flash—out of synch with the metered strobe and having nothing to do with their lover's frenzy, it took Sarah a moment to realize—lit up the sky outside the lighthouse.

"Shit." Logan's whole body had turned rigid. He tugged his pants on and shot up from the floor. He cupped his hands against the black glass and peered out. "Time to go," he announced.

When he turned back toward her, Sarah saw his pupils were the size of saucers. He made a mad grab for the litter and began stuffing trash randomly into the cooler.

"Logan, what's wrong?" A sudden chill reminded her she was half naked and she began to reassemble her clothes. She rose to her feet, her legs still liquid and unsteady from the almost lovemaking. She managed to grab Logan's arm and spin him around to face her. He was trembling and twitching. Then she knew.

The lightning. The storm.

"Wait. You can do this. *We* can do this," she said, her hands hard on his forearms. She knew he knew exactly what she meant: *stay*.

"No!"

"Yes!" Sarah wrapped up bunches of his shirtsleeves in her fists and shook him. "It's just like with me and Spot. Don't run from this, Logan!" A flash sparked outside, briefly illuminating the black sea. The leader bolt seared itself into Sarah's peripheral vision, even as she focused on Logan's face. Both of them froze, waiting. A peal of thunder rippled through the iron members of the tower, vibrating the floor beneath their feet. Seven seconds. The storm had moved incredibly fast.

He made a lunge for the stairs. Sarah hung on grimly, grabbing the back of his belt with both hands. "Don't!"

He twisted around toward her and his eyes were wild. White at the edges like Spot's when he was about to go for her throat. Somehow thinking about Spot made her stronger.

"I. Can. Not. Do. This." Each word was a bitter slice, hacked out of him. "Tried before."

She knitted her brows. *Before?*

"Alone, once. Couldn't"—he slumped and she got her shoulder under an armpit—"get up . . . the stairs."

He was too heavy to prop upright. She let him sink to the floor.

What an idiot coming out to the lighthouse by himself. Thinking he could climb up here and lick Spot, or something like him, single-handedly. He had no idea.

Sarah got him into a sitting position with his back to the wall.

"Get me . . . down!" he pleaded, looking toward the stairs. Another flare lit up the room, inserting itself between the regular flash of the strobe, then *boom!*

About three seconds. Jesus, the speed of the thing. Sarah couldn't imagine being up in an airplane with this kind of crazy shit going on. Logan started screaming. *Really* screaming. Then he lashed out at her. Not at her specifically, she understood, but at the storm, the pain, the guilt, whatever it was. He was pummeling the air in front of him. Unfortunately, she occupied most of it, but she kept her head down and her body on top of his.

Flash—*boom!*

He was like a caged animal. As a writer, Sarah reflexively rejected trite expressions, but there was no other way to say it.

Flash—*boom!* To Sarah, locked in what felt like hand-to-hand combat, it seemed to go on forever, the psychedelic kaleidoscopic pastiche of blinding white pulses—some on the beat, some syncopated—its musical score violent, frenzied, and deafening.

Logan fought and she hung on grimly, cursing Fate or whatever had thrown them together into the tiny tower room in the middle of a gargantuan nightmare, hoping all the while that she was doing the right thing in keeping him there. But the way through shit was through it. You hit it head-on. She learned that in the Cessna, a little bit when she first got in it and a whole lot more right after the bridge miss.

She prayed Logan was learning that right now, too. She ducked yet again to keep her head from being bowled across the tiny room. Weird, but she found herself a tiny bit jealous of him at that moment, of where he *was*. As miserable as he must have been feeling, he had his hands on Friend of Spot's throat. Wrestling *mano a mano,* hand to . . . paw. And Logan was fighting—she could hear it in the anger and desperation in his cries—giving as good as he got.

The storm gradually spent its fury, and as it did Sarah sensed Spot's buddy accept defeat and lope down the stairs back to the wild. Logan calmed down by degrees until he became a rag doll under her.

Damage assessment. She gently shook him. "Hey."

"Hey, yourself," he croaked, lifting his head. "You look like crap, you know?"

"It's hard work helping a guy deliver a baby." She brushed sweaty tendrils of hair out of her face.

He chuckled. "So this is how it feels?"

"You're asking me?"

"Shit." His head went back down onto the deck. "We ought to get back."

He was completely wiped, Sarah realized. Not that she was feeling exactly peppy at the moment, either. "Let's give it a minute, though, huh?" she suggested.

"Right. And Sarah?"

"Mmmm?"

"Thanks."

"Any time."

She pulled herself in close beside him and closed her eyes just for a minute.

Chapter 19

When Sarah woke up, bright sun was streaming through the windows, catching on the prisms of the Fresnel lens and shooting dancing, colored beams around the room, which nicely complemented the ones inside Sarah's skull. She must have groaned.

"Good morning," Logan said, to the accompaniment of a "scritch-scritch" sound that was obscurely familiar to Sarah.

She gingerly opened her eyes. He was perched cat like on the narrow shelf surrounding the lens, scratching at his jaw. The stubble on his chin glistened reddish gold in the early light. "My mouth feels like the floor of a subway car," Sarah said.

Logan handed her a squirt bottle of now warm water. She rinsed, and realizing there was no place to spit, forced herself to swallow. She levered her aching body up on two elbows. She'd never walk again. The only part of her that wasn't screaming in agony was perhaps the tip of her nose. She scratched it and then sniffed herself. "Whew, I stink. And I really need to pee."

"I just knew sleeping with you would be great," Logan said.

She had nothing to throw at him, unfortunately, and seriously doubted whether she could raise an arm high enough anyway. She flopped back down onto the metal deck. "If I shut my eyes will this all disappear?"

"I tried that last night. It didn't work."

He got up and loomed over her. "C'mon, honey, get up. We're all packed and the bellboy has the suitcases down at the car." He extended his hand. Sarah grabbed it and he pulled her to her feet. Good thing he was there. Otherwise the Tidal public works crew would probably have found her dried-up skeleton right there on the deck when they came in to change the bulb.

They climbed down from their ivory tower. Sarah grudgingly interjected to herself that it was really more of an, okay, dirty-white tower. But that seemed to suit the both of them. They hiked back to their cars and went separate ways for some much needed freshening up. Although Sarah, after the taillights of what passed for a car in Logan's eyes had disappeared behind the sand dunes flanking the parking lot, had dashed back into the brush to take care of some personal business that wouldn't wait for indoor plumbing.

Sarah and Logan met back at the airport at ten o'clock. The morning's lesson went particularly well. To Sarah's delight, Logan finally let her fly south along the coastline almost as far as Boston. From five miles out, she took in the network of runways crisscrossing Logan International Airport. And then a light went off in Sarah's head.

Logan must have picked up on it because without her even opening her mouth he made a weary admission. "Yes, it isn't just a coincidence. That is in fact where my name came from so don't even bother asking."

"Really?" Sarah marveled. At the man or the airport, she wasn't sure. Maybe both.

"Yes. Now watch your heading. I don't want any Nasty-grams from their approach controllers."

She couldn't let it go. "Really . . . ?"

"Just fly the damn plane."

She didn't share with him that she found his exasperation completely endearing. On the northbound leg they toured Salem Harbor, the belching smokestacks at the power plant—the spoilsport wouldn't let her buzz through the smoke chimneys—the beaches along the Swampscott and Lynn shores. She had a chance to remind herself that Marblehead Neck and Nahant really were barrier islands, sculpted by the same hand that had fashioned Pear Island. It was all there and all beautiful.

And then she knew for sure that she'd passed some kind of final exam in Logan's mind. After they'd landed and tax-ied to a stop he said, "There's someone I want you to meet."

Her first thought? *His mother?* Yikes. Then she remem-bered what he had told her in the tower about his mom.

She nevertheless braced herself for the worst and fifteen minutes later they were in Logan's "car" headed north on scenic Route 127.

"Logan, what do you call this thing, anyway?" Meaning his mode of transportation. Sarah tentatively let her forearm down to rest on the cracked vinyl covering of the passenger-side armrest.

"A car."

"No kidding. What *kind*?"

"It's an El Camino."

Sarah laughed. "More like an *Old* Camino." She snorted. She really was hysterically funny sometimes.

Logan looked over, deadpan. "Ha-ha."

"Seriously, Logan. This is well and truly a complete piece of shit." The gummy residue from—Sarah peered closer—*some*thing malingered in one of the cup holders. "It ought to be condemned."

Logan just pointed to the inspection sticker on the corner of the windshield.

"But still," Sarah said, "big wheel like you? Shouldn't you be driving some honking SUV something or other with 'Noah Crossly Airport blah, blah, blah' blazed onto the side?"

As soon as the words left her mouth, Sarah felt the sting. There it was. The Thing Between Them. The pin that could let the air out of a perfectly good day. Or a perfectly good lay, for that matter. But it was more than that. Or could be. What the hell was she talking about, anyway?

"Maybe I'll just shut up now," she said.

"Maybe that'd be a good idea," Logan said, without rancor.

Delightful vistas beckoned on the right as the Atlantic played peek a boo behind the old trees and expensive houses that lined the ocean side of the roadway. Sarah had her hand out the passenger window of the Camino, surfing the airstream with her palm, when Logan asked her what she was doing.

"An informal investigation into the aeronautical action of moving air across the surface of an airfoil," she said.

"No, really, what are you doing?"

She laughed. Playing with him in a nice way was so great. "Oh, nothing. I was just wondering what it might be like to be a bird. Having your own wings, feeling the air rushing over your body? In complete control of yourself hundreds of feet up in the air?"

At that moment, with her hair blowing in the slipstream, a goofy smile on her face, and the ring of one of Logan's rare spontaneous laughs in her ears, she felt like a little kid again. What happened to people as they got older anyhow? She had a very sophisticated theory about that: somehow layers of crud built up over what was essentially the very simple business of living. She suddenly appreciated how sad the boy in *Polar Express* must have felt when he realized that even his sister could no longer hear the sound of the First Bell of Christmas. Beth, Sarah thought, could still hear it. She always would.

"Actually, I don't think I've ever thought about being up in the air without an airplane under me," Logan said. "But I'll tell you, you want to feel as close to a bird as you can without growing tail feathers? I'd love to hook up with another Pitt and—"

"I'm all ears," she said. *Go for it*, she silently urged. He was walking right up to *it*.

But, like herself in the Cessna, he'd traveled too far, too fast. He clammed right up. "Well, maybe not a Pitt, but something else. I'll think about it."

Sarah quickly changed the subject. "So tell me. Your place is up this way, right? You must have millions secretly stashed to live around here." She gestured out the window at a stucco mansion with generations-old climbing ivy and a red-tiled roof sliding by to starboard.

"Oh, yeah. Didn't I tell you? My other car's a Ferrari. I just use this heap when I want to drive like an asshole."

"I'll bet. Although I must say I appreciate your staying under the legal limit."

"See? I can be thoughtful."

A few more miles and he slowed and pulled off Route 127 and onto a gravel drive. "Here we are," he said. "Home sweet home."

Sarah gasped. "Cripes, Logan. Are you running drugs or something?"

The narrow roadway opened to a circular drive that led to a porte cochere attached to the largest shingle-style Queen Anne house cum mansion that Sarah had ever seen outside of a design magazine. Towers, turrets, columns, fish-scale shingles. It even had little eyebrow windows let into the roof.

"Don't get your hopes up," Logan said, veering off the drive just before the house. "Old friend of my grandfather— I just recently found *that* out—lives in the main house. Down back here is really an ideal spot for me." He squeezed the El Camino between two stone pillars and onto a road with two well-worn wheel ruts and a crown of grass gone to seed. Stones pinged off the undercarriage of the vehicle as it negotiated the steep grade.

"The royalty lives back there," he said, doing a poor imitation of a Cockney accent while tossing his thumb back over his shoulder. "But us commoners live"—the car gave a lurch as they broke from under the lush cover of overhanging ornamentals and bounced between a gap in a border of tall poplars—"here."

"Here" was a decrepit, landlocked cabin cruiser sunning itself up on blocks.

Sarah was speechless. A rarity, yes, she could admit. But, jeepers . . . "Oh, how . . . nice. You live on . . . sort of a . . . boat?"

"It's not sort of a boat. It *is* a boat. Only it doesn't float. At least, not anymore."

"How . . . interesting."

"Not exactly the swinging bachelor pad you expected, eh?"

She didn't know how to break it gently to him that she had never really thought of him as a swinging bachelor. More like a very grumpy old man decades from retirement.

"No, not exactly. But anyway, that's not the main reason we're here, right?"

"Ah, yes: Gertrude." The person he wanted her to meet was named *Gertrude?* Not his mother, alas. Then an alarming picture formed in her mind's eye: Maybe Logan'd done a Norman Bates sort of thing with her up in the main house. No. Too much late-night TV on her part.

Gertrude. A maiden aunt, then, perhaps?

"Oh, boy are you gonna be surprised," he said, throwing the Camino into Park and killing the ignition.

Oh, boy, she hoped not.

"Hey, I know," he said excitedly, coming around to Sarah's side of the car and wrenching open the protesting passenger door. "Close your eyes and I'll lead you to the surprise. You'll get a better first impression that way. Okay?"

This was the guy she trusted with her life in the air? But, then again, how could she refuse? He was like a little kid showing off his new bike.

"Ah, Logan . . . I'm not sure I . . ." She got out of the car slowly. He still had the maniacally expectant grin on his face. She sighed. "Oh, all right. Yes, you can lead me to the surprise." *There's a good boy.*

Sarah shut her eyes and held out her hand, waggling the fingers. "You wouldn't let me walk off the end of a pier or anything just to be funny, now, would you? I mean, I'd really have to kill you if you did that," she said, entirely pleasantly, but meaning every word.

He sniffed sanctimoniously. "No trust. You've been hurt before, haven't you?" Sarah stuck her tongue out. "Kidding, kidding. On with the tour," he said, like an emcee.

He led her down a slope and across the crispy, broad-bladed kind of salt grass that grows ubiquitously along the ocean's edge. The footing changed to smooth stone steps, then sand. They ventured across a creaking, swaying metal gangway, finally ending up on rough planking.

"Okay," he announced, "open your eyes."

Sarah blinked in the dazzling light reflecting off water.

"Well," he said, "meet Gertrude."

"Oh, my . . ." Again, speechless. Logan seemed to have a knack of doing that to her.

It was an airplane. Not the snazzy, sleek-looking machine that you might have expected from a guy like, well, Logan. Not at all. This was winged water sprite. She—no question in Sarah's mind on the feminine denotation—rocked gently on the calm surface of a protected cove carved into the granite ledges of the Manchester shoreline. The airplane nuzzled the fenders of her finger float.

Sarah watched her palms press themselves to her face in a very un-Sarah-like way. Like a gesture one of her aunts might make right before she pinched Sarah's cheeks and kissed her. Sarah realized she was that delighted. "Logan, she's absolutely adorable!"

"Aw, I'll bet you tell that to all the floatplanes," he said, but he looked pleased.

Sarah drifted closer to the amazing . . . what? *Machine* wasn't right. *Airplane* didn't begin to describe it. *Creature*, she settled on. Tentatively, she reached up and brushed her fingertips along the bottom of a wide sheltering wing. Beneath her caress, the metal felt warm and somehow . . . alive, as if the shiny aluminum belonged to a sentient entity that responded to touch. She stroked it again. Maybe an eddy bumped against the old girl's dock right then, but darn it if the wing didn't seem to quiver. Sarah half expected it to curl up cartoon fashion and gather her into its gentle embrace.

Reluctantly, Sarah broke the contact and stepped back to

take in Gertrude's entire length. She was something out of an old black-and-white war movie, rescuing downed aviators ditched at sea. Kind of an airborne version of a benevolent Saint Bernard minus the keg of brandy.

Her dimensions weren't that much larger than the Cessna 150's, but this gently bobbing bird was solid and substantial. Twin engines mounted above the wing, pontoons on struts suspended below. Her best feature was her nose. People often said that about Sarah, which she never really understood. Gertrude's was upswept like the front of a boat. In fact, the whole front section of the plane was sculpted into a serene, dolphin-like grin.

Actually—Sarah backed up and tilted her head critically—Gertrude's expression kind of reminded Sarah of Dr. Loo's enigmatic smile. Sarah wondered if Logan would let her have a bronze likeness of Gertrude cast for the coffee table. Sarah laughed and clapped her hands. As if she owned a coffee table. "Logan, this is too much. She's an absolute doll."

Logan desperately aimed for nonchalance as he stuffed his hands in the back pockets of his shorts and bobbed on his toes.

"She's enough to make any woman in your life jealous, you know," Sarah said, teasing. "Any other female would always take a backseat to this gal."

He made a pretense of scowling, but the plane obviously meant a lot to him and Sarah thought he was glad that she'd taken a shine to Gertrude so quickly. Again, the mental balance sheets Sarah had been grinding out on Logan didn't tally anymore. Him and this darling old plane? It was like finding out a known mobster gave Sunday organ recitals at a little old ladies' home.

Sarah watched Logan do some more hands-in-the-pocket

action, this time stuffing the front ones. She wondered what the The Good Doctor would make of it all. Logan sidled up beside her.

Sarah asked him, "Do you have to go to the bathroom?"

"What?"

"You're jiggling."

"Sorry." He cut his glance tentatively toward her then slid it possessively back to Gertrude. "Want the rest of the tour?" He was *really* excited.

"Definitely. But, Logan, how did you"—"get her" seemed like the wrong phrase—"meet her?" Sarah could see a creature like this was never really bought by anyone. You never really *owned* it in the usual sense of the word. You ended up with a Gertrude in your life the same way you came home from a shelter with a particular cat: it picked you.

"She was a mail-order bride," he said, smiling.

"I . . . ?" Sarah tried to make her expression something other than completely blank.

"From a picture in a magazine," he explained. "It was love at first sight. She's what's called a Widgeon. Baby sister in the famous Grumman Flying Boat line. Her older siblings were the Goose, the Mallard, and a really gigantic old dame called an Albatross. I was reading an article about World War Two amphibious aircraft in *Flight* magazine and, *voila*, there she was."

"But how did you know she was available?"

"Because she was rusting away on the top of a pile of scrapped B-twenty-fives in an aircraft graveyard in Arizona."

"Oh, how sad . . ." Sarah patted the fuselage just below the cockpit windows. "Poor baby, yes . . ." Call her crazy. She never got attached to flesh-and-blood critters that easily.

"She's a certified veteran of World War Two rescue and reconnaissance missions too numerous to mention," he continued. "Some people think her matronly lines are ugly, but I like to think of her as 'utilitarian.'"

"Cute, even."

"No, *not* cute. Utilitarian. Built for comfort, not for speed. She is not cute."

"Men. Ugh. It always comes down to a female's shape."

"You just kill yourself, don't you?"

"That's it, all right." Sarah stood on tiptoes and peered into the cockpit through the big Plexiglas side windows. Dual controls up front, another couple seats in back, and plenty of room toward the tail for cargo. "Boost me up," she said, wiggling her fingers behind her.

Logan fished his hands out of his pockets and came over. He laced his fingers together. He stooped down and paused. Sarah glanced back expectantly. He seemed to be making a detailed study of the pockets on the rear of her shorts; then—and this is the best way she found to describe it—he made a noise like *harrumph!*

Now, in her experience only old guys "harrumphed." Her grandfather was a harrumpher, the little she remembered of him, and he did it when he was flustered. Which was a lot of the time.

So Logan was flustered. Why?

"Er, I've got a better idea," he said, a little too quickly. "Let's just hop in."

"This is so exciting," Sarah said, meaning it. Her feet were dancing *her* around the float. "Oh, please, please can I have the keys and take her for a spin?" she heard herself beg. "Pretty please?"

"Yeah. Sure. Just get in, okay?" He held open the fuselage door and made a big deal of appearing not to look at her as she contorted herself through the narrow hatch, but she felt his attention nonetheless. Once inside, she made her way in a semicrouch through the passenger seats and forward into the cockpit. Out of habit, she slid into the right-hand seat.

"Move over," Logan said. She felt his touch on her shoulder. His fingers were sun warmed.

"What?"

"Get in the other seat."

She scooted over and he plopped himself in the copilot's chair.

"You're letting me drive?" she asked, incredulous.

"Do I look that crazy?"

"So you're gonna take her up from that side, huh? So cool." She was literally shaking.

"Uh-huh, absolutely. I'm gonna take her up right now, right this minute. No preflight, nothing." He snorted. "You *are* nuts."

"Boy, no sense of adventure."

Logan snapped back at her. "For God's sake, I figured you as having more brains than that. Haven't you learned anything about safety? You can't just go traipsing off into the wild blue yonder without a preflight check. Without—oh, I don't know—a *flight plan*?"

What got *him* so cranky all of a sudden? Sarah pretended it didn't bother her. She flashed him a smile. "Relax, I'm just yanking your chain. Don't get all excited." Like she was.

The control yoke beckoned. Sarah gently torqued it side to side. Gertrude answered with a faint shudder and squished a fender against the dock. *Squeak.* A surge of excitement rippled from her toes to her scalp. She reached out, gripped the twin throttles, and whooped for the sheer joy of it.

"What?" Logan asked, looking at her like she'd lost her mind.

"No one but my dad knows this," she said, remembering nights as a kid when she'd stayed up way past her bedtime in his shadowed study, "but know what my favorite TV show was when I was a kid?"

"I can't imagine."

"Reruns of *Twelve O'Clock High*."

"No way."

"Way. Now, sitting here, in Gertrude like this? Man, I'm in the show. What a treat, Logan. Thank you." She reached over and squeezed his hand. He flopped his hand around, bumping hers, but he didn't squeeze back.

"No problem. It's . . . uh . . . want to turn her over?"

"By that I presume you *don't* mean capsize Gertie, right?"

Logan laughed, a little too loudly, Sarah thought.

"I mean spin the props," he said. "Not start her up or anything. I like to reserve that for when I'm actually heading out. You know, spare the neighbors and all that. Gertrude's a love, but she's loud."

"I can just imagine," Sarah said. "We used to go watch air shows up at Hanscom Field. You know, in New Hampshire?" Of course he knew. "The noise of the jets was terrifying. But thrilling in another way, too. Like the people flying the planes were doing something big and important and I wanted to do something like that, too. Anyway, what do I do now?"

"First check your fuel switches."

She scanned the instrument panel. "Where are they?"

"You find them."

She systematically toured the myriad of dials, buttons, and gadgets set into the instrument bank. The Cessna panel was about as complicated as a microwave's compared to Gertrude's overwhelming array. On the third scan she still hadn't found what she needed. Logan pointed up.

Overhead, on a console protruding from the ceiling, were the fuel switches, clearly labeled.

Gotcha. "They're off," she said. "Check magnetos, too?"

He nodded. "You're getting it."

She couldn't keep the smile off her face.

"Mags off," she said. Several silent seconds passed. "Logan? Did you hear me?"

"Um, yep. Fuel off."

"No. I said the mags were off."

"Oh. Right."

She looked at him. He was beet red. "You all right?"

"Uh-huh. Fine. Clear right and left," he said. "She's a twin engine, remember."

"No—really?" Sarah said.

He frowned. "You'd be surprised how many people forget basic things like how many engines they've got. They'll be flying along and have one engine go dead because they forgot to switch the fuel feed to the other side."

She had done it again. "Once again, Logan, I am sorry," she said formally, lightly touching the back of his hand. That seemed to be becoming a habit for her. All of a sudden, *whabam!* her hand would be out there before her mind knew she'd moved it. "I keep making fun of you when you're actually telling me really important stuff. I do listen, just so you know. It all gets filed away even though it might not seem like it."

"Okay, okay. Let's keep going," he said.

Testy. She twisted around in her seat for a quick peek out the side window toward the open ocean. The relatively narrow cove entrance, carved out of the sheer Manchester cliffs by eons of sea action, restricted the view, but she spied whitecaps. A thirty-something-foot sloop was beating upwind, close hauled, probably trying to hit Misery or Baker's Island on one long tack. As she leaned to get a last look, she felt a slender, silky strap slip down her right shoulder. When she turned to fix it, she discovered Logan in deep contemplation of it. She looked herself. She had to admit that the purple satin contrasted nicely with the tanned, round little ball of her shoulder muscle. Hey, she worked hard to stay in shape. That earned you every stare you got.

Sarah pretended not to notice Logan noticing. She looked past him to the right wing and hiked the strap back up.

When she finally met his gaze, she was struck anew by how intensely green his eyes could become. The irises were huge, like saucers again, like a cat's when it's tracking something. He was trying not to show it, but he was edgy and intense.

Hell, so was she. Meeting Gertrude had gotten her juices going and now she and Logan were *again* jammed together in a tiny space. She was suddenly intensely aware that Gertrude's engines weren't the only things she badly wanted to spin.

But tough luck. Been there, done that—incinerated her front door—and Logan had backed down. Thank God, probably. And that night at the lighthouse? Tension, danger, self-revelation did weird things to people. Foxhole sex, almost. Damn the storm.

So once again she stashed the Logan fantasies deep within the nestled cluster of drawers she kept next to Spot's water dish. At least where his water dish *used* to be. She had a lot of respect for Logan now; she could finally say that. Especially after the tower deal. And despite the rock-hard floor of the beacon room, she'd had a great night's sleep next to him. And she thought he finally respected her. He wouldn't have brought her to see his baby otherwise.

This respect stuff was all good, albeit frustratingly platonic. But she wasn't going to risk messing things up just for the sake of some stupid, casual, completely spontaneous and uninhibited—enough! Her imagination had overflowed its container like a stopped-up sink.

Oh, also—lest she forget in light of Logan's recently revealed charms—the cautiously developing roadway known as Their Relationship was inching inexorably toward an abrupt termination at a cul de sac called The Second Runway. There was no getting past the one, simple fact that Logan wanted to destroy something she loved. No, that wasn't strictly true. He felt *honor bound* to do something that would eventually destroy what she loved. What did motives really play into it when all was said and done, though? Whatever the reason, the inescapable bottom line was that the preserve would be history.

Any way you sliced or diced it, getting caught up in Logan's traffic pattern would make for all-around dangerous flying.

At the moment, however, he appeared to be very interested in hers. That was a puzzler. She was cantankerous and argumentative, only *metsa-metsa* looking—except for her oft-complimented nose, of course—and had given him more crap in the few short weeks he'd known her than he'd probably ever gotten from all the women he'd ever dated in his life put together.

Yet he'd been gawking at her bra strap like some pizza-faced kid in a coed health class. She seriously hoped he didn't have a thing for women's underwear. But enough with the speculation.

"So, we ready here or not?" Sarah asked. She was chomping at the bit to see Gertie do her tricks. "I found the starter switch."

Me, too, she thought she heard Logan mumble. Again, she hated mumblers. "What?"

"Nothing."

"Still clear, then?" she barked. A tone of command had crept into her voice. *God, she loved this shit!*

"Clear," he said. Then, "Hit 'em, Captain."

She took a deep breath and stabbed both ignition switches.

Gertie coughed and shuddered. Sarah looked up through the big canopy windows toward the huge engines mounted on the wings just above and to either side of the cockpit. The props kicked over like upturned bicycle wheels rotated by hand, spun freely, but hinting at their true power. Sarah was intoxicated. The cylinders were patiently waiting for but a breath of fuel and touch of spark and they'd explode into life.

Of course, Logan would let her give them neither. And she wasn't sure she'd dare to even if he gave her the okay. But just to see them free spin . . . It thrilled her to the marrow. She let up on the starters and the blades wound down.

"Whoa . . ." Awesome. A throwaway word through no fault of its own, but in this case it was completely right. "That's about the best time you could have with your clothes—ah, I mean, in a tethered airplane."

"I don't know," Logan said. He had a truly goofy smile on and he was watching her with those cat eyes again. She swore she felt him insinuate himself into her thoughts. "I've never flown without clothes."

"Pervert," Sarah said, amiably. She relaxed her neck and let her head come to rest against the high seat back.

They sat there for a while longer, as Gertie swayed in the tide and gently nuzzled the dock, not speaking, but Sarah didn't feel they had to either. She was moved to occasionally brush her fingers over some part of the cockpit array. The ancient Bakelite knobs on the instrument panel were especially fascinating. To think that the stuff had disappeared from use decades before either she or Logan had been born. Sitting there, she was caught up in a time warp.

She was the first to break radio silence.

"Ah, Logan, this has been so marvelous. I *get* this whole thing, now." She gestured around the cabin. "The flying, I mean. The thrill of being up there."

"Once it hooks you, you're done for," he agreed.

"I see that now. Once I lost the fear." She turned in her seat to face him. "You know, Preston Lewis really sucked."

Logan cracked up.

"What are you laughing at?"

He doubled over, snorting and having a grand old time. She smacked him on the arm. "What, for God's sake?"

He pounded his chest and coughed. "Say what you feel, you know?" he said, gasping. "Oh, boy." He wiped his eyes with the back of his hand. "But yes, yes, I agree."

She'd never seen him laugh so hard.

But she couldn't let go of the bone. "Preston never really understood me. No, that sounds stupid and whiny. What I mean is, he never really just let me be *me*, you know? I wasn't chicken to go up; I was just really afraid. There's a difference."

That sent Logan over the edge. He completely devolved *again*.

"Logan, stop it." She was indignant. The man was a puddle. "I'm trying to make a point here. Please, stop."

"I know, I know," he said, pleading. "Seriously, I'm trying to." He gulped. "Okay, okay, there." He sat up straight and wrapped his hands around the control yoke on his side of the cockpit as if to steady himself. "Remember, I'm not laughing at you; I'm laughing *with* you."

She was not impressed.

"Put that eyebrow down," he said. "Go ahead, I want to know, really."

She tried to frame how she felt. "It's just that I had to be a mess before I got better, you know? I just needed time to work through all that crap from crashing when I was a kid. I think I could be really good."

Logan squirmed in his seat and said something she didn't catch.

"What? Don't mumble," she said, gritting her teeth. "*God*, I hate mumblers. You obviously want to say something, so go ahead."

"I'll bet you'd be good," he said. "A good pilot, I mean."

And she thought she was the whack job. "Are you feeling okay, Logan? You've been strange ever since we got here."

"And how is that any different from the rest of the time?"

She was lost. Her copy of the script must have lost a page.

He said, "Anyway, what I mean is that I wouldn't have let many students take over the plane after they almost downed us."

"And that means what?"

"Just that you're a good—could be good—" He stopped and got this really weird look on his face. Like he was an ant frying up under a magnifying glass. "Come on, let's get out of here."

"No," she said, laying a restraining hand on his arm. "Not until you tell me what's going on."

But he was intent on ending the conversation. He gently but firmly pushed her arm aside and rose. Exasperated, Sarah swung into the narrow space between the chairs at the same time but forgot about the step-down. She tripped over her own feet and her legs tangled with his. They crashed lengthwise into the aisle and Sarah landed on top of him.

"Ow . . . You've got a head like a rock," she said. She pushed off his chest and rubbed her forehead. "Jeez." Then she noticed Logan looked to be in some kind of distress.

"Oh, you all right?"

"Oof—"

"What? Speak up!"

"Ungh—" He pointed frantically.

Her knee was driven into his anatomy just south of the belt line, robbing him of coherent speech.

"Oh! Sorry. That better?"

He sucked in air and gingerly rolled her partway off him. "God, you were busting my . . . never minds."

"Again, sorry. Better now?"

He swallowed and his eyes refocused. "Barely."

Sarah grinned down at him. Her position had a lot to recommend it. "So now that I have you at my mercy—" She shifted her leg a fraction, just to show him who was boss. He grimaced. She shocked even her*self* at times. "Now you can appreciate how I feel when my instructor is not very . . . forthcoming about my capabilities." She wriggled her hips. Why? She didn't really know. But it felt terrific.

"Yes, I can see how you, uh, feel."

With the length of her lower body pressed tightly against him, he had little choice. Not that Sarah heard him complaining. She felt his lack of complaint hard against her leg.

"Experiencing a little turbulence, Captain?" *Stop now*, she told herself. Her self didn't listen. "Hmm?" She brought her face directly over his. "So give . . . how am I doing?"

"I think you're doing . . . great," he said, his breath ragged.

He stretched his neck up and whispered against her lips, "I think you're doing just great."

"Oh, yeah?" she whispered back, touching her nose to his. Hey, it was just noses. Eskimos did that stuff all the time.

"Yeah. And you'll probably get even better with a little more experience," he said, gently brushing his lips against hers.

Breaker, breaker, we have contact . . . "You're a pig," she said, without malice. She increased the pressure of their lips. Same lips she'd kissed one evening at her front door. Nothing new. And at the top of the lighthouse. Old ground.

"Oink. I meant as a pilot," he murmured. "Experience as a pilot."

"Yeah, right."

He hadn't shaved since the lighthouse, either, lazy bugger, but she loved the rasp of his beard on her fingertips and the touch of his hands on her cheeks. For breathless moments, a snapshot of the last few amazing weeks fluttered through her mind: Logan after her lesson with Preston Lewis. The wheel of the Cessna, his hands resting lightly on it. Her in tears trying to hold level flight while Spot lunged at her throat. The bridge reaching for them. The pullout, the toast. The thrill of his hands on her breasts last night in the tower.

To Sarah it seemed they remained connected for an eternity but in reality it was probably only seconds, lips barely touching, the narrow space between them filled with portent and promise, dilemma and disappointment.

Squeak. One of Gertrude's fenders.

She broke away first this time, her breath short and quick. Logan gazed up at her, cradling her face in his wide, warm palms.

"Crap," she said. "This complicates things, doesn't it?"

"No, this is fine, I think," he said, surprising her. "I don't get it, but it's fine. It's amazing, actually. It's you being my student that complicates things."

"What about the preserve?"

"I'm not backing down on the runway."

"I know that. I'm just saying. And what about the article? That's not going away either."

"Understood. But one thing at a time, okay? First, you're not my student anymore."

"Okay." They kissed enthusiastically to seal the deal.

"Mmmm, I love graduations," she said. "Do we shake hands or something now?"

"Or something . . ." He raised his head for another smooch. He swept his palms down her rib cage and encircled her waist.

She shivered like the temperature had dropped twenty degrees. His touch was glorious. Then she stiffened.

He looked at her quizzically.

"It's not you," she said, unsteadily. She kissed him again, hard and deep. To think some people drink to forget. She pitied them. "Oh, God"—she couldn't catch up to her breath—"it's not you . . ."

It was Rick.

In typical Sarah fashion, she'd left her options open, stayed flexible. Read: *done nothing*. Now, in her rush to escape from a burning building—or maybe to fling herself into one—she was ensnared in all the dangly little loose ends. Poised on the threshold of the future, she was hog-tied by her past. Dr. Loo had warned her it would come to this. Joan, too, for that matter, and her services were free.

She couldn't tell Logan what she was thinking. "It's just that"—she forced herself to go through with the lie—"Gertrude's watching. You know?"

He laughed. "I do. Gertie's a dear, but I'm about as comfortable doing this here as I would be in my mother's parlor. But there's a problem: I can't stay in this holding pattern forever." He wiggled telegraphically beneath her.

An iron pipe, warm and wonderful, pressed against her thigh. It got more difficult to remain focused on Rick. There was nothing like a joystick to get a girl's mind off her troubles. She giggled into Logan's neck.

"What?"

"Nothing. It's just that I never realized how many opportunities for double entendres the field of aviation offered."

"Huh?"

"Double entendres. Plays on words. Like *the stick*. Or *cockpit*." She squirmed against him to make her point—and to feel his.

Logan groaned and pulled her closer. With her mind's eye

she grabbed one quick last look at Rick—at a photo of the two of them, actually—she had carried in her wallet for a long time. They were leading a flotilla of canoes down the Allagash Waterway, way the hell up in Maine. Rick was paddling the lead boat, her just behind in another, both of them aping for the camera. It had worked then.

Key word: *then*.

She refocused on Logan's face. Reason waned; Want became Need; the rest was history. They plunged over the falls together.

She insinuated a hand between their bodies and lightly traced his hard length with her fingertips. Logan hissed in a sharp breath, looked at her for a long moment, then, as if a decision had been made, slid his palms up the outside of her shirt to just beneath the curve of her breasts. He stretched his thumbs to tease the peaks through the thin fabric of her bra.

"You say anything about 'high beams' and I'll trade my hand for my knee," Sarah murmured, searching for the tip of Logan's tongue with hers.

"No, ma'am. Never. Besides that'd be more in the automotive field, ma'am, an area I am less than familiar with . . ." He made a quick grab with his teeth and captured the prize.

Her eyelids drooped. Then, somehow, Logan had gotten his hands underneath her bra and was reconnoitering the hilly terrain. He seemed to become instantly familiar with the unique features of the area. "Gaahd, Log . . . ung . . ."

"Sorry?"

She wasn't, but who had the mumbles now? Her lips felt too heavy to work right. Sarah felt Logan do some kind of magic thing with her nipples, and her back arched of its own free will. She felt herself turn to taffy. Daffy taffy. *Good grief . . .*

"Logan. Stop. Oh, God . . . not here. Where can we go?" There was a plea in her voice.

"The boat . . ." he said.

A boat? Take one out to sea? "No!" It would take too long to get far enough away from shore. "I mean, God, I want you"—she gritted her teeth—*"right now."* Although feeling the ocean swell beneath them as Logan did likewise inside her did have a certain appeal. She tugged on the front of his shorts and a quiet snap rewarded her efforts.

"Not on the ocean, you nut," he said, panting. "The boat I live in. Where we parked."

Ah, yes. The cabin cruiser.

Good thinking. *In a minute.* She tugged his shirt to up above his pectorals and ran her hands across his chest, kissing his nipples. She nipped at what little extra skin there was around his navel.

"Uh-huh . . . the boat . . . could work . . ." she said between mouthfuls. She ran her tongue along his abdomen just above the waistband of his shorts. Then she went for broke and insinuated a hand up one leg hole.

"Now," Logan gasped, "must go *now."*

"Mmmuf . . ." she said. Her lips were busy against the straining hardness she'd discovered with her mouth. She nibbled away and blew hot breath through the tautly stretched fabric. He liked that, she realized. A lot. That made two of them. She blew again.

"Aagh—" Logan pushed her away and rolled Sarah gently from beneath him. "Now . . . come on . . . now . . ." he said. Their vocabulary was regressing.

"I'm with ya," she told him. God, she was *so* ready.

Good *God*, ready, ready, ready. Ready, set, *go!*

Logan rose and hauled her up with him, then hastily straightened her top. That simple gesture, of him putting her back together for the short hop to his place, took her completely apart. Any lingering reservations she had about him vanished in a puff of affection, appreciation, and take-me-now-before-I-gnaw-my-fucking-hand-off lust. Rick *who?*

Never, *ever* in her whole life had she felt like she did right then about any guy.

The man in front of her was a raging river to be run. You strapped on your helmet, cinched up your life jacket, and tossed your kayak into the flow. He wasn't for the faint of heart. But, oh, what a ride!

She couldn't keep her hands off the long muscles of his back as they made their way between the passenger seats.

He was a breathless free fall, the biggest bungee jump in the world. And she just couldn't wait to jump him. She pinched his tight little behind. Laughing, he reached back and captured her hand.

He was a great big, tantalizing box of white chocolate bricks with almonds. She *had* to pop the lid. She slid her free hand along the inside of his thigh on the way out the cabin door. Then around to the front for a quick, preflight check.

"Don't—" He shoved her hand away and tugged her out the cabin door into the bright sunshine. "Keep that up and we'll get premature liftoff."

She laughed and he started up the gangway first, pulling her along behind. With a whoop she leapt onto his back. He grabbed her ankles and she dug in with her knees, her arms locked around his neck. "Giddyup!" She slapped him on the rear end and started a not-so-gentle suction on his neck.

"I can't believe you," he said between pants as he took the ramp in giant steps.

"Me neither," Sarah said, mumbled by flesh. She was only dimly aware of the crunch of gravel beneath his feet, engaged as she was. However, she did take time to appreciate the firm, flexing haunches of her steed as he vigorously mounted the stairs. Would that he did same to her, *pronto*.

She came up for air and realized they were at the front door—front *hatch?*—of his boat-slash-house.

Logan threw their weight against it and it abruptly gave way. They tumbled inside together.

Chapter 20

Fortunately for them, the floor—or did one say deck?—was carpeted. Logan kicked the door shut, then his mouth descended on Sarah's.

Things happened fast after that. They made short work of their clothes, and then Logan became completely still.

Sarah prayed he wouldn't stop. She couldn't take another replay of the front hall scene.

He just held her. She slowly realized he was giving her every chance to reconsider. There was so much keeping us apart, she thought then. And Logan knew it. The preserve, the article, Rick. She suddenly understood there was no turning back for Logan once they took the next step. He was a military man, trained for missions, accustomed to putting his life on the line to achieve an objective. And now here he was, poised above her, throttle fire walled, standing on the brakes, waiting for the go-ahead to catapult.

And *she* was his objective. He was putting everything he had on the line for *her*. His eyes were clear and deep, like windows to his soul. Finally to know what that phrase meant.

He wanted *her.* Over all others. He had seen her slathered in boogies, half hysterical. Witnessed her egotistical pride and her self-centeredness at its worst. And still he wanted *her.*

Her eyes filled.

What a clown she was, degrading the great love scene into a leaky, salty mess. Logan wiped away a wet track on her cheek with the ball of his thumb. And still he waited.

Then she understood that it was the bridge deal all over again. Logan wasn't going to let her off easy by taking charge of where they were about to go. She had to get there under her own power. She felt truly lucky he'd be traveling with her. Next to her. Not ahead or behind, but next to her, right into the fire. But she had to fly her own plane.

Again she wept, like an idiot. Logan held her.

Opening her blurry eyes an eternity later, Sarah found his eyes. They were chock full of riches. The mat of hair on his bare chest called to her. She plowed her fingers slowly through it. She pulled him greedily onto her, heart to heart, heat to heat.

He buried his face in her hair, nibbled her earlobes, trailed kisses. A gentle nip on her neck. Then lower. And lower still. He was through waiting.

Ooooh! He'd gone right to the heart of the matter and he was breathing heat right through the last thing left between them: her best, silkiest, pastel panties. Subconsciously, she'd made a good call that morning.

"Mmmm . . . ugh!" she babbled. Inconsequential nothings, urging him on, the threads of need gathering deep in her belly.

He rolled off the last scrap of her clothing, torturous millimeters at a time, all the while brushing back the downy hair with facile fingers, suckling the swollen folds with inquisitive lips, finally settling in to tease the very most sensitive center of her with an astonishingly nimble tongue.

A whorl of sensation centered where his busy mouth met her. A raging torrent built, surged, then burst to overrun all rational thought in an intense, unstoppable deluge.

When her strength came back, Sarah pulled Logan's hips toward her. Her hand curled around him like a lover of years, stroked him, felt his pulse jump under her fingertips. She moved lower and teased him with her mouth. Finally a chance to return the exquisite pleasure he'd given her, twice now, asking nothing in return. When he was gasping, incoherent, unable to stand more, he abruptly pulled away. They kissed with lips that tasted of each other.

"Now," Sarah said, her breath in his mouth, suckling his tongue.

He settled himself between her thighs. She shifted her hips, brushing his hardness between her swollen folds. He groaned and slowly inched forward into the velvet. She stroked his buttocks with her heels. He popped completely inside.

His whole body went rigid then and Sarah watched a magical change come over his face. The shutters in his eyes, drawn even in the brightest of times, suddenly flew open. He became newly minted, glowing from within.

The enormity of the power she wielded over this man inside her was staggering. Power he freely imparted. Power to heal, to reassemble his scattered parts. She squeezed him tightly, intimately, and was rewarded with a smile of such lust and longing that she began to set the tempo of the lovemaking.

Infinitely gentle at first. Slow movements with tender caresses. Reaching to stroke the globes that bumped gently against her as they rocked.

Somewhere along the way her careful choreography fell

off the beat as she subtly passed from incredulous observer to fully involved participant. Logan must have known she'd watched his demons flee, because she felt what she could only envision as a message written in searing white light, passing swiftly from him to her: *You are mine.*

Every nerve in her body rejoiced. Joy stole her control and bore her up and away on angel's wings. From then on she existed in a world of pure sensation: breathtaking plunges, soaring updrafts. Clear air, open spaces, endless blue vistas. They flew so high and so fast that they shattered the sound barrier.

Their world exploded in a million glittering pieces.

Chapter 21

"*Aye carumba . . .*" Logan said sleepily, his breath tickling Sarah's shoulder.

Sarah was stroking the back of his neck, fingering the hair at the nape, trying to brand the feel of him into her memory.

Because she was already disconnecting.

Logan got himself up onto one elbow. "What's wrong?"

Staring off into space after making love is always a tip-off to one's lover. "It was beautiful, Logan. It really was," she said.

"But what?"

"But nothing. Don't ruin it by picking it apart." She sat up and hugged her knees. Nature had screwed with her royally. Hope made you do stupid things.

"Tell me I'm wrong," Logan said. "Tell me you *don't* want to run for cover right now."

Sarah reached for her shirt and tugged it on.

"Question answered," he said. "Shit."

"Logan . . ."

"Tell me it isn't true."

Sarah waved vaguely. "The ball is over, Logan. It's midnight. The coach is changing back into a pumpkin. I have to go back to the scullery. You've got to go back to your . . . enchanted airfield."

"Sarah, this isn't a fucking fairy tale." Logan sat all the way up. "We've got differences, sure. But we can work them out."

"Really? You think so?" Her tone was cruel. "That's hormones talking. Yours and mine. Don't listen to them. That's what got me here in the first place."

"And where exactly is that?"

"Sitting bare ass on your floor. Turn your back." She hiked on her panties and shorts and stuffed her bra in a pocket. "It's just that this is so damn sad, Logan, you know? *We're* so damn sad."

"Uh, just give a few minutes, here. To recharge. I can go again."

"Logan . . . please."

"I know, I know. The shit between us." He sighed. A very heavy one. "What the hell ever drew us together in the first place?"

"I don't know. It's way too . . . Joan."

"Say what?"

"Joan. My best friend." For a few glorious minutes Sarah had had the crazy notion that Logan could become her *best,* best friend. "She believes in predestiny. Karmic loops? Fate? Call it what you will."

"Ah," he said, like he understood, but she didn't think he really did.

"Sarah, all I know is that I hadn't felt anything—I mean I was *dead* inside—in an airplane since the accident. And up until I met you, I didn't think I'd ever feel anything again anywhere on this planet, either. But when I saw you getting in with fucking Preston Lewis, and I saw what you were trying to do, a little bit of it—the way I remembered *I* used to feel—came back to me, you know? Something moved around inside me—I don't pretend to get it—but that's what it felt like."

So maybe he did understand.

He looked up to see if she was listening. To every word. But her ear was all she had left to give him.

"The time I spent with the Air Force shrinks before I was discharged? Never got me anywhere close to that point. But then I met you and I heard what you went through and saw what you were doing about it. And I thought about me, and what I went through and what I *wasn't* doing about it. And I thought that if *you* could do something about it, well, maybe I could too."

Logan braced himself with straight arms back to the floor. "And . . . that's part of the reason I agreed to give you lessons. I thought maybe if you put one nearsighted person together with a blind person they could get where they needed to." He sighed heavily. "Not that I really understand this."

Although he probably didn't realize it, by so precisely describing what would never in a million years be within their grasp—she could absolutely see that now—he was cutting her heart out with a dull spoon.

"But . . . this is never gonna work out, is it?"

The look on her face told it all, she imagined. Her turn to sigh. "Logan, we are never, ever going to be on the same side. That fact is the giant heartache in this whole thing." She sat and gathered her legs under her Indian style. "I can't back down on the preserve. You can't back down on the runway. You wouldn't be : . . *you* . . . if you did."

"Tell me about it. The field led me to you, although what good that's done me I don't know because it's also making it impossible to be with you. This is a fucking mess, Sarah."

Misery loves company, but it was cold comfort, Sarah knew from experience. She felt the death knell for them reverberate down the frigid, barren corridors of her heart. She laughed, not bitterly. "Logan, the fat lady is *so* done."

"We never should have let it get this far," he said.

"You really feel that way?" she asked.

"No. You?"

Sarah shook my head. "Not for a second."

"This sucks," he said.

She summoned a smile, her tear ducts brimming. "You have no idea."

"Meaning?"

"Nothing." She hung her head. If she'd had long hair she'd have hid her face within its tent. She pretended that she could. How did you say to the stubborn, cantankerous, opinionated man sitting unconcernedly naked in front of you that *He* did *it for you?* She didn't casually give away what she'd just given him. Her head *and* heart agreed: he was The One.

Big fucking whoopee.

"I loved meeting Gertrude," she said, looking up.

"She felt the same about you." He gathered his clothes together. "You've always got visiting rights."

"That's nice."

They went on like that for a while, two people chatting, treating each other civilly at last. That was part of the waste. To have come so far for nothing.

Sarah cried. Yet again. It was beginning to feel like that was all she ever did around Logan. "I'm sorry," she said. "This wasn't supposed to be part of the deal."

He brushed a few stray hairs from her face and tucked them behind one ear. "Neither were you."

That didn't help. Hack her open, again, why didn't he?

They held each other while Sarah sniffled. They dozed off lying flat on the floor, something they were getting good at. When they woke up, the world had turned gray and a fine drizzle was falling.

Logan dropped her off at her place.

Sarah didn't see Logan again for almost two weeks. Life went back to what passed for normal before she'd met him.

A.C., the period in her life after the African crash, became A.L., After Logan. No, she didn't schlep around the house wearing one of his old jumpsuits, but she missed him. And flying.

Planes would drone past overhead, and if she were outside she'd stop whatever she was doing to gawk up at them. Iverson called about the article, but she blew a little smoke and he went away. She just couldn't get going on it.

Joan came by about a week into her self-imposed exile. As usual, the news was a spicy mix of the completely unbelievable, the hideously real, and the downright indecent. Her friend worked her way backward through the flavors this time.

"So about the airport, Michael says—he's Logan's lawyer, you know? You saw him that night, at the meeting in town hall? We went out. Whoa!" She rolled her eyes. "That man is a *wealth . . .*"

"Joan . . ."

"We were barely in the door to my place and—"

"Joan!"

She looked around her like Sarah had announced the room was on fire. "Oh! Was I at it again?"

"I'm afraid so. What does Michael say about the airport?"

"Logan has almost all his financing in place for the second runway."

"Too bad. But how did you come by this little tidbit?"

"What was that old movie with Rock Hudson and Doris Day?"

"*Pillow Talk*?"

"Exactly."

She shuddered. "Why do I suddenly want to wash out my ears?"

"Anyway, it looks like your Mr. Donnelly is poised for takeoff."

"He is not *my* Mr. Donnelly. He is nobody's anything. He will do exactly what he wants to do and no less." Double damn, she missed him.

Joan rounded her hands above Sarah's kitchen table like there was a crystal ball upon it. "Hmmm. Let me see . . . The future holds many things. I see . . ."

"Joan."

"The mists, the mists!"

"Joan . . ."

"But what's this? A blond, pain-in-the-ass pixie with a classic nose? Hmmm . . . Wait! Enter a tall, dark stranger in . . . *ta dum* . . . Columbia, all-terrain, side-zip cargo pants—"

"Joan, stop now before Auntie Sarah has to kill you." Joan really listened to everything Sarah said and, unfortunately, never forgot any of it. "And my hair? It's really dirty blond."

"Ever consider highlights?"

"No."

"Having it layered?"

"Please . . ."

"Okay," Joan said, suddenly serious. "I'm done. But note that I said earlier that Mr. Donnelly has *almost* all of his financing in place. Never count your chickens, etcetera, etcetera. My lawyer toy says there's a little glitch."

Sarah's head shot up. "Really?" Glitches could be good. Her heart did a funny little skip.

Joan gave her the scoop.

Chapter 22

The second informational meeting was televised. WKAX out of Boston had a camera crew set up in the rear of the hall. Joan and Sarah arrived early to get seats within chair-heaving range of the stage.

Most of the panel members seated at the long table up on stage had been there the last time, Sarah remembered. Logan looked neat—no tie, heaven forbid—but he was wearing a sport coat with an open, collared shirt. Susan Crawford's hair looked wonderful, lustrous even, in the lights. A future Helmet-head of America, no doubt. Joan's little lawyer friend was seated next to Susan and the money guys filled out the flanks.

Joan pointed to one of the suits. "You know that guy? Second from the left?"

"No."

"Roger Baines. Loan officer of Tidal Savings and Loan. Major player in Logan's deal. They're in for like forty percent."

"Ah, no wonder I don't recognize the guy, me being a

renter and used car owner." She hated banks and, by extension, bankers.

"I hope you don't feel the same about lawyers," Joan said.

Really, how did her friend do it? "Did I say something out loud?" Sarah asked.

"No, I read your mind."

"Large print?"

"Something like that. By the way, your hostility is practically precipitating in the atmosphere tonight." She said this offhandedly, as she was ogling her sensuous solicitor. His hands were busy under the draped table, probably sharpening the crease in his trousers, Sarah thought. Or he was touching himself impurely. Little need for that, though, based on Joan's all-too-graphic reports of their time together.

"Speaking of the atmosphere," Sarah said, "cloudy toward evening, chance of shit storms around eight."

"Try to contain yourself, dear." Joan cocked her head left, then right, like a robin hunting worms. "Big stuff's brewing. I can feel it."

"Oh, boy . . ."

"Keep your wits about you, Sarah. I mean it."

Mrs. Harker had done a pretty good ad hoc job controlling the first, unanticipated skirmish, but the big guns had been wheeled in for this second, high-stakes battle. John Woodley, Tidal's elected moderator, opened the meeting. "Welcome, everyone."

He introduced the panel, then got down to it. "I want to reiterate, ladies and gentlemen, the purpose of tonight's meeting. You've all had an opportunity, I hope, to examine the proposed plans and the three-dimensional model of the new runway at Crossly Field."

Sarah hadn't, even though Joan had reminded her several times that renderings of the new runway, as well as maps and a three-dimensional model in a Plexiglas case, were on display in the palatial lobby of the newly remodeled Tidal Savings Bank. So maybe she was passive-aggressive. All the drawings and fancy architectural whatnots were now displayed on an inclined table stage right.

Woodley said, "This evening is intended as the second in a series of informational meetings, the purpose of which is to answer any questions and address any concerns individuals or groups may have regarding the construction of the second runway at Crossly Field."

Sarah barely heard the remarks of the moderators. She couldn't tear her eyes from the display. Intellectually, she knew, from the numerous drawings published in *The Coastal Press*, how devastating the new airstrip would be to the preserve. It inserted itself into the green, wooded space like a long, dirty finger. As if that weren't bad enough, paved access roads to the navigation lights placed in front of the runway, along the intended flight path of incoming airplanes, effectively cut the narrow preserve in half. On the published maps and the renderings, the engineer's superimposed pen strokes slashed through the heart of the preserve.

But none of that compared to the impact made by the three-dimensional mock-up of Pear Island showing the second runway installed. On the model, it looked as though someone had crudely blowtorched a black stripe right down the middle of the gently rolling, verdant, albeit Styrofoam, topography.

Joan whispered something. Sarah didn't hear it because part of her was busy dying. Oddly enough, she was thinking of her dad. Specifically, of his photos of the animals and the scenery in Africa. Every time she looked at the black-and-white pictures, they seemed to burst with ripe color because the beauty of the place—in spite of the horrors they had encountered there—had emblazoned itself on her heart. Like the black stripe on the model.

"You look like crap. You gonna be able to do this?" Joan was referring to their little plan.

Sarah realized her jaws ached from clenching and her fists were balls of stone. She cared deeply for Logan, but she couldn't live with herself if she allowed—she glanced over at the charred scar bisecting the island of green—*that*. "Yes."

She stood up.

"Order! Order!" John Woodley barked at her. "Weren't you listening, Ms. Dundee? I just finished reminding everyone that this meeting will be conducted *only* in a civil fashion. Sit *down*, Ms. Dundee."

Not fair. She was only halfway to her feet.

"Any further outburst without chair recognition will be grounds for expulsion. Do I make myself clear?"

Sarah sat down, frustrated.

"Center yourself, kiddo. This one counts," Joan whispered, out of the corner of her mouth.

Did it ever. And here she was, *way* outside her comfort zone. Exposed. A neophyte knight, all thumbs, with an uncooperative jousting helmet and a nervous steed. Had the TV cameras caught her gaping like a fish when Woodley told her to chill?

She glanced at the model again. Anger gave her strength.

She zeroed in on Roger Baines from Tidal Savings and Loan, representing the 40 percent contributor and final holdout. He was there to take the temperature of the townspeople. To sniff out pockets of potential resistance that could delay, or possibly even abort, the second runway.

Prior to the meeting, Sarah had convinced herself that it was her job to provide him with clear evidence of that resistance. *Attack, attack, attack!* The wicked witch sending forth her malevolent, flying monkeys.

She waved her hand perkily in the hush that followed the moderator's admonition. Teachers used to hate that.

"Yes, Ms. Dundee, you are recognized." John Woodley already sounded weary.

She stood up. "Mr. Moderator, as this meeting is of an informational nature, I request that Mr. Donnelly provide us with some." She let that hang out there for a minute to torque up the level of drama. It didn't. Overhead fans squeaked.

"Ms. Dundee? You were saying?"

She checked out the crowd. For sure the Friends were following along, and the money guys on stage for sure, but the great undecided making up the majority in the hall seemed comatose.

"Yes. Thank you, Mr. Moderator. This supposed improvement to Pear Island"—she gestured toward the model with contempt—"will, in fact, lead to the eventual, if not imminent, collapse of the ecosystem of the preserve. I wonder . . . what might prompt any individual to precipitate such an environmental catastrophe?"

That prompted a stir in the crowd. Logan rose, but Michael Brophy placed a restraining hand on his arm: *Wait. She's not done yet.*

Which she wasn't.

"It's odd that such an obviously"—Sarah considered him in the stage lights—"*experienced* individual as Mr. Donnelly would act so callously, don't you think?" She fought to keep her mind off just *how* experienced he was. "After all, a man of his varied background. The military . . . his wilderness training . . . growing up in the wilds of New Hampshire. Surely these life experiences would have sensitized him *somewhat* to the beauty and vulnerability of the natural world?"

"Yes, I wonder about that, too," said a resonant baritone in the rear of the hall. People half stood and turned around.

What the hell? Sarah went up on tiptoes to see. Holy crap.

It was Robert Iverson.

The crowd buzzed. "Order! Order! The speaker has the floor," said Woodley. "Do you surrender it, Ms. Dundee?"

"Well, I . . . guess so."

Joan asked, "Your freaking boss?"

Sarah nodded, dumbfounded.

"Thank you, Mr. Moderator," Sarah heard her freaking boss say. "Ms. Dundee . . ." He gave her a casual wave like they were old friends. Her legs sat her down.

"Folks, I'm Robert Iverson. From *Natural Spaces* magazine?" He dropped the name like he expected everyone in the hall would instantly recognize it. Statistically speaking, a few people might have, but even people who Sarah was *sure* didn't seemed to feel compelled to nod knowledgeably.

"He's got strong mojo," Joan whispered.

"Great. Let's bring clarity to the situation by offering free psychic dipsticking," Sarah whispered back.

Joan made a disparaging noise.

Iverson meandered casually up the aisle toward the stage. Sarah bet that he wouldn't stop until he got to the exact middle of it. She was right. He picked up a mobile microphone resting at the edge of the stage.

"Thank you for inviting me here tonight," he said to the assembled. Sarah wondered who had, because no one said, "You're welcome."

"I also have some questions of Mr. Logan Donnelly." Sarah saw Logan make to rise, but Michael Brophy checked him again.

"Is he . . . *afraid* of the outdoors, I wonder?" Iverson asked.

Jeepers, get right to it, why don't you. Sarah was reminded of his pointedness from their phone conversations.

Iverson raised his shoulders theatrically, hands palms up, reminiscent of Jack McCoy from *Law and Order*. Sarah got the feeling Sam Waterston used the gesture with permission from Iverson. "Maybe he just doesn't like . . . bugs?" Iverson let his hands flop to his sides.

Oh, slam. Chuckles drifted through the hall. Logan's cronies coughed behind their hands. Roger Baines looked constipated. Sarah actually felt bad for Logan.

"Mr. Iverson, I don't think—" Woodley began, but Logan stood up.

"John, thank you, but I've got this." He glanced deferentially toward Woodley. "If Mr. Iverson yields."

"Please . . ." said Iverson. He made an expansive "the-floor-is-yours" gesture. Sarah wondered if Logan knew who Iverson was.

"Things are getting weird fast," Joan said to Sarah.

Like she needed to point *that* out.

Logan rose and shot a withering glance at Sarah.

How did you tell another person with just a look that you only wanted to trip him up, *not* knock him out?

Logan brought a microphone with him to center stage, where he towered above Iverson on the floor. Despite their differences, Sarah found herself cheering for Logan. Not his cause, but him.

"In spite of attempts to portray me otherwise," Logan said, "the efforts of the Friends, their concern regarding the future of Pear Island preserve, their love of nature, the planned contribution to *Natural Spaces* magazine, etcetera, etcetera are not lost on me."

A swell traveled through the crowd: *Sure . . .*

"He's powerful," said Joan. "Dark, but powerful."

Silly Sarah. She'd left her light saber at home.

Logan continued. "I have a great affinity for the outdoors. I . . . appreciate it. I value it. I completely empathize with your concern for it."

Iverson cut in. "And *I* say that that is a patent fabrication,

Mr. Donnelly. Your pretense of being a nature lover is a sham. You are no woodsman. You are, in fact"—he made another *Law and Order* move, whipping around to deliver his pronouncement to the audience—"completely incapable of sustaining yourself in the wilderness. You, sir, are a 'nature' Nazi."

The crowd went wild, by Tidal standards. A reporter from *The Coastal Press* clicked his pen and turned a new page in his notebook.

Woodley fired up the gavel. "Order! Order!"

"Really weird . . ." Joan said, doing the birdlike head tweak again.

"Hel-*lo* . . . ?" Sarah said. "You're way off the FM dial. Clue me in here."

Joan silenced her. Then, to even Sarah's amazement, she began to hum. Not the attention-getting, comb-kazoo kind; just a gentle, unnerving, off-key keening. Sarah looked around to see who might be listening.

Joan went on tonelessly for the few minutes it took for everyone to settle back down into seats. Several hundred people could give pretty good mutter. Woodley, exasperated, gave up on formalities. He pointed his gavel at Logan: *Go.*

Logan nodded. "Thank you." He turned to use his greater height to advantage. "Mr. Iverson, while I am certainly not a *Survivor* contestant, —*his* money guys sniggered—"I can certainly hold my own in the woods. When I was in the Air Force—"

"Prove it," Iverson said.

Suddenly you could have had your pick of any seat in the house because no one was occupying any of them.

"Order!" Woodley called.

"John . . ." Logan said into the mike, holding up a hand to quiet the crowd.

Iverson squared himself to Logan. David, the underdog,

facing down—rather, up—Goliath. The cameras would eat it up. Sarah would have, too, a few weeks ago, she had to admit. "Why don't you put your money where your mouth is, Mr. Donnelly?"

"What are you proposing, Mr. Iverson?"

"A challenge, Mr. Donnelly."

"Order! Order!" More staccato gavel work. "Mr. Iverson," Woodley said, "this is entirely inappropriate. Kindly refrain—"

Logan said quietly, "Describe it."

All eyes swung to Iverson. If he'd worn glasses, right then would have been a good time to peel them off and chew thoughtfully on the bows, Sarah thought. Instead, he slowly paced back and forth, considering his shoes. Sarah bet they weren't made from an endangered species.

Finally, he spoke. "Fine. I'll wager that you couldn't go into the woods and take care of yourself and one other person, oh, say, Ms. Dundee?"—*Hey, ho, hold on there, Tex,* Sarah thought, shocked—"for one week. Maintaining her in the style to which she is, no doubt, accustomed."

Woodley had his gavel suspended in midair, ready to smash down on the block, but no one in the humid hall seemed to know how to react. Sarah included herself in that group.

Logan was the first to break the silence. "Pardon?"

"It's very simple, Mr. Donnelly. You and Ms. Dundee live in the woods for one week. You set up camp. You pitch the tent. You cook. You cut the wood, Mr. Donnelly, while Ms. Dundee, metaphorically speaking, holds the lamp. Or lantern, as the case may be. You. Do. It. All."

Sarah looked at Logan. He caught her eye. She shrugged: *Beats the moose out of me . . .* Little did she know then how prophetic that random expression would turn out to be.

Logan cut his eyes back to Iverson and said, "Mr. Iverson, I can't see what—"

The idea might have died right then and there had not the woman to Sarah's left broken off her bilabial concerto to pipe up, "I think it's a great idea."

Damn it. It was, yes, her new *ex*–best friend, Joan. Sarah grabbed Joan's arm to shake some sense into her—or maybe just break the arm—but Joan shrugged Sarah off. She spoke directly to Logan. "Mr. Donnelly, don't allow these people to do this to you. Give them what they want. Clear your name. Take the bet."

"Hear, hear!" made the rounds. Woodley exercised his gavel.

Sarah was about to rip Joan a new body orifice when she noticed the look on Logan's face. Now, Sarah had been in some pretty hairy situations with him—her going nuts in the air, him going nuts in the lighthouse, their death kiss of the bridge—but she'd never seen a look on his face like there was at that moment. It rattled her.

He turned to his money guys.

Some nodded: *Reasonable idea.* Others just watched like birds of prey just served up a reheated entrée of small mammal. They were getting just what they came for: an airing of the real dirty laundry. Some of them chuckled openly at Logan's discomfort.

"What's a good place to set up our little experiment, Ms. Dundee?" Iverson queried. "Ms. Dundee . . . ?"

Sarah realized Iverson was addressing her. How long had she been standing there numbly? She snapped back into reality, desperate for something to grab on to. Something to steady her. Something familiar like . . . like . . . "The Allagash," she said.

Sarah knew that sometimes a drowning person will clutch at something really stupid just because it's familiar, but it ends up pulling her down like a brick. Her mind had grabbed on to a place the old her remembered well.

The Allagash Wilderness Waterway. *Way* the hell up in Maine. One hundred miles of winding river meandering through a series of connected lakes running from the Moosehead Lake Region north to the Saint John's river at the Canadian border. Rick and Sarah had led tour groups there. It was where they had first . . . um . . . where they had first gotten to know each other.

A woman behind Sarah called out, "The Allagash?"

You'd have thought she'd said, "The dark side of the moon."

"Up in Maine?" the woman persisted, incredulous.

No, lady, the *other* one. Next block over? Cripes.

The woman wouldn't let go of the bone. "If they go all the way up there, how will we know if Donnelly came through or not?"

The crowd, suddenly a crew of pirate extras, *arr-arr*ed.

Regrettably, the woman had a point. A guy who looked like a model for the L.L.Bean summer clothing line chimed in, "Yeah, we need more than one person's say-so."

Dork. He even *sounded* like a condo owner.

But his tone convinced Sarah that the coziness between Logan and herself had been duly noted in Tidal. Like she gave a shit. Amazing, though, to think her credibility was in question solely because of her association with Logan. People actually believed she'd sacrifice her own principles because of her feelings for the man. Would that she could pass on her heartache to them like the common cold.

A third person chimed in, "Mr. Moderator?"

Despite originating from the very rear of the hall, the new voice had the piercing quality of a line judge's at a tennis match and carried easily to the stage area.

Oh, no. In her mind's eye Sarah could picture the engaging wave. She thought she heard thin bracelets jangle on a slim wrist. John Woodley pointed his gavel at the air over her head.

"Yes, thank you, Mr. Moderator," her mother said.

Sarah tried to imagine what she had done in her life that was horrible enough to warrant the events of the evening. Good God in heaven. Violet involved in the Battle of the Preserve? Her idea of public spiritedness was to buy a couple extra tickets to the garden tour every June.

Then Sarah figured it out: the Hillary Harker connection. Violet and Hillary were lifelong buddies. Sarah mentally smacked herself upside the head for being so oblivious. It had been only a matter of time until Violet would join the fray. Sarah wondered if her mother knew any good jail jokes.

Her mother continued. "As a lifelong resident of Tidal, I think Mr. Donnelly's performance is a matter of public record. In light of this, I suggest that each person in attendance tonight is entitled to arrive at their own conclusion regarding his claim of being a wilderness advocate."

And she was going *where* with this?

"To that end, is there not some way a photographic record might be made of this . . . adventure?"

Violet somehow made the word *adventure* come out like *circus*. A sick feeling in Sarah's stomach transported her back to ninth grade. She and her classmates were lined up like penguins at the front of a packed-house, baking-hot high school auditorium, ready to begin the end-of-year choral recital, when mother dearest dashed up and pinned the limp, sweaty hair out of Sarah's face with a barrette. She'd spent the next three years living that one down.

"A wonderful suggestion," Iverson said. "Perhaps WKAX might provide us with a camera crew?"

A talking head Sarah had seen doing cover interviews outside the hall before the meeting gave Iverson a vigorous thumbs-up.

"Very well, then," Iverson said, clapping his hands together once. "We'll have a public review of the tape at a third public meeting, date to be announced. Any more details to wrap up?"

Sarah had some details she'd like to fucking wrap right around his neck. Parking her rage on ice to be picked over later at leisure, she contemplated strategy. How did you walk the razor-thin line between alienating your brand-new boss, encouraging your mother, and abandoning your . . . Logan . . . to the wolves? "Oh, Mr. Iverson . . ." she trilled, in an eerie echo of her mother. She waved engagingly. "I'm not sure this is quite fair—"

A smattering of boo erupted. Sarah raised her voice. "After all, Mr. Donnelly—"

The smattering acquired substance and became a raucous wave.

Sarah shouted. "This is nothing but a crock of—" *Whoosh!* She was inundated in castigation. The crowd wanted Barabas. She caught Logan's eye and made a face: *I tried.*

Sarah realized Iverson must have picked up on her telepathic message because she felt daggers shoot toward her from the stage area. It wasn't too difficult to imagine them skewering little pink slips into her chest.

Don't push it, his eyes said. *Go along like a good girl. You wouldn't want to lose that national soapbox, now, would you?* Suddenly she didn't like him even a little bit. But she'd go along, all right. To make sure Logan got a fair trial, she'd go along.

A man's deep baritone cut through the din. "Uh, excuse me, Mr. Moderator?" Woodley stabbed the handle of the gavel at him and nodded. "In the spirit of public good, my company, Adventure Ventura, will donate all the required camping gear."

Thank you, fucking Rick. Was everyone she'd ever been in

therapy for in the hall? Just clap her into the public stocks, already.

"And at the conclusion of the expedition, the gear will be donated to the Tidal Boys and Girls Club," her ex-fiancé said.

Applause. Gavel action. What a guy. Everybody instantly fell in love with him. Made that mistake herself once.

"I'll also supply canoes for the party's use and personally guide the expedition down the waterway."

This she heard, but betrayal she felt. *Rick.* Did we have *nothing* together? He heard Allagash and it rang his bells. Or a couple of other dangly little things. He couldn't leave her alone to decide on the direction of her life. Her love life, to be precise.

"All I ask," he said, "is that my company logo be allowed to appear on the sides of all the canoes and tents."

Then she suddenly got it. It was all so clear. Ha-*ha*! Son of a bitch . . . His offer didn't have anything to do with her, or them, or what they once had. It was all about *him.* It was all about his frigging business. A few weeks ago that insight would have been a body blow. Now, it came as a breath of fresh air. The truth hath set her free.

Woodley gunned his gavel at someone else. All Sarah could see was a raised hand.

One of the few people in the hall she hadn't spent hours counseling on with Dr. Loo spoke up.

Maura said, "I have complete confidence in Mr. Donnelly. He's taken my son, Eric, on a lot of hikes and he's been a wonderful influence on the boy." Sarah located Maura—and it looked like Eric—tucked way back in the crowd.

"They've spent real quality time together and what with all the survival training Mr. Donnelly had in the service—" She abruptly stopped. Sarah could see Eric was tugging frantically on his mother's sleeve. Maura held up her hand

and placed her head close to him. He whispered intently in her ear. The look on her face deadened and she looked like she'd unexpectedly swallowed something unpleasant. She squared herself and waved dispiritedly at Woodley. "Ah . . . that's . . . uh . . . all, Mr. Moderator."

"Mr. Moderator?" Another male voice, close by. Sarah caught a whiff of his cologne before she saw him.

Woodley recognized Lloyd Higgins.

"Yuk," Joan said.

Sarah said, "Don't you dare speak to me."

"Mr. Iverson, on behalf of the newly opened Crossly Field Flight School—" Higgins began.

He pronounced the school name like you'd say, "The Father, Son, and the Holy Ghost."

"I'd like to provide air transportation to Maine for the crew and all their gear. The cameras. The whole shooting match. Ms. Dundee, Mr. Donnelly, too, if they want."

"We don't want," Logan interjected.

The "we" was royal. Sarah would sooner walk to Maine barefoot than have Lloyd—and Preston, presumably—fly her anywhere.

"Ms. Dundee and I will provide our own transportation."

Interesting . . . She connected the dots and mouthed *Gertrude?* Logan nodded. At least something positive would come out of this.

"Your generous offer is duly noted, Mr. Higgins." Woodley said. "Now, if there's nothing else, we can adjourn—"

Logan broke in. "There's one more thing. Mr. Iverson?" he said. "Should I somehow manage against all odds to convince this august assembly of my credibility, I want your assurance that Noah Crossly Airport will no longer be persecuted by your magazine."

"I resent the implication that—" Iverson began.

"I'm not finished."

Iverson actually shut up for once. There was a subtle menace in Logan's voice that Sarah had never heard before. She was suddenly *very* glad he was not talking to *her* like that. The savage inside her half hoped he'd completely lose it, jump off the stage, and whop her new boss's ass right in front of everybody.

"You agree to abandon the article," Logan said.

Iverson, the cunning bastard, apparently had seen that coming. He glanced over at Sarah, his eyebrows raised, with a look that clearly shifted responsibility to her: *Well?*

Mrs. Hillary Harker waved her arms frantically, making slash marks across her throat. Sarah didn't think she'd swallowed her gum and was signing for an emergency tracheotomy. *No deal*, Hillary meant.

If by some miracle Logan pulled his ass out of this jam—and Sarah truly didn't believe he could—he deserved to be let off the hook. She nodded back to Iverson: *Sold*.

"Agreed," Iverson said.

Having hit an all-time-high watermark for drama in sleepy Tidal, the meeting wound down quickly. Honestly, Sarah didn't know much more you could throw into the fan in one night.

Joan and Sarah walked out together. Anyone watching them would have thought they were still speaking to each other, Sarah thought. That person would have been dead wrong.

"Whew," Joan said when they were clear of the crowd malingering in the circular drive.

The evening was beautiful. Red sky at night, sailor's delight. Joan tried again. "Gorgeous sunset."

Sarah walked faster.

"Sarah?" Her mother had pulled even on the starboard side.

"Mother."

"Sarah, it was necessary. We must find out for the good of the preserve where Mr. Donnelly is coming from, as you would say. He'll have a fair chance to prove himself."

"Really."

"Call . . . me . . . kiddo?" Joan said, from several steps behind. She was starting to puff.

Sarah picked up her pace. Violet, too, fell away. Rick took his shot next. He ambushed Sarah from behind a tree, inserting himself into her path, bringing her up short.

"Sarah?"

She set an angled course between some cars in the parking lot. Rick kept pace on the far side of a row. "Sarah, wait a minute, will you?"

He circled the hood of a beat-up Jeep Wagoneer and cornered her. "That was nothing to do with us in there and you know it. It was just business."

Sarah laughed and found she couldn't stop. The look on his face was priceless. For everything else—like tents and canoes and camping gear—there's Mastercard. "Finally, we're on the same page, Rick. Yes, yes. I completely understand what you're saying."

Now all she had to do was put that understanding into words. She waited for herself to do that. *Tic, tic, tic . . .* Nothing.

She shut her eyes and halloed down into the depths of herself: *Sarah . . .*

No answer.

She realized with a desperate sadness that she didn't want to surrender her tickets to a game even though she couldn't possibly attend. Couldn't give up her seat on a bus that was going somewhere she couldn't. Stupid, stupid, stupid, but there it was.

"Rick . . ." she started, then dropped her hands in frustration. When she opened her eyes he was already walking away. By the time she reached the Rav, he had disappeared completely.

Numbly, Sarah fired up the Rav and merged with the line of cars exiting the lot. A traffic jam at the gate penned her in. On the sidewalk, maybe fifty feet away, she spied an out-of-shape woman trudging slowly homeward. Joan *who? Piss me off* . . .

Suddenly, Logan was at Sarah's window.

"Hey," he said.

"Hey, yourself." The words echoed in a hollow place the size of Montana in her chest. "You're the enemy, you know. I shouldn't be talking to you."

"Person'd have to stand in line to be your enemy tonight, I'm figuring."

A goofy little giggle escaped her. Tension. The evening's escapades had stripped her of mental energy, leaving her bereft of her usual glibness. She became nervous, unsure what to do with her hands. She watched them flutter around the steering wheel like moths. Here, now, alone, just the two of them, there was so much she wanted to say but couldn't. So much she wanted to do, too.

"The Allagash looks beautiful from the air," he said, falling directly onto the point of the sword the town had thrust into the veils between them. "Been by it a lot."

Translation: *flew* over it. She *so* missed being in a plane that the longing was like a physical pain. "No pizza runs up there," she said.

He laughed politely. God she missed *them*. Like comedians say about Cleveland, she spent a lifetime there one day. *Budda-bing, budda-boom!* Laugh track.

Only she didn't feel like laughing. Titles for a sorry little article about them ran through her mind: "Goofy Girl Gives All for Guy," or maybe "Frightened Femme Flips for Flyboy."

The Greeks had it right thousands of years ago. The two masks were just opposite sides of the same coin.

She raked her hand through her hair. Not like beautiful women do on shampoo commercials—hadn't conditioned in *days*, so busy, you know—but like she was ready to sear it all off with the glowing tips of burning branches and go into grieving like she'd read some West Coast Native American tribal women did.

"Stop," Logan said.

"What?"

"Doing that. You're creating a federal disaster area." Reflexively she'd slap any other male who dared make a comment like that to her, but Logan had seen her at her worst. Nose goo hanging off her sleeves, pine needles in her teeth, the unabridged history of Spot writ large across her face. And she'd seen him when his tanks weren't exactly topped off. So it didn't really matter. That was part of what made this all so hard.

He pulled her hand out of something that probably looked like a roof-thatching job gone bad and intertwined her fingers lightly between his. Sarah peeked around to see who might be looking. Consorting in public with him. Again. Her insides got warm and sloshy when the feel of his hand reminded her of the consorting they had done in private. Her body announced that she was *definitely* not done with him yet.

Traffic moved and she had to inch forward. "Watch your feet."

"Need them to land on."

"You better hope. Don't expect any help from me."

"No quarter given, eh?"

"Don't get me wrong. I hate what they did to you—to us—in there. But we're still on opposite sides of this."

"Unfortunately, yes."

He wasn't done with her, either, she realized. She'd have to use a curling iron on her tongue later if that turned out not to be true, but with as much certainty as she'd ever felt about anything in her life, that's what she thought then.

Sarah prayed a little prayer for them. Their physical bodies were in the hospital waiting area, sitting on crappy plastic chairs and reading magazines three months out of date with their recipes torn out, while their hearts languished on life support. The situation demanded a last-minute miracle or one of them had to get real brave real quick and start pulling plugs.

Right after she finished memorizing every callus on his hand. A few thousand years ought to do it.

She so missed digging at him. He was a joy to bait. Maybe she'd wait and give him up for Lent. That'd mean about eight more months of comic setups.

"*Sooo, grasshopper,*" she crooned, "if a pilot survives a night in the woods and no one sees it, has he really done it?"

"Oh, plenty of people will see it. Rumor has it the town hall's renting stadium seating for the premier of the video."

Sarah laughed.

"You don't think I can pull it off, do you?" he asked.

"Got it in one."

"Have it your way. But 'Grizzly Logan,' that's what they'll call me after it's over. I can see it now. Lake beautiful in the early morning, mists just clearing, me making a gentle cast out over the still waters—"

"Hooking the Coleman lantern on the backswing, dragging it through the smoldering campfire, and setting half the virgin timber in upstate Maine ablaze . . . Oh, yeah, it's gonna be great. Can't wait."

Logan snickered.

Sarah said, "You do realize what that'll mean? I mean, if you look like a klutz up there in the woods? Your credibility's shot. You'll lose your financing."

"I won't even ask how you came by that information."

She blushed. He had the good taste not to comment.

"You remember your part of the deal?" he asked.

"You shine? I—or rather my boss—kills the article."

"Can you live with that?"

"I'll have to."

His brow furrowed. "Which means what, exactly?"

"Damn if I know."

"Which pretty much brings us back where we started." He toed the asphalt and looked at his feet.

"Pretty much." It was hard.

So naturally she avoided it. She forced her hand to let go of his and windmilled her scrawny fists in his face. "Care to make a friendly side bet?"

"You don't do friendly."

"Chicken."

"Fifty bucks," he said.

"That you'll screw up?"

"No, that I shine."

"Fine. I'll call and raise you. A hundred even says you implode."

"Fine."

"Fine." Sarah pretended to spit in her hand and stuck it out the window.

He shook it. "Fine."

"Fine," she said.

He clammed up, looking uncharacteristically worried.

After a moment Sarah said, "Now you say 'fine' back."

To her enormous relief he chuckled. "I'll call you as soon as everything's set up. It won't be long. Your boss is all fired up to move on this and I might as well strike while the iron is hot. Hey, how do you stand him anyway?"

She didn't know if she'd be able to, long term, after what had just transpired in town hall. "No comment. It'll be great to go in Gertrude."

As she thought of Gertrude, possibilities grew large in her mind. "We'll be landing on the lakes, won't we . . ." *Ooh . . . I could see it all:*

Like the migrating Canadian fowl of its namesake honking in low over the trees, our floatplane, dubbed "Gertrude" by Logan Donnelly in a rare moment of whimsey, skims the sparkling waters of Eagle Lake and gently touches down. . . .

What a story.

"Call me soon," she said.

Traffic moved on.

Chapter 23

Gertrude was flying too high for Sarah to make out specific features of the terrain unrolling below, but one thing she could see were the logging roads. They were the only straight lines visible in any direction, cutting with geometric precision across the endless green carpet of upstate Maine. Plumes of dust on the narrow tan bands marked the passage of log carriers barreling sixty miles an hour along the rutted gravel roads.

Trip outfitters and guides took their lives in their hands hauling clients and their rented canoes miles out into the wilderness along those roads. The smart ones kept the two-way radios in their vehicles tuned to the truckers' frequencies to avoid becoming roadkill at a blind corner.

Logan glanced down at the ground and noticed the dust plumes.

"Rangers?" he asked through the headset.

"Truckers," Sarah said. "Some guides, too, bringing canoeing parties to the waterway."

Lulled by the drone of the twin engines, Sarah let her

mind drift. The takeoff from the waters of Salem Bay an hour and a half earlier had been spectacular. They'd left Manchester earlier than they really had to, but they needed the tide on their side. If they'd waited three hours, Gertie would have been mired in the mud at the end of Logan's dock. They had made their run-up about 500 yards out from the cove. The plan was to rendezvous with Iverson et al.— the guest list of the imminent fiasco was still sketchy—on Eagle Lake, one of the many lakes that connected to the water-way and contributed about eight miles to its length.

Logan's hands were resting in his lap, letting the autopilot do the work. He laughed.

"What?" Sarah asked.

"Just thinking about my hundred bucks."

"Dream on," she said. And then she did.

About Gertrude: the Amazing Amphibian who lifted them from the unforgiving deep off the rocky Manchester shoreline into the calm morning air. Spray kicking up, mo-tors roaring balls to the wall, sea swells thumping the hull. Then the sudden leap into airy blue.

About Logan: Hard to imagine that just a month or so ago she was whacking him with a sign. A few weeks later she was whacking him; she forced herself not to indulge. She watched him at the controls. Now she was falling—too late: *fell*—for a guy that she could never, ever be with. Her life had turned into a Ricki Lake episode.

All that aside, Logan had proved to be a fascinating pack-age. Full of inconsistencies, riddled with compulsions, but somehow intensely alive. He had something that she didn't. Sure, she'd been known to mince along the rim of the pre-cipice, but she took holidays on flatland. Without even know-ing it, Logan lived every moment on the edge, like one of those fools who hung their sleeping cots from pitons halfway up a sheer rock face. She tried to imagine him letting out a war whoop after pulling off an outrageously difficult and dangerous maneuver in a stunt plane. No way. Never. Too disciplined. To him, the real joy lay in the quiet doing, not in the noisy celebration.

He was a man of the moment, too, mostly, but sometimes, just like her, he'd be forced to sit through a movie trailer in the private screening room in his head. But something had shifted with that, too. What, she couldn't say exactly, but something.

"I know I'm going on and on about it," she said, looking down at the unrelieved forest below Gertrude, "but I just cannot believe the view from up here." She was in constant amazement at some new thing she saw. She wondered if a person ever took the perspective for granted.

"It's something you never get tired of," Logan said, doing a Joan thing with her thoughts.

Joan. Another casualty in the War of the Preserve. They hadn't talked since the second meeting. In all the years the two of them had known each other, they'd never been on the outs for this long. Sarah counted up the bodies and realized they were piling up: Joan, Rick, her mother, Mrs. Harker—Hillary wanted to stone her for agreeing to abdicate on writing the article if Logan exonerated himself—and Logan himself.

On the horizon to their right, a blue fingertip of water scrolled toward the plane. That would be Telos Lake. Chamberlain Lake was a little beyond, then Eagle Lake, their destination.

A few more minutes went by, the reassuring rumble of Getrude's twin engines a constant backdrop. Curiously, Sarah realized the steady thunder never registered as an assault on her eardrums—and sanity—like the whine of the Cessna's little four-banger engine did. Gertie purred like a very large cat.

Sarah checked the ground again. From the air, the linked lakes leading north from Telos, the southernmost point of the waterway, looked like glittering gems in a sparkling sapphire necklace laid casually across a viridian jeweler's mat. Sarah had paddled the waterway, swam in it, drifted on it, and been unceremoniously dumped into its Class Three rapids at least a dozen times. She could probably pick her way blindfolded through its sinuous 100 miles of interconnected lakes, rivers, ponds, and backwaters. But to see huge parts of it, all of a piece, from Gertrude, was breathtaking.

Except for the brown scar that mirrored the sinuous, twisting track of the river barely a hundred yards from it.

"Holy shit."

"Progress," Logan said.

Sarah had read about the so-called vanity strips of undisturbed green. Paper companies strip-mining Maine for the next ten million rolls of toilet tissue left a few hundred feet of woods, immediately adjacent to the river, intact to conceal the slash and burn being done to the forest just beyond. From their altitude, the visual impact of the damage was something else. Environmental groups must have fought their asses off to preserve even those thin bands of natural forest. Canoeing down the waterway, you'd have no reason to never know what was happening just on the other side of them. Sarah thought about Pear Island.

The headphones crackled and Logan's voice tickled her ear. "They'll replant, won't they?"

He meant the paper companies. "Sure. The last thing they do before they leave a stripped-out lot is drop off a crate of seedlings."

"That's good, isn't it?"

"Yeah, provided there's enough money to hire workers to replant the seedlings before they dry up and turn into the world's most expensive tinder. And if you don't mind waiting twenty years for the space to fill in again."

"Getting close?"

"To what?"

"Where we're going."

"Right." Sarah had to tear her eyes away from the destruction. A sectional map was spread out on her lap.

"Tell me exactly where we're headed," Logan said.

She checked the printed compass rose against the floating ball on the instrument panel. "Bear northeast, ten degrees."

Hard to believe that a few weeks ago she would have pointed and said "over there" like you'd identify an available parking space at a mall.

Logan nodded and nudged Gertrude onto the new heading, shedding altitude in the process. As they descended, new perspectives were revealed.

Was that Telos Dam? Yes. And to the northeast, the tiny body of water with the improbable name of Coffelos Pond, courtesy of an upstate Maine wag. She explained the joke to Logan.

He laughed. "Now there was a guy with way too much time on his hands."

"Around here that's *all* you have if it's too muddy to log."

"Yeah, but does that really ever happen?"

"Thus spake the smart-ass techno-geek."

"Tree-hugging, backcountry hick."

"Just fly the plane."

He smiled an adolescent smile, one she was unfortunately growing quite fond of. A nice little "mix and match" was going on with Logan. He was letting things leak out of one bucket into another. Something really was changing for him. But, unfortunately, from her perspective, it was like she'd heard people say about houses: just when you had one all fixed up the way you wanted it, you had to sell.

"There's Chamberlain Lake," she said, pointing. She *was* excited. She'd gotten them where they wanted to go.

Cumulus clouds wiped mottled shadows across its surface. In the middle, a deep blue reflected, with lighter shadings of tan and greens in the shallows near the shore.

"I can't believe I got talked into this," Logan said, as he scoped out the view. She glanced at him and saw what? Desperation? Longing?

"*We* got talked into this, remember? We both got set up."

He'd been on a quick commercial break. Even if they had had more time together, Sarah wondered if she'd ever really find out what was featured in those home movies behind his eyeballs. Suddenly, a hot flood of desire for him surged through her. Her eyelids drooped. Her cheeks got warm. Yes, courage always was an aphrodisiac for her. But what wasn't, she wondered, shifting restlessly in her seat.

"Airsick?" Logan asked.

"Not exactly."

"We'll be down soon, yes?"

Sarah referred again to the map, not that she really needed to. The waterway was hers. But Logan's training ran deep: *check everything twice; then check it again.*

"Yes."

She scanned the ground, comparing the printed version with the landscape unrolling below.

"There—" she did point—"about ten degrees left. At the end of Telos Lake. There's a one-lane bridge over what they call The Thoroughfare. It leads to Chamberlain Lake, which is about ten miles long. Nasty when the wind is up."

She tried to pick out whitecaps but couldn't. Maybe they were still too high up, or maybe the mercurial lake was in a receptive mood.

"Eagle Lake is where we're headed, just above Chamberlain. At the north end, toward the western shore, is Farm

Island. Home sweet home. I make it about"—she measured the distance on the map with her finger, then figured in Gertie's airspeed—"three minutes."

"Got it." Logan backed off on the throttles. "I'll circle around a couple times to check the approach. What do you know about that stretch on Eagle? Sandbars, stump fields, stuff like that?"

"We should be okay this time of year. It's still early in the season. By August you're poling through some parts. They regulate the flow downriver, but if it's a dry year, there's not that much water to work with. Rip out a canoe bottom."

"Just as long as we don't do that to old Gertrude, here."

"Don't worry. I wouldn't let a single feather of hers get ruffled." Sarah stroked a finger along the control yoke on her side of the cockpit. She caught Logan watching.

"I can't believe you waited this long," he said. "Try it. Get the feel of her."

Sarah longed to but felt like she needed an invitation every time. Gertie was Logan's baby, after all. She rested her hands lightly on the yoke and followed the inputs Logan made to the matching one on his side of the cockpit. An electric thrill went through her fingertips, up her arms and made her scalp tingle.

"You okay?" Logan asked.

"Wow, this is a trip."

He chuckled.

Captain Joe Gallagher, you're relieved. I got the con. Or was that submarine talk?

A few minutes later, or a few hours later, for all she knew—being part of Gertie in flight was magical—Logan said, "Well, well, well. Lookie down there."

It was a frigging armada. Five, no, six canoes were just entering the narrow, white-water passage that connected Chamberlain Lake with Eagle. Even though Gertrude was still pretty high up, too high to make out fine details, Sarah would have bet every one of her hundred-dollar wager that the canoes would have Adventure Ventura emblazoned on its sides.

"How damn many people does it take to make a simple video?" Logan said.

"Are you making a joke? Like, how many psychologists does it take to change a lightbulb?"

"No."

He wiped at the side window as if it were fogged. "How many, by the way?"

"Only one, as long as the bulb has a sincere desire to change." Sarah batted her eyes.

He scoffed and continued to stare down at the canoes.

She pretended she didn't care about them. "There it is. Eagle Lake."

Logan located it and nudged Gertie a few degrees east.

"Can I take her again?" Sarah asked.

"Go."

Flying above the deep blue of Eagle was . . . what? She'd run out of superlatives. Campfire smoke along the west shore of the lake drifted lazily into the sky. Wind wouldn't be a consideration on landing.

Yikes, she was thinking in "pilot." If college French had come to her like that she'd be on permanent assignment at the Sorbonne.

They were a mile or so away from Farm Island when she handed the controls back to Logan. He said, "We're going to do one flyby. Check the landing area. Look sharp for anything that might be a problem for us coming in."

He eased back on the throttles and Gertie, lined up now on a pass parallel to Farm Island, slowed and sank through the crisp air like the bird of her Grumman namesake. Logan leveled her off at 100 feet. "Check the water along this line.

Look real good. We don't want anything coming up through the hull when we touch down on the next pass."

Hell, yes. Sarah got a cold chill. You could never afford to let the raw beauty and joy of flight mask the fact that your very existence lay in the palm of your hands in the air, or water, in Gertie's case. Mismanage anything and your future would change very quickly.

So she looked really, *really* well.

"Anything?" Logan pulled back on the yoke and added throttles to pull Gertie over the tree line at the end of the flyby. Sarah was pressed backward into her seat.

"Deep blue all along the line, no apparent obstructions. I think we're okay. Like I say, it's deep along there. Any logs are on the bottom minding their own business."

"Nobody around to come paddling across our path?"

"Nope. There are campers along the edge of the lake, but all the canoes are pulled up high. They look settled in. Nobody on Farm Island, either. We're good to go."

"Okay, coming around for real. Let's get her feet wet."

Logan cleared the area, banked 180 degrees west onto a downwind leg, then turned 90 degrees west again. They flew for about a minute.

"Flaps ten degrees," he said.

Sarah engaged the hydraulics. Servos whined and the airframe shimmied. "Flaps down ten."

Before they had taken off from the harbor, Logan had given her a run-through on the main systems of the Widgeon, which was not a problem because she had been passionately interested in every aspect of Gertrude from the very first time she'd set eyes on her. Logan explained that should anything happen to him when they were flying together, knowing the controls would give Sarah a reasonable chance of piloting the plane down in one piece.

She'd take reasonable over none.

"Carburetor heat on," he said.

"Check. Carb heat on." She'd never forget that as long as she lived. Catchy epitaph, actually: Here Lies Sarah Dundee: She only forgot her carb heat once.

Logan turned onto final approach, lining Gertrude's bow cleat up on Eagle Lake again.

"Gear down."

"Roger, gear on its way." Sarah reached for the red lever near her left knee but stopped as soon as her hand touched it. Logan, the sneaky bastard, was setting her up. Put the gear down for a water landing and there'd be two great big rubber donuts cluttering up the pristine byways of Eagle Lake.

"Ha-ha. I hope Gertie thought that was funny. I didn't."

"Good job. Give me thirty degrees on flaps. Really."

She reached up to the overhead panel and slid the dual levers forward another notch. "Thirty degrees flaps, really."

She took a look outside the cockpit and instantly became alarmed. They were coming down way too close to the Farm Island beach. "Logan, for Christ's sake, you've got the whole width of the lake through here. Get the hell off the beach."

"The water's dead flat, like a mirror. I can't judge how high we are and I need a reference point."

"Fine." But Je-*sus* it looked like they were landing in the sand. Gertie settled lower, with the island off her port bow.

"Full flaps."

"Flaps forty degrees."

As the flaps whined down, Gertie wallowed, surfing the still air with the added wing area. Sarah had the fleeting impression of webbed feet feeling for water contact.

Logan said, "Even close to the beach this is a bitch. Watch the altimeter and call it out from fifty feet on down. Is it always this calm?"

"Ah . . . no." She remembered wild, water-over-the-gunwales, heart-in-your-mouth canoe trips. Times when her and

Rick's parties had to hunker down in the lee of Farm Island or the shore of Eagle Lake to wait out the winds. "Usually the only way to beat the wind is to start out before dawn. It can blow all day. Flat water's not the norm." She checked the altimeter. "Fifty."

Logan reached overhead and cut back on the throttles. "Loosen them up a bit, will you?"

Sarah stretched and backed off the throttle friction settings. Standard procedure during takeoffs, landings, and taxiing, Logan had told her. During cruising flight the pilot usually keeps the response tight, but during delicate maneuvering the pilot backs off the friction to get more control.

"Forty."

The yoke in front of her twitched and rocked eerily. Sarah lightly touched it, tuning in to Gertie. Like a baseball player in the on-deck circle swinging at pitches in time with the batter at the plate. Gratifyingly, the inputs she would have made seemed to match up pretty well with Logan's. Gertrude was a good girl. A female spirit with the heart of a lion.

"Thirty."

The trees on either side of the lake loomed in Sarah's mind like enormous pickets on a gigantic fence as they descended closer and closer to the surface of the lake. The roar of the twins reverberated off the solid, gray-green trunks, throwing waves of sound back at the plane, immersing Gertrude in a solid wash of sound that Sarah could hear—and feel—despite the headphones.

"Twenty."

Spots of bright color on the far shore broke the unrelieved greens and browns of the lake edge. Tents.

"Ten," Sarah called.

"Lift your feet. We're in," Logan said.

The lap belt dug into Sarah's waist as Gertrude settled

matronly into the lake. The pontoons dug in and threw curtains of white spray. Water flung from the props misted the windscreen and Logan called for the wipers. As Sarah flicked the switch, she felt Gertie's bow drop as she morphed from bird to boat, and suddenly Sarah could see over the nose again.

"We want the beach on Farm Island, back to our left," she said. "It should be easy to sneak in there."

"Right. I'll head us around."

Being back there again, on Eagle Lake, where it all started with Rick, brought up curious emotions. Relief that she could finally do a free release, return him to the river. She'd finally seen the truth about him and their relationship. She didn't feel cheated or compelled to have to hunt him down and kill him in anger. If either of them had committed the sin of deception or, to be more accurate and less accusatory, *delusion*, it was her. Because Rick had given her, in good faith, exactly what she asked of him. Unfortunately, with Spot constantly gnawing at her ass and the sun creeping inexorably above the yardarm of her third unmarried decade, her clarity, the little she had ever possessed, had been compromised. But no crime here, no victims.

Just a little sadness: she was left without so much as the appearance of having a dance partner.

"Is it?"

Logan's voice in the headphones. He was talking to her. No, he was barking at her. "Is it *what*?" she said.

"You with me here? Is the water clear on your side? Pay attention, will you?"

Pay attention, will you? she mimicked to the glass in the side window.

"Clear this side," she barked back. Thinking about herself had made her cranky. Dr. Loo always said that try as you might to run away the one thing you could never leave out of your suitcase was your own ego. Hers could be a real party pooper.

Logan cut back on the starboard engine and goosed the port engine to fishtail Gertie around facing Farm Island. He gunned both engines and she galloped right along. The spray across the windscreen lessened. The fine art of floatplane taxiing was something else Logan had filled Sarah in on when they were leaving his cove.

"Taxi fast or taxi slow, but not in the middle," he'd said. "Slow, they don't kick up much water. Fast, most of it blows off to the side and the plane outruns it. In the middle, spray gets thrown over everything, especially the engines. Not good. Especially salt water. Rots the hell out of everything. Go ahead and try it."

Sarah had discovered that piloting Gertie at full gambol across the chop off the Manchester coast was no cakewalk. It was how she imagined driving a hovercraft might be. Gertrude behaved like neither fish nor fowl.

Plus, she'd had to watch out for channel markers, ubiquitous lobster buoys, and curious jet skiers. The activity level around the plane made her feel like they were in the middle of a Richard Scary illustration entitled "A Busy Harbor." All in all she'd found the whole experience disconcerting and quickly handed the controls back to Logan.

They were coming up on Farm Island. Logan's eyes were glued to the surface of the lake in front of them. He said, "At least Gertie's getting a good rinse off of all that salt water from Salem Bay."

"Yeah, and we've probably irrevocably altered the ecosystem of the waterway by introducing a foreign substance into it."

For a millisecond, Logan took his eyes off the view out

front and gave her one of his Dark Darcy looks. She shrugged: *Just kidding.*

Another minute brought them within hailing distance of the island. Logan cut back on the throttles and Gertrude obligingly settled in the water. His voice crackled through the headphones. "Unplug your headset and pop open the front hatch. Take the phones with you."

"Roger." She knew the drill. They'd gone over this before, too, in Logan's cove. Sarah yanked her headphone cord out of the connection on the instrument panel, unbuckled her seat belt, and crawled forward into Gertie's hollow bow section. Groping overhead in the dark, she released the forward hatch dog and levered it open.

Cool, pine-scented air rushed in. Beautiful.

Sarah acknowledged that while she was completely besotted with Gertie, she could be the tiniest bit claustrophobic. Or was it the company? Sarah maneuvered her upper body through the opening and stood for a moment, hip braced against the side of the hatch. She tilted her head back, savoring the breeze blowing through her hair.

Back to business. She felt around inside the hatch coaming for the audio jack and plugged in her headset. Then she turned and waved gaily to Logan through the windshield. "Sound check. One, two, three . . ." Being outside in the fresh air had instantly whisked away her crankiness. She *was* a nature girl, through and through.

"Yeah, yeah, I hear you," he said, his disembodied voice trickling down into her ear. She couldn't see him because of the reflections bouncing across the cockpit glass. He sounded martyred. "Hang on. I'll take her in as slowly as I can. Watch for obstructions."

She waved in response and turned to face front. She felt like the figurehead of a clipper ship, proudly poised at the bow of the craft. She leaned out over the bow a little more and hoped the rear view was getting to Logan. Nature always got her going—again, what didn't?—and, hey, she might as well pass the favor forward.

Gently, Logan played the throttles and Gertie crept closer to the beach. Sarah hung on to the forward cleat, peering down into the green depths. Nothing but shafts of sunlight disappearing into the gloom. Suddenly there were weeds, gently waving. Pebbles materialized. She signaled with her free hand: *Cut!* Logan killed the engines. With a quiet *shoosh*, Gertrude snuggled onto the beach.

For better or worse, they'd arrived.

Chapter 24

Sarah had to give the lad credit. He did okay setting up his tent.

Yes, he did permanently crimp one of the aluminum poles when he forced it into an unnatural, bordering-on-perverse contortion, but to her surprise he was able to fix it with the repair sleeve the manufacturers of the good stuff always included in the stake bag.

Her tent was identical to his, and he elected to wait on setting it up until the video crew, and whoever else comprised the remainder of the floating invasion force, arrived. It had to be a really weird situation for him, having to get credit for everything he did correctly over the next few days. Iverson had wanted a week, but not even WKAX went along with that. The Nature Nazi might be hot local news, but he wasn't exactly Ben and J-Lo, either.

Rick had prepacked plastic boxes of gear for Sarah and Logan, and they hauled them out of Gertrude and up onto the beach. Sarah helped Logan safely moor Gertie fifty feet or so off the beach. Knowing from experience that Eagle Lake could kick up waves when the wind was right, she told him to get a really good bite with his anchor thrown off the bow. That set, they ran a stern line back to a tree on shore.

Each container Rick packed was stenciled "Donated by Adventure Ventura, Inc." in a letter size you'd use on a school bus, Sarah noted. She wondered if the labels were negotiated items or if Rick had done the stenciling on the sly.

Logan parked himself on a rock and arranged the containers on the sand in a semicircle around him. He popped the watertight lids and rummaged through each box carefully, like he was expecting something to spring out at him, then, one by one, he pulled the items out of each box and examined them.

Sarah made herself comfortable on a nearby log and simply observed the proceedings, which was difficult because when Rick and she ran tours together she had always been the one buzzing around setting everything up and making everyone comfortable. On the river, toward the end of the day, she'd often leave Rick with the main body of the generally slow-moving group and race ahead solo to the campsite they'd chosen ahead of time. Arriving forty-five minutes or so before the party, she'd rake out the area, gather up firewood, get a blaze going, and wrap potatoes and corn in tinfoil, ready to be tossed on the coals.

Water purifier, storage containers, stove, fuel, kitchen set, and first-aid kit. The list of things Logan dredged out went on and on. All spanking new. Nothing but the best with old Rick.

No item was in its original container, not surprising as Rick knew well what a pain in the ass carry in/carry out could be, but none of the stuff had any operating instructions included, either. Sneaky. Sometimes even she had laminated the info sheets and stuck them in the carry sack of some of the new, ever-trickier gear she was planning to test. You just couldn't keep up with the constant innovations.

Logan clucked when he examined the propane lantern. Both mantles were missing. Again, sneaky. Every lamp Sarah had ever used was shipped with the little silk bags installed. Points to Logan for having discovered it ahead of time. Not fun tying in new mantles by flashlight.

He dug around in some of the small mesh storage bags and found replacements. He took the lantern apart, tied on one mantle, and held his handiwork up to admire it. Then he untied the mantle and put everything back the way he had found it. He looked at her and grinned.

She laughed. Rick had better watch his back. A steady flash of light out on the lake caught her eye. "Find any binoculars in those tubs?" she asked.

Logan rooted around and produced a pair of minis in a Neoprene traveling case. Same kind she'd dropped and fallen upon all in the name of writing next month's "Gear Review." She dialed in the focus on the remarkably well-protected lenses. The field of view was a bit tight at . . . she guessed half a mile. But she could well enough pick out sunlight rhythmically reflecting off of canoe paddles. The flotilla of canoes spelling doom for Logan was making steady progress toward Farm Island.

"What's up?" Logan asked, although Sarah thought he already knew the answer.

"It ain't Lewis and Clark, that's for damn sure." Sarah brought her knees up and braced her elbows on them. The boats were jumping around in the narrow field. Gentle reminder to self: don't get in the lazy habit of testing new equipment in only one environment. These little babies should have been dry run somewhere other than in just the limited confines of the preserve. She was getting sloppy. "It's them. E.T.A.? Twenty minutes or so."

"Lovely. So now we wait."

"I guess so." She unwrapped the new nylon lanyard she discovered in the binoculars case and threaded it through the tie ring on the housing of the glasses. "Hey, you're not doing too bad so far, sorry to say. How'd you get so good so fast?"

"I can read up on stuff, too."

"Touché." She handed him the binoculars.

He stowed them away in one of the tubs, then stood up and stretched, sizing up the dense greenery that surrounded the clearing on the beach. "I suppose I ought to scout out the terrain."

Sarah laughed. "Ex-military, right?"

He shot her another Dark Darcy.

"Just take it easy," she said. "Remember: you're just trying to convince people you like nature, not that you can dominate it."

And, why, pray tell, was she helping him? Answer: because she was still so incredibly torn. Her mouth had moved before her mind was in gear.

"I'm going to look for firewood," Logan said. Sarah watched him crash off through the underbrush.

"Be careful," she called. No response, although she knew he must have heard her. Sarah relaxed in the sunshine. She must have dozed off because the next thing she knew a spray of sand shot into her face.

"What the f—" She spit out half the beach.

"Did you see it? Did you? Holy shit!" Logan was dancing around her spastically, waving his arms and babbling.

"See . . . *cagh!*"—Sarah hacked up granules and *p'tu-ied* inelegantly into the sand between her boots—"what?"

She wobbled to the water and blindly kicked off her sandals—her eyes had gotten blasted too—and rinsed.

"Logan—*cagh!*—what is your fucking problem?" The

threat of silicosis and permanent vision loss was enough to make anyone testy.

"The fucking moose? Did you see it?" He followed her knee deep into the water, oblivious of his boots. "Holy shit . . . biggest fucking thing I ever saw." He waved wildly at the woods.

Sarah filled in the dots.

A moose. Logan had seen a moose. Now he was a kid with a new toy. She loved all woodland creatures, for sure, but she'd had—she had to think about it for a moment—conservatively, 200 Moose Moments in her life. Watching Logan, though, brought back the thrill of her first time.

"I'm so happy for you, Logan, making a new friend on your first day away from home. But he plays rough, so watch out." Moose, bear, coyotes—hell, even fisher cats and raccoon: you didn't screw with them. They owned the place, humans just rented. Sarah waded back to shore.

"Jeez . . . unbelievable," he said.

Maybe there was hope for him yet, Sarah thought, picking balls of grainy gunk out of the corners of her eyes. Unfortunately, God, she hated feeling like a cheap bedsheet tugged in two directions.

"Oh, shit," Logan said, shading his eyes and peering out toward open water.

Sarah tried to focus blurry, teary eyes, but no go. "What?"

"Hallo!" carried to the beach.

"Don't tell me," she said, sifting through possibilities. "Iverson?"

"Oh, yeah. Lead canoe. But it gets better."

Sarah squinted. Her eyes felt like they'd been reinstalled by an auto-body technician. "How much better?"

"*Sa-rah!*" A woman's voice.

"Oh, no," Sarah said.

"Oh, yes," Logan said."

"*Oh, hello, dear!*" her mother trilled, Violet's piercing tones carrying easily over the water.

Wasn't life just full of surprises? Feeling the phantom scrape of barrettes against her scalp, Sarah secured a few tickling hairs behind her ears and scrunched her eyes up— *ouch*. The bobbing boats swam into some kind of focus, with Violet occupying the lead seat of the lead one. No surprise there.

Three guys in the next boat. She wiped away tears. Two she . . . didn't know, but one face she instantly recognized from the *The Eleven O'Clock News*.

Behind them a woman, dark hair—*ow*, pain—Maura Winslow and a man, no, a boy—her son Eric. He'd grown three inches in like two weeks. Next in line . . .

Boats started hitting the sand. Out of one stepped a broad-chested guy whose name, it suddenly occurred to Sarah, rhymed with *dick*.

"Sarah? How are you?" Broad Chest said. "You didn't call. Gear working out? Tax deductible contribution, so careful with it." Laugh track. Everyone except her—and Logan— joined in.

"Hello, Rick," Sarah said.

The middle section of his canoe, as well as any open spot in anyone else's, was piled high with watertight boxes identical to the ones Logan and Sarah had already unloaded. In the front seat of his boat perched a woman whose silver hair glinted beneath an enormous sun hat that would have fit nicely in a seaside remake of *Gone with the Wind*. Given the different surroundings, it took Sarah a moment to recognize the woman. It was her old-home griddle jail mate, Hillary Harker.

The final craft, straggling in quite a ways behind the main

force, contained the loose-lipped, slim-hipped, legal expert Michael Brophy, Esquire, at your service; a small mountain of gear; and her ex–best friend Joan, who waved her paddle halfheartedly. She and Michael both looked sunburned and exhausted. An alert group leader would have picked up on that.

Iverson's canoe ground onto the beach. The whole landing operation had been conducted with military precision.

Sarah kissed the air around her mother's cheek, shook Iverson's hand, exchanged "hey's" with Maura and Eric, nodded to the film guys, ignored her ex-fiancé, kicked off her sandals, and dove into the lake.

She swam out to Joan's canoe, grabbed the painter; and after a few one-armed strokes found her footing in the shallows and towed their boat onto the beach. She shouldered her way through the milling crowd to the expedition's chesty, fearless leader.

"Get water and sunscreen out for everybody *now*," she growled at Rick. Then, as an afterthought, added, "*Jerk.*"

The camera crew had finally finished hauling equipment cases out of their boat and up onto the sand. Sarah watched them take off lens covers and check light meters. The guy with the very familiar face pulled on a clean shirt from a waterproof duffel.

"So, Logan? Find everything you needed?" Rick asked, wading ashore with his hands full of waterproof boxes. Logan squared off, facing him, hands on his hips. Rick paused, holding the boxes against his stomach.

One of the video cameras whirred softly. A newsreel clip to entertain the folks at home: George Patton confronts General Montgomery on the shores of Sicily.

"You bet, Rick. Nice of you to . . . ah, set me up."

Rick gave him a look Sarah well remembered. An un-adulterated, testosterone-saturated Completely Male look. Paired up with nice dark eyes and all kinds of ripply things going on under the tanned skin of muscular forearms, it used to work for her. It seemed like another lifetime though, like another woman entirely had felt that way. Nowadays, a light in the attic cranked her engines. But she'd seen buck deer go after each other with less eye contact.

"Rick, say, how about helping Joan and Michael with their stuff? And Logan"—Sarah said this in her best Ma Cartwright voice—"that second tent needs tending to."

But the two men held their gaze, Rick looking like he could drop the box and be on Logan before he drew another breath, Logan standing with his feet evenly spaced in the sand. *Bring it.*

"Firewood," Sarah said, loudly, pointing to the woods. "Now."

Better to have the two guys go beat the shit out of each other in the woods, away from the camera and the audience. She realized everyone in earshot was staring at her, oblivious to the standoff.

"Go!" she said again, shooing Logan and Rick away with her hands.

Without taking his eyes off Logan, Rick set the boxes down. Sarah watched him and Logan walk up the beach in lockstep, never varying the distance between them and never taking their eyes off each other. They faded out of sight into the underbrush.

The camera guy and the Talking Head guy, their sensitive antennae undoubtedly picking up the scent of blood in the water, got up and followed.

To Joan, Sarah said the first word they had exchanged in what seemed like years. "And, no, I *don't* care what the crystal ball says about that."

Joan was drinking deeply from the Nalgene bottle Maura had given her and Michael. "Too bad," she mumbled around slurps. "You might be surprised."

"By what?" Sarah's mother asked. Sarah jumped. Violet cruised around on ball bearings for all the noise she made behind a person.

"I've got to get the rest of this stuff up the beach, Ma," Sarah said.

"Don't change the subject, and don't call me 'Ma,'" Violet said.

Ah, the public airing of the Mother/Daughter Bone of Contention Number Twenty-six: The Proper Form of Address. Sarah had heard the teenage years were the hardest, but in the case of she and Violet, they looked to have been the best.

"Violet? I could use a hand over here." Sarah silently thanked Iverson. He was at least good for something. Sarah smiled and waved, the dutiful almost employee. Sarah was shot with one of Violet's patented dirty looks. Her mother stalked away.

"Gonna be a fun trip. I can tell already," Joan said.

Sarah grimaced. "Make sure she finishes that bottle off," she said to Michael. "And down another one yourself, too."

"Will do. Thanks."

Polite man. A commodity in short supply this trip. Sarah decided that she didn't have to share her Dead Lawyer joke series around the fire ring that evening.

She grabbed up a plastic tub and started on her way up the slope of the beach toward the relatively flat tenting area that countless seasons of concentrated human habitation had wrested from the deep woods bordering the lake. Huffing and puffing, she reached the fire ring, then dropped the container onto the packed earth. Maura and Eric had already lugged most of their gear up from the boats and were going through boxes that had their names written on them. Sarah watched Eric dig out the tent and shuck it out of its bag.

Suddenly, something that sounded a lot like a strangled human cry emanated from the underbrush in the direction the Hardy Boys had disappeared. Sarah froze, praying there wouldn't be much blood involved.

Eric and Maura also stopped what they were doing and looked in the direction of the woods. They had heard something, too.

Sarah could only imagine what the camera guy and the announcer type—whose name she *still* didn't have—were capturing on film. She glanced to her right. The third and obviously junior member of the video crew had been left behind to shove containers around by himself, but now he, too, had stopped in midgrunt and, with a look of longing on his face, was apparently listening intently. To Sarah's left, Mrs. Harker was sitting on a log, daintily pursing her lips at a compact mirror and touching up her lipstick. The casual observer would never guess at the wonderfully foul mouth on her.

No more noise came from the brush. Sarah relaxed. Everyone else eventually did, too, and went back to what they were doing. Sarah found herself doing what came naturally to her: helping people get set up.

All in all, things were progressing nicely, Sarah thought, and she was just heading back down to the beach for another load of boxes when Announcer Guy leapt out of the underbrush not ten feet from her. He snagged his feet on a corner of the tent Eric was laying out and he pitched head over heels into the center of the campsite clearing, almost cracking his head open on the boulders forming the fire ring. Camera Guy came out of the shrubbery next—backward—filming something.

Then Logan exploded from the underbrush as if fired from a circus cannon.

You'd never have imagined he normally gimped around a bit, Sarah thought, because now in his arms he carried—to Sarah's open-mouthed amazement—Rick. Rick's legs were bloody and with every step Logan took they bounced up and down like the appendages on one of her old Raggedy Ann dolls.

"Moose!" Logan screamed. The announcer struggled to his feet, but the tent was still wrapped around a foot and he went down again like a wet sack of dirt.

"Huge, fucking moose!" Logan screamed, like everyone in upstate Maine hadn't heard him the first time. He skidded to a stop at the campfire ring. Mrs. Harker's lipstick tube froze in midswipe. Violet was carrying a box with Iverson. She dropped her end of it. Iverson cursed creatively but softly. Eric tugged on his tent possessively and Maura—never taking her eyes from the woods—groped blindly for the guy on the ground, trying to help him up.

A moving tree erupted from the forest behind Logan and came right for him, the leafless branches sprouting from its head bayoneting the air. They enthusiastically slashed to and fro, dangling green streamers that whipped the air furiously.

Pond weeds, Sarah realized. For a second they reminded her of the gaudy plastic things kids used to stick into the ends of the handlebars of bikes. Except these slimy things were adorning a nine-foot-tall, six-foot-wide walking Swiss Army knife. Death on the hoof.

It was indeed a—

"*Fucking moose!*" Sarah yelled.

The moose swiveled his huge head and looked right at Sarah like she'd called it by name.

"Get into the trees!" she yelled to the shocked onlookers.

No time to assess personal escape options—she had to buy other people time. She locked eyes with the enormous beast and slowly sidestepped away from the main group. *Look at me, bub. I'm the most interesting thing out here. . . .*

Out of the corner of her eye, Sarah saw Maura grab Eric, who shoved hard on the announcer, which finally untangled him. To his credit, the guy then ran for Violet and dragged her along with him to the nearest oak.

"*Sarah . . .*"

Someone was whispering to her, Sarah realized. She signaled *Go!* in the general direction of the voice.

The moose abruptly broke eye contact with Sarah to track the sound and leveled what could only be called a loving gaze on the individual who had obviously become a human Rocky to his Bullwinkle: Logan.

Logan's eyes became as large as dinner platters. He was evidently not prepared to make a serious commitment because he—still cradling Rick—made a dash for the beach. Apparently Bullwinkle was not a moose who gave his heart away lightly, because he pawed the ground and snorted beckoningly. Off to the side of the clearing, Iverson was struggling to boost Violet up onto the lowest branches of a big birch. Better than nothing.

To avoid becoming hoof gunk, Sarah dashed for a shag bark hickory she'd scouted out. Not that there was a tree of choice if someone ever found herself in a similar situation because there wasn't. The hickory just happened to be small enough for her to wrap her legs around it and shinny up. She was about eight feet off the ground when Bullwinkle charged. He blew past her perch and he was, as she could all too clearly see, as reported, frigging enormous.

Good thing it wasn't her he'd booked a play date with because given the height of her precarious perch, the uppermost point on his enormous rack would have gone right up her—she shuddered and climbed higher. She had never, in any of her Moose Moments, been anywhere close enough to one of the little darlings to get a whiff of their actual scent. It was nice to know she had missed absolutely nothing. She wrestled with her gag reflex as the back draft hit.

She tracked Bullwinkle's path toward the beach with her eyes and extended an imaginary line straight out from his nose. It intersected . . . shit! Joan. Reclining on the sand, facing the lake, her back propped against a shaded boulder and her boots off, she was oblivious to the danger.

"Get out! Paddle out! Now!" Sarah yelled to her and gestured frantically. Joan didn't stir, but Michael's head popped up from the other side of the rock. Ivy League training evidently prepared a body for a multitude of life events because he grasped the situation instantly. He and Joan grabbed their grounded canoe fore and aft and slid it double time into the water.

Logan by then had dumped an irate-looking Rick onto the sand and was trying to drag a canoe—still half filled with gear—into the water. Sarah prayed that he hadn't suffered some sort of head wound and was just acting crazy, because that's what it looked like, but she guessed he figured he could never get a wounded Rick stuffed safely up a tree. *Dump out the fucking gear!* she silently screamed.

Reaching the head of the beach, Bullwinkle jammed on the brakes, shooting cascades of sand from his hooves. He sniffed the air—delicately for such a huge creature—then pawed the ground menacingly, blowing woofies the size of handkerchiefs from his nostrils. Which brought to Sarah's mind a spin-off of the old credit card commercial: How do you stop a moose from charging? She couldn't remember the answer.

So she screamed, "Hey, Moose!"

Bullwinkle bellowed and shook his head violently. That evidently wasn't the punch line.

Logan had the canoe about halfway to the water. Something looked to be wrong with one of his arms and his limp was more pronounced than Sarah had ever seen it. She wished she were better at math and could calculate angles and intersections, but a quick eyeball of the situation led her to one inescapable conclusion: Bullwinkle would be on the boys before the boys were in the canoe.

She mentally clothed herself in Ninja black and shinnied backward down the hickory.

"Sarah, have you lost your mind?" a voice hissed from the big birch. Her mother.

Of course, Violet might say the same thing if she had caught her daughter eating a sweetened breakfast cereal, so Sarah just touched a fingertip to her lips. *Silence.* The party was over. Bullwinkle needed to be immediately served his second after-dinner coffee pointedly without sherry. If she waited, he'd food process the luckless lads.

What would scare him off? A bigger moose? Rocks, maybe. But then how fast could she really run?

Flares.

Rick always used to pack them on their trips. If she could get to the right box, they'd be in business. Her feet touched sandy soil. She peeled herself from the tree. Ouch. Nature's depilatory. She'd never get the pitch off her inner thighs. She glanced toward the beach, where Logan had given up on the canoe-launching idea. Now he was rolling the boat on top of Rick, who was flopping around among the gear boxes like a wounded baby seal. She was still quite far away, but Sarah did hear snatches:

"Get the fuck under there." That was Logan.

"That fucker's gonna gore you something good." Rick.

"*I'm* gonna fucking gore you if you don't shut up and get under the fucking boat."

And so on.

Sarah would have peed her pants if the situation wasn't so serious bordering on deadly. She reached Maura and Eric's stuff and ransacked one of their boxes.

"The other one! The other box!" Voices from on high. Maura and Eric were pointing furiously. How nice when everyone was on the same page. Sarah popped the lid on the second container. *Flares . . . flares . . .* Her kingdom for one fucking—ah! pay dirt. She grabbed the waterproof pouch and commenced to sneak up on Bully's backside, staying low like Lenny Brisco on *Law and Order* did when he was on a raid. You really went to your strengths when the pressure was on.

Of course Lenny wouldn't have tripped over something hollow and metallic and extraordinarily noisy on his way past the fire ring. With her eyes on the prize instead of the cluttered ground in the clearing, she'd managed to jam her foot into a two-quart cook pot. She yanked at it but the bail caught on her sandal strap, so she was forced to abandon subterfuge and clank along on her peg leg like Captain Ahab.

Oddly enough, this was how a one-hundred-and-not-much-more-than-fifteen-pound woman scares the shit—literally—out of a thousand-something-pound moose, Sarah discovered. Bullwinkle's head whipped around to size up the clanking threat—which no doubt sounded like a mechanized tank division to his ears—then squirted what looked to be a typically vegetarian lunch out his exhaust and bolted. Right at Logan and Rick.

Not what she'd had in mind. Not at all.

Logan hopped over the upside-down canoe to avoid the charge. Horrified, Sarah watched Bullwinkle lock up the brakes, then, with a flick of his rack, flip Rocky's—Ricky's—damn it, she was terrified—*Rick's* flimsy shelter into the air. The knucklehead tried to make a run for it but his legs lost all compression and he collapsed in a heap. His ankle wouldn't take any weight.

"Logan!" Sarah screamed.

Logan glanced her way and she hurled the package of flares at him. They sailed over his head like the mayor's opening day pitch and plopped into the sand half a dozen yards away. Out of options, Logan turned and faced down Bullwinkle, waving his arms and making threatening—in human terms—noises, drawing the animal away from Rick.

Sarah was impressed, but not for long. Logan snatched up a hunk of driftwood from the sand. It looked remarkably like a moose antler. He jabbed it at his new friend and bellowed.

But hell hath no fury. Bullwinkle charged.

Logan made a beeline for the woods, scooping up the flares on his way by, his half-ton honey in hot pursuit. Sarah plopped herself inelegantly down onto the dirt and wrenched the pot off her foot. Free at last, she yelled at everyone to stay put and dove into the underbrush.

It was dim and dark and full of screams in there. Scratchy things tore at Sarah as she ran following the trail of sound. Suddenly, the Fourth of July arrived eleven months early. The forest ahead of her exploded in shimmering orange light. A ball of fire whizzed by her head. She ducked behind a tree. Another burst of kaleidoscopic color off to her left. A ricochet off a branch showered her with sparks.

Then the Portland Express barreled by on Track Nine. Bullwinkle, sounding like an entire company of especially lead-footed but highly motivated sumo wrestlers, thundered by her, making perhaps the most piteous sound she had ever heard in her life. Unrequited love seasoned with abject terror was only an approximation.

She peered into the dimness of the forest in the direction the locomotive had come from.

Not a creature was stirring, not even a Logan.

Sarah had heard people say that at a moment of crisis their heart stopped. It was true, she realized. Nothing moves in your chest. There's this numbing, frozen lockup deep in your guts.

Then she saw a dirty, bleeding forearm fling itself over a downed, moss-covered pine trunk about a hundred feet in front of her. A little gear inside her clinked. Next, a head revealed itself, then all the rest of the parts of a body. All in the right places. All apparently working.

It was only then she felt her heart go thump.

"And . . . cut!" someone called, behind her. "Got it."

The camera guy.

She spun around.

He slid his video camera off his shoulder and cradled it in the crook of one arm. He gave her a cheery thumbs-up and headed back to camp.

One brave, stupid bastard. Just like the one rising to his knees in front of her. She walked over to Logan. The overwhelming concern she felt for him had taken her by surprise, but smacking him upside the head seemed to come pretty naturally. "What the hell is *wrong* with you?"

Logan rubbed his scalp.

Sarah rubbed her palm. He had skull like granite. Like she didn't already know that. "Crissakes. You've been here what? Not even an hour? And you've already pissed off one of the most amicable animals going."

Logan struggled to his feet. Sarah didn't offer assistance.

"I had help." He said this like she was Sister Mary and it wasn't really all his fault because an accomplice had assisted him when he dumped the frogs in the holy water.

"Oh, so that makes it okay?" She didn't wait for a response.

Back at the campsite, people were coming down out of the trees, just like their ancestors had done two million years ago. Sarah snickered. *Sometimes I slay me.*

Her mother was kneeling next to Iverson, who was slumped against the base of the tree they'd scaled. That *wasn't* so funny. Eric was with them.

Down at the beach, Joan and Michael were bending over Rick. Sarah met Maura heading there. She carried a first aid kit. "Logan?" Maura asked.

"He's okay."

"Figures. He has nine lives."

Sarah fell into stride with her.

"How *do* you piss off a moose?" Maura asked.

Sarah laughed. "Tell you later."

"Men?"

"There you go."

Rick's injuries looked worse than they actually were. Maura got an Ace bandage around his ankle and cleaned and taped up everything else. She fussed over him more than Sarah might have thought she might, and he seemed to want her to more than Sarah might have expected.

Logan stumbled over. Sarah pretended they'd never been introduced. Maura gave him a once-over. "You'll live," she said and tossed him the first aid bag.

Rick, standing with the help of Joan and Michael, flung himself onto Logan.

Ding! Round Two, Sarah figured.

"Oh, my God . . ." Rick said. "You saved my life, man. You fucking saved my life." He hugged—Sarah was dumbstruck. Yes, as in, actually wrapped his arms around— Logan.

Logan patted Rick's back like Rick had a communicative skin disease.

"That's . . . uh, okay. Okay. Okay—get *off* me, Rick."

It was a weirdly touching, very strange moment for everyone.

Eric came running down the beach. "Mom! It's Mr. Iverson!" He stopped and pointed back toward the campsite. "Something's wrong with him!"

Maura and Sarah got to Iverson first. The Second Camera Guy and The Announcer—Sarah made a mental note to sometime learn the guys' real names—already had Iverson lying down, his feet and head elevated. Her mother was frantic.

"It's his heart . . . his heart." Violet reached into a small tote bag and pulled out a prescription bottle. "He usually takes two of these—" She glanced at Sarah guiltily.

Usually? Sarah thought.

"And it goes away."

"Angina?" Maura asked, taking the pill bottle from Violet and reading the label.

"Yes."

How would her mother . . . ? Sarah struggled to keep her attention on Iverson. He didn't look good. Pale, sweaty.

Maura said, "Eric, get me my knapsack. And a sleeping bag. We've got to keep Mr. Iverson warm." She pressed her fingers to the inside of his wrist and monitored her watch. Fifteen seconds later, her brows knitted. "How you feeling, Robert?" she asked, with that slightly too loud voice professionals seemed to use when addressing the ill.

"Been better."

Violet squeezed his hand. "It was the shock. The shock of seeing that damned . . . *creature*." Sarah hoped she didn't mean Logan.

Eric brought the sleeping bag, and with many hands making light work, they bundled Iverson into it. Maura tugged a blood pressure cuff and a stethoscope out of her knapsack. She wrapped the cuff around Iverson's arm and pumped the bulb with practiced ease.

"What don't you do?" Sarah asked her.

"Shhhsh . . ." She concentrated on the gauge.

Joan, Michael, Rick, and Logan joined the group huddled around Iverson. Stupid But Brave Camera Guy came over also, mercifully with nothing on his shoulder. The cuff hissed and Maura tore it off.

"How's he doing?" Logan asked. Sarah shrugged, then realized he was asking Maura.

"You're doing fine, Robert," Maura said, rising. "Just take it easy."

She turned to the group. "He's responding to the nitroglycerin. He should be fine if we keep him quiet for a while. Violet, you've got plenty of those pills, yes?"

Sarah's mother—who had a lot of explaining to do, as far as Sarah was concerned—nodded.

Everyone breathed a sigh of relief. They'd weathered another brush with The Infinite. The camera cranked up again, the unloading got done, and Logan made pretty fair work of supper on the portable stoves. After dinner, Sarah decided to take pity on him—from the way he was moving it didn't look like he'd be out dancing anytime soon—and unobtrusively wandered off to wash the dishes, but a camouflaged Camera Guy captured the evidence of her favor on film. The hanging jury in Tidal would have a field day. Exactly *who* they'd hang remained to be seen.

They bedded down their wounded, and just after sunset everyone turned in for the night.

* * *

Robert, Violet allowed, in a terse conversation with Sarah over morning coffee—before she had stalked back to her tent dragging Hillary and two cups of java along with her—passed a peaceful night.

Robert, now, was it? Sarah thought moodily. The man she knew only as her new boss thankfully looked pretty much back to normal from the quick assessment she'd made of him as he moseyed past the fire ring munching on a bagel. He was on his way down to the beach to join the rest of the lads. They'd left the high ground to the females. Sarah smiled politely at him in passing, but one of her planned activities for the day was to pin her mother's feet to the floor over the matter of one Robert Iverson.

Sarah shifted her butt to a more comfortable position on the log she was perched on and curled her fingers around the warmth of the coffee mug. Her new boss was her mother's what? *Boyfriend*? Sarah pictured them sitting in the dark on her couch eating her potato chips and watching cable TV that she paid for. Boyfriend didn't work.

Significant other? Good for a tax return but damn little else. Beau? Maybe. The situation between them was extraordinarily confusing to the little girl in Sarah. The adult was pretty shaky about it, too.

And speaking of shaking, the ground beneath her feet should have been, Sarah realized. The coffee had kicked in and with the buzz it also had ushered the sounds of a two-man ripsaw to the forefront of her brain, mercifully interrupting her bleak reverie. Sarah identified the source of the sound. In their tent, set up in a natural pocket of clear ground a few yards back into the woods, Joan and Michael were sleeping the sleep of the just—and the exhausted. Dr. Loo would have commended them on their deep breathing. Nice couple they made, Sarah had to admit.

Maura wandered groggily over to the fire ring. Sarah

watched her pour herself some joe and arrange herself on the opposite end of Sarah's log. Aside from brief "morning"s, they sipped in silence, which, after several minutes, began to feel strained. Maura finally set her empty cup down and bent over to straighten out the laces on one of her lightweight hiking boots.

"Rick tell you about the trains?" Sarah asked. In the twenties, two locomotives used to haul pulpwood between Eagle Lake and nearby Umbazooksus Lake. The rusting remains of the two giant, steam-powered beasts, abandoned in the woods not far from Eagle Lake, were a popular day hiker destination.

"Yeah, they sound wild. That's where we want to go today."

"We" didn't sound like it would stretch nearly far enough to constitute an open invitation. It sounded like teams were already picked: if you hadn't come together you didn't play together.

"How's Rick doing?" As tour group leader, Sarah meant.

"He's not himself."

"Is that a good or a bad thing?"

"The final tallies aren't in, but I'm thinking . . . good." Maura's face was screwed up in concentration. It wasn't that hard to untangle laces.

"And who better to know than you, eh?"

Maura cut her eyes to Sarah.

Sarah remembered eighth-grade gym class again. "Sorry. I didn't mean that the way it sounded." Actually she did.

"For that I'm glad," Maura said. "Because I would have thought less of you for it." The tongue on her boot refused to lie flat and she scowled. "Do not consider me an enemy unless you want a bad one."

Touché. The girl had game. Even though Sarah had a sudden inkling of a pending plot twist, she wasn't sure she could ever truly dislike Maura.

"End of speech," Maura said, lightening. "Whew." She made bunny ears and double tied the loops. "You going to the trains?"

Before Sarah had a chance to answer, a barnyard squabble broke out in the tent just behind them.

"Violet, you're stepping on my bags!"

Nylon tent walls bulged and contracted like the skin of a digesting anaconda. Sarah looked at Maura and each of them broke up in silent laughter. "Ladies, how we doing?" Sarah called to the tent.

"Hillary, if they weren't hanging so low to begin with I wouldn't have stepped on them!"

Rude rejoinders, then cackles. "You're as red as the tent," Maura whispered to Sarah.

"It's not *your* mother in there. With *your* elementary school nurse, for Chrissakes."

Maura soundlessly cracked up again. "Ah, folks," she said to the undulating tent side, "we'd like to get there sometime today. Could we get a move on, please?"

"Simmer down, sweetie, before I put a move on you. Hah!" The tent twitched violently as Violet made some kind of karate-style slash across the fabric. Giggles galore followed. Sarah just shook her head. You do your best. You try to bring them up proper, but the minute they get involved with boys it all goes to hell in a handbasket.

"Hey! That's my underwear you're putting on," Sarah's dignified, pillar-of-the-community mother said.

"So what's it doing on my side?" her school nurse answered.

Maura tried. "*La*-dies, we do have to get a—"

"And I said hold your horses, missy. We'll get there when we get there." Violet.

More rudeness transpired.

Maura said pointedly, "Damn it all . . . Like I need this?"

That cracked Sarah up. "Hey—how'd you end up on customer patrol, anyhow? Rick's not completely impaired." Physically, at least. She glanced down to the beach where he was reenacting, to the guffaws of the assembled, what looked to be the moose charge. The scene had a definite posthunt, Cro-Magnon flavor to it. For the hundredth time: *men.*

Maura rolled her eyes and sighed. "Because I'm an idiot." Then she became serious. "Look, really. How are things between you and him? I mean, he proposed to you or something, didn't he?"

"Or something."

"I'm not trying to be nosy or anything—okay, maybe I am—I'd just like to know where it stands with you guys."

Hushing noises and giggling from inside the tent.

"Truthfully," Sarah said, leaning in and tapping ash from an imaginary cigar, "it hasn't stood up between us for a while." She couldn't help it. She was caught up in the Cabaret moment.

Maura snickered. Someone in the tent dropped the F-word. Whatever.

"Sounds like they're having a liquid breakfast," Maura said.

"Yeah."

"They get out into the woods and they turn into Amazons."

"Uh-huh." Waiting, waiting.

Maura kicked the heel of a boot thoughtfully into the sandy dirt. When she had a depression that exactly conformed to the rounded rubber sole, she looked toward the beach and then back at Sarah. "Look, I was straight with you about

Logan. Be straight with me about Rick. Bottom line. What gives?" She crossed her arms.

Yikes, trapped like a rat. Sarah struggled to come up with a way to make Maura understand that for her giving up Rick was like knowing you couldn't go to the concert but hating to give the tickets up to someone else. Stupid, but there it was.

"All . . . right, all right," she finally said. "We're nowhere. Absolutely fucking nowhere." She raked her hands through her morning-mess of hair.

To Sarah's surprise, Maura chuckled. "And you, carrying on with Logan?" she said. "Tsk-tsk."

Sarah shuddered. She was being Joaned to death everywhere she went. It got worse.

"Sarah," Maura said. "You've got to end it once and for all. You know Rick's not going to go away until you tell him to. He'll continue to make our—I mean *your*—life hell. He's incredibly loyal to you. Egocentric, selfish, boneheaded—sorry, he is your ex-fiancé and all—but that's how he is."

Sarah crossed *her* arms. "And you have reason to know all this about him based on sharing a stretch of rapids?"

Maura kicked the dirt again. Sarah waited.

If Maura started tugging at a splinter in the log Sarah knew she was screwed.

"Okay, that's not all we shared," Maura said, finally.

Sarah felt herself become the nasty girl in gym class. It must have been obvious.

"Calm down, calm down," Maura said.

"Fuck." Sarah scratched her head.

"Whoa, not hardly. When I said he was loyal I meant it. Nothing happened."

Sarah didn't think she'd lie. "But you only met him that one time at the field, yes?"

"No."

"Secret rendezvous?"

Maura's eyes flashed. "Again, no. It was at Crossly Field. All very innocent."

"Wha—how?"

"He came out there all the time to watch you fly."

This was a new wrinkle. Sarah had only seen him there that one time.

"He wanted to make sure you were okay. After a few visits, I let him come up into the control tower. That day you almost bought it at The Rip?"

Sarah nodded mutely, remembering all too well.

"He was a mess. We practically had to mop him up off the floor. It wasn't pretty. Spying was stupid—I'm not proud of helping him with it, by the way—but his motives were pure. You gotta give him credit."

Sarah growled in frustration. She was seven years old when she found her first Barbie box under the Christmas tree—*"Yes! My dream come true!"*—only to realize that the doll was dressed in a square-dance costume and not the chic New York outfit she'd pictured her in. Almost right. That's what it was like with Rick. Almost right. But she wouldn't settle for the country outfit this time around. If she dared to risk ending up with no toy at all.

"Look, I'm not exactly impartial in this," Maura said. Sarah sensed she was choosing her words very carefully, gauging Sarah's reaction. "But you know in your heart that you're never going to get what you really want with him."

Yes, Maura fit nicely in the front row of the Greek chorus, right between Joan and Violet. Sarah parried pointlessly. "No shit, Sherlock."

"Hey, don't be all over me just because I'm saying what you already know." Now Maura was the gym class girl again.

The center section of the birch log/seat was polished to a satin finish by the touch of countless behinds over countless seasons, but at the ends there were still tiny strips of bark ripe for the picking. Sarah tore off a paper-thin section.

"I really thought it would work out, you know?" She smoothed the translucent parchment against the skin of her thigh. "He had it all. Successful, devoted—albeit in his own smothering way." She looked up at Maura. "And now he's yours."

Sarah flipped the gossamer peeling into the light breeze and watched it flutter away. It became tiny and she lost sight of it. She stood up and faced the wall of brush surrounding the clearing. Hot tears filled the corners of her eyes. They weren't really for Rick, she was honest enough to remind herself.

Maura and Rick. The snoring duet of Joan and Michael. Her mother and Iverson, for God's sake. Two by two onto the ark.

But Logan and Sarah? *Tilt!* Red lights flashed; horns blared.

"I should probably have my head examined," said Maura, awkwardly.

Sarah wiped her eyes on the sleeve of her Appalachian Trail T-shirt. No fuss. No prob. She was Nature Girl. Riding solo but riding hard. Cranking out those scintillating gear reviews. Now maybe something bigger. Things could be worse. "Don't bother," she said. "I did it for years and it never took."

From inside the tent, the mayhem reached a crescendo. A brassiere shot out and landed on the ground between Maura and Sarah.

"I'm done with that damn thing," came a garrulous female voice, raised in triumph. Hillary Harker's. "All it does is give me chaff. Phooey."

"More information than we really needed," Maura said, wincing.

"Uh, yeah."

"Sweetie, I hear you." Violet. A second bra slingshotted out of the tent doorway.

You had to laugh. So they did.

Iverson, despite his perky start, slept away the remainder of the day. Sarah stayed behind at the camp with Hillary Harker, while everyone else made the trip to the trains. Robert—Sarah was somewhat resigned to that moniker— had pleaded with them to make Violet go on the hike.

The group returned in late afternoon full of high humor. Sarah felt bad for Logan having to make supper for everyone, but she wasn't willing to further jeopardize the bet for the sake of being a nice guy—girl, rather. He made corn on the cob and baked potatoes in the coals and flash broiled some defrosted steak tips over a fast, hot fire of pine boughs. You had to give the lad credit. She did wince and look away when an errant ax strike clunked off the side of his boot. He seemed genuinely jazzed up about the hike and seeing the trains.

Later, the coolness of the evening drew the entire expedition to the fire ring. People swapped stories and Mrs. Harker organized a very unorthodox but completely hysterical game of charades. Maura covered Eric's ears at one point, although he looked like he'd heard it all before. The crowd gradually thinned as people made their sleepy way toward their tents. Gradually the blazing inferno Logan had built reduced itself to flickering flames casting deep, moving shadows onto the wall of woods surrounding the clearing. Maura, Rick, Eric, Logan, and Sarah were the last holdouts.

Half asleep, stretched out with her back to a log seat, Sarah remembered a scene from the Serengeti: her dad sitting by the fire long into the night. He had looked completely at home: a tall, thin, white man—or maybe not so white, since they'd been in Africa for several months by that time—seated cross-legged and shoulder to shoulder with dark-skinned, long-limbed native men. The slow beat of a drum set the cadence for a hymnlike song with words in a beautiful, singsong African dialect. She'd pretend to be asleep, but she, too, would be up long into the night, watching, concealed behind the flap of her tent.

She glanced at Rick from under the pulled-down brim of her cap. He was across the ring from her, his legs stretched out and feet crossed at the ankles. He appeared to be asleep, but she caught the glitter of his eyes as he scrutinized . . . Maura.

That hurt. So long had she herself been the apple. Now another had taken her place. *O, Cecelia* . . .

Abruptly, Rick's eyes switched back to her. They had a calculating look about them, not at all the unabashed puppy love she'd come to expect to see in them.

Poor Rick. Just like her, she realized. Skewered by his own indecisiveness. Good. Let him swing in the wind for a while, see how much *he* liked it.

Logan was also pretending to be asleep. Who was he sizing up? Sarah watched him breathe for several minutes. He began softly snoring. *Jerk.*

That left Maura, staring into the dancing flickers, apparently not a player in the cozy fireside passion play. "About that time," she offered. She stood and stretched. "C'mon, junior, sleepy time," she to Eric.

"Aw, mom, can't I just—"

"Nah, we got another hike tomorrow. We need our beauty rest or we'll be cranky."

Logan snorted and woke with a jerk. He mumbled "g'night," waved vaguely, and took off.

The darkness prompted his retreating footsteps to sound unnaturally loud. Once they fell away, Sarah felt the silence settle heavily between her and Rick. Now was the chance for them to settle things once and for all. He had probably been biding his time, too, waiting for just such an opportunity. They'd have to keep their voices down, of course. No screaming, yelling, or rending of garments. No backbiting, no vindictiveness, no—

"Well, think I'll turn in, too," Rick said. He got to his feet.

Son of a bitch. That was it? The famous final scene she'd agonized about for months? The bastard had just stolen it out from under her with half-a-dozen words.

"Yup," she said, "me, too." What else was left to say?

He disappeared into the brush.

Sarah counted off ten seconds, then sprang to her feet, a woman scorned. Her rage ate up the distance to the beach, her sandals attacking the sand. She was surprised the water around her feet didn't sizzle when she waded into the lake. The water reached her knees. She was still burning up. Got more pissed when she realized she was standing in the exact spot where it had all started with Rick.

She had to cool down. She got back up on the sand and had her shirt and bra stripped off and her hand on the zipper of her shorts when she heard a moan. Not the in-pain kind, either. It was coming from the direction of Rick's tent on the far side of the beach.

A high-pitched giggle, then a female voice, honeyed with love, but still bent on getting its own way, drifted across the still night air. "Whoa. Slow down, big boy. We got all night." Even cast in shadows, it was plain to see Rick's tiny one-man tent had become a two-person. "Push over, why you're at it. The goodies are getting crushed . . ."

One side of the nylon bulged out in the shape of a familiar posterior. Sarah fought down the impulse to sneak over and kick it hard.

"I mean it, damn it, shove over!" A now angry female voice. The rear end twitched and tent fabric stretched to the bursting point.

A deep voice said, "Okay, okay, easy honey . . . I'm trying . . ."

Sarah doubled over in silent hysteria. Feeling lighter than she had in years, she stripped off her shorts. The moon shimmered across the flat water, reaching silver arms toward her, beckoning. A splash to her far right made her jump.

It was the Great One himself, waist deep, scooping water over his chest, washing himself. For a guy who professed no great love for the outdoors, Logan looked pretty damn fine naked in it. Jeez, you could just make out the crack at the top of his miniscule butt as he bent over.

Something in her combusted. Wind shift or something. Needed to get in the water, get wet. *Lord, already am*, she realized, as she shed her underwear. She waded out, none too quietly.

Logan turned at the splashing, smiled a slow incendiary grin, silver traces of moonlight running down his limbs, beading on his chest, and as she got closer, his eyes were actually twinkling.

She trailed her fingers in the lake like a Siren, bones melting and her will as languorous and supple as the quiet lake surface. Logan held out his hand and she took it and pressed it between her breasts. He lowered his mouth to her and her legs liquified.

She swept her hands possessively along his tiny rear, caressing, squeezing, shocked by the intensity of her body's response to him.

The hard length of him pressed against her and she found

him with her hand, stroked him gently, pumped him excruci-
atingly slowly. She felt tremors course through him as he
fought for control. He slid his lips down her neck to her
breasts, his lips cool, to urge her nipples into exquisitely
sensitive points. She shimmied to force more of her into his
mouth. He drew her deeper out into the lake until the water
covered her breasts. She became weightless when he slipped
his hands beneath her and held her suspended, completely
vulnerable and open.

The heated tip of him brushed her silken, swollen folds
and her head lolled in bliss, a mythological mermaid, posed
with her lover: fluid, ancient, and primeval.

Her lover. Logan. He was. Whatever else there was between them, this she could not deny. For this moment in
time, they would be one.

He stroked with long fingers, found the swelling bud. She
clung to his arms desperately. "Don't stop—whatever you
do, don't—oh, God!—don't—oh!"

She came in a blinding flash, imagining the heat vaporiz-
ing the cool lake water, surrounding them in clouds of
steam. "Do . . . It . . . Now. Damn it, Logan—now!"

He entered her, the head bridging her tight opening. A
groan of satisfaction—not quite right. *Ungh*. More intense:
redemption—that was it—was ripped from him.

Sarah floated down his hard length, coming to rest
against his belly. She forced her eyes open and was greeted
with the same look of surprise and amazement on his face
she remembered from their first time.

"Question of altitude . . ." he mumbled.

"Wha—?"

"Ungh, attitude, I mean . . ."

"Yeah. Oh, God . . ."

"Yeah."

She found his testicles, afloat beneath them. She massaged, teased. Sweat beaded his forehead despite the cool water. An indrawn breath, then "Sssss . . ."

"Say?"

"Don't screw with me here," he pleaded.

"Too late."

Sarah felt the pressure build. Life, rushing to fulfill itself, danced beneath her fingertips. She went over the edge then, too, in a red-hot fury, riding a bucking Logan. His legs eventually gave out and they sank down, noses barely clearing the surface, hugging each other, suspended weightlessly in their own personal womb.

"You gotta love the great outdoors," he said.

"See?"

"Yeah, *now*."

Nice to hear, but she didn't let it get it her hopes up.

The next morning dawned cold and rainy. Sarah was sleeping like the dead, alone in her tent, when Eric awakened her in a panic. "Sarah! It's Mr. Iverson. He's really sick. My mom says come right away."

She yanked on whatever clothes she could hastily pull from her pack. Everyone was anxiously gathered around Iverson's tent when she arrived. Why was she always the last to know anything? She heard Hillary, inside, say, "You're not in any immediate danger as far as I can tell, Robert."

"What's up?" Sarah asked Maura.

"More of the same as yesterday, only worse."

"Something is seriously wrong with him?"

"We'll find out in a minute."

Hillary backed her way out of the tent and Logan helped her to her feet. "We need to get him home," she said, in a low voice. "As soon as possible." She waved Violet over. "His doctor's located . . . ?"

"At St. Anna's." A regional medical center, arguably the best north of Boston, in Newburyport, north of Tidal.

Maura looked at Logan.

"We'll take him in Gertrude," he said. "Two hours and he's in Emergency."

"Good. I'll go with you," she said.

"You can't. Rick's got a bad ankle. He needs your help getting the group out of here."

"I'll stay with the group," Sarah said.

"No, you I need in the right seat."

"I'll go."

You could have knocked Sarah over with a feather. "Ma . . . no . . ." she said.

"But I'm . . ."

Violet faltered, but Sarah was truly dying to hear the rest of it. "Yes?"

"Responsible for him."

Then again, Sarah thought, maybe she really didn't need to know all that badly. "How did this happen, Ma?" "This" was an unexploded bomb. Violet wrung her hands and looked away. The Violet Sarah knew did not do such things.

"Well, Sarah . . . after your father died, things were very . . . hard." Her eyes teared up. "I was lonely and you loved your father so much . . ."

My God. She and Iverson *were* an item. Violet had hid that fact from her, thinking to protect her, or because she knew her already nutty daughter would go completely crazy if she ever found out her mother was replacing her beloved father with another man. Violet got that right, Sarah realized. Which was totally stupid because her mother was a grown woman who'd lost her husband way younger than she should have and who was she, the woman's only surviving daughter, to keep her mother from having any happiness. *Shit.* Sarah felt her eyes fill, too.

"Oh, Ma. How long?"

Violet blinked. "Seventeen years."

Seventeen—? How blind could you be? "So all those visits to your 'school chums' . . . ?"

She nodded.

"And the weekends to New York for gallery openings?"

"Yes, I'm afraid so."

Sarah had thought her mother had just been a great fan of art.

"And you care for him?"

Violet bit her lip and nodded.

Sheesh, what's a daughter to do? "He'd better be good to you or I'll kick his ass," Sarah said, then hugged her.

"Yours, too. Or the same," Violet said, to blank looks on the faces of the assembled. Violet hugged Sarah back—hard. They held the clench for a good long time. There was something in the air in Maine that's good for people, Sarah thought, not for the first time.

"Don't worry about Robert," Sarah said, finally releasing her. "We'll get him home in one piece."

Logan looked at her strangely. *Robert?*

Sarah stuck her jaw out and bugged her eyes at him. She couldn't call Iverson "Iverson" anymore, now could she? The guy was practically her step—no, she wasn't ready. Maybe by Thanksgiving dinner, but not yet.

Sarah felt moisture on her face. She and her mother had stemmed the waterworks, so it wasn't that. She tilted her head back and a fat raindrop hit her right in the kisser. Over the tree line, Sarah saw a dark wall of cloud advancing toward the camp. A cooler breeze kicked up and she watched Gertrude swing on her anchor, her stern line tightening.

"Well, folks," Sarah said, "we're in for a blow." Rick gave her a look that said: *No shit.*

She sent one back that said: *Bite me*. She was proud of her and Rick. They were moving ahead in their lives.

Maura said to Mrs. Harker, "We'll get Robert set to go." She directed Logan and Sarah to get Gertrude ready. "Eric, help those camera guys open up our blue tarp and get it strung up. You," she said to Rick, "get off that ankle before you make it worse. I'm *not* paddling your canoe."

Rick sat. Sarah was impressed. Within ten seconds everyone was working at their assigned task like an obedient army of ants.

"Go," Maura said to Sarah.

"But what about you? Can you manage everything on this end?" Sarah asked, feeling like she was running out.

Maura's snort made Sarah remember that in her day job Maura was used to having a lot of things in the air at one time. Literally. "We're going to get the tarps up and wait this out," she said. "Stay another day if we have to. But you hurry up and help Logan. I want Robert out of here ASAP."

Sarah had to admit that Maura was good. Sarah saluted respectfully and caught up with Logan halfway down to the beach. A long peal of thunder rolled across the lake and boomed hollowly among the trees. Logan stumbled, but she chose to assume it was because of the many roots underfoot. The lake had kicked up right on cue. Short, choppy waves broke against the undercut shoreline. Farther out, they were spanking Gertrude's hull and floats.

Somewhere to the south, a leader of light flashed. Logan shivered. Sarah hoped it was because he'd just stripped his shirt off. "Get on that stern line," he called to her over his shoulder as he waded out into water. She got it free and dug her heels into the sand to check Gertie's swing. Logan was half swimming, half pulling himself out to the plane by the line.

He reached the passenger cabin door, yanked on the release handle, and heaved himself over the threshold and into the plane. He waved her off. She ran back to the campsite to help with the gear.

Three plastic tarps were already strung up. Robert was comfortably enthroned on the picnic table on top of a pile of sleeping bags, and Violet was busy arranging and rearranging a pile of fleece jackets beneath his head. Mrs. Harker looked to be trying to keep Robert's mind off of how incredibly annoying Violet was being. Mrs. Harker was surreptitiously taking Robert's pulse. Announcer Guy and Brave But Stupid Camera Guy were under an umbrella attempting to ignite a pile of tinder in the fire ring. Camera Guy One was heating up something that smelled terrifically good on one of the stoves. Joan and Michael were making disgustingly intimate goo-goo eyes and masturbating each other's hands.

Only Rick was sitting by himself, his bad foot propped up on a stump.

Sarah sauntered over and plunked herself down near him. "Sulking?" she asked.

"No."

"Which means yes."

"It's not the same," he said, a little kid in his voice.

"What isn't?"

"This trip. It's not like we used to do it."

She considered that for a moment. A flurry of raindrops tattooed the tarp. "You're right. Maura's not running around taking care of everyone else *and* you the way I used to."

"Was it really that bad?"

He was talking about more than just the trips. "Honestly? It's better now," Sarah said, gently. Gertie's engines roared to life down at the lake.

"Holy shit," Rick said, startled. Then those terrific dark eyes got sad. Kind of like a beagle's do when he begs and you tell him, "There's a good dog, but no, you can't have my dinner roll." She told Rick Maura was good for him. "She won't let you wear her out, like I did."

"How did you know?" That he and she were an item, he meant. He had the good taste to look a little guilty. People change.

Sarah punched him on the arm and bounced her eyebrows, thinking he needed a good laugh right about then. "Maura gives pretty good tent, huh?"

Once he figured it out, he howled, looking younger than he had for a long time. You had to like the guy.

Ten minutes later Logan nosed Gertie into the sand at the shoreline.

"Time to go," Maura said and set people to work transporting Robert to the shore.

She had some unfinished business to attend to before she left, Sarah realized. She cornered Joan. "Why are you here?" she asked. Then she held up her hand. "No, that came out wrong."

Joan looked behind her, then pointed to herself. "You talking to me? The woman who paddled her not inconsiderable ass all the way up here just to watch her best friend's back?"

"Joan, don't bust my—"

"To what do I owe this honor?" She feigned wide-eyed appreciation. She was hardly ever sarcastic-mean. Sarcastic-funny, yes, but not mean.

Michael, sensing trouble, said, "I'll meet you, sweetie?" He pointed toward the beach.

Joan waved to him, her eyes never leaving Sarah. She randomly punched another button on the eight-track cassette that replaced in her cerebral wiring what most people would refer to as their train of thought. "Hmm . . ."

"What?" Sarah said.

"Your aura's funky."

"I know, I know. I've been meaning to have it looked at for weeks, but with one thing and another—"

"Don't fool with me." She grasped Sarah's arm at the biceps and squinted at something above her head. Even if she owned a make-up mirror to look up there with, Sarah knew she wouldn't see anything.

"Look, Joan, I feel really bad about what happened. I just couldn't believe that you would side with Logan."

"All part of the plan. Don't worry about it." Joan continued to squint at the air just above Sarah's head as if a double coupon for loofa sponges were suspended there and she desperately needed to know the expiration date.

"Whose plan?"

"The 'plan.'"

Sarah loved their little talks. "How could you have possibly known how things would turn out?" It was unnerving trying to have a conversation with someone who only looked you in the third eye.

"I don't and that's part of the problem."

"'The problem.' Would that be in capitals, like 'The Plan'?"

"You're fooling with me." Joan hovered both palms inches away from the crown of Sarah's head and shut her eyes, then turned white as a ghost.

"Joan?"

She pressed her hands to her chest. "Oh, my."

"What?"

She turned her open palms to face Sarah. Not as in Throw Me the Ball, but as in Stop.

"Joanie dear, you're upsetting Sarah."

"Oh, Sarah, you are such a dear friend." Joan's grip on Sarah's left shoulder was so hard she reminded herself to check for bruising later.

Okay, now she was scared. Openly expressed heartfelt affection? That ran completely counter to the code universally respected by all divas of The Dig. "What do you see that's so terrible?"

"No." Joan shut her eyes.

"Joan . . ."

"Uh-uh." She shook her head like a sheepdog.

"For once I'm actually asking you and you won't give? What gives?"

"Go. You must walk the last mile alone." She looked at the ground and pointed toward the beach.

Honestly, people. Sarah kissed her on the forehead. "I'll see you back there." In Tidal, she meant. "Or up there," she pointed heavenward, mimicking Joan's gesture. "Or down there," she continued, trying to lighten the mood.

Finally, Sarah made a six-gun with her hand and cocked it at Joan. "But I'm not done with you."

Joan still wouldn't look at her.

"Michael seems nice, by the way," Sarah said, as a benediction of sorts.

Joan lowered herself down to the picnic table bench, looking old and infinitely sad.

Even Rick hobbled down to the beach to see the plane and its passengers off. Robert was already loaded into the cabin by the time Sarah got there. She saw Logan in the cockpit. Michael asked her where Joan was. Sarah rolled her eyes. He laughed. They'd do fine.

Maura was coming out of the cabin hatch as Sarah was headed in. "You've got one extra passenger," she said.

Sarah looked inside. Mrs. Harker.

"She retired from nursing."

"Don't I know it." Sarah scratched her scalp.

Logan barked something from the cockpit. He was probably up there obsessing over the preflight.

"Yeah, yeah," Maura yelled back. I didn't think she even knew what he was going on about. "Men."

"It always comes back to that somehow, doesn't it?" Sarah said. "But isn't it funny how you one day get pissed off and throw the Monopoly game into the air and all the little playing pieces come down in different spots?"

"Yeah, you ended up with the race car and I got—"

"The boot?"

They had a good laugh over that one.

"Didn't I ever," she said, "But he's a good boy. Responds to discipline."

"I saw."

Logan slid open his side window. "Maura, for Chrissakes, shove us off this frigging beach, will you? The weather's not getting any better."

"Yeah, yeah, right away." She casually flipped a middle finger in the general direction of Gertie's nose after the slider snapped shut. "Hey, you guys," she called to the assembled on the beach, "get ready to shove us out."

The window slid open again. "Maura, I mean it. Let's go."

"Best of luck," she said, crossing her eyes and tipping her head toward the front of the plane.

Sarah laughed. "You, too."

Maura hopped out. Sarah hopped in. She dogged the hatch shut behind her.

The passengers were belted in. Sarah realized with a start that it was the first time she'd be flying with anyone other than Logan in the plane with her. Robert was tucked into the back row, his seat fully reclined. Mrs. Harker across the aisle from him, stethoscope and cuff at the ready. Violet just in front of Robert, her neck already in a twist from peering at him anxiously.

Sarah's stomach tightened. *A three-hour tour . . .*

"Welcome to Allagash Air, ladies and gentleman," she said. The low cabin ceiling compromised the showmanship of her speech. "I'll be your hostess, waitress, and copilot today. If at any time during the flight you require assistance, please don't hesitate to push the call button located on the arm of your chairs. Our in-flight movie today—"

"Sarah—" Robert croaked. He weakly motioned her over to him. She slid sideways down the aisle and crouched next to his seat. His eyes were bleary and he looked completely drained. She hadn't realized what tough shape he was in. With what looked like great effort, he reached for her hand. "Not the way I wanted this to work out. Any of it. Your mother—"

"Save your strength, Robert," Mrs. Harker said.

"Is a wonderful woman. That Logan. Better man than I thought, but we can't—"

Sarah cut him off. "I know. He won't. You rest, now. We'll have you home in a jiffy."

Hillary smiled indulgently, which brought to Sarah's mind a time she'd bandaged her up after she'd lost an argument with the entire boy's kickball team.

Sarah's mother grabbed Sarah's forearm as she passed by Sarah's chair. "Sarah, how are you doing all this?" Violet waved her arm to take in the entire plane.

"A person who's as nuts as I am showed me how." Sarah smiled and checked her mother's seat belt. "Wouldn't want to lose you, *Mother*." Sarah made crazy eyes at her.

"Oh, Sarah, don't do that, your eyes—"

Sarah finished, "Will stay like that?"

They shared a tentative chuckle. The first since B.C.: Before the Crash. It was a start.

Chapter 25

"You took long enough with your gabfest," Logan said as Sarah slid into the right seat.

"And if you were a woman I'd call you something right now that rhymes with 'witch.'" She clapped on headphones and dialed in the volume.

Logan informed her the weather service had issued a caution on violent thunderstorms forming all along the front passing just south of the waterway.

"And you're just finding out about this now?" she asked.

He scowled. "I knew about it two days ago. What I *didn't* know was we'd be leaving *here* to go *there* right *now*."

Like it was her fault. He stuck his arm out his side window and spun his hand in a circle. Maura and company moved in. Gertie slid backward into deeper water, then slowly pirouetted until her nose faced the lake. Sarah's head nodded back as the beach crew gave a final shove off. Logan waved everybody away and snapped his window shut.

He launched into the litany Sarah had heard when they'd left his cove what seemed like another lifetime ago. "Magnetos on . . . supercharger low . . . mixture . . . throttles . . ." He touched everything as he went through the list. "Clear left. Your side?"

"Roger, clear right."

"And start." He jabbed the ignition buttons.

Gertie coughed once, twice, then spat exhaust from both engines. She groggily spun her props, then cleared her throat and settled into her trademark roar. Logan toggled down the propeller RPM.

A brilliant flash split the sky, followed seconds later by a tremendous bomb burst above the lake. Light flooded the dim interior of the cockpit for a brief second. The front was moving faster and on a more northerly route than predicted.

Logan thumbed something on the control yoke he'd explained was a "coolie switch"—it *had* seemed pretty cool to her at the time, which is why she remembered the name of it, not that she had a clue as to what it did—and wiggled the rudder. Nothing seemed to happen.

"Stupid shit," he muttered to himself. "Hydraulics pump's supposed to be set to 'Engine.' Missed it. What an idiot."

"Don't let it beat you."

His laugh was a little too loud. He knew exactly what she meant. "What was it you said? *Ruin a good pair of underwear and move on?*"

He nudged the throttle and the engine rumble rose back up to a dull roar. Gertie waddled forward, her aluminum hull slapping the waves. The sound echoed hollowly within the cockpit.

Logan pointed and said, "Flip that toggle marked 'Cabin.' No, no. To the left, near the radios. Uh-huh." Gertie rode up the spine of a particularly large roller and slammed down the other side. Logan put two hands back on the control yoke. "You're on speaker now. Tell the passengers to buckle down tight. It's going to be a rough ride for a few minutes. Get

Robert's chair all the way upright. They can put it back down when we're airborne."

Thunder boomed again and blinding light split the sky. "Maybe."

She made the announcement. It was weird hearing her disembodied voice filling the cabin behind them.

"Like the bad old days, out here today," Logan said. "We used to fly search and rescue in the service. Skimming the waves on piss-poor nights. Good times, good times . . ." His smirk looked a little thin.

Sarah glanced at the low, scudding banks of gray at the far end of Eagle Lake. "What's it like up there today?"

"IFR all the way, but once we get on top it shouldn't be too bumpy. And Crossly can route us around the worst of it."

"Call ahead for an ambulance to meet us at the field?"

He nodded. "We'll radio for one. Give me more wipers."

He had his hands full. Waves pitched and tossed the plane around as we slogged ahead. Water lashing the windshield made visibility almost nil despite the high-speed flailing wipers, but in a few minutes Gertrude was in deep water, lined up nose to the wind.

Logan finished more checks, then said, "It's now or never. Let them know in back."

Sarah toggled "Cabin" again and made my speech. "All set."

"Help me with the rudder till we're up; then work the flaps on my signal. Get the gear up as soon as we break out."

The *landing* gear? "Logan, have you lost your—"

"Just checking." He flashed her a smile. The world righted itself for an instant and everything seemed possible.

"You are such an—"

He nailed the throttles.

Sarah was pressed backward into her seat. The din of the twins rendered conversation temporarily impossible, even with the headphones. Gertie gamboled gamely ahead, throwing spray like a cigarette boat, fighting to get up on the step and shake her feet free of the lake. The tree line on the opposite shore rapidly approached as Gertie waged her personal war on the laws of physics.

There was a nice clearing along the far shore there, at the foot of the trees, right along the water's edge. A nice spot for a picnic, Sarah thought. Maybe if we all lived through the fucking takeoff we could come back some day, right to that very spot.

The bow lifted slightly. They raced closer. Sarah could now see a dozen yards or so of sandy beach—for the Allagash, a vast expanse indeed of waterfront real estate. A good place to dip your feet in the cool water. Reeds to either side, awash in the waves and bent almost horizontal by the wind. Just when she was calculating how her meager possessions would be divided postdemise, the spray from the pontoons fell off.

Logan's knuckles were white on the control yoke. "C'mon, baby. Git up . . ."

Suddenly the teeth-jarring slams magically ceased as Gertie broke free of the lake and morphed into a creature of the sky. A gust caught her in the armpits and boosted her, spinning the altimeter. Now all Sarah could see over the bow were the crowns of the trees.

Towering pines they were, too. Merely pinecones a century ago most of them, they'd patiently waiting a hundred years for their chance to tear Gertrude from the sky. And Logan didn't seem to be doing anything to avoid them.

"Logan, shouldn't we be . . . ah . . . *climbing*?"

"Watch the airspeed. When it gets in the green zone on the dial, call it out."

Was that pinecone clusters she was seeing on the branches? "*Logan*, we're getting *close*—"

"The speed, damn it! Watch it!"

Seconds turned to hours, but Sarah watched, having nothing better to do in what she anticipated would be the final moments of her life.

"Coming up on green . . . now!"

Logan hauled back on the yoke and Gertie obediently climbed, clearing the pines by yards. "That's why most Widgeons have been retrofitted with turboprops."

But not *their* Widgeon, of course. "You fricking waited long enough to pull up," Sarah said, snappishly. There were times when you just didn't care about all the technical shit.

"We were surfing the ground effect—water effect, in our case. Biding our time, picking up speed, which is hard to do given the head wind."

And he thought she cared about this why?

"I pull up any earlier we drop right into those trees."

"Oh." Okay, maybe some of the techie crap was important.

He smirked. "Next lesson. Got the sectional?"

She already had it open on her lap. "Yep."

"Turn it upside down. That way a landmark on your left is on your left on the map, too. We're going to fly instruments, but keep your eyes peeled for the ground. If we ever get a break in the cloud cover, try to match something up down there with a landmark on the map."

Sarah looked down and around and only saw shifting blankets of gray. Less than a minute's climb and their world had become a hazy, dark place. "There's nothing to see."

"Do your best. Service says there's intermittent breaks in the cover. I'm getting a strong TO/FROM indicator on number one navigation radio right now—we're on a radial from Crossly Field—but who knows if we'll keep it all the way in."

Yeah, right, who knows? As in who knew what the fuck

he was talking about. Sarah was profoundly glad to be in the right seat.

"With all this electricity flying around the signal might get lost. Then you gotta go hunting for it."

Sure. Uh-huh. Where? She looked around the instrument panels. The dials, gauges, and gizmos were still an untamed wilderness to her, like the West before the railroads.

He said, pointing, "On the clipboard—" The control yoke shivered in his hands as Gertie caught some bad air and he clamped both hands around it.

"Yes?"

"All the frequencies we're going to need are written down. Pull it out."

"Got it."

"Tune in to Whitefield. Get a weather update."

Sarah dialed in the frequency and moments later the pre-recorded bulletin played.

"Sounds sucky," she said.

"Nice to see you coming up to speed on some of the more technical lingo."

"Thank you."

"At least the winds will be dropping off some. Still not weather I'd fly in by choice."

A crack of lightning and a peal of thunder underscored his point. Gertie twitched, but not before Logan did. They flew on through pea soup. Time lost meaning among the shifting gray curtains. Gertie's engines droned on, punctuated by rolling peals of thunder. Occasionally, a flash would light up every corner of the cabin.

Sarah glanced over at Logan. He was anxious. She suddenly understood how Dr. Cynthia Loo must feel about her patients. She routinely ripped them open, rearranged the guts, sewed them back up, then kicked their sorry asses out her office door. Did Cynthia ever worry about her needlework holding up through the rest of her patient's day/weeks/ lives? Sarah wondered if the patches that had been bubble-gummed onto Logan in the lighthouse would hold through the storm or if he'd blow out like an old inner tube.

Might as well run the bike over a few bumps and find out. "How come you never told me about your phobia until that night in the tower?" she asked him.

He adjusted his headphones. "Every relationship needs a few secrets to keep it fresh."

"I showed you mine. Scared to show me yours?"

He tore his eyes from the instruments. "You're a strange person, you know that?"

"Don't avoid the question."

"Okay. Truth is, I didn't want to think about it."

"Until you had to."

"Yup."

"Like right in the middle of a thunderstorm."

"Yup."

"Planning not your strong suit?"

"Uh-huh."

He could make her laugh at the oddest times. It appeared the patch job was holding up.

He flipped the "Cabin" switch. "Would one of you nice people back there put on the set of headphones you'll find hanging next to the door? Thank you."

"Very friendly," she said. "I'm impressed."

"Friendly's what I'm all about."

Sarah made a face. Her headphones crackled. "—ello? Anyb—there?" Hillary.

"Hello, Mrs. Harker, this is Sarah. Pull the little micro-phone near your mouth."

"Oh, yes. That's better. I can hear myself."

"How're things back there, Mrs. Harker?"

"Robert's holding his own for now, dear. Are all your takeoffs . . . like that?"

Logan said, "Tell her, sorry, next time I'll remember the JATO bottles."

Jet-Assisted Takeoff. Sarah had a vague idea they were some rocket-type things you stuck on the side of planes to give them a boost into the air. But damn sure not any plane *she* was in.

"Ha-ha," she said to Logan. She reached across the narrow aisle and backhanded him on the arm. She keyed the intercom. "Um, yes . . . Mrs. Harker. I know what you mean. It's just all part of the, ah, adventure of flying antique airplanes."

"I suppose. Your mother's not happy, by the way."

"What's up?"

"She's having some kind of a . . . wait a minute. Violet!" There was static, then the soundtrack to the LA street riots rolled.

"Violet—no, you're not!" More static and the connection became intermittent "—right now. Violet! Sit dow—"

"Did you hear that?" Sarah asked Logan.

"Check it out. But hang on."

"Hang on, Mrs. Harker. I'm coming." Sarah unbuckled and unplugged and lurched her way through the door in the bulkhead separating the cockpit from the cabin. Gertrude hit what she and Beth—when they were kids, riding along rural roads in the backseat of the family's old station wagon—used to call a "thrill." The down force knocked Sarah off balance and the sudden rise smacked the top of her skull into the door header.

Pinwheels burst behind her eyeballs and she staggered into the cabin like a drunken rock star into first class—*oof!*—colliding with her mother. "Ma, what the hell?"

"This is unacceptable, Sarah." Violet was using the seat backs to claw herself forward. It appeared her destination was the cockpit, no doubt to personally lodge a complaint with the management.

Over Sarah's—and possibly everyone else's—dead body. "Sit *down*, Mother."

Violet tried to shoulder her way past. "Sarah, get out of my way. We are stopping this nonsense right now."

"Uh, hello, Mother. Remember why we're here? Robert?" Sarah cut her eyes to him. He looked to be dozing. She hoped that was a good thing.

"This"—Violet sputtered—"*situation* is not safe for any of us. I demand your friend take us down." She made like a linebacker again, but Sarah got her hip into her and bumped her into an empty chair. "Buckle up."

Violet tried to get up but Sarah slung one of her legs over her lap. "Now."

"But—"

"Do it."

Mother was not one to give up, but neither was daughter, and after all, Sarah reminded herself, she was over twenty years younger. In certain situations that counted for something. Brimming with indignity and rage, Violet strapped in.

"Don't make me come back here again," Sarah said, pointing.

Sarah thought her mother growled at her as soon as her back was turned, although what she thought she heard might actually have been a talking telegram from Spot. He probably missed her and wished she were there. Sarah hoped the person he was presently torturing was somebody truly evil and deserving.

"Everything under control?" Logan asked as Sarah slid into the right seat.

"As much as ever."

"Iverson?"

"Sleeping, I think."

He nodded. "I guess we've had our little upset for this trip."

That made her remember the scene in the movie *Apollo 13* in which Tom Hanks corrects for an engine misfire, then says something just like that. She thought of Joan, and how weird she had acted just before Gertie took off. Sarah wondered if Logan ever saw *Apollo 13*. Or if he even liked movies.

"We're getting breaks in the cloud cover," he said. "Check it out."

Sarah peered out the side window. Below the plane, a silver river snaked through an unrelieved green carpet. Ahead, the river split, widening to create an oxbow. A town materialized, springing as if by magic from the deep pile of the endless, encroaching forest. A toy town. A Christmas village you set up on your fireplace mantle at the holidays, complete with white-steepled church, a tiny common, even a long, red truck pulling out of what must be the firehouse.

"Rocky Falls," Logan explained. Sarah had temporarily forgotten her job was to match landmarks to the sectional map.

"It's so perfect it looks fake," she said. "God must spend his long weekends down there."

"We can stop sometime."

"The river's wide enough to land on?"

"It's called the Mohasset. And, yes, you can."

"But it'd be easier with turboprops, huh?"

He laughed and grabbed the radio mike. "Crossly Airport, this is LZ one-eight-five-seven. We have a visual confirmation on position and our ETA for your location is approximately one hour, twenty."

"LZ one-eight-five-seven, Roger that. We have contacted

your patient's physician as requested. He agrees with your plan and is expecting you. Please advise us as to status of your patient."

"Holding his own, presently, Crossly. Please arrange for ambulance to meet us at the runway. LZ one-eight-five-seven out." He returned the radio microphone to its clip. "Well, that's it till our next checkpoint. About twenty minutes I figure."

Sarah looked down. The break in the clouds had disappeared as quickly as it had come. It was as if she had imagined the town, the meandering river. "So, we're going to be in and out of this soup all the way, huh?"

"That's what I'm hearing. Crossly will keep us updated on what the storm's doing and vector us around the worst of it."

He'd already said something like that before they took off. Sarah wondered if he was saying it again to reassure her or himself. A few minutes later, the answer didn't seem to really matter because they had gained a temporary reprieve from the storm. Gertie trundled along placidly and the miles to Crossly Field—Sarah still couldn't bring herself to legitimize it by referring to it as an airport—ticked down. They were still blanketed in clouds, so there was absolutely nothing to see or keep track of. Things became so peaceful that she drifted off.

She awoke with a start, how much later she didn't know. *Idiot.* "Where are we?" she asked Logan. "God, I'm sorry." She wiped her drooly mouth.

"I let you sleep. It's been hectic. About fifteen minutes out of Crossly."

"Robert?"

"As of about fifteen minutes ago, fine. Sitting up and talking."

"My mother?"

"All quiet. Everything's looking good."

Now why did he go and say that? Why invoke the ancient curses? Something always screwed up right after you said stuff like that.

The headphones crackled. "Hello?"

"Yes, Mrs. Harker?" Sarah asked, holding her breath.

"Could you come back here for a minute?"

Could she call it or what? Sarah slipped out of the copilot's seat. "Back in a sec."

It wasn't her mother this time. It was Robert. His skin was gray. "How are you doing?" Sarah asked, not really wanting to know the answer.

"Ah, Sarah. Another bedside visit. How nice." He winced in pain. She hoped it wasn't because his latest employee had showed up.

Hillary gave Sarah the bad news in an aside. "I don't like this at all, Sarah. His BP's down and his pulse is weak and way up. We've got more on our hands than we bargained for."

"I'll let Logan know. Anyway, we'll be home soon," Sarah said, turning back to Robert. Violet was holding his hand in both of hers and barely noticed when Sarah patted her shoulder on her way back to the cockpit.

"Your mother losing it again?" Logan asked, conversationally.

"No, it's Robert." Sarah filled Logan in.

"This gets better and better doesn't it?" He unclipped the radio mike and keyed it. "Crossly Airfield, this is LZ one-eight-five-seven. We are declaring an emergency on board. Our sick passenger is presently semiconscious and worsening." He relayed the symptoms Mrs. Harker had described to Sarah. "Please contact patient's physician and advise us as to any change of plans. Over?"

"Roger, LZ one-eight-five-seven. Stand by."

Thirty seconds later the reply came. "Patient's physician advises you reroute to Boston. We're vectoring you to Logan Airport."

Logan frowned. To Sarah he said, "That was a quick decision." He keyed the mike. "Roger, Crossly. Reroute Logan understood. Please advise as to weather between here and Boston. Over?"

"LZ one-eight-five-seven. Sorry, more of what you came through up north. After handoff, Logan approach will issue vectors to move you around it."

"Crossly, please advise Logan control as to immediacy of our passenger's situation. We'll put up with some bouncing to get down sooner. The more direct the route the better."

"Roger, LZ. Understood. Stand by."

"Shit," Logan said.

"You shouldn't have said it," Sarah said.

"What?"

"That things were going okay."

The radio crackled again. It was Crossly Field, handing them off to Logan approach. They wished them luck. Sarah would have given a lot to hear Maura's voice on the line.

Almost immediately, Logan Airport approach came on. "LZ one-eight-five-seven, this is Logan International Airport approach control. We have you on radar and understand you have sick passenger on board and are requesting priority landing. Over?"

"Roger that, Logan approach."

"LZ one-eight-five-seven, we are issuing you vectors around local low-pressure cells. Please stand by."

"What about your request for a direct route?" Sarah asked.

"Crossly made it clear to them. When Boston says go around, it's because *no one's* getting through."

Approach control came back on the horn and Sarah

watched the needles swing as Logan brought Gertie onto the new heading. And still she saw nothing outside the cockpit windows except shifting veils of gray. To think human beings flew around in this shit every hour of every day without people on the ground even being aware of it. Maybe it was just her who hadn't been aware of it. Pretty soon she'd have to book herself on an airliner. She'd been living in the back of her closet for too long.

Logan said, "Tell everyone to buckle up tight again. We're in for another round."

Sarah made the announcement. Something Logan had a minute earlier came back to Sarah. "It *was* a quick decision on Robert's doctor's part, wasn't it? The reroute to Boston, I mean. Don't you usually think if you hear someone's been sent to Boston that there's something seriously wrong with him—something that couldn't be handled at a local hospital?"

"And how did his doc diagnose Robert was in trouble based on the limited info we forwarded?" Logan said.

"My thoughts exactly."

"Sounds like there's a lot more to the story."

"No doubt."

And no doubt her mother would be right in the middle of it. Lightning crackled, off to Gertie's left.

"We're getting into it now," Logan said.

Life suddenly paralleled a stage set from one of her beloved *Twelve O'Clock High* episodes. A thunder boomer exploded like an antiaircraft shell just above Gertrude, eerily illuminating the cockpit and slamming her sideways and down. With no visual reference outside the plane for orientation, Sarah scanned the instruments. The dials went nuts for a moment, ticking off impossible numbers. She grabbed the side of her seat, in shades of the day with Preston Lewis. Logan wrestled with the controls. Gertie painfully clawed her way back to an even keel as he jockeyed the control yoke and the rudder pedals.

"Holy crap, Logan, what the hell was that?" She was drenched in sweat. "The freaking pontoons were alive for a minute there. Glowing, like in a bad Frankenstein movie." She looked out again. Now they were just everyday, ordinary floats. "Cripes . . ."

She heard him mumble, "Fucking lightning. I hate fucking lightning."

The headphones crackled with a new voice. "Um, sorry to bother you, dear. I know you're probably very busy right now, but we've got smoke—" Mrs. Harker coughed demurely—"back here. And an unpleasant smell."

Oh, boy.

Logan fiddled with some knobs on the panel, then snatched off his headset. "One fucking thing after another. Tell her I'm coming."

"As in *leaving?* But—"

"She's on autopilot. I'll be right back."

"You're leaving me in charge of this thing?" All alone with the plane, Gertie had suddenly become a thing in Sarah's mind. "What the hell do I do?"

"Nothing. Just sit there."

Logan slipped out of his harness and squirmed into the aisle. "Don't touch anything."

Right. Good safety tip. Otherwise, she might impulsively snap Gertie through a couple Immelmanns just to see what she was really made of, while her maniac pilot was someplace else doing God knew what. If she wasn't scared completely shitless the whole situation would make a great screenplay. Any second now a hollow-eyed, much younger William Shatner should burst into the cockpit crying, "There's some*thing*—out *there*—on the *wing*!"

Sarah cinched her harness tighter and scanned the myriad dials and levers and gadgets. She completely understood the function of only a handful. The control yokes and rudder pedals—all on their own—moved back and forth, back and forth. She thought about twiddling her fingers and whistling. Or maybe she'd just stand up, stretch, and go for a nice little walk.

White chunks bounced off the nose and windscreen, startling her. *Hail*. The wipers slowed as they loaded with ice. She heard herself laugh shrilly.

Hail, hail, the gang's all here.

She wondered if slapping oneself in the face was as effective as having someone else do it. Were there university studies? Through the headphones, snatches of conversation from the cabin drifted to her.

". . . I don't know, but it's gone now . . ." Logan said.

His voice was comforting. Sarah rested her hands lightly on the control yoke on her side of the cockpit and followed it through its ghostly, autonomous movements, pretending Logan was still in the left seat.

Abruptly, Gertie dropped into an unmarked pothole in the sky. The autopilot rammed the control yoke into Sarah's knees. Her shoulder straps bit into flesh and her head was thrown forward. She swallowed hard at the bile that rose in the back of her throat. Gertie lurched again, this time rocketing upward. The yoke shot forward to check her climb.

Gertie rode out a few more dips and doodles before finally leveling off.

Holy Mother of—

"Dear, we've got a problem." Mrs. Harker.

"No shit," Sarah said, to no one in particular.

"Something like that, dear."

"Sorry. I'm right here, Mrs. Harker."

"It's your Mr. Donnelly."

He would never be that—hers—but she sensed a bigger point. "What's wrong with him?"

"He's unconscious."

"Really . . . Imagine that."

The pilot was unconscious.

The only person on board qualified to fly the plane was in La-la land.

Sarah stared out the windshield. The pattern of hail rushing at her formed a white cone, a seductive tunnel with no end. *Step into the light, children . . .*

"Sarah?"

Did the hands on the controls belong to her?

"Sarah, dear, please answer."

Didn't you usually wake up from nightmares about now?

"Sarah!"

It felt like her brains just about flew out her nose. "*Jesus,* Mrs. Harker. I heard you." And possibly nothing else ever as long as she lived. All the rock concerts she'd made it through as a youth. What a waste of earplugs.

"I'm glad, dear. I'm assuming you don't know how to fly the plane?"

"Well, I could probably fly it. Just not land it."

"I see. We'll need to think this through very carefully, won't we?" She said it like she once said to Sarah after she'd barfed all over the cafeteria floor, "We'll have to call your mother, don't you think?" Sarah hoped that if she ever lived long enough to grow up she could be just like Mrs. Harker.

"Mr. Donnelly won't wake up, huh?" Sarah asked. Funny, calling him Mister Donnelly. The last time she called him that was at the town meeting.

"No, dear."

Oh, dear. "Is he bleeding?"

"Yes, but nothing I can't handle."

What couldn't she handle? "Have you tried telling him he's never getting that second runway?"

Sarah clicked the intercom switch. "Mrs. Harker?"

"I'm glad to see you've still got your sense of humor, dear. Now think."

How could she when she'd suddenly become obsessed with every miniscule movement of the controls? How long would they keep moving on their own? If she stopped watching them would they stop doing their job? And what difference did it make anyway? *They* couldn't land the plane. They were just delaying the inevitable—

"Sarah, dear?"

"Yes?" A human voice. Thank God. How narrow the line between sanity and complete craziness.

"Are you thinking?"

Sarah knew that Mrs. Harker knew the answer.

"Because *I* am, Sarah. Violet's told me about your flying lessons with Mr. Donnelly."

This is so not happening.

"So, Sarah?"

Fingers in my ears. Sorry, not listening la la la . . .

"Sarah!"

"Yes," Sarah heard herself croak.

"You can fly us down."

It was the *Flight of the Phoenix* all over again. Proving that she was a real sicko, for the last ten or twelve years Sarah had been periodically torturing herself by renting a grainy copy of it from the video store downtown. It's about these British soldiers whose plane crashes in the desert and this scrawny, dislikable little civilian claims he can reconstruct the broken plane into a smaller one that can fly them all to safety. Just before takeoff, they almost kill him because they find out all he's ever worked on are model airplanes.

Well, she was that little guy. Buzzing around clear skies with a skilled instructor in a single-engine four-banger was a whole lot different from instrument landing a fully loaded—*God*, she wished she were at that moment—twin-engine antique at a major metropolitan airport. She hit Hillary with the abridged version of this.

"But, Sarah. A plane is a plane, yes? You've driven a large truck before without special training, correct?"

"Yes, once. When I moved. But you remember what I did to Mrs. Murphy's steps? Well, this would be much, much worse."

"Very well, then, Sarah. We'll just . . . sit. Sit and wait and hope Mr. Donnelly wakes up. What's that?" She spoke to someone else. "No, Violet, she says she won't."

Sarah heard static, then, "I tried, Vi, but she won't."

Jeeeez, kill me, why don't you? Sarah vividly recalled how Violet used to guilt her into doing door-to-door collections for the heart fund when she was a kid. She hated it. Violet would order her to do it—"Think of all the good you're doing, of all the people you're helping, Sarah"—and of course she'd refuse, little shit that she was. But it was the "Fine, do what you want" as she walked away that got Sarah to assemble that little cardboard collection box.

What the hell. If you was going to die it might as well be by your own hand. As for everybody else? She was the best chance they had, like it or not. You dances with the one who brung ya.

Oh, for God's sake. "All right," Sarah said.

Chapter 26

"Excellent, dear. I'm sending someone up there to help you," Mrs. Harker said.

Wasn't it Sherlock Holmes who said that if all the impossible solutions were eliminated, the remaining one, no matter how improbable, had to be true? Sarah mentally ticked off who was available from the cabin—taking into consideration who was conscious and who wasn't—and discovered she didn't like the answer she came up with.

"Hello, Sarah."

"Mother."

The shaking in her voice was off the Richter scale. "Ma, I really don't think you should be up here."

"That makes two of us, dear. Do I sit there?" She pointed to the left seat.

"Ma, you're not sitting anywhere. Go."

"How nice."

"What?"

"Hillary obviously doesn't want me back there, and now

you don't want me up here. Maybe I should just jump out of the plane. What do you think?"

"Ma . . ."

"Maybe I'll just do that. Just jump right out."

"You'll jump nowhere. You couldn't even get the hatch open."

"That's what you think. You just watch me." She turned to go. Sarah didn't think she'd do it, but then again . . .

"Ma, wait." Her mother wore her out. "All right. You can stay."

Violet headed for the left seat.

"No," Sarah said. She unbuckled, and taking great care not to touch or bump or nudge anything, she slid into Logan's chair. "You sit there." Sarah indicated hers. She leaned over and helped Violet strap into the harnesses. "Put these on." She helped her mother with the headphones.

"What are we listening to?"

"Each other." *That will be a nice change*, Sarah thought.

Violet took in the cramped cockpit. "There's not very much room up here, is there?" she said. "I always pictured where the pilots sat as bigger, somehow. Of course, I haven't been on a plane since . . ."

Her forced breeziness disappeared.

"Ma, we're not going there right now."

Too late. She was staring catatonically out the windscreen.

"Do you know it's been twenty years?" she said.

"Ma?"

"Since your dad and . . . Beth."

"Hell, yes." Like Sarah herself hadn't been, in one way or another, counting every fricking hour since.

"And here we are again," Violet said. "Right back where we started."

That Sarah would not listen to. "Mom, that's pure, unadulterated horseshit."

"You watch your mouth, young lady."

"You watch yours, Ma. We've been victims long enough. Both of us."

"Victims." She said it like a swear word. "Your father and Beth were the victims. Don't tarnish their memory by giving us that title."

"But we earned it, Mom, didn't we? We pay for it every fucking day."

"Sarah, if you don't watch your mouth I swear I'll—"

"What? We back to jumping? Save yourself the trouble. Wait a few minutes."

Her mother dissolved.

"Ma . . ."

A full-fledged meltdown.

"Ma, for Chrissakes."

Tears, goo. The Dundee women always brought so much to the picnic.

"Ma, look, I'm sorry."

Sarah leaned over. Better for her mother to slap her. Which she did, right in the face. She was swinging lefty, but she got good wood on it and she was pissed. It really hurt.

Then, feeling like a complete idiot, Sarah burst into tears: *Her own mother. Right across the kisser . . .*

"That . . . hurt," Sarah said, blubbering.

"Good. You deserved it."

Sarah hiccuped and rubbed her cheek thoughtfully. It really hurt.

"And I'll do it again if you talk that way about your father or your sister."

"Look, Ma—"

"I told you, I don't like 'Ma.'"

"Mother, I—"

"Mom is fine."

Sarah suddenly didn't want to talk anymore.

"You were never like this when you were younger," Violet said. "You were the sweetest child."

Yeah, before you *turned into Dragon Lady*, almost escaped Sarah's lips, but she realized that she didn't want to get whacked again. "You used to be nicer, too."

"The crash—"

"Mom, no. We're not going there, I told you. The end. Period. We can't spare the time for that now." But if not right then, when? Their future was, to say the least, uncertain. She reconsidered. Hey, she was nothing if not flexible. "Never mind, go ahead."

Violet splayed her fingers, then curled them into ladylike fists. "I didn't think I wanted to live after we came back from Africa and the . . . ceremonies were over. When we were left alone, just the two of us."

Bing. Right back at you.

"I was mad at your father for taking us there in the first place and I felt guilty for being mad at him. And you—you were such a—"

"Such a what?"

"A little shit, pardon my French."

Sarah laughed so hard her stomach hurt.

"Oh, Ma, I still am." She reached across the aisle and touched her mother's hand. It was ice-cold. "Mom, look at me."

Violet just kept staring, like Sarah had caught herself doing not too long ago, at the tunnel of white racing toward the windscreen. Sarah touched her mother's cheek and Violet turned her face toward her.

Sarah met her mother's eyes across an ocean of memories. Violet was still in Africa.

Self-disgust made Sarah want to fling open the hatch and hurl herself into the slipstream. Could she really have been so criminally stupid for so many years? Spot had had the Dundee women enrolled on the family plan, a two-for-one deal. She and her mother had both been running from him. And each other. And themselves. Everybody running, nobody making a stand. It was insane.

"Mom . . ." Her mother's face was blurry around the edges. Fresh tears stung Sarah's burning cheek.

Violet said, "You and I made it, didn't we?" like it was occurring to her for the very first time.

Sarah nodded and salty drops bounced into her lap. "Sometimes things just work out like that. There's no figuring."

The burning plane. The searing heat. Dad. Beth. The pilot. Her mother was the only one left after the plane had skidded to a stop. Loss consumed Sarah. The engines droned. But she still had her mother. It didn't matter for how long, right then, only that she had her.

Sarah couldn't imagine the kind of courage—and love for Robert—her mother must have, volunteering to come along in Gertrude. The little girl in Sarah wondered how her mother's love for the man in the cabin behind them compared to what she'd felt for her dad. Sarah told that little girl to grow up or go to her room.

Sarah felt her brave mother squeeze her hand, then release it. Violet's eyes were back in this hemisphere.

"Go," Violet said. "Get us home."

"Done, Mom."

But that was easier said. Sarah's eyes darted around the cockpit, peered out the side window. She realized she could be looking at the last sights of her life right then. Suspended between heaven and earth, the fate of everyone on board was tied to her and the fragile cocoon she must take control of.

With all its electronic gadgets, its pretensions of mastery, its . . . its . . . hat.

Logan's hat was hanging off his headphone hook. He must have stuck it there in his mad rush to the rear of the plane. That fucking hat. The same one that had so irritated her when she'd first met him weeks ago. The rage she'd directed at him had been a tonic for my soul. Some of that anger came back to her and the unfairness of their situation fanned the flames into a white-hot fury.

They weren't going out like this—not yet anyway. She had not come from a far shore to make peace with her mother only to have it come to naught.

"Mom, look. These things aren't supposed to happen. Not to good people, anyway. And we are. A little screwed up maybe, but we're okay. You with me here?"

Violet nodded, watching. She was.

"I hate to be blunt, but we're not dead yet," Sarah said. "The situation isn't good. You know that, right?" Like she had to ask. Her mother knew the score. "But 'almost' doesn't go on your permanent record. We're going to get through this, me and you. Understand?"

Her mother nodded again, grimly. Sarah sincerely hoped her speech had worked. It was her best work to date.

A red light on the instrument panel caught her attention. The right engine was running hot. Cylinder head temperature in the red. Oil pressure down. All stuff Logan had warned her about on the Cessna, but she assumed that they were not good things in any plane. Poor Gertrude.

She felt a little silly to be concerned about the comfort of a mechanical system, but it was, after all, Gertie. Sarah would never want to see her suffer needlessly. *Ashes to ashes, parts to parts.* She stifled a hysterical giggle, for her mother's sake, and cut back on the throttle. A klaxon wailed.

Sarah had learned that a klaxon is a loud, obnoxious,

impossible-to-ignore alarm of the kind that invariably sounds in the movies whenever John Wayne sights an enemy torpedo heading for his ship. The alarm must have gone off because she touched the controls. Sarah glanced at her mother. Violet's lips were moving but in the headphones there was only silence.

A flash outside and, then, immediately after it, a rolling crash of thunder. Retribution sent by the God of the Old Testament. The autopilot bounced Gertie across unevenly spaced railroad ties. She shuddered through a series of rolls, pleading for help, desperate for a human's touch.

Unfortunately, the only human available wasn't remotely qualified to touch anything, Sarah thought.

Still, something had to be done.

Sarah eyed the autopilot control panel, wondering if it worked like the cruise control in the Rav. If she cancelled it, would it ever come back on again? Then again, why would she want it to? She must have been talking out loud.

"It can't land for us, can it?" her mother asked.

Sarah knew what she meant. "No, a human has to do that."

"Meaning you."

"Yes."

Violet seemed to think about that for a moment. "That horn noise is horrible, Sarah."

Okay, what the hell. The frigging alarm was making her nuts, too. Sarah grabbed hold of the control yoke with both hands, orientated her feet to the rudder pedals, and punched the autopilot "Off" button. The quiet hurt.

Violet smiled gamely. "That did it."

Did it ever. The control yoke turned meaner than a one-eyed mechanical bull in a country western bar. Sarah leaned into it, the tendons in her forearms standing out like ropes. "Come on, you old biddy!"

"Excuse me?"

"Sorry, Mom"—Sarah gritted her teeth—"the plane."

She found herself struggling to reach an agreement with Gertrude. Compared to the Cessna, Gertie handled like a Mack truck. Not that Sarah would ever share that observation with her. Finally, Gertrude let her win and Sarah got them flying in a way that felt straight and level.

The hail abruptly stopped, leaving behind an angry and battered sky splotched with ugly black bruises. Dusk conditions prevailed in the cockpit, Sarah realized. She flipped on the panel lights.

A thousand dials illuminated, all demanding some action from her. In the artificial horizon, the little plane was tilted thirty degrees to starboard. The seat of her pants had lied to her. Big time. They were in a steep bank.

She nudged the wheel left and the wings on the little plane mercifully leveled. She checked the altimeter. More bad news. They had lost almost 500 feet of altitude in the few moments she'd been in charge. Her ass would fly them right into the ground if she didn't start relying on the instruments. All of a sudden she got it: flying on instruments meant, well, flying using the instruments.

She hauled back on the yoke. A hawk couldn't have kept a closer eye on the rate-of-climb needle. The little plane symbol got away from her again and she corrected. "Mom, keep an eye on those little wings. When they get crooked tell me."

"They've been crooked for most of the time you've been driving."

"Ma . . ."

"Fine."

After a tense two minutes they'd only climbed 300 feet. They were underpowered.

A quick check of the right engine temperature confirmed it was back in the green. Barely. But it had what they needed.

"Baby, I hate to do this to you." Sarah winced and shoved both throttles to their stops. The RPM of both engines increased, but she detected a vibration she'd never felt before, as if the two engines were fighting against each other.

The climb indicator inched up. The altimeter responded. thirty-five hundred feet. Four thousand.

Bingo. Back where they started.

Sarah sudenly felt so good about life that she kept up the steady climb. Logan had said there'd be clean air on top. At 8,000 feet the clouds thinned. Nine thousand: weak shafts of sunlight cut through the gloom. At 10,000 feet, Gertrude outran the vertical reach of the storm and broke into dazzling sunshine.

"Glory be," my mother said.

"Yes?"

"It's a hymn. Don't you remember?" she said.

"Ah . . . it's been a long time, Mom." Since Dad and Beth's . . . No. Stop. Get back on track. She reached for her sunglasses. They were gone, too, tossed aside by another random act of aviation. She squinted and reached for the radio microphone. "We have to check in with Boston."

Her hand had just touched the mike when something just over her head went bang. The shock wave violently rattled the plane.

"That doesn't sound right," Violet said.

"I know, I know, Ma. Hang on."

Another alarm went off and enunciator lights on the right engine panel lit up. Gertie slipped into a thirty-degree bank to starboard.

The cylinder head-temperature on the right engine pinned against the stop on the high end. Sarah knew that was really,

really a bad thing. Oil pressure read zero and manifold pressure—whatever that was—was also nonexistent. She slammed the right-hand throttle to idle. The headphones came to life. "Sarah?"

Like she had time to chitchat right then. "Yes, Mrs. Harker."

"I can't see out the right-side window."

Sarah glanced out. The sky was clear as a bell. "Say again?"

"The right-side window. I'm sure you know your business, but it's covered with what looks like . . . oil. I thought you might want to know."

Anything for a rearview mirror. Sarah strained to look backward through the clear panel in the cabin roof, but the edge of the fuselage cut off any view of the starboard-side engine. Think: big bang plus no oil pressure plus oil all over the place equaled what?

They blew the right engine. Had to be. Shit.

Mrs. Harker came on, coughing. "—Smoke—back here."

Her being an ex-nurse and all, Sarah didn't figure she was asking permission to light up a butt. Clearly, they were on fucking fire. That's what was happening.

Twelve O'Clock High time again. Memories of being a kid, awake way past her bedtime, hiding out from Violet, the lights dimmed in the study, TV volume down low, she and Dad watching the black-and-white reruns. Just the two of them huddled up under afghans on the couch—she could still smell the old leather—watching Joe Gallagher will his wounded B-17 bomber home while flames trailed from one of the engines.

Think! What was it Captain Joe always did about that little—holy shit, *she* could smell the smoke now—problem?

Feather the engine! That was it. Basically, shut the damn thing off and let the prop free spin. Sarah skimmed the panel for anything that might help with that operation. Nothing screamed "Yank me."

"Talk to me here!" she yelled.

"What would you like me to say, dear?" her mother asked.

"No, Mom. I'm talking to the plane."

"Aren't you still seeing . . . what's her name . . . ?"

"Dr. Loo. And, yes, I am."

"Mmm."

Sarah finally looked overhead. There they were, along with every other switch she could never seem to find: two red T-handles, one for each engine, labeled "Feather." *Aviation for Idiots*. She twisted and hauled on the right one until it yielded and locked in a down position. She did remember where the switches for the magnetos and the main power to each engine were located. She shut down the ones to the starboard engine, but not before she made triple-damn sure they belonged to the right engine.

Obediently, the right engine shut down. Sarah crossed her fingers and keyed the intercom. "Mrs. Harker?"

"Better—" followed by *cough, gag, gag, cough*. Sarah took her word for it.

She looked back to the horizon in time to see a towering cumulonimbus, its edges filigreed silver by the sun, slide sickeningly across Gertrude's bow. They had been losing heading while she'd been playing fireman. Certainly she hadn't moved the controls, so what was up?

Ah. With the right engine out, Gertie would naturally pull to the right unless constantly corrected with the rudder pedals. If she had a free hand she would have dope slapped herself. She *had* to start thinking—*anticipating* things—like a pilot.

So she did.

She'd need help with the rudder pedals if they had to be constantly worked. Sarah looked over at her mother. Her mother was sitting as far back from the controls as the seat would allow—just like she herself had done on her first time in the Cessna—as if Violet were afraid the yoke was a snake and wanted to bite her.

"Mom."

Sarah realized she'd lost her again. "Mom! You were supposed to be watching the wings on that little airplane. What the hell's wrong with you?" Two could play the guilt card.

Her mother flinched. "Yes. I'm sorry. It's just so hard."

"I know. I do. But I need your help here."

Violet shook herself. Sarah recognized that move. It was called Dislodging Spot.

"What do I do?" Violet asked.

"I shut down the right engine, so the plane wants to keep turning to the right."

"Should you have done that? I mean, don't we need two engines to fly?"

"Well, it'd be nice but—Mom, please. No explanations right now, okay? I just need you to put your feet *gently* onto those pedals that are moving around down there." Sarah pointed to the floor.

"I can't reach them."

"Pull that lever on the side of your seat and scoot forward, like in a car."

"Okay." The seat ratcheted forward. "I'm putting my feet on them."

Sarah felt Gertie twitch. Her mother grimaced like the pedals were hot coals. "Relax, Mom. Just follow what I'm doing. See?"

"I can do that."

"Good. Now, I need you to watch something else besides the little plane. See the compass?"

Violet's eyes scanned the panel. She pointed. "Right there?"

"You got it. Now watch this." Sarah eased up on right rudder and the compass swung. Then she brought them back on course. "See that?"

"Oh, yes! I do."

"Now you make it do the same thing."

Her mother did it.

"Ma, nice job. I'm proud of you."

Her mother smiled a real smile. "You're a good teacher."

Right. At the Nearsighted Leading the Blind School. "Now, Mom, every time we get off course I need you to move the foot pedals and make the compass go where it's supposed to. Okay?"

"I think I can do that."

"I'm counting on you, Ma. Everybody is." Sarah gave her a raised-eyebrow look that said, "You know what I'm saying here?"

"I can do it," she said.

"I'm calling Boston. They're probably wondering what the hell's going on up here." Sarah made the transmission.

"LZ one-eight-five-seven, good to hear from you again. You have been flying erratically."

Yeah, no shit.

"We have a new vector for you. Make a left turn to heading . . . two-zero-five. Over."

"Boston, LZ one-eight-five-seven. A left turn is impossible. We are a twin-engine Grumman amphibian with right engine out. Repeat: left turn impossible."

There was an incredulous pause. "LZ one-eight-five-seven, please repeat last message."

She did.

"LZ, please provide full details of your present situation. Are you declaring an emergency?"

"Well, I hate to cause trouble, but, yes, I think we should. The pilot of record is unconscious."

There was an even longer pause.

"That man seems concerned," her mother said.

"Well, he should. It's his job."

"LZ one-eight-five-seven, message understood. Please squawk seven-seven-zero-zero on transponder."

Great. The last rites for an airplane: General Emergency Status. Sarah hit the switch. It would highlight Gertie's blip on Boston's radar.

"Thank you. We register you strong and clear on our radar, LZ one-eight-five-seven. You have been granted emergency status. Request you change frequencies to a dedicated channel, 124.7. Repeat: 124.7. We will join you on the new frequency."

Sarah twiddled the radio tuner. "Boston, this is LZ one-eight-five-seven. Do you copy?" She'd waited her whole life to slip that phrase into a conversation.

"Roger, Boston here. New heading is right turn to one hundred ninety degrees. Begin now."

She horsed a cranky, complaining, recalcitrant Gertrude around the bank like they were on a trip to the glue factory. "Give me more on the rudder pedals, Mom." Sarah's legs shook from strain and tension.

One hundred ninety. *Finally*. Not pretty, but on the numbers.

"LZ one-eight-five-seven, nice job. Maintain one hundred ninety degrees and present altitude for . . . oh . . . about seven minutes." A quieter voice on this new frequency. Seemed more casual. Relaxed, even. Undoubtedly the guy they assigned to talk down the nutcases. *Hey, if the shoe fits . . .*

She scanned the gauges.

"The little airplane is straight and we're heading the right way," Violet said.

"Nice, Mom." Good. They were holding their own. Level flight, basically. Fuel, temperatures, pressures okay. *In the only engine!* her mind screamed. She told it to shut the hell up.

Except for the cramps in her legs from all the rudder work and the crappy, sluggish, lethargic, mushy handling, it was your average, everyday flight with one engine out, the pilot unconscious, and a seriously ill person in back. And not to forget the really thrilling part: a student pilot with her mommy in the right seat.

The radio crackled. "LZ one-eight-five-seven. What's your fuel situation?"

"Well . . . with just one engine operating, it'll probably last well into next week."

The guy laughed, humoring her. Then she asked him the million-dollar question. "You given any thought to how we're gonna climb down through all the crap underneath us?"

"Ah . . . Roger that, LZ. Given your maneuverability issues and lack of instrument training, we propose to divert you to an alternate field in Connecticut. Does this work for you?"

"Hold on, Boston."

Cripes. Decisions, responsibilities, and more decisions. That was what Logan was talking about when he said that you were the captain of the ship when you were flying. You were the master of everything and everybody on board. You made the life-or-death calls. No one else—*you.* And you lived with the consequences. If you lived.

Well, damn it, she might be captain by proxy, but she was sure as hell entitled to at least a consult.

She clicked the cabin intercom. "Mrs. Harker?"

"Right here, dear."

"Has Mr. Donnelly come around at all?"

"Just a minute, dear."

There was rustling in the headphones.

"Whaa . . . ?"

A consult with a drunk was not what she had in mind.

"Logan, listen to me. The right engine's out—"

"Ungh?"

"Yeah. And Boston wants to divert us to another field. So I don't have to land on instruments."

"Cream, no suggy . . . uh-huh . . . uh-huh . . . big cup, big cu—" *Clunk.*

"Sorry, Sarah, he's not very rational right now."

Good thing Mrs. Harker told her, otherwise she might never have guessed. "Yeah, well, we tried, Mrs. Harker. How's Robert?"

"Not good. I don't want to pressure you, dear, but I think things may be very serious indeed in another half hour."

That did it. Sarah keyed the radio. "Boston, this is LZ one-eight-five-seven."

The same calm voice answered. "Roger, LZ. Boston here."

"Boston, diverting is a no go. Repeat: no go. I've conferred with our captain and he . . . agrees." Robert was walking—actually, lying—death, and Logan belonged in a giggle coat and might be seriously hurt, for all anybody knew. Their chances of landing safely at another field, even if she could fly VFR, were probably only incrementally better than their chances at Logan Airport. And flying to freaking Connecticut on one engine? She wasn't pushing their luck that far.

"Understand, LZ. Your call."

Would that it weren't. "Boston, do you have a name?"

"Jim, LZ. And you?"

"Sarah." Nice to be declared an emergency. You got your own cozy little channel and a soothing, infomercial voice.

"Anybody in your right seat, Sarah?"

"My mother." She motioned to her mother, *Say hello.*

"Hello, Jim."

Either he was from a Midwestern state originally or he

hid incredulity extremely well because he said "Nice to meet you" like they were talking over brownies in the church hall after Mass. Sarah realized he was probably just the kind of guy her mother wished she'd meet.

"Jim, what have you come up with? How you gonna get us down?" she asked.

"Well, Sarah, that depends on what you got on board. You said you were driving a"—paper crackled—"a twin-engine Grumman. Goose? Mallard?"

"Close. Widgeon."

"Ah. She have a name?"

"Gertrude."

"Mmm . . . Gertrude . . ." He mulled. "Cute."

"Not cute. Utilitarian."

"Say again?"

"Never mind."

"Ah . . . okay, then. Sarah, you know if the pilot was using Loran or VOR?"

Or onomatopoeia or iambic pentameter? He rattled off a few more acronyms that meant even less to her than the first two, but she gathered that they were talking about navigation.

"He said he was on a . . . radius, I think." she said.

"A radial?"

"That's it."

"Okay. We could go that route. But tell me about your experience. You're a . . . novice pilot?"

"Actually, that's generous of you, Jim. I'm a student. There won't be a quiz at the end of this, will there?"

His chuckle trickled into her ears. You'd think we were having a laugh over a beer, the guy sounded that calm. That made one of them.

"No, no quiz. What I was thinking was you could follow what we call a 'vector' down through the clouds. A vector is

a beam of radio waves that Boston sends out. We send them
out in all directions around the airport, like spokes in a bicycle wheel. You guys would pick up the right one and follow
it down."

Right. And find a cure for world hunger, while I was at it.

"LZ, come back. Did I lose you there?"

"I got the bicycle part, Jim. Sort of. Look, all that's great,
but I got my hands full up here. Engine out, likewise one
passenger and the pilot. Is there a plan B?"

Jim laughed softly again. "We got as many letters as you
need."

Really, the guy's voice was hypnotic. If he said, "Sarah,
jump off the bridge," she'd be the first up on the rail.

"Plan B is you just fly the headings I tell you to. But, any
way we go, you have to be prepared to do an instrument
landing."

Gulp. "No sweat. I love this plan. I'm excited to be a part
of it."

"*Ghostbusters*?"

"One of my favorites."

"Me, too."

"Say, Jim, before we get in too deep here, give me a pre-
view of the instrument landing part."

"Okay. I get you close to the runway by giving you headings, clearing traffic out of your way, etcetera. You picked a
good time for this to happen, by the way. Nobody else is up."

Go figure.

"I bring you within a mile of the runway. From there, you
find some markers, stay on a glide path, and, presto, you
drop through the bottom of the pea soup and see runway
lights. We watch you, tell you what to do, you're down.
Simple."

It was never that simple. Simple was someone qualified

doing it on a clear, dry day with two good engines. Not simple was film at eleven.

"Is there a plan C?"

"Do you really want the answer to that?"

"Again, I love plan B."

"Good girl."

"How much longer on this heading?"

"Another five. How's your good engine doing?"

She scanned the gauges. "Okay, so far."

"Worth trying a restart on the bad engine?"

"Negative. Oil's covering the whole side of the plane. It's lunch meat."

"Uh-huh, understood. Ah, Sarah, your next turn will be to port." Port. A full bottle, please.

"That's to the left, Sarah."

"Got it." She decided not to share the joke.

The intercom crackled. "Sarah, Vi, I'm sorry. Robert's slipped completely into shock. We've got less time than I thought."

Sarah thumbed the radio.

"Ah, Boston any way we can speed up our ETA? We're very concerned about our injured parties."

"Understood. Initiate turn heading . . . one-zero-five . . . now."

Getting Gertrude's nose around was a Herculean task. "Boston—done." She was panting. "Good job, Mom."

"Looking . . . good, LZ. We're lining you up for our longest runway—we think. Depending on wind direction when you arrive. We've got about eight minutes to decide."

Long was good. At a time like this length *did* matter to a girl.

"We're factoring your inability to turn to the left, so flying approach is taking a bit longer than usual."

"Okay, Boston. You're calling the shots."

"Airplane handling like a bag of cats right now, huh?"

"Worse."

"Feet giving out?"

"Glad I'm wearing my Hush Puppies. Thank God for my mother." Sarah gave her a wink. Her smile was still real. It was uncanny how good old Jim seemed to be right in the cockpit with her, Sarah realized, understanding exactly what they were going through in the plane. No wonder he worked the Panicked Pilot Hot Line.

"Part of that sluggishness you're feeling right now could be loss of hydraulics," he said. "The bad engine might have been running the fluid pump. I'm not familiar enough with the setup of your particular airplane to say for sure."

"Roger." To whatever he just said.

"Sarah, we're going to start your descent now. Listen carefully to my instructions and watch your instruments. It'll be like wandering around with a blindfold on. You've got to trust other people."

Historically a strength for her. *Not.*

"Ready, LZ?"

"As I'll ever be."

"Here we go. I want you to throttle back until you get an airspeed of one-twenty. Maintain level flight."

Cutting power to the one good engine took every ounce of her willpower. Millimeters at a time she eased back on the lever. "Set."

"Good. Fiddle with the mixture till you get the most RPM at that setting."

She fiddled. "Done."

"Good. Now you're going to drop the nose about ten degrees. Try for a descent rate of about five hundred feet per minute. Watch your airspeed. Keep it at one twenty."

They had a final glimpse of sunshine moments later as

Gertie once again submerged into an ocean of cumulonimbus. The cabin plunged into darkness. It took a few moments for Sarah's eyes to adjust, even though the panel lights were still on.

"Mom?" Sarah pointed to the mixture control for the left engine. "That doohickey adjusts the engine to get it smooth. One of your jobs is to play around with it—carefully—when I tell you. Get it so you get the most RPM"—Sarah showed Violet the tachometer—"at whatever engine power we're at. See? Follow the little needle."

"So that's three things I do."

Sarah assumed she was complaining. "Ma, for Chrissakes, I got my hands full here with just steering and working the radio. The least you could do is—"

"Sarah, I'm just asking so I can keep track of everything." *Sheesh.* "Sorry."

Sarah watched her mother run her fingertips lightly over the mixture-control knob and then the tach, her lips moving. Satisfied, Violet sat back. "It is nice to be in control of these things, even if it's just for a little while, after being afraid of them for so many years," she said. Then her brow furrowed. "Does that sound stupid?"

Sarah laughed. "Not at all. I know exactly what you mean. And 'this thing' has a name. It's Gertrude."

"I thought it was a girl." Violet evidently hadn't been listening to the conversations with the controller. Sarah wondered what *had* been going on in her mother's head during all the exchanges. "Pleased to meet you, Gertrude. I'm Violet." She patted the armrest, just like Sarah herself had done what seemed like a lifetime ago.

Violet looked outside the plane. "Uh, Sarah, dear. Do you know we can't see anything?"

Sarah laughed again. "Yuh." Really, the woman was a hoot. "We're on instruments, Mom." She pointed to the instrument panel in front of both of them. "These babies are the only things we need to see. Oh, and Mom, I want you to watch this dial here, too. It's the airspeed—how fast we're going. Tell me if it gets more than a few miles an hour above or below one-twenty. Okay?"

"All right. Four things . . ." She touched the airspeed indicator, then the tach again.

Jim came on. "Sarah, Boston. Altitude, please?"

"Seventy two hundred."

"Good. That's what we mark you at on our scope. Maintain present rate of descent. Sarah, I need you to find a dial that says DME."

"Mom?"

"Right . . . there, dear."

Her mother was quick. "Got it, Boston. Reads . . . twelve . . . and a bit."

"Great. That gadget tells us how far away from the airport you are. We also mark you about twelve miles out at this point. Hey, good news for a change. Weather's improving down here. Gusts below forty."

Forty? "ETA on us, Jim?"

"Seventeen minutes, with all the jockeying we're doing." Sarah prayed that would work out for the boys in back. And for her. Cripes. Seventeen minutes until the most harrowing experience of her life, probably. Her mother's life, too, undoubtedly. Taken together, she and her mother's past traumas were hard to top, but Sarah had a feeling Africa would shortly lose the crown.

The drone of the engine lulled. Inside the belly of the whale, time stood still. What a great idea she'd had, learning to fly! She'd met interesting people: Logan, the unconscious sack in back. Robert Iverson—hmmm, also unconscious. Didn't she just have that effect on people around her?—her new boss, and apparently much more than that. Lucky bastards, though, the two new guys in her life. They weren't worried about the next—she checked the clock—sixteen and a half minutes.

She'd seen all manner of neat things: rivet heads tattooing the Tidal Bridge, the inside of a thunder cell at—she checked the altimeter—6,700 feet. And to top it all off, very soon she might die. Here in an airplane she couldn't really fly. Really, she had the best ideas sometimes.

"Sarah?"

"Yes, Mom?"

"I came with you to be with Robert."

"Yes . . . ?"

"But also to help out. Any way I could. And here I am feeling so useless I can hardly stand it. Are we really going to be able to do this?"

Her mother. Pulling her back from the brink. "Yes, we are, Mom. And you have a very important job. You're keeping me glued together. Now, fiddle with the mixture, will you?"

The engine smoothed. The woman had skills. "You're going one hundred twenty-five, by the way," Violet said.

Sarah teased the throttle back. One-twenty.

Altitude? Sixty-two hundred feet. Temperature? In the green. Pressures? Good. Alternator? Okay. Easier job checking just one side. Even the ride was better now. Gertie was still slopping around the sky like a bucket of wet plaster, but no hail, no elevator shafts or rocket rides. Everything was coming up roses.

Peace, for the moment.

Sarah realized she was exhausted. She could only imagine how everyone else on board was feeling. If they were unlucky enough to be conscious.

"Sarah? Boston." The radio. She snapped to.

"You're about ten minutes out," Jim said. "We've cleared

what little traffic there is out of your way so you just concentrate on your flying. We've got another course change. Ready?"

"Shoot."

"Right turn to course nine-zero. Repeat, heading nine-zero."

The headphones crackled and Sarah thought she heard mumbling on the cabin channel, but she forced the distraction out of her mind. She beat on the control yoke and finally Gertie responded. She'd deserve a nice treat after everything was over. What did you get the plane that had everything? Hah! An engine overhaul. "Boston, I'm on it."

"Altitude should be about . . . three thousand feet?"

"Boston, thirty-one hundred."

"Close enough. Continue present rate of descent for approximately two minutes, then we'll have another change for you."

"Roger that, Boston. Uh . . . Jim?"

"Here."

"Sometime soon there's going to be a moment of truth, right? I mean, I gotta land this thing."

"Good time to talk about this, Sarah. You have some experience landing, correct?"

"Yeah, but it was VFR in a tiny, little—"

"Then you can land . . . ah . . . Gertrude. You're doing ten times better than most people in your situation would be doing. Really. And you actually are going to land visual. We've lifted our ceiling to five hundred feet. The trick is to get you right to the runway threshold on instruments then transition you to visual. Copy?"

"Right. So you're saying I have about five hundred feet to screw around with where I can actually see what I'm doing?"

"Correct."

Their chances of making it soared to like two in a million.

"Now, Sarah. Let's go through your prelanding check."

The intercom sparked. "Sarah?"

"Mrs. Harker?"

"It's Robert. Pulse thready, BP way down. We are losing him. I am so sorry, Violet."

"Working on getting him down. Soon," Sarah said. It could go like dominoes, their situation, she knew. Lose Robert? She'd lose her mother. Then she herself would just plain lose it; then everybody loses. Big time.

She thumbed the radio. "Boston, this needs to be a one-shot deal. No flyovers, no go-arounds." She watched her mother out of the corner of her eye. "We're losing one of our injured. Needless to say, you'll have an ambulance at the runway, yes, Boston?"

"Roger that."

The slight hesitancy in his voice said, *And a whole lot more.* Sarah had seen all the disaster movies. She figured foam trucks, fire engines, an entire fleet of assorted emergency vehicles.

"Sarah? Jim here. We've been filled in on your heart patient by Crossly. To make things simpler for you, I'm handling you all the way in. No handoff to tower. Remain on this frequency."

"Sarah?" Mrs. Harker.

"Yes?" She braced herself for the worst. She sensed her mother stiffen in the seat beside her.

"Your Mr. Donnelly's awake—in a manner of speaking. Just a moment . . ."

Heavy breathing over the intercom. Great, Logan picked now to place an obscene phone call.

"Logan, what is it? I'm busy here—"

"Tell 'em no . . . " His voice was a croak.

"No? No what, Logan?"

"No standing here—" Then, just like the first time, there was a clunk and the line went dead.

Great, another country heard from. Sounded like he learned his lesson: don't be standing up in a plane in the middle of a thunderstorm. Nitwit. Go back to sleep.

"Sarah? Boston. Can you find flaps and landing gear?"

"Got them." She really did. She remembered Logan's minilessons in Manchester.

"Your help all lined up?"

"Mom?"

"Good to go, as you young people say." How she was doing it Sarah didn't know.

"Right on, girlfriend." Sarah sat up straight, cracked her back, and flexed her fingers on the yoke. "Okay, Mom. More jobs. Landing gear"—she stabbed a finger—"and things called 'flaps.'" Another finger. "There're big wing extension things that help us land. They're marked off in increments. See? Like five . . . ten? I call out the numbers and you move the levers to that number, okay?"

"I think so. Six things . . ."

"Right."

Violet bent forward for a closer look and caressed the levers like worry dolls. "It seems simple enough. You're going one-fifteen, by the way." She toyed with the mixture knob and the RPM picked up. "There."

"Nice, Mom. And did you catch what Logan was babbling about?" Sarah asked.

"Something about not standing up, I think."

Good. She wasn't going crazy.

"Sarah, Boston. It's time to tune the radio labeled NAV one to our instrument-landing frequency. It's 113.9. Repeat: 113.9."

She dialed it in. "Got it, Jim."

Two needles twitched and formed a crosshair that crowded into the upper-left corner of a dial on the panel.

"Sarah, Boston. Level out at two thousand feet. Repeat: two thousand. You're about seven miles out. Be home soon."

"Can't wait to soak my feet—but not in Boston Harbor, you know what I'm saying, Jim?"

"Got it. Did you see any needles moving around when you tuned the navigation radio?"

"Yes."

"Good. You've intercepted our localizer."

Whatever the fuck that was.

"Now I need you to turn right to two-seventy."

Gertie was only too happy to comply, taking advantage of the tendency of her left engine to race ahead of the rest of the plane. The nose slid around to almost 360 before Sarah regained the correct heading. "Done, Boston."

"Sarah, you are now on final approach."

Could have fooled her: the scenery hadn't changed.

"Let's get stabilized on ten degree flaps; then we'll get your gear down."

"Move the flap lever to ten, Mom."

Gertie whined and settled back onto her tail feathers.

"The speed is going down, Sarah."

"We're okay for now, Mom."

The radio crackled. "Airspeed?" Jim's voice was clipped. He was feeling the pressure, too.

"Dropping to one-hundred."

"Okay, no lower. Maintain one-hundred. Watch it like a hawk. Gear down, Sarah, when you're ready."

"Mom, new airspeed here. Below one-hundred miles an hour you yell. Loud. Twist the landing gear lever now."

A clunk under the floor confirmed the wheels had released.

"Boston, flaps ten and gear down."

"Good, now the interesting part," Jim said. "On the dial with the needles, tell me what's happening. Where is the vertical one?"

"Pushed way to the right."

"Nudge Gertrude left and watch the needle."

Holy shit! It moved, centered, then stuck far left. It was a homing beacon. Sarah persuaded the controls back the other way and got the needle to center.

Damn. Maybe all this mumbo jumbo did make sense. "Boston, I got it figured out! We're on course!"

"Congratulations. What's the other needle?"

Sarah pushed the nose down and the horizontal needle slowly floated up to center. She pinched off the shallow dive and the needle centered. The vertical one drifted. "Shit . . ." She corrected and the horizontal rose. Okay, so it wasn't exactly a piece of cake, but at least she had the basic idea.

"Boston, I think we're okay. The needles are roughly centered. I still can't see a damn thing, though."

"Good, Sarah. If those needles are crosshaired on the center dot, you're on the glide slope. That'll lead you right down to the runway threshold. Depending on head winds, another minute or two should bring you into the clear at about five hundred feet. You got almost two miles of asphalt to set down on. The tricky part is transitioning to visual the second you see our lights—"

"Mom, new job." Sarah realized she was barking and softened her voice. "Sorry. You're doing great. New job. Look below us. You see lights, ground, *anything* down there, you yell." She cut back on the throttle.

"Check."

Sarah stole a look at her mother. Maybe weren't many left. Exhaustion tugged at Violet's features, but she was positively lit from within. "You hanging in there, Mom? You still my rock?"

"Still here, dear."

"What's your secret, Ma?"

Her mother laughed, sad and happy at the same time. "I spoke to your father and Beth a little while ago."

Sarah would have scoffed if Joan had said that. "Really. What did they say?"

"Well, nothing, dear." Violet looked at her as if she was wondering if her daughter's sanity was suspect. "But I told them to wait for us."

"Any mention of for how long?" Sarah had to get back to flying, but this she had to know.

"I told them we didn't know yet." Violet reached over and put her hand on Sarah's. "I'd really like to go home now, dear. One way or another."

"Ma . . ."

"It's been wonderful spending time with you, Sarah."

"Me too, Mom." It came out in a croak.

"Let's go," she said.

Sarah nodded. Together they jockeyed and cajoled the Widgeon along the glide slope, straining their eyes for the merest glimpse of the earth below.

"Sarah, Boston. We have you at our middle marker. Runway threshold three miles ahead. Keep it nice and steady. Thirty degree flap now. Wait for her to settle, then go full. Minimum airspeed, eighty."

"Mom, flaps to the thirty. I'll watch the speed now." Sarah felt Gertie wallow as she spread her wings wide, the scent of earth reaching her. "Push the lever all the way . . . Now."

Her mother cranked the lever to the last stop. With no landmarks for orientation, the sensation of free-falling was unnerving. Sarah kept her eyes riveted on the airspeed and fought the urge to add power. Gertie drifted right and, as one, she and her mother jammed the rudder full left.

The horizontal indicator dipped. Sarah added a touch of power. *Come up, Gertie . . .* "There."

"Looking good, Sarah," Jim said. "Now I want you to fly the needles all the way down. Forget about the altimeter. Trust the needles."

She sneaked a quick peek at the altimeter anyway. Six hundred feet. They should break through the bottom layer of soup any second.

She felt some of her mother's sense of peace, of calm alertness, of—

Fucking A, there it was!

The longest, most beautiful stretch of asphalt she had ever seen. Lit up like a freaking Christmas tree.

"Sarah! Water—no! Land! There it is!" her mother screamed, almost blowing out Sarah's eardrums. She cringed.

"Sarah, we see you," Jim said. "Repeat: we see you. Beautiful job . . . just keep it coming. Forget the instruments now. Just fly the plane . . ."

"Off the pedals, Mom!" Sarah screeched. God, what a load. Every muscle and fiber in her body strained to take up the slack in the controls, to keep Gertie tracking down the dotted centerline. Whitecaps on the harbor vied for her attention, but she blocked them out. Must focus completely on the runway.

The controls were worse than ever.

They were coming in high, not settling. Too fast. She chopped the throttle back to idle, expecting Gertie to start her patented low-speed waddle that signaled she was ready to stretch her feet. The plane continued to shoot ahead like a diving starling.

Jesus H. With full flaps, the gear dragging, one dead engine? Think! What do we have to do, throw out a fucking anchor? Slow down you—

The intercom rasped.

"Slow standing here . . ." Clunk.

Fucking Logan. Can't stay out of it. Got us into it, can't stay out of it. What the fuck is he—

"Sarah! This is tower. Abort landing. Repeat: abort landing!"

Like hell, after coming this far? She said no go-arounds and she meant it.

"Uh, Sarah, dear?"

"*What*, Ma?" The ground was looking better and better.

"I think your Mr. Donnelly just said 'no landing gear.' Maybe you ought to listen to that man in the tower.*"*

One hundred fifty feet.

Sarah could see rain lashing across puddles. To come this far and fail in the last hundred lousy feet?

The radio crackled. "Sarah, you're waved off! Repeat: wave off. Your gear didn't drop all the way. Go around. We'll figure an approach for a harbor landing."

One hundred feet.

Yeah, right. A harbor landing was sunshine up her skirt. A quick glance out the left window confirmed that. Huge rollers, residuals of the storm, smashed against the rock fill where the edge of the runway met the bay. To the right, sailboat masts swung a dizzying dance in the water off the Winthrop yacht club. And it was calmest in close here. Suicide farther out.

Fuck!

Sarah slammed the throttle forward and hauled the yoke back, leaving the runway—and any chance Robert might have had—behind.

She was numb.

Without warning, Gertie turned up her nose. Sarah, on principle, didn't object to the old girl having her own opinion, but at their altitude it would be her last. Sarah crammed the yoke forward, but Gertrude reared, ignoring her. Sky filled the windshield. They were underpowered, still set up for the blown landing, carrying too much wing, flying too close to the ground. Prescription for disaster.

Violet must have sensed Gertie's distress. "Sarah, this doesn't feel right."

"No shit, Ma. Pull the flaps all the way up." Violet got on them.

Servos in the wings whined, clunked, and then fell silent. Gertie continued to wallow dangerously. "Mom, let's go, let's go. We're frigging dying here . . . Get 'em *up*."

"Sorry, dear. It's no good. They seem to be"—she grunted—"stuck."

Sarah pried one hand from the yoke and hauled on the lever herself. Nada. Zilch. Bupkis.

Fuck!

Caught like rats in a low-altitude trap. Even if they wanted to, they couldn't escape back up into the IFR conditions overhead. Gertie had declared her climbing days were over. Sarah pulled back on the yoke to give her one last opportunity. Gertie said no. They were fast running out of options.

The radio crackled. "Sarah, tower. We've figured out your problem. Your bad engine ran the hydraulic pump for the gear and the flaps."

Nice to know what they'd die from.

"You had no fluid pressure in the system. The wheels free-fell a little way, then jammed. Probably sounded like they'd locked down. You were fast coming in because the flaps didn't completely deploy, either."

Which meant that they'd never retract again, either. Little wonder Gertie was inclined to do shit-all she asked. "Yeah, so? What do we do?" Sarah wondered out loud.

"You're going to fly around the airport in circles while your helper hand pumps the wheels down."

Logan had told her about the backup deployment system. It was foolproof, he'd said, if you had time. It took something like a thousand hand strokes to lock the gear down. In a thousand strokes Robert would be a memory. She would not allow her mother to be robbed of anyone else by another fucking airplane. *Sorry, Gertrude, nothing personal.*

"Nice talking with you, Jim." Sarah snapped the radio off.

There had to be a way.

Chapter 27

Gertrude passed over the far apron of the runway, then left the blinking lights behind. Infinitely slowly, she limped higher into the air.

Think! Sarah implored herself.

"Sarah?"

"Mom?" Sarah struggled to maintain an even tone. Common courtesy dictated you be on speaking terms with people with whom you were about to share eternity.

"You can land this type of plane on water, can't you, dear?"

"Yes. What's your point?"

"Land there." She pointed.

Ahead of them, maybe a mile away and just to their right, a corpulent silver snake wound its leisurely way through the heart of Metropolitan Boston, the ordered streets of the bay on its southern shore and the historic congestion of Cambridge to the north.

Land on the Charles? The Charles *River?* Was her mother crazy?

Land on the Charles.

Cripes. It had one, two . . . four bridges across it that she could see from—she checked the altimeter—400 feet. Still dangerously low.

Out of the question, landing on the Charles. It was completely, totally—

Huh . . .

It *was* relatively calm down there. That beat hell out of six-foot swells in the harbor. There was no reinforced concrete runway to rip apart the hull on a pancake landing. And her resume did feature near-death bridge approaches, something not everyone could boast about.

What would have happened if she and Logan had been in Gertie instead of the Cessna when she screwed up the approach into Crossly? Instead of climbing their way to safety could they have bailed out of the stall by descending? In other words, by shooting over the bridge like they did but then land on The Rip?

Her mind shifted into mathematical mode, computing speeds, gauging the distances ahead of Gertrude. Take away the stall and you take away the speed you needed to pull out of it. Good, because they had damn little control over how fast they could go. Lower the angle of attack, factor in what little flap they had. What kind of room did Gertie really need to get her ass down if her life—and theirs—depended on it? Sarah struggled to conjure up a visual picture of the run out she and Logan had made after touching down on Eagle Lake. She should have paid more attention at the time, but who knew?

"Mom, I'm liking this idea. Help me get the nose over." Violet slid her feet back on the pedals and pitched in on the control yoke. Sarah hardly felt her inputs, they so followed her own, but it felt like Gertie suddenly acquired power steering. As they wrestled her gamely toward the river, one of the advertised forty-plus-mile-per-hour gusts caught the plane in the underbelly and they ballooned up to 600 feet.

Cut throttle to baby her down. Watch the altitude. We stall: we dead. Maintain the bank. Hold it . . . hold it . . . get the nose to line up on the river.

The turn took forever. With two good engines they'd have been through it thirty seconds ago. *C'mon, Gertie, for Chrissakes!*

Sarah glanced over her right shoulder. The space between the bridges didn't look big enough to turn the Rav around in. *Tight, tight, tight.*

But she and her mother forced Gertrude through the turn and Sarah switched the radio back on. "Boston, I need distances off your sectional. Give me miles between the Longfellow and Harvard Bridges. Also Harvard to B.U."

"Understood, Sarah. But please advise us as to your intentions." Jim had become considerably more formal during their hiatus. No controller liked a loose cannon in his airspace.

"Just do it, Boston."

"Hold on." The airwaves hissed. Sarah hoped he hadn't gone to lunch. Or called up an air strike against them.

The radio crackled. "Ah, Sarah? We read Longfellow to Harvard at . . . 2.9 miles. Harvard to B.U . . . 2.8. Again, please advise us as to your intent."

"I'm putting us down in the river. Meet us with ambulances for our two injured and any emergency equipment you deem necessary somewhere between Harvard and the B.U. Bridges."

"Er . . . Sarah, we advise—"

"Thanks." She killed the radio again.

She dropped the nose fractionally. A three-mile corridor of open water—if you ignored the bridges, Sarah reminded herself—materialized beyond the bow cleat. Up close and personal now, the expanse of the Charles directly in front of them beat the length of the best runway at Logan Airport by almost a mile. "Mom, you're a genius."

"Nice to finally be appreciated, Sarah. You're at four hundred feet."

And she always thought she got her smart-ass sense of humor from her dad. "Descending to three hundred, Mom. Call it when I get there."

Ahead, a lone toy truck with its lights on was crawling across the Science Museum Bridge. The weather was keeping people off the roads. Good.

A half minute later Sarah could pick out individual cars. They were *still* fighting their way through the last few degrees of most time-consuming turn since Orville and Wilbur. Her legs were twitching. *Gertie, it's now or never. Git over . . .*

"Altitude, three hundred."

Gertie finally settled on a course that led her straight to the heart of the Charles. "Descending to two. Call it, Mom."

The spire of the Science Museum Bridge flashed past below them. Ahead were two spots to get wet. Same lengths give or take. But the stretch after the Longfellow was too close given their protracted turn. Sarah remembered her hard lesson about cutting the corner on approaches all too well. A flyby over the Longfellow, then. Use it as a warm-up. Gauge the space; then do the dirty deed just after the Harvard.

"Two hundred feet," her mother said.

"Try to get the gear up," Sarah said. Logan would be pissed if they survived but then broke something off his precious toy in the process. Sarah realized she would gladly snap something off *him* right at the moment.

Violet wrenched the landing gear lever back and forth. "Dead as a doornail, dear."

"Figures. We're going low over the first bridges, then we're dropping in right after the second."

"Sarah," he mother said, tentatively, "I've really enjoyed flying with you."

"Me too, Mom, me too. Let's do it again sometime." Sarah peeled a damp hand off the yoke and extended it. Her mother shook it.

"We did good, didn't we?" she said.

Sarah laughed. "Better late than never."

Violet laughed.

"Now, Mom, keep calling altitude. I want two hundred till we're in between the first two bridges."

"Roger, dear."

Sarah felt Gertie tremble as they closed on the Longfellow. A sneaky gust like a giant hand shoved them downward. "Mom! Altitude every ten feet now!"

"One-ninety . . . one-eighty . . . one-seventy . . ."

The glow of street lamps now. The Longfellow hunkered on solid masonry support columns. An immovable stone monolith with the muddy waters of the Charles swirling beneath it. A low parapet along the edge of the walkway, but thankfully no pedestrians braved the crappy weather.

"One-seventy and holding . . ."

A driver just entering the bridge proper in the northbound lane must have spotted Gertrude. The car locked up its brakes, skidded for perhaps forty feet, and came to rest sideways across the roadway. A beer truck—Sarah could plainly see the giant bottle painted on its side—pulled up short in the opposite lane and traffic behind it accordioned to a halt. She fervently hoped the beer guy wouldn't go too far. She'd need a cold one—or two, or 500—once they landed.

The Longfellow came and went in a flash, snapping the fine hairs on her neck to full attention. She shrugged her knotted shoulders and cracked her spine. Gertie aimed her bow along an imaginary line running down the center of the river. Sarah leveled the wings perpendicular to the Harvard

Bridge just ahead. Below the plane, most of the small boats had been pulled up onto shore, but a few remained anchored off the docks, enough to tell Sarah by their drift that the wind was from behind. They'd run high and hot on the landing.

Seconds ticked by. The frayed, gray-green tapestry they were floating above twitched and bunched as the fabric of its surface was erratically sueded by the unpredictable winds. The Harvard Bridge—even from a mile away—loomed, appearing to rise farther into the air than Gertrude's flight path. Sarah prayed it was merely an optical illusion.

"Mom, I'm gonna kiss the railing of this next bridge if I can; then we're setting her down. Call Hillary on the intercom—that switch right there—and tell her to pull the belts on herself and everyone else as tight as she can. Tell them to bend forward at the waist, protect their heads with their arms." Again, Sarah had seen all the movies.

Her mother did quite a nice job of it, considering she could have been saying good-bye to a dear friend for the last time.

"Cinch up your harness, Mom. As far as it'll go. And keep calling altitudes."

When Sarah was a kid she was consumed with reading biographies of famous people. People who started out ordinary enough, but went on to accomplish extraordinary things in their lives. There was always this great defining moment when whatever these seemingly average people were actually made of came to the surface, when their light first shone. As a teenager she'd desperately sought that magical illumination. But since the crash, it had stubbornly remained dark.

At some point in her twenties—around the same time she gave up on Santa Claus and the Easter Bunny—she gave up on The Light. From then on she'd artificially manufactured challenges to measure herself against. Kayak the killer rapids, rappel down the sheer granite face. Then write about it so the world could go out and buy the best gear in which to follow her footsteps. All this had been processed ad nausaum with Dr. Loo.

But Fate was a patient hunter and she had found her girl at last, Sarah suddenly realized. The exact same impartial, impersonal, universal force that had chosen Logan to be the instrument of an entire family's demise—and ruining his life in the bargain—had stuck Sarah Marie Dundee in his seat at the controls of his airplane. That force had drawn her, despite long odds, to Logan in the first place. The same Fate had set Sarah's light in the waters of the Charles River just beyond the next bridge.

She felt a change come over her then. A cool, detached part of her, far from the cramps in her legs or the churning in her stomach, rose from her . . . what? Her guts. Her vitals.

It filled her chest, narrowed her eyes. She became someone else.

Logan Donnelly? Captain Joe Gallagher? Hell, maybe even Captain Kangaroo.

Or maybe just *herself*, at long last.

But the who didn't matter. There was a job to be done and like it or not she was the most qualified person on board to do it.

Her death grip on the controls loosened and she let her mind relax, inviting Gertie's input. The yoke twitched in response. Sarah remembered the countless times she'd watched that happen with Logan. Gertie told her to take off power. Her nose obligingly came down. Pressure on the wheel lessened. Sarah eased the wheel to the right. Gertrude ran straight and true and all vibration ceased.

"One hundred sixty feet..."

"Thanks, Mom."

Sculpted stone arches supported the Harvard Bridge, a

study in Victorian architecture. It had to be what? Forty-five feet mean elevation?

"One hundred fifty . . ."

Two dark objects near the center point of the bridge took flight parallel with the roadway. Big birds, maybe. Gulls? Cormorants? The two objects separated.

They were people, foreshortened by distance. Running from the plane. Just like at Tidal Bridge. Flashing yellow lights and strobes on the Cambridge riverbank, then, moments later, on the Boston side, coming toward the bridge caught Sarah's eye.

Backup forces. No need to foam the runway now. Sarah hoped they had a rowboat with them.

"One hundred forty feet . . . one hundred thirty . . ."

How much room did she need to leave over the Harvard? Fifty or 60 feet meant staying at 110 feet. Nice to be lower. But with the wind? Better stay where they were.

Some of the strobes stopped a mile or so beyond the Harvard Bridge. Optimistic bunch they were, thinking she could drop Gertie that close.

Other flashing lights, blue ones, stopped at the shore ends of the bridge. Traffic control. Minimize the collateral damage in case the chick bites granite.

Like the Longfellow Bridge, the Harvard was gone in an instant. Focused down river, Sarah sensed it rather than felt it rush under them.

Airspeed? *One hundred ten. Hot.*

She brought the throttle almost all the way back to the stop but kept her hand poised to slam it back on when they touched down. Didn't Logan do that in Maine? Couldn't remember, but for sure they'd need some steerage control when they hit water.

"One hundred thirty feet . . . one hundred twenty . . ."

A gust tickled Gertie and she bounced up.

"One hundred forty . . ."

Nice to have full fucking flaps about now . . .

"One hundred thirty . . ."

"Settle Gertie, c'mon . . ."

Airspeed? Still a hot 110.

"One hundred twenty feet . . ."

They zoomed by the rescue vehicles lined up on either shore.

"One hundred ten . . . one hundred feet . . ."

The River Street Bridge filling the horizon ahead was relatively plain, architecturally speaking, compared with the previous two. Not that its more modern lightweight construction wouldn't obligingly shear the wings off an antique amphibian.

"Ninety feet . . . eighty . . . Sarah."

Sarah remembered a calendar page she'd ripped out and stuffed in a drawer at home. Full of colorful hot air balloons, the photo was, all of them in a pack, crossing the Great Divide. She felt right then now like she was flying one of those gas bags.

"Still eighty feet . . . Sarah. I can see the next bridge clearly . . ."

"God damn it, Gertrude, I'm ashamed of you! Get *down*!"

There were blue lights on either side of the River Street Bridge, too.

"Seventy . . . sixty . . ."

The last fifty feet saw all the fight go out of Gertrude. She settled and stretched her webbed feet for the Charles. The sudden five-story drop took Sarah by surprise, leaving her no time to flare. When they hit the water at over 100 miles per hour, her mind was still flying an airplane fifty feet in the air. The transition from airborne bird to hurtling, waterborne projectile was instantaneous and jarring.

Sarah's spine wrenched violently and somebody's headphones flew across the cabin. The waves and swells raked Gertrude's flanks. Something outside the plane slammed against the port side of the fuselage, then set up an unrelenting thumping. Gertrude recoiled in shock and took to the air again, a wounded bird seeking the safety of the sky.

But Sarah wouldn't permit it. She killed the throttle completely, then wrestled with the yoke as it threatened to buck itself free from her hands. Gertrude fell again, not quite parallel to the line of travel, jumping this way and that like a skipping stone. Spray covered the windscreen, blocking all view of the outside world, giving the illusion they were back up in the clouds again, flying blind.

Gertie threatened to pinwheel. Sarah slammed on the left engine. The airplane leapt to the right, skimming over the water at an even more oblique angle. She tried to compensate, but Gertie had a mind of her own. Sarah's head connected solidly with the left window, stunning her. She groped groggily for the throttle lever, wasting precious seconds.

Quick glance at her mother. She was slumped in her seat, held fast by her harness, but her head flopped around like a rag doll's. *Africa.*

The lone engine roared, louder on the water than in the air. Seconds later the spray dropped off marginally as Gertie's skeg found a tentative bite on the water and she skipped along the choppy river in something vaguely resembling a bow-high plane. Sarah somehow found the wipers. Careening off the tops of the waves, they were racing in a broad uncontrolled arc toward the Cambridge shoreline.

Five hundred yards ahead of them bobbed a boat dock, then just behind it the shore itself: solid concrete retaining walls extending down into the water. Sarah curled her fingers around the ball of the left engine throttle lever and yanked it back toward her with what little was left of her strength. The bow slid down off the step, but Gertrude was still charging straight for the dock.

One hundred yards . . .

Fifty yards . . .

There was nothing left to do. Sarah let go of the yoke and shut her eyes.

Chapter 28

Damn the media. You'd think they *owned* Gertrude.

And him, and Sarah, and everyone else involved in the incident. He refused to call it an "accident." The tabloids called it the "Greatest Landing Since Lucky Lindy."

For two days, the TV variety shows had been calling Crossly nonstop. "Come on the air," they'd tried on him. Fly you first class, wine you, dine you. Just tell all.

You couldn't flip to a TV news station without inadvertently tuning in to some coverage of the crash. A bio of Iverson had featured just that morning, Maura told him. Along with the thousandth slow-motion replay of the river landing and the scenes of Gertie being disemboweled with cutting torches. Or the heart-stopping moment when Sarah was extracted from the twisted cockpit through the gaping hole that used to be the left windscreen panel.

Sarah . . .

It was easy enough to avoid the television. He never watched much anyway. But those damn reporters were like gnats.

Sarah . . .

At least Iverson had escaped the endless requests for interviews—but only just—by being out of commission for three days recovering from heart surgery. Sarah's mother—*God,* that woman could talk—on sentry duty in her hospital room adjacent to Robert's, reported that a film crew had barged into his hospital room moments after he had regained consciousness.

Hillary Harker had come through the collision with flying colors. "Pun not intended," he could hear Sarah say. Hillary was unsinkable. In his book, she could have swapped her school nurse uniform for field hospital greens any day.

He himself had made it through okay, too, physically. Bumps, bruises. He, Hillary, and Robert had been far enough back in the fuselage that they were cushioned from the major force of Gertie's impact with the dock and the concrete retaining wall just behind it.

Not everyone on board had been so lucky.

Every morning he'd visit the hospital. Every morning the doctors told him the same thing.

"She's had a bad go of it. The body takes time to heal."

Brain swelling. Artificially induced coma. He knew all that.

But what he didn't know, he came away every day never getting: a guarantee of her return to health. To wholeness. Together with, or even apart from, him. Their future together was so much less important than her having a future at all.

If only.

If only he hadn't decided to chase down that burning smell right when he did. If only he hadn't lost his balance and blacked out when he did. If only he'd come around long enough to land the plane.

If only.

He was trying not to be hard on himself—Sarah would

have reminded him of his own words to her: you make the best call you can at the time, then live with the consequences—but old habits died hard.

Sarah . . .

Gertrude was in pieces in the adjacent hangar. After she had been forklifted down from the flatbed and dollied into the shed, he'd hauled the rolling doors shut and locked her in. He found solace in puttering on the Hellcat in the afternoons, after he'd returned from his daily visit to St. Anna's.

"Hey."

He pulled his head out from under the fighter's instrument panel and peered over the cockpit cowl. Maura.

"Hey, yourself."

"We got another call." She handed him up a Styrofoam cup of coffee.

"Tell them not interested. I've already got two busted-up airplanes sucking up hangar space. I don't need any more."

"This guy was from California. His secretary put it through. He's some big mucky-muck out there and he's got an . . . Avenger? Yes. That's what it was." She reached up her hand with a slip of paper in it and held it out for him to take.

He wouldn't. He busied himself prying the lid from the coffee cup.

"It's all Greek to me," she said.

Part of his brain registered the name. *Avenger.* "Torpedo bomber, WW Two Pacific. Amazing amount of them still flying."

"Really. Anyway, he wants it put into flying shape, pronto." Her hand was still extended.

He grudgingly took the slip of paper from her, read the notation, and scowled. What did these people think Crossly Field was? An elephant graveyard for old Grummans? Because Maura had brought him coffee he felt obligated to make conversation, but it wasn't going to be about airplanes.

He stuffed the note in the pocket of his jumpsuit. "How's Rick?"

"Being Rick. Never around." She laughed, but not bitterly.

"Eric? I haven't seen much of him."

"He's been steering clear of the field. He doesn't want"— she looked away, as if she'd publicly revealed a secret— "Sorry."

"To see me like this?" He scoffed, as much at himself as anyone else.

"Well, I mean, Logan, it's hard. On you, I know. But nobody else is having a grand old time with this, either. You're . . . scary lately."

"Like the old days, huh?" He breathed at her. "No booze, this time."

She cocked an eyebrow.

"Don't worry, Maura, really. I—meaning we, everyone— will get through this."

"Now piss off, right?"

"Thanks for the coffee."

She gathered herself. "She's not dead, you know. You have to hang on to that."

It took every ounce of willpower he possessed not to hurl his coffee across the hangar. But Maura wasn't the enemy. "Look, I gotta get back to . . ." What? His life before he met Sarah Dundee? The moment before they'd slammed into the dock?

"Don't lose it again," Maura said, cryptically. She stepped away still facing him, surveying him critically.

He ran his fingers over the welded patches that ringed the fuselage skin around the cockpit like stones in a necklace. She meant his sanity. Would that someone could weld *him* back together.

Sarah . . .

He set his coffee on the staging next to the plane and buried his head in the gloom beneath the instrument panel. It was a disaster under there. A dark, shadowy place filled with a maze of wires crossing and doubling back on themselves, their insulation cracked or missing entirely. A corroded tangle. The first step was to sort things out. Map out what connected to what. He chose one wire at random. He felt his way along and traced it with his fingertips into a place he could not see.

His hand closed on what felt like a Ziploc plastic bag.

Shit. If Eric had been using the airfield as a convenient place to hide drugs he'd damn well better make himself scarce . . .

Logan teased his discovery into the light of day.

The bag contained an envelope addressed simply "To Logan Donnelly." Inside were several pages of neatly folded heavy stationery.

The paper crinkled as he unfolded it. The pages were written in a careful, but obviously weakened, hand. A photograph fluttered to the dusty floor of the cockpit. He reached for it. It was a black and white of a young man standing in front of an airplane.

Logan eased himself down onto the plastic crate he was using as a temporary seat.

To my Grandson, the letter began.

> *So, you have found this. Please excuse the melodrama, but as you are probably quickly learning, to be a Crossly invites it.*
>
> *I am writing this as an old man who has been told that his days are, quite literally, numbered. This news does not bring me sorrow, as I have felt, since World*

*War II, that I have been living on borrowed time. So
many who flew in the Pacific alongside me never returned.*

*You may have surmised that the individual who spi-
raled his plane into Crossly Field in the early seventies
was your father. I took great pains at the time to pre-
vent this information from becoming generally known
throughout the community, first, because I have always been, as you have undoubtedly discovered, a
person who jealously guards his privacy, and second,
because I was ashamed of my son, your father.*

*You may conclude, as everyone else in Tidal has,
that I was simply a bitter, eccentric, rich—do not forget the wealth of our family, because that has played a
major role in bringing us to where you and I are
today—man who was intolerant of weakness and failure. Please understand that time has taught me many
lessons.*

The writing broke and resumed at a different, more
abrupt slant. The letter had been written over a series of sit-
tings.

*With the hindsight of advancing years, I came to
understand that my son's war was a different thing altogether from, the war that I had fought, or your great-
grandfather's World War I. We were welcomed home as
heroes, as you and those of your generation were from
the Middle East. The burdens on your father were in
many ways harder to bear than were our own. This—and
may God forgive me, my disowning him after his dis-
missal from the service—contributed to his early death.*

After your father's death, I kept in contact with you

and your mother, often employing the services of private investigators to be my eyes and ears. I made sure that you wanted for nothing. Your mother, becoming so ill herself—I hold myself at least partly responsible for this as well—did not question the regular checks from the "Serviceman's Trust Fund."

When you entered the service and displayed such exemplary conduct in the Gulf, I thought that the cloud of tragedy that had loomed over our family had been dispelled. When you had your difficulties and left the Air Force, I knew it had not.

I again paid to have information about you gathered. I discovered you living out your father's life and I was determined to intercede properly this time. I asked an old friend to offer you a place to live that would accommodate you and your Gertrude. She is a marvelous old bird, by the way, and I can personally attest that her kind was a most welcome sight to an aviator downed at sea.

I saw in you, underneath your despair over the death of the four family members—yes, the investigation was very complete—the love of flying that I once had and that runs through all Crosslys. Including my dear and youngest brother, Phillip, killed at the airfield just after the war. To survive the dreadful attrition over Germany only to perish in a routine landing in one's own backyard. It seemed the gods were against us.

You, however, were unaware of the Crossly family history. You represented a fresh start, a chance for us to get things right my last time around.

I pressured you to make the airfield a success because you needed a project to pull you out of your de-

spair. Like all Crosslys, you chose duty and obligation over personal comfort and convenience, and that, I hope, has turned out to be your salvation.

Crossly Field is yours now. It is up to you to decide how to make it successful in your own way, as yours is a complicated generation that has gone far beyond my far simpler world. I do not pretend to understand it. As you have seen, I have struggled at—and did poorly at—comprehending even one generation, beyond my own.

The town has been harassing me mightily and will probably continue to do so, right up to the hour of my demise, regarding that damn nature preserve. I personally do not see the immense value they place on an apparently worthless spit of sand and brush. On the other hand, the developers are keen to make an expanded Crossly Field serve the newcomers, a "crowd" about whom I have decidedly mixed feelings.

I am enclosing the original of the "long lost" document drawn up many years ago that will automatically convey title of the preserve land to the town upon the death of the last surviving Crossly. I hope you do not come to regret its return to the light of day.

From my limited and aged perspective, I offer you one piece of advice dearly gained, one that, even with all my fortune, I was unable to purchase: Follow your heart. You are on the right track thus far. It has led you to the rusted hulk of one of my dreams.

Your Grandfather

Logan examined the photograph again. It was World War II vintage and printed on thick paper with scalloped edges. Palm trees in the background, a Quonset hut. A single-seat fighter in the foreground. A young man was casually posed, with one arm draped along the trailing edge of the wing. Logan squinted.

Holy shit.

The plane was a Grumman Hellcat. With a scattering of neat, round holes just below the open cockpit bubble.

He was sitting in the plane in the picture.

He shivered and tilted the photo to cut the glare. He stared backward through the decades at the young man whose face was shaded by the bill of what had to be an officer's cap. The expression, even more than the features, were reminiscent of framed pictures of his father, some of the few things he had kept when he had gone through his mother's things after she had passed away.

He was looking into the face of young Noah Crossly.

His mind raced to flesh out the chronology: World War II ends, Noah returns home. He somehow gets hold of the bird he'd flown in the Pacific and has it shipped to Crossly Field. That would be about . . . 1947, '48. The single-seat prop war birds didn't hang around for long after the big one was over, so Noah must have paid a pretty penny to beat out the salvage guys. *Wealth played a role . . .*

Noah and Phillip plan to reopen Crossly Field as their private playground using old Micah's money, but Phillip dies tragically at the field. Noah loses heart in the reopening project and forsakes the field. In the seventies, he tries to persuade his son to reopen it, but Todd cracks under the pressure and delivers one final message to Noah.

Enter me, *Noah's lost cause.*

Logan rose creakily, suddenly feeling his age. He perched on the edge of the cockpit and thoughtfully caressed the necklace of smooth patches on the fuselage. On the cockpit side, sharp crowns of metal exploded inward from each neat, round hole. Someday he'd take a grinder to them. It was probably hard for a guy like Noah Crossly, who had nine lives, to realize most people only had one. And a fragile one, at that.

Sarah . . .

Logan wearily flexed his bad leg, sunk back down onto the crate, and closed his eyes.

Fourteen months ago, the corpse of the Hellcat had been the first thing to catch his eye when Lloyd had given him a tour of the neglected, weed-infested wreck that was Crossly Field. Speaking of Lloyd, he had to have been in with Noah up to his eyeballs. Was no one who they appeared to be?

But the Hellcat. Called to him just like Gertrude had when he'd seen her in the magazine photo lying abandoned. Instant attraction. It had taken him two years of constant work and most of his Air Force retirement money to restore Gertie, but he'd had no choice. He couldn't not. There was no rational way to explain that. And she had repaid him by saving his sanity. Now the Hellcat was a dike holding back a raging river of craziness.

He reached for the dregs of the coffee, tilted back on the plastic milk carton, and stared up at the airy rafters of the hangar. The usual crowd of little sparrows? Finches?—Sarah would know—flitted from one steel cross tie to another. One intrepid bird broke away from the pack, swooped down, and landed feet away from him, right above the instrument display where the gun sight used to sit. The bird cocked its head, its bright eyes seeming to expect something.

"Sorry, just coffee today." *I used to just talk to planes*, he thought.

He rubbed his head where it rested against bare metal. His scalp was still tender where Sarah had nailed him with her protest sign. The memory curved his lips in a smile, cracking what felt like rust at the corners of his mouth. What had the sign said? Something about *The Plane Truth* . . .

He tilted forward so fast his forehead banged against the cockpit coaming.

Eureka.

Noah Crossly *had* gotten it right the last time around.

Chapter 29

Sarah thought she heard Logan's voice. But it sounded canned, like it was coming to her down a long, echoing corridor. Maybe it was Dr. Loo calling, just to check in. Sarah's head spun.

It was all too tiring. She slipped back down into comforting darkness.

Sarah awoke to a blinking orange light and a persistent beep. *Holy shit.* Landing gear busted? Flaps jammed? Dinner ready in the microwave?

God, she was starved. Someone clearly said, "She's awake."

She wondered if they meant her. She hoped she was conscious, seeing how she was in the middle of flying—

No, that was a minute ago. Now she—no, *they*. Someone else had been with her. In a plane. She shut her eyes and remembered something about a . . . a skull? Not as in a macabre, grinning Halloween kind of way, thank heavens, but like . . . what? She struggled to make sense of the idea. Of anything. She drifted off.

Intermittent conversation punctuated her dreams, but Sarah didn't catch any of it. She was seeing a river. With sculls floating on it. Aha! She had it. Sculls were boats. Teams of people rowed them. Sarah pictured long, skinny boats. Someone in the backseat of one of them yelled through a megaphone at her: "Too fast!" Or maybe it was the person with her in the plane. Who was *that*? She couldn't pull the face into focus.

She—they—were going fast, all right. Right at the little boats piled up like cordwood on a dock. The person with her in the plane said "Too fast" one last time. Sarah shut her eyes and unconsciousness swept her away.

"I can't believe Logan actually did it," someone said.

"I know, neither can I," another voice responded.

Finally a conversation she understood. "Me neither," Sarah said.

"She's coming around," she distinctly heard someone say.

The mountain, she finished. She couldn't wait to meet whoever they were talking about. But first she needed a little nap.

For a guy who once claimed he'd never thought about flying around without an airplane, Logan seemed to be doing pretty well for himself. Because there he was, hovering over her with no visible means of support. Maybe he was suspended from the apparatus above him. No, Sarah realized. *She* was. By one arm and one leg.

White plaster. Shiny aluminum frame.

She scratched the spot where she remembered her nose used to live and discovered plastic tubes had grown in its place. Logan stretched down from on high and took her good hand in his.

She heard the reassuring chirp of rubber tires on asphalt. She hauled back on the control yoke and flared the plane. The radio crackled.

"Welcome back," he said.

"Thank you," she said. "The flight was a real bitch."

Logan chuckled. Sarah felt his lips brush her forehead.

Her head spun. This time, though, she stayed awake through everything.

Epilogue

The film of the Maine trip was a hoot, Sarah was the first to admit. Robert, after he had recovered from surgery, had confiscated the raw footage from the WKAX guys and personally directed the postproduction. The gimpy-Logan-carrying-a-wounded-Rick sequence, slowed down and set to a musical score, had everyone crying in their champagne at the reception. It nicely broke up the real sobbing.

Sarah thought her mother looked as beautiful as she had ever seen or remembered her looking as Robert met her at the altar. Sarah was sure Beth was crying right along with her. Her dad, she thought, approved: Robert was a good man once you looked beyond the master manipulator.

And at his knee, Logan was learning fast. The plucky lad actually *asked*—a major milestone, Sarah thought—for Robert's help and, together, the unlikely pair had arranged an exclusive interview on WKAX. They told the whole story of Crossly Field—the *whole* story—right on TV. Logan held nothing back about his life. Sarah watched the tape three times and still didn't know how he did it.

It was that very televised interview that she'd heard when she'd finally regained full consciousness—after *four weeks* of being gaga, people told her later. She cut those missing days out of her Eastern Mountain Sports calendar and had them framed as souvenirs of her mental holiday.

The Crossly Airport story was syndicated and picked up by a couple of the big morning shows; then the phones started jumping off the hook at the field. Maura manned them for a solid week. Some calls were reporters requesting additional interviews, but most were from people with antique planes. What were Logan's rates for airframe renovation? Did he have long-term storage facilities? Did he upgrade avionics? Would he recertify antiques for airworthiness?

Sarah glanced at the poor guy pitifully scrunched up beside her in the passenger seat of the Cessna. He was dead on his feet from all the work of reconfiguring the airfield. Exhausted, but happy. She was too.

Gertrude was coming along swimmingly, although she was still "in hospital," as old Preston would no doubt say. One of the wings was welded back on and the windscreen on the pilot's side where Sarah's skull had gone through it was as good as new, as was Sarah's own. Thank God it was just one little boat and not the whole dock that had joined her in the cockpit.

And, Sarah reminded herself, lest she forget to count her blessings, as an unanticipated bonus of her full recovery, both Preston and Lloyd had moved their operation to an airfield in southern New Hampshire—once it appeared inevitable she would eventually regain all her senses. Fear was a great motivator for change.

The best news of all was that she managed to salvage enough of her brains to become a certified pilot. IFR was still a mystery, but she had time. Definitely a new way to feel.

Logan snorted and rolled, searching for a more comfortable position, which didn't exist in the cockpit of the little Cessna. Good old LD 108. Their reliable second car, but Sarah missed Gertie dearly.

In case people thought that all she had been doing with Logan since the accident was watch him sleep, Sarah would like to set the record straight. These pages would spontaneously incinerate if she went into detail about how they'd spent the last six months since her discharge. The docs had told her to stretch regularly and vigorously to gain flexibility in her gimpy arm and leg, and she and Logan had assiduously followed orders. Stretch and flex, stretch and flex. *Yum*. They now shared two aphrodisiacs, planes and the great outdoors, and they spent *mucho* time around both.

The second runway? That issue was dead. As in buried—literally—under the slabs for the new storage hangars and workshops. Crossly Field was now an officially licensed antique airplane restoration facility. FYI: if you bring in an old Grumman you automatically qualify for a 10 percent discount. The regional high school even donated money toward some new bench and test equipment in exchange for use of one of the shops as a vocational training site. Around school, Eric was a hero.

Someone else was, too, in Sarah's book: Logan. He framed up the original letter deeding the preserve land to the town of Tidal and gave it to her as an engagement gift. Cheap bastard.

The girl jokes. She couldn't imagine anyone giving her anything more precious to her.

A really close second, though, was the ring he presented her with in the hospital on the day it appeared she had most of her marbles back in the bag. He had waited a long time for *that* particular moment, he'd explained, because he wanted to be sure that she was completely clear on who was proposing to her. The ring was silver, an "amalgam" he called it, which made her regard him suspiciously until he explained that it was a composite of silver and Gertrude, melded together by a jewelry genius downtown. It had cumulous clouds adorning the outside and a microscopically small inscription on the inside. He wouldn't tell her what it said.

Home for the first time in eight weeks, she fished out the magnifying glass from the drawer in the hall table. *To SMD,* it said—Marie was her middle name—*From LGD.* She would never reveal to anyone what Logan's middle name was. He'd kill her. The inscription read: *You*—this is the part that really choked her up her every time—*you gave me back the sky.*

Logan snorted and sat up abruptly "Heading two-eighty," he said, scanning the instrument panel. "You're flying two-seventy-eight. We'll miss the way point."

Cripes. She gave the guy the damn sky back—metaphorically speaking—and now he thinks he's acquired absolute title. Couldn't he just let her play in it for five fricking seconds . . .

"Go to sleep, will you? Chrissakes . . ." she barked, nudging the yoke and watching the compass needle gently swing.

God, what an irritant he was. But it all just went to show, didn't it?

Some things never change.